TREACHERY OF THE HEART

Brigid O'Donnel had staked all on concealing the truth about her past when she came to the isolated army frontier fort in the violent year of 1876.

To the commanding officer's family who employed her, she was a sweet, demure young lady.

To the young officers who flocked around her, she was a delightful creature who would make a perfect bride.

To the common troopers, she was a tormentingly untouchable vision of femininity.

Just one person knew her secret . . . a man whose tongue could destroy her fragile hopes and dreams . . . a man whose lust still had the power to set her afire . . . a man who made her fight against him and against herself, in a no-holds-barred struggle that she dared not lose . . .

Also by Oliver B. Patton and
available in Popular Library editions:

THE HOLLOW MOUNTAINS (08462-6, $1.95)

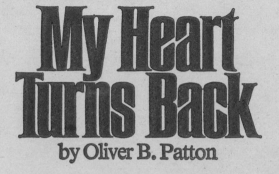

My Heart Turns Back

by Oliver B. Patton

POPULAR LIBRARY • NEW YORK

MY HEART TURNS BACK

Published by Popular Library, a unit of CBS Publications, the Consumer Publishing Division of CBS Inc.

ISBN: 0-445-04241-9

Printed in the United States of America

10 9 8 7 6 5 4 3 2 1

To Anabel

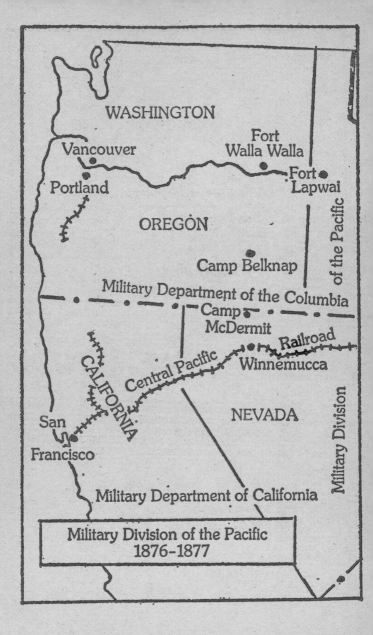

WASHINGTON

Vancouver

Fort
Walla Walla

Fort
Lapwai

Portland

OREGON

of the Pacific

Camp Belknap

Military Department of the Columbia

Camp
McDermit

Railroad

Central Pacific

Winnemucca

CALIFORNIA

San

NEVADA

Francisco

Military Division

Military Department of California

Military Division of the Pacific
1876–1877

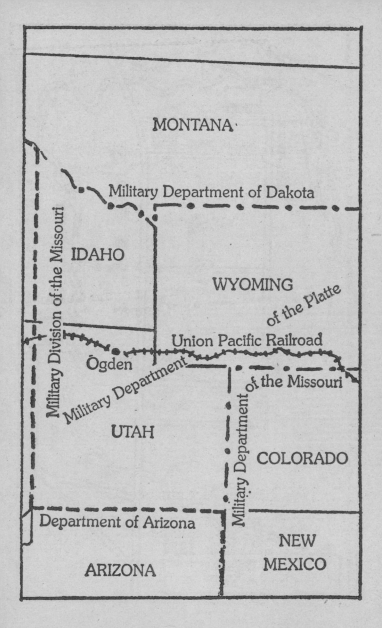

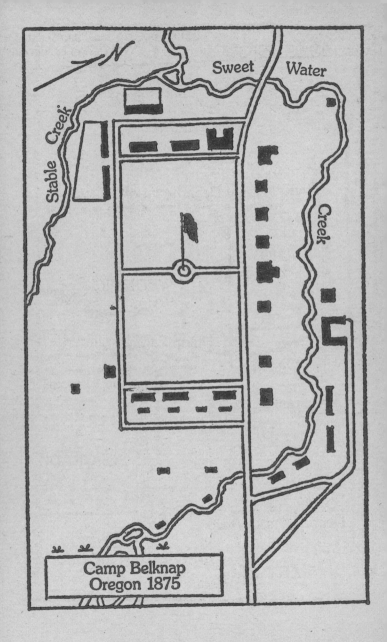

Sweet Water

Stable Creek

Creek

Camp Belknap
Oregon 1875

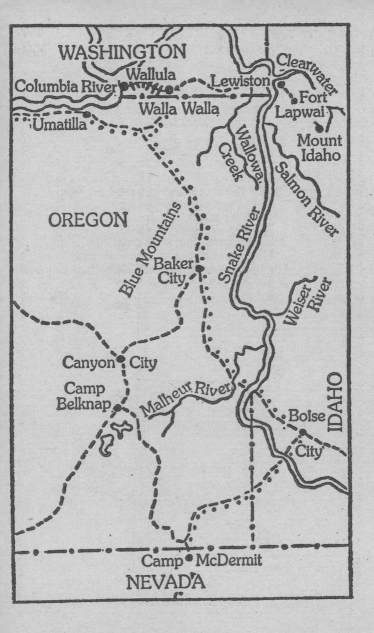

Oh, the dames of France are fond and free,
  And Flemish lips are willing;
And soft the maids of Italy,
  While Spanish eyes are thrilling.
Still, I'll not fall prey to all their wiles,
  Their charms shall not ensnare me,
For my heart turns back to Erin's isle,
  And the girl I left behind me.

A soldier's song

PREFACE

This is a story about an Irishman who came to America in 1864 and was drafted into the Union army for the last year of the Civil War. After that war, when he had tried civilian life for a while, he enlisted in the regular army of the United States. If there was actually a Private Michael Brennan in the post–Civil War army, he was not the Brennan of this story. Neither this Brennan nor his girl, Brigid O'Donnel, are of historical record.

There were a lot of Irishmen in that army. For ten years after the war, half of the men who enlisted in it were foreign-born and twenty percent of them were Irish. Another twelve percent were German, and from these two groups came most of the army's noncommissioned officers. A private's pay of thirteen dollars a month doubtless lured a lot of these Irish- and German-Americans to the recruiting office, but those who stayed on, hitch after hitch—as the five-year enlistment was called—had something else in common. They liked soldiering.

The strength of the regular army at the end of 1876 was close to 28,500 officers and men, all but about three thousand of them in the line—the infantry, cavalry, and artillery. The remainder, scorned and envied by the line, made up the staff.

A small increase in army strength was authorized in 1876, inadvertently procured by Lieutenant Colonel George Custer. Since 1874, the Congress had been tacking onto each army appropriation bill a proviso that no more than twenty-five thousand soldiers could be enlisted, and since no units were deactivated, this simply meant that there were fewer privates in most companies of the army. Then in midsummer came the disaster that removed Custer and five troops of his regiment from the army rolls, and the Congress relented, specifying that cavalry companies—not officially "troops" for another seven years—could be filled up to one hundred soldiers each. It took General of the Army William Sherman until August to convince the legislators that if this were accomplished within the twenty-five-thousand-man ceiling, there would be less than twenty men left in any infantry company. Again the Congress relented, and an increase of twenty-five hundred soldiers in the army was authorized.

The Army staff performed a bewildering variety of jobs, not all of them immune to combat. They manned the departments and bureaus of the army in Washington, and they also provided officers and noncommissioned officers for the staffs of the Divisions and Departments into which the country was divided for administrative purposes. Included among their number were the Engineer and Signal Corps, which had small troop units.

The Engineers were more concerned with civil than military works. West Point still trained the best engineers available, and they excelled at the improvement of rivers and harbors, coast and lake surveys, and the monumental task of mapping America west of the hundredth meridian. The Signal Corps—not yet a permanent establishment—was also cultivating civil works. Its scattered soldier-telegraphers tapped out daily local observations which were consolidated centrally into our earliest national weather reporting.

General Sherman viewed this occupation sourly. "They are no more soldiers," he said, "than the men at the Smithsonian Institution. They are making observations of the weather, of great interest to navigators and the country at large. But what does the soldier care about weather? . . . Good or bad, he must take it as it comes."

Sherman's relationship with the army staff in Washington was terrible. By law the discipline and military control of the army was his, but its political, administrative, and fiscal affairs were reserved to the civilian secretary of war. Secretary Belknap issued orders affecting individuals and units which Sherman did not learn about until he read them in the papers. Frustrated by this arrangement, Sherman simply took himself and his personal staff off to Saint Louis in 1874 and stayed there until a new war secretary, Alfonso Taft, lured him back to Washington in 1876 by putting the Adjutant General and Inspector General under his control. Taft, however, retained the rest of the departments: Quartermaster, Subsistence, Ordnance, Pay, Medical, and Military Justice; and the Engineer and Signal Corps.

Recruiters were not supposed to enlist married men, but this was far from a womanless army. In 1876 the only women on an army post with a status defined by regulations were the laundresses, but there were more—wives and daughters of officers and senior sergeants, women of the post trader's family, and a few servants of officers' families. All except the laundresses fell into a category vaguely defined by military law as "retainers to the camp," generally and less attractively called camp followers.

From 1802 to 1878, every army company was entitled by law to one or more laundresses, each to have a soldier's rations, a roof over her head, and transportation when her company changed station. They established by negotiation with the company commander what a soldier had to pay them for washing his clothes, they were affectionately known as "spikes" and the quarters provided for them were almost always called Suds Row. By 1876, not surprisingly, all of them were soldiers' wives. They offered just about the only chance for a low-ranking soldier to marry and keep his wife with him on the frontier.

No soldier could openly take a wife without his company commander's permission, and this was not freely granted on the frontier, where there was usually no place for her to live near her husband's post. An exception might be made if there was a vacancy among the laundresses of a soldier's company, which his bride could fill. Her rations, income, and legal status made marriage and children marginally possible on the pay of a private or corporal.

Some frontier posts had a few houses for married soldiers other than those whose wives were company laundresses, and these were occupied by senior sergeants with pay enough to support a family. Officers' quarters were built, insofar as possible, to accommodate wives and families, though the occupants deemed many of these houses uninhabitable. Sometimes they were adequate or better, but often they were no more than adobe huts or framed tents.

An officer's family generally had a servant of some sort, which inclined observers to doubt the austerity of their lives. The fact was that if he were doing his job he had little time to help about the house, and his wife—usually an educated young woman from a well-to-do family—had difficulty performing all the daily tasks of a frontier household—cooking, washing, caring for children, tending stoves and fireplaces, cleaning and filling lamps—the list was endless. Most officers bent the regulations and employed a soldier orderly or cook. Some who could afford them hired a civilian servant. When a family hired a girl to go with them to a Western post, they usually looked for an unattractive one, hoping to delay her inevitable marriage to one of an instant horde of suitors, military and civilian. The hope generally proved fruitless even if the girl had the looks and temper of a dragon. Marriageable women were scarce on the frontier.

Why men and women like Michael Brennan and

Brigid O'Donnel joined the army of 1876 is not hard to understand. The great financial panic of 1873 was still felt, and jobs were scarce; and most were ill-paid for long hours under miserable conditions. Why they stayed in the army is something else.

Some officers' wives expressed their attachment to the service in letters, diaries, or memoirs. A few expressed it well. One, who traveled and studied in Germany before she married an infantry second-lieutenant, may have summed up their feelings. *"Glaenzendes Elend,"* she called her frontier life—glittering misery. The glitter must have been powerfully attractive.

Soldiers' wives and girls, less articulate or even illiterate, have left few explanations of their devotion to the army. Their lives must have had more misery than glitter. Why did they stay? Maybe just as a means of survival, but more likely for love of a man.

There were twenty-five regiments of infantry, ten of cavalry, and five of artillery in the regular army of 1876. Two cavalry and two infantry regiments had black soldiers with white officers—defended against charges of segregation by the claim that if there were no units specifically for blacks, the recruiting parties would not enlist them, and there would be no blacks in the army at all.

The infantry regiments were numbered First through Twenty-fifth, numerical order having little to do with the age of the regiment. Since the Revolutionary War, the infantry had undergone so many reorganizations that few regiments could trace their own ancestry. In 1815, for example, forty-five regiments were collapsed into eight and renumbered according to the seniority of the colonel commanding.

An infantry regiment in 1876 was authorized a colonel, lieutenant colonel, major, two staff lieutenants, a few staff noncommissioned officers, and ten line companies. Each company was supposed to have a captain, a first and a second lieutenant, a first sergeant, four sergeants, four corporals, and somewhere between six-

15

teen and forty privates. The average in the field that year was thirty-five.

The army's combat troops were distributed in response to two immediate requirements—"reconstruction" of a shrinking portion of the late Confederacy, and protection of citizens exposed to hostile Indians. The latter was more pressing, and by the end of 1876 all the cavalry, ninety percent of the infantry, and more than a third of the artillery were west of the Mississippi River.

America was divided into three Military Divisions: the Atlantic, the Pacific, and the Missouri. The last was the largest, commanded from Chicago by the Lieutenant General of the Army, Philip Sheridan, embracing on the east all the states and territories bordering on the Mississippi and Missouri Rivers and reaching west to include substantially the entire Rocky Mountain chain. East and west of it lay the other two Divisions.

The Atlantic was commanded from New York City by Major General Winfield Scott Hancock; the Pacific from San Francisco by Major General John Schofield until July of 1876, when he became superintendent of West Point and was replaced by Major General McDowell.

All three Divisions were subdivided into Departments, and when the total number of these exceeded the number of line brigadier generals available to command them—six in 1876—a Department might be given to the senior colonel commanding one of its regiments. In 1876 there were few regimental commanders who could not sign their names "Colonel and Brevet Major General." When the army was reorganized in 1869 it had more than a hundred brevet major generals.

Brevet rank in theory is simple—a temporary or honorary promotion above regular rank for gallant or meritorious service. In combat it served a useful purpose. A young officer who rose by bravery and competence to a command above his actual rank could be

16

given speedy brevet promotion to the rank he deserved. George Custer, entering the Civil War as a regular first lieutenant, by its end commanded a cavalry division with brevet rank of major general—six brevet promotions above his regular army rank.

In the postwar reorganization all such officers lost rank—generally not all of it. Custer, for example, was reduced to the regular rank of lieutenant colonel, second in command of the Seventh Cavalry. Until 1870, however, they were permitted to wear the uniform and insignia of their highest brevet rank, and the effect was an army that appeared to consist largely of generals. That year Congress ruled that all officers must henceforth wear the insignia and uniform of their regular rank and be addressed officially by it.

But those brevets were prized awards, and no matter what the Congress decreed, the army addressed all its officers socially—and often officially—by their highest brevet rank. The ramifications of this system were understood perfectly by the army, but by few civilians.

Private Michael Brennan of this story belonged to the Twenty-first Infantry regiment, stationed in the Department of the Columbia, Division of the Pacific— Major General Irvin McDowell's command. McDowell was a tall, corpulent man in his late fifties, prickly and formal in manner and often testy with subordinates. He was a good soldier, though often called the unluckiest regular of the Civil War.

Commanding the mob of militia and volunteer regiments forming the first Union army, he had been forced to commit them to combat at Bull Run in Virginia before they were ready. He survived that disaster to encounter another on the same field a year later.

His greatest misfortune that time was to be one of General John Pope's corps commanders. To incompetence Pope had added the singular distinction of being the only Union general for whom the great Confederate leader, Robert Lee, ever voiced a personal dislike. Lee said Pope needed "suppressing," and, catching him beyond support by McClellan's army in August of

17

1862, he and Jackson suppressed him with skill and thoroughness.

The extent of the defeat demanded sacrifices. Pope was bundled off to the Northwest to watch Indians, and some of his subordinates suffered worse. McDowell was cleared of charges of disloyalty but relieved of his command. The army remembered he took this injustice manfully without complaining or string-pulling, and by 1872 he was one of the army's three regular major generals. He gained a reputation for querulous competence and elegant hospitality—financed by a personal fortune that enabled him to indulge in some unusual cultural interests: art, music, architecture, and landscaping.

In the Division of the Pacific in 1876, McDowell commanded six regiments—three infantry, two cavalry, and one artillery—distributed among three Departments: California, Arizona, and the Columbia.

The first, consisting of the states of California and Nevada, had no separate Department commander, that function being a part of the Division Commander's office. Arizona was really back of beyond. It included Arizona Territory and a desolate piece of southern California, and there were no rail connections—east or west. A single military telegraph line linked the Department headquarters at Fort Whipple near Prescott, Arizona, to the rest of America via Yuma and San Diego. At Whipple, Colonel August Valentine Kautz commanded his Eighth Infantry regiment and the Department. In recognition of the lethal nature of Arizona's Apache Indians, Kautz had two full regiments—his own and the Sixth Cavalry—plus three companies of infantry detached from peaceful California.

The Department of the Columbia, in which Michael Brennan served, included Oregon and the Territories of Alaska and Washington plus the western half of Idaho. It was commanded from Portland, Oregon, by Brigadier General Oliver Otis Howard.

Forty-six years old, Howard was a true eccentric—a

18

deeply and overtly religious man who could resist no opportunity to preach or hold a temperance rally wherever he found an audience—on a street corner, railway platform, or steamboat deck. He was known as the Praying General.

"General Howard is an excellent speaker," wrote the wife of one of his officers, "has a charming voice and uses beautiful language, but he does all his good in such a queer way, he gives people something to smile at."

Regulars knew him for more than an eccentric. They remembered when he had led the Sixty-first New York Infantry into the charge at the battle of Fair Oaks in 1862, his shattered right arm flapping at his side. The arm had to be amputated, but Howard finished the war commanding Sherman's right wing on the devastating march through Georgia. Assigned after the war to head the new Bureau of Refugees, Freedmen, and Abandoned Lands in Washington, his innocence of politics landed him in serious trouble. Congress found his management of the bureau inefficient—to use the mildest term applied. When he was finally cleared of charges of corruption, the army transferred him to Oregon.

Portland was a metropolis of eight thousand inhabitants. It could be reached by steamer from San Francisco, and there was a rail connection with only one gap. A branch of the Central Pacific reached north to Redding in California, linked by daily stages to the southern terminus of the Oregon and California Railroad in Roseburg, Oregon. The two hundred and seventy-five mile gap was also spanned by a telegraph line connecting Division and Department headquarters.

Michael Brennan's Twenty-first Infantry was scattered among seven of the twelve posts in the Department. Seven troops of the First Cavalry, whose headquarters was in California until McDowell sent it mournfully to Fort Walla Walla in Washington Territory, provided the Department's strike force, and five companies of the Fourth Artillery manned the Alaska

19

posts and the forts guarding the mouth of the Columbia River.

These twenty-two companies and the Department staff added up to a few more than a thousand soldiers. Of the ninety-six officers assigned to the Department in the summer of 1876, twenty-eight were absent on detail, detached service, or leave. General Howard considered his infantry and cavalry strength inadequate and his five companies of artillery unsuited for Indian warfare.

Congress had a quirk of economy about artillery. Of the five regiments in the army, only one company of each was designated a Light Battery and equipped with horse-drawn guns adaptable to wilderness operations. The other eleven companies of each regiment were organized to man coastal defenses or heavy siege artillery. Congress found the light batteries inordinately expensive, and army pleas for more of that arm fell on deaf ears.

The five existing light batteries were not only scattered all over America but were equipped with guns that were antique by European standards. Most of them had the twelve-pounder smoothbore bronze Napoleon, workhorse of the Civil War and, of course, a muzzle loader. As a concession to Indian fighting there was a quaint little mountain howitzer procured in 1841 from the French. It was also a bronze smoothbore muzzle loader, but it would come apart into four pieces, which could be packed on three mules. This antiquity, at top performance, could lob a nine-pound shell about a thousand yards.

Though Indians had yet to attack from the sea, General Howard's five companies of coast artillerymen lived under constant threat. They made acceptable infantrymen, and when trouble occurred they were turned out in that role to fight Indians where they did attack.

Of the three posts in Howard's Department inaccessible by steamboat, only Fort Boise in western Idaho was located on a stage route. Coaches of the Northwest

Company departed daily from Kelton on the Pacific Railroad in Utah and ran north to The Dalles on the Columbia River, passing through Boise City—three miles from the fort. Fort Boise's status was enlarged by the telegraph line running through it from Winnemucca on the railroad in Nevada to Fort Walla Walla on the Columbia, where it joined a line running east along the river from Portland.

That left two posts—Fort Klamath and Camp Harney—in southern Oregon, served by neither steamboat, railroad, stagecoach, nor telegraph. Their garrisons got into and out of them by private, hired, or military conveyance—when the roads were open. Mail and telegrams came by mounted courier.

Like Private Brennan, the Camp Belknap of this story is not to be found in army records. Historians and frontier-army buffs may note a similarity between Belknap and historical Camp Harney, but Belknap is not simply Harney renamed. It is a composite of various Oregon army posts of 1876.

Michael Brennan's army existed primarily to cope with the American Indian, and it is important to remember that as it performed this task it was viewed by Americans with everything from detestation to pride. Even more important to an understanding of the army's view of itself was the attitude toward Indian warfare taken by the United States Congress.

Until the advent much later of a profusion of medals and ribbons, brevet promotions and a single Medal of Honor were the only awards for heroism on a battlefield available to the army. When it tried to award brevets for action against Indians, the Congress balked.

When President Grant in 1876 nominated some officers for brevets in recognition of heroism against Indians, Senator John Logan, chairman of the Senate Committee on Military Affairs, bottled them up.

"I have opposed all the time," he said, "the brevetting of men for making assaults on the Indians on the ground that the law recognizes brevets only in time of war for gallant conduct in the face of the enemy." The

21

Congress, he continued, has never declared war on the Indians, and "if the Senate will not recognize glory in Indian warfare . . . there will not be any glory in Indian warfare."

The army kept trying, but more for the record than with any real hope. After his troops had caught and captured the last fighting remnant of the Nez Percé Indians, Colonel Nelson Miles reported that he would once again submit the names of officers and enlisted men who deserved Medals of Honor or brevet promotions for gallantry in battle. He concluded with a wry comment:

"I am aware that this service has been regarded by some as not coming within the purview of Section 1209, Revised Statutes of the United States, but those who endure the hardships and encounter the dangers of a service in which there is no middle ground between success and death by torture, are unable to give it any name less mild than war."

As Private Michael Brennan would have put it, the Indians weren't the only ones between a rock and a hard place.

Book One

1

"Payday! . . . Payday!
  What will ye do
With the drunk-en soljers?
  . . . Payday!"

Smigocki was whistling the army's favorite bugle call,
and Michael Brennan sang the doggerel verse soldiers
had put to it.

"Hot damn!" chortled Smigocki. "The eagle has
screamed!"

The regularity with which a paymaster appeared at
Fort Columbus never ceased to surprise Michael. In
Kansas, where he had served his first enlistment, payday was a sometime thing, always late. But Fort
Columbus was almost in sight of the Military Division
headquarters in New York City. With a ferry running
hourly, even a division staff officer could make it across
the half mile of water between Manhattan and Governors Island on time.

He resumed his shaving, working carefully around
the scar that began under his right cheekbone and fur-
rowed the smooth, pink skin to a triangular notch in
his ear. He traced it with his finger and sighed happily.
Explaining an arrow scar to the girls of New York was
a pleasure. Razor poised, he studied his face in the
mirror over the zinc-lined wooden trough of the
washroom in the barracks sinks.

He was a big man—broad-shouldered and slim-
hipped—perhaps an inch over six feet and seven or
eight pounds over the army limit of a hundred and

eighty for infantrymen. No one questioned that, with his height. He had thick black hair and dark eyes under bushy brows, in a lean face distinguished by a great hawk's beak of a nose. It was a paradox of a nose for an Irishman.

Hitching his suspenders over his bare shoulders, he rinsed the razor and wiped it dry on the seat of his trousers. He had another scar, longer and uglier, marking the passage of .50 caliber Indian bullet across the muscles of his back below his shoulder blades. It was ugly, but when he got down to it most girls found it just as glamorous as the one on his cheek.

"Come on, Smig," he urged. "We're on our own time, man!"

He took the ringing iron steps two at a time to the second floor of the barracks and the small room he shared with Smigocki. Stripping off canvas work trousers, he brushed his shoes and put on a clean shirt and his undress uniform: light blue trousers and dark blue coat, piped around the collar and cuffs with infantry blue. A half-inch dark blue stripe down the trousers and sky-blue chevrons on the coat sleeves proclaimed his rank of corporal. He paused to admire the chevrons. Brennan, he said to himself, you are a hell of a man. How many soldiers do you know with two stripes and not six years service?

The orange light of the setting sun across the Upper Bay just topped the roof of the western side of Fort Columbus's quadrangle. It slanted into the room, bringing with it the smell of salt and excitement from Manhattan a half-mile distant. Thinking of the city, Michael patted a slim bulge in his coat pocket.

Twelve dollars. Charges for laundry, tobacco, and a haircut had lifted five of the seventeen the army paid a corporal in his second enlistment. But those things had been more expensive in Kansas. Crazy, he thought—it cost less to live a thousand yards from New York City than at Fort Wallace; but that was just another bit of the good fortune that had spilled into his lap this year past.

Smigocki joined him and hurried into his uniform. The sun had sunk below the opposite roof, and Michael prodded him to move faster. Lieutenant Harper had granted full weekend passes for the first time in months, and it was a sin to waste a minute of this bounty. Picking up his forage cap, he frowned at the brass crossed rifles above the visor.

After wearing a hunting horn for forty years, the infantry had suddenly adopted a new insignia. As an added annoyance, the order prescribing the change was all screwed up, directing brass numerals identifying the wearer's regiment to be pinned above the rifles and a company letter on top of them—an impossibility devised by some idiot who had failed to measure the space between the visor and the peak of a forage cap. While they waited for Washington to unscramble that mess, soldiers mounted the numerals above and the letter below the new insignia and their officers condoned the solution.

They went down to the orderly room on the ground floor of the barracks, and Brennan extracted his pass from the Charge-of-Quarters—an envious private who regarded him sourly.

"You're supposed to be back by retreat on Sunday, Corporal."

"Permanent party don't stand retreat, you nipplehead. What's the matter with you?"

"That's what the first sergeant said to tell ever'body goin' on pass."

"I'll take care of the First Soldier, son. Just you dip that pen an' leave me have it."

Signing his name in the pass book with a flourish, he handed the pen to Smigocki and admired himself again in the mirror on the orderly-room door. Once in a while, he thought, a man ought to wear his uniform in the city. You had to wear it to get off post, but old soldiers exchanged it for civilian clothes as soon as they reached New York. Dress uniform would be better except the New York police complained about the belt.

The army's leather belt with its heavy metal buckle was a lethal weapon in a saloon fight.

He hurried with Smigocki along the walk by the arsenal fence, past the brick post headquarters building to the wharf at the northern end of the island. The quartermaster steamer was tied up for the night, and there was no sign of the civilian ferry that shuttled between Governors Island and the Battery at the foot of Manhattan. Smigocki swore, but a soldier waved from a small boat at the dock. The post barge was still running.

It nosed into the carpet of debris bobbing offshore—offal, carcasses, mattresses, and more exotic garbage from harbor shipping. Every day a detail of recruits scavenged the beach, burning or burying the accumulation of unpleasantness. It was a thankless task, for each day brought fresh delights.

The barge labored though the wake of the Staten Island ferry, just pulling into its slip, and nosed into a small wharf below Battery Park. The passengers scattered, Brennan and Smigocki crossing the park to State Street and around to Pearl. A few doors east on Pearl Street was Morrissey's saloon, and George himself greeted them from the bar when they entered.

"Draw two, gentlemen?"

Michael nodded. "To the brim, Jarge."

Taking his beer, he made his way to the back of the room. It was too early for a crowd. A few customers stood at the bar—dock workers and crewmen from the ferries whose slips were clustered east of the Battery.

Morrissey offered a service that drew soldiers from the army post on Governors Island. In a back hall he provided a row of lockers in which a man could keep his civilian clothes under his own padlock, ready for use when he had a pass to the city. It made business, but Morrissey's generosity did not extend to lighting the hall. When he had changed clothes, Michael returned to the bar mirror to knot his cravat.

"That's a handsome suit, Corporal Brennan," said Morrissey. "Another beer?"

"Sure, Jarge. Why don't you put a light in that damned black hole back there?"

"You can have a lamp for the askin'. If you brought a few more regulars, maybe I could afford a gaslight in there. What about you?" He looked at Smigocki, who shrugged.

"I got no use for a locker till I got clothes to put in it. When I make real corporal I'll buy me a suit of civvies like Brennan."

Smigocki's status in the recruit depot at Fort Columbus was tenuous. There were never enough noncommissioned officers to give even the brief instruction the recruits received before being shipped off to a regiment, so the officers made acting corporals of the best privates in the recruiting detachment, to help. None of them had ever been promoted to the actual rank, but there were rewards beside the chevrons sewn on a removable brassard. The best was a chance to share a room in barracks set aside for real noncommissioned officers, and that was how Acting Corporal Smigocki had become Michael's roommate. He could not afford a civilian suit because his temporary rank brought no increase in his private's pay of thirteen dollars a month.

Michael ignored this exchange. He was adjusting his cravat and admiring his stylish suit in the mirror. It was dark gray wool with a two-button coat, close fitting with narrow lapels and cut away at the bottom to expose a bit of the vest. The trousers were gray with a strip of black braid on the outer seams, and his shirt was white with a starched collar and a magnificent cravat of gray silk. He wore no jewelry, because the tailor who had made the suit had given sound advice on that subject.

"If you can't buy a good stickpin, don't wear any. That's a elegant suit, soldier. Don't crap on it with fake jewelry."

There was only one flaw, which Michael tried to ignore—his shoes. He had spent all his money on the suit, and until he saved more he had to wear his army-issue brogans. Well-blacked, they were passable, but as soon as he could he would buy himself a fancy pair— two-toned leather and low cut.

He drank his beer and chuckled to himself. Funny that his worst problem was a pair of quartermaster shoes, when less than a year ago he had been flat on his stomach in the Fort Wallace hospital, his back ripped open by an Indian bullet.

Morrissey's place was filling now, the nearest table taken by an ill-matched couple—a bold-looking woman with a little man who kept his derby on his head and scowled at Brennan. He was angry because his girl was smiling invitingly at the big Irishman.

"Goin' to see the elephant?" asked Morrissey.

"Coney Island? Nah . . . takes too long to get there."

"Don't have to go to Coney."

The huge wooden restaurant on Coney Island, built in the shape of an elephant with big glass eyes illuminated at night, had become so famous a pleasure spot that the question could mean two things—actually visiting the thing or just seeking entertainment in disreputable quarters anywhere.

Michael winked at the girl, who was listening avidly to their conversation, and her derbied escort pulled at her arm. He's probably carrying a knife, Michael decided; and besides, I can do better than that.

"I'm goin' uptown, Jarge. Satan's Circus for me. You comin', Smig?"

His companion looked doubtful. "I ain't got much money, Mike."

"Just got paid, didn't you?"

"Any friend of Corporal Brennan's is good for a dollar or two on the cuff here," said Morrissey hopefully.

"Yeah," replied Michael. "After you're broke, Jarge'll give you a bed or a shakedown upstairs, an' put that on your tab . . . unless you can pick up a whore with a room. Come on, an' I'll show you how to get one free."

"You're an evil man, Brennan, tollin' the lad into

30

that wickedness. You think the French madam'll let you stay the night in her sink without a charge?"

"I said nothin' about a cathouse, Jarge. When I have to buy me a girl, I'll not be needin' a bed in this town. I'll be too old an' feeble to get off the island."

"I guess I'll go with Mike, Mr. Morrissey," said Smigocki. "I thank you anyway."

"Another beer before you go?"

Michael shook his head. "No thanks, Jarge. That woman yonder is lustin' after me, an' I'm afeard her little man will have his knife out if I don't put this temptation out of her way. Let's go, Smig."

They walked up Pearl to Whitehall Street and north to the elevated railroad at Bowling Green. The cars were crowded and odorous, and it was a long ride to Sixth Avenue and Fourteenth Street. Fastidious passengers had opened a window or two, but they admitted more smoke and cinders from the engine than fresh air.

At Fourteenth Street began the part of New York described by a noted Brooklyn minister as Satan's Circus—a "gaslit carnival of vice" extending to the intersection of Sixth Avenue and Broadway at Thirty-third Street. This was Michael's goal.

"Did you see the girls wavin' from the windows on Sixth Avenue?" demanded Smigocki excitedly.

"Sluts, Smig. Panel-thieves. Stay away from that kind."

"What in hell's a panel-thief?"

"A whore with only one chair in her room. You put your trousers on it, an' soon's you're in bed, her pal in the next room sticks her hand through a hole in the wall an' lifts your wallet. She puts it back with enough to pay your shot an' a greenback left over maybe. You don't find out till you're on the street, an' if you take that tale to the cops they laugh you out of the station. Just stick with me an' I'll show you how to get it for the price of a supper."

"Go on! What kind of a whore does it for a supper?"

"I told you," said Michael, "I'm not lookin' for a tart. This town is full of pretty girls, Smig, who work for

31

their livin' but not on their backs. They don't make enough money to eat very good, so when they've a night out they want decent company that'll buy 'em a nice supper an' maybe a show or some dancin'. After that, they'll likely want a little lovin' too."

"But you gotta take that kind to a hotel!"

Brennan looked at him pityingly. "You're dumb, Smig. You got to find one that's got her own room. Come on, I'll show you."

They drifted up Sixth Avenue to Sixteenth Street, passing any number of unattached women whom Brennan ignored. They wore a bodice too low or skirts too short; cheeks with an indelible blush or lips too bright. But suddenly he pointed, like a bird dog scenting quail in a fence-row.

"There!"

Two young women had paused at the curb, waiting for a break in the stream of hackney cabs entering the avenue. They were nicely but not expensively dressed. When they stepped off the curb they lifted their skirts enough to show a flounced petticoat and a glimpse of shapely ankles in clocked stockings. Michael beamed, and as if they had received some mysterious signal they both looked back. At sight of Smigocki's uniform their heads turned away, noses high.

Michael knew that reaction. "Smig," he said irritably, "why don't you get the company tailor to make you a suit?"

"He wants ten dollars—twelve if it's jaw-bone—an' I got to pay that in two months."

"Hell!" muttered Michael, but his eyes followed the pair of young women. "Whisht, now!" he warned. "Stop here a bit."

The girls had paused to look at something in a store window, and two men closed in behind them. It was hard to see what was happening in the dim light of the gas street lamps, but a feminine voice, raised in anger, came through the street noise.

"Get on with you now!"

One of the men stepped back, propelled by the tip of

32

a rolled umbrella in his midriff. His withdrawal gave a better view of his quarry: One of the girls was tall and dark-haired, the other shorter, with a flame of red hair beneath a flat, rakish hat. She used her umbrella skillfully to back off her annoyer, but he had not given up.

"Come on," said Michael. For all his bulk he moved swiftly, and he was between the redhead and her target before anyone was aware of his presence. He smiled down at the man, who backed up again, only to collide with Smigocki. The soldier was smaller than Brennan, but he was stocky and muscular and his close-fitting uniform showed that.

"Jeez!" said the trapped civilian. "What the hell is this?"

His companion faded into the crowd and Smigocki grinned at him. "You gonna let him just walk out on you? You better go get him."

"Yeah . . . I guess I will."

Michael turned to the girls. "Sure an' I hope they gave you no trouble, ladies," he said solicitously.

The dark one smiled at him, but her companion's face was hard and watchful. The point of her umbrella shifted to Brennan's broad chest, and he had to withdraw a little to make them a formal bow.

"My name is Michael Brennan an' this is my friend, Cas Smigocki. At your service, ladies."

"Thank you, Mr. Brennan," said the taller girl demurely. "We're obliged."

The redhead's eyes, green and sparkling, shifted from Brennan to Smigocki and back.

"You're a soldier too?" she asked.

"I have been," he replied smoothly. "You don't like soldiers?"

"I didn't say that."

"Ah! Then maybe you ladies would help us."

"Doing what?"

Michael's expression was pained. "We're just lookin' for a good place to get supper, an' we thought you might tell us of one."

The girls consulted in whispers, and after a moment

33

the redhead said doubtfully, "Harrison's is nice. We've been there. But it's not cheap."

Michael dismissed that with a wave. "That's no matter at all, ladies."

"Well . . . you go up to Eighteenth . . ." She pointed. "And then west for about a block an' a half, an' then . . ."

Michael groaned. "We don't know this part of the city, miss. Couldn't you show us the way?"

She looked more doubtful than ever, but Michael smiled at her. "I've got a grand idea. We'll go an' find it, and you ladies will be our guests for supper. How's that, now?"

There was another consultation, longer this time, and finally the dark-haired girl smiled at Smigocki.

"All right. We'd like that." She put her arm through his. "I'm Maria. What did he say your name is?"

"Cas. It's Casimir but everybody calls me Cas . . . or Smig. My last name's Smigocki."

She giggled. "I'll call you Cas. All right?"

Brennan crooked an arm, and the redhead engaged it lightly with her fingers.

"And you are Miss . . . ?"

"Brigid."

"Ah, I thought so! Michael Brennan's in luck this night."

"Ummn," she said noncommittally.

Harrison's was a forbiddingly expensive-looking establishment with a dark-paneled wood front and leaded glass windows. One look at its interior confirmed Michael's suspicions. Brennan, he told himself ruefully, you have been bagged. This redhead has never been in here in her life—and never would, had you not stuck your thick Irish head in the noose. There was a wicked twinkle in Brigid's eyes as she settled into the chair held for her by a waiter, and Michael gave her a knowing grin. All right, my pretty Bridey, he thought, there'll be more than one great reckoning to be settled this night.

"Cocktails for the ladies?" asked the waiter. Michael looked blank. He had heard of this new fad, but he

34

hadn't the foggiest notion what it might be. Brigid was no help.

"I'll have a glass of white wine," she said primly, and Maria followed her lead. Smigocki looked relieved.

"Rye whiskey and a beer for me."

"I'll just have a beer," Michael told the waiter.

After a study of the menu, both girls ordered steak and potatoes, the most expensive meal on the card. Michael shrugged and asked for the same, but Smigocki looked worried. He ordered knockwurst and cabbage.

A weedy looking young man played a piano in a corner of the restaurant, and several couples circled decorously on the small tiled dance floor.

"Will you dance?" Michael asked Brigid, and she rustled off with him, still looking very prim.

But he was a fine dancer, and after a little his redhead relaxed a bit. Indeed, she seemed to enjoy herself, and they continued to dance—leaving Smigocki and Maria to their drinks—long after the other couples returned to their suppers. The pianist winked at Michael and shifted to one of the new, slower tunes that permitted a man to hold his girl closer. Brigid seemed to like that too, but suddenly she stiffened in his arms.

"What's the matter?" he asked in surprise.

She was gone without an answer, and he stared after her as she ran for the table. Smigocki was going out the door and Maria was nowhere to be seen. Brigid caught up her umbrella and followed them. As Michael reached the door the waiter appeared with their meal. Seeing this exodus of his customers, he slammed down the tray and grabbed for Michael.

"No, you don't! Come back here!"

On the sidewalk, Smigocki and Maria seemed to be wrestling with each other.

"Smig!" shouted Michael. "What the hell are you doing?"

The waiter's grip on his arm delayed him, and Brigid reached the struggling pair first. She brought her umbrella down on Smigocki's shoulders so hard it flew from her grasp.

"Leave her be!" she shrilled.

Smigocki shrugged off the blow and wrapped his arms around Maria. "Wait . . . wait! Just listen a minute, will you?"

"Get your dirty hands off me!" she shrieked. "Let me go!"

Far from disarmed by the loss of her umbrella, Brigid doubled a small fist and punched Smigocki scientifically just over his liver.

"Ow!" he yelled, whirling on his attacker.

Michael tried to get between them, but again he was too late. Maybe Smigocki really meant to strike the green-eyed little fury or perhaps he was only defending himself. She must have thought he threatened her, for she attacked again and Smigocki howled in pain.

His upraised hand was pinned to his shoulder by her foot-long hatpin thrust through his palm and into the shoulder. He stared at it in horror.

"Oh, Jeezus! I'm stabbed!"

"All right, now . . . break it up!" The blue coat and brass buttons of a policeman elbowed aside the gathering crowd of onlookers.

"You . . ." he warned Brennan with a tap of his long nightstick, "you stay right there. The rest of you move on." His stick twitched irritably and they moved.

The hatpin came out of his shoulder as easily as it had gone in, but Smigocki seemed too appalled by the six inches of slim steel protruding from either side of his hand to remove it.

"What's the matter?" the policeman demanded of Maria.

"He . . . he . . ." She pointed a shaking finger at Smigocki and sobbed noisily.

The waiter thrust his bill at the policeman.

"They got to pay! They didn't pay yet."

"I'll pay you, man," growled Brennan. "Just shut yer yap, will you?"

The policeman was studying the two girls suspiciously, and Maria dissolved in tears. Brigid bristled.

"You needn't look like that! We're decent girls, we are!"

"So? What's the matter with her, then?"

"He chased her! He was goin' to hurt her!"

Everyone looked at Smigocki, and Maria began to sputter again.

"He did! He said somethin' dirty to me an' then he chased me!"

"I'm bleedin'!" said Smigocki in a hushed voice.

The policeman gave him a disgusted look. He whipped the hatpin out of his hand and made as if to throw it away.

"No!" wailed Brigid. "Give it to me!"

"It's yours, is it?"

"Yes, it's mine. Give it here!" She reached up to snatch the hatpin from his hand.

"How did this get started?" he demanded.

There was no answer, and he looked around for the waiter, who might explain.

"I paid him," said Brennan, "and he went inside. You want him back?"

The policeman was not listening. He was watching Brigid. She picked up a scrap of paper, wiped her hatpin carefully on it, and threw the paper away. Then she restored the pin to her hat. He shook his head wonderingly.

"Let's see," he said, pointing at Smigocki. "You said something she—" a gesture toward Maria—"didn't like, so you—" he looked at Brigid—"stabbed him. That right?"

"He was goin' to hit me!" snapped Brigid.

"What did you do to him before you stabbed him?"

"I never hit her," said Smigocki. "I was tryin' to get away from her. First she hit me with an umbrella, then she punched me with her fist, and then she stuck me. She's crazy!"

The policeman's face grew red. "What about you?" he demanded of Brennan. "What were you doin' while all this happened?"

"Nothing except tryin' to stop it."

37

"To hell with that!" snarled the policeman. "I'll not spend all night tryin' to get sense out of you clowns." Thrusting the nightstick into his belt, he produced a pencil and notebook.

Both girls wailed simultaneously. "You're never goin' to book us!" exploded Brigid. "That's no fair! It was all his fault!" She shook her fist at Smigocki. "I told you, we're decent girls. We'll get in terrible trouble if you do that!"

Her anguish was so urgent the policeman paused to look at her in surprise.

"I wasn't goin' to run you in, but I want your names and where you live." He interrupted Brigid's protest with a warning shake of his notebook. "Any more sass out of you, miss, an' I'll take you to the station for sure. Now, what's your name?"

His threat silenced her. "I'm Brigid O'Donnel," she said in a choked voice. "One sixty-three West Twelfth, over the store . . . front room."

He extracted similar information from a sniffling Maria and waved the two of them away. They disappeared immediately.

"Give me your pass," he said to Smigocki, who pulled it out awkwardly with his left hand. His eyes searched Brennan and came to rest on the telltale shoes.

"You still in the army?"

Silently Michael handed over his own pass, and the policeman examined it. Pulling a watch from his pocket, he noted the time and poised his pencil to write on the pass.

"Wait a minute," said Michael in alarm. "My friend here made a little mistake, I guess, but give him a chance . . . he can explain it."

The policeman spat in the gutter. "I bet he can, only I don't want to hear him. Goddamn candy-ass city soldiers. I put two hitches in the army and the biggest town I ever saw was Julesburg, Nebraska. You two fat tomcats—loafers, ghosters, coasters, an' floaters—you live in New York City an' you ain't got sense enough to stay out of trouble. You make me sick to my stomach!"

Scrawling something across both passes, he thrust them at Brennan. "I'll give you a choice, soldier. Get your ass back to the island an' turn those passes in, or spend the night in a cell an' I'll take you back tomorrow myself. Which is it?"

Michael took the defaced passes and shook his head. "We can't get a boat back to the island this time of night."

"Then swim, dammit! And turn those passes in just like they are. I'm goin' to check your company pass book next week, an' I'll find out if you don't."

He stalked away, swinging his nightstick angrily, and Michael swore.

"Smigocki, what in the name of God did you say to that damned woman?"

Smigocki belched and nursed his punctured hand. "Guess I shouldn't of had that second drink. I didn't think she'd take on like that."

"What in hell did you say to her?"

"Only asked her could we go to her room."

"Jesus, Mary, and Joseph! Couldn't you wait till after supper?"

"You said after they had supper they'd want to go to bed with us. I didn't have money enough to pay for her supper, an' I was afraid when she found out she wouldn't go at all. That's why I asked her."

2

Brigid O'Donnel's knowledge of her origins was small and doubtful. Even her name had been given her by the Sisters of Charity in Boston who had raised her. And it was a guess by Sister Mary Monica, to whom in August of 1859 a Boston policeman brought two little girls he had found asleep under some steps.

The older of the two denied any relation to the red-headed waif with her. She said the child was called Biddy O'Dee and her mother was dead. She had more to say about the mother, but Sister Monica did not record it. Irish herself, she guessed Biddy was short for Brigid, and O'Dee she translated into O'Donnel. She saw no reason to burden the child with a double L on the last name.

Brigid's earliest memory of the orphanage was a fight with the girl found under the steps with her. "Your Ma was a *hoor*," the girl said. "She went to sleep drunk in the shed behind Cooley's and froze to death."

That taunt had cost her a broken tooth and Brigid a memorable session with Reverend Mother Felicitas, but when Brigid demanded tearfully of Sister Monica if it was true what her tormentor said, Sister Monica swore it was not.

She told Brigid she had tried to find out about her mother. Whether the good sister had actually asked questions in Cooley's saloon or simply made up the story Brigid never knew, but she accepted as fact what Sister Monica reported.

"I think," she said, "you were born in Ireland, an' after a bit your da came to America to make his fortune. Something happened to him. Nobody knows. Then your ma came on to Boston with you . . . God knows how, poor soul! That must have been a year past. She died last Christmas-time."

"How?" Brigid had demanded.

"How what?"

"How did she die?"

"A man told me she took the typhus fever an' died of it," Sister Mary Monica said firmly.

In 1870, when Brigid was probably sixteen, the sisters found her a job as kitchen maid with a good Catholic family in Boston at wages commensurate with her status. It was obvious to Brigid that in Boston she was not likely to improve that status.

From the sisters she had learned to read, write, and do simple sums. She had an encyclopedic knowledge of the lives of selected saints and a certainty that if she did not go to Mass regularly she would go to the Devil. Along with this she learned thrift, industry, and the hard necessity to get ready before you jumped. It took her four years to accumulate enough money to jump.

She departed Boston in 1874, avoiding difficulty with her employer and the Sisters by giving no notice of her intention. New York was her goal. She began as dishwasher in a restaurant near the infamous Five Points of the Bowery. She moved from that to chambermaid in a hotel on Great Jones Street, and a year later achieved the transition from servant to working girl at Lord and Taylor's department store.

That was no small achievement. A cash-girl at Lord and Taylor's was paid four dollars a week, and on those wages Brigid prospered. She moved at once from her basement room, shared with three other girls, to a room of her own—a dream realized.

One sixty-three West Twelfth Street was a three-story building of chocolate-colored brick scarcely fourteen feet wide. Its neighbors were identical. The first floor housed the work and show rooms of *Charles Pfalz and Son, Tailors*; the second was living quarters for the Pfalz family, and on the third were two rooms for rent. Brigid had the third-floor front.

There was neither a Charles Pfalz nor a grown son. The widow Pfalz supported herself and two children making tailored suits and costumes for women and selling a small line of the ready-made undergarments just coming into fashion. Both of her tenants were women. The third-floor back, the larger of the two, was occupied by a middle-aged woman who was a cashier at Arnold Constable's department store. Brigid envied her. If a cash-girl caught the eye of her superiors she might rise to be a sales clerk, and beyond that was the lofty status of cashier. It took years to get there.

Her room was small and ill-furnished but it pleased Brigid. It offered privacy she had never known before and it was very convenient. In fair weather she walked to work—east to Fifth Avenue, up Fifth to Twentieth, then a block east to Broadway and Lord and Taylor's ornate new store. In rain or snow she could take the Central Cross Town horsecar at the corner of Twelfth and Sixth Avenue and ride to the top of Union Square, leaving only three blocks up Broadway to the store.

The title of cash-girl at Lord and Taylor's was a misnomer. It derived from a minor function—taking the money given a clerk by a customer to the cashier and bringing back the change. The greater part of Brigid's work entailed the unpacking, distribution, and shelving of merchandise, plus whatever other assistance was required by clerks, cashiers, and managers. The cash-girl was at the bottom of the structure. She served everyone else and she was fined for sitting down during working hours, talking to a friend, or lingering in the washroom.

There were compensations. For Brigid, Broadway was an endless fascination. Lord and Taylor's was near the upper end of the famed "Ladies' Mile"—most fashionable shopping district in the city. It reached from

Eighth to Twenty-third Streets. At Ninth was A.T. Stewart and Company, filling an entire block. At Eleventh was James McCreery, and at Eighteenth the vast marble establishment of Arnold Constable, where Brigid's third-floor neighbor on Twelfth Street worked.

Among these giants were dozens of smaller shops of high repute and higher prices. During afternoon shopping hours this stretch of Broadway was jammed with elegant vehicles—victorias, landaus, broughams, and coupés. Their passengers crowded the sidewalks—handsome women, beautifully gowned, holding their long walking dresses a careful inch above the dusty pavement.

There were other attractions of the room on West Twelfth also. Brigid could brew a cup of tea on the gas-ring—carefully hidden when she was away—and breakfast on a penny roll, or she could have coffee and a roll for three cents in half a dozen nearby shops. Neighborhood restaurants provided a filling supper of soup, stew meat, bread, pickles, and pie—all for fifteen cents.

Sunday Mass was no problem. Saint Bernard's was two blocks west on Fourteenth Street and Saint Francis Xavier's Church on Sixteenth a bit closer. The Jesuits there made Brigid nervous—they were too stern—and most Sundays she walked to Saint Bernard's, feeling greatly superior to the giggling troop which erupted from Saint Zita's Residence for Girls a block away and was marched to Saint Bernard's by the Sisters of the Congregation of Mary who managed the home.

Fiercely proud of the place she had made for herself in New York, Brigid never forgot it depended entirely on respectable employment. The job at Lord and Taylor's, or another as good, was essential. The episode in front of the restaurant on Eighteenth Street threatened her comfortable existence because if her superiors at Lord and Taylor's learned of it, there could be trouble. Saturday, All Fools' Day of 1876, dawned bright and sunny, but Brigid viewed it apprehensively. In her opinion she had celebrated it one day early.

43

She left her room for work in time to loiter a little in Union Square. The gracious old homes that once surrounded the little park had long since given way to shops or been converted to office buildings, but for Brigid the shops were a happy distraction. She liked looking into the windows of Brentano's Literary Emporium, and Tiffany's awed and enthralled her. There the rich and fashionable folk of New York bought their jewelry, silverware, and the engraved cards, notes, and invitations that ordered their beautiful lives.

The day passed uneventfully, but that was small comfort. Brigid knew it could take a day or more for word of her escapade to reach important people at Lord and Taylor's, and that thought spoiled her Sunday. But Monday and Tuesday passed without incident, and closing time on Wednesday found her so confident that she bid the timekeeper good evening with a cheerful smile. He gave her a sour look.

"The Super wants you, O'Donnel. In his office."

Brigid's heart froze. Mr. Gilpin, the Superintendent, was the ultimate authority visible to employees of Lord and Taylor's. The timekeeper was a petty tyrant who could impose fines for minor offenses, but Mr. Gilpin employed and discharged them. If he wanted to see her it was about no trifling thing.

Slim, fastidious Mr. Gilpin intrigued and awed the girls of Lord and Taylor's. He had a sixth sense which led him to any difficulty before it got out of hand. Suave, polite, soothing or haughty as the occasion demanded, he dealt with customers who were troublesome. Not one of the hundreds of young women under his command had ever gained his favor though many had tried. He spoke to them only to correct them, and they whispered to each other that Mr. Gilpin's refined tastes did not include women. That conclusion did not diminish his authority.

Brigid knocked on his door and after a long minute was summoned. She entered apprehensively. Mr. Gilpin was writing at his desk and did not even look at her.

After a while he said casually, "O'Donnel, a police officer was here today to ask a question . . ."

Another pause. Ask a question about what, she wondered frantically. There could be only one policeman with an interest in her. She waited cautiously until Gilpin looked up with an expression of mild curiosity.

". . . about you."

It was that damned cop. He must have found out from Mrs. Pfalz where she worked. But what did he want? She had to find out before she could defend herself.

"Yes, sir?"

"You were arrested by the police, O'Donnel?"

"I was not! I've never been taken up by the police. It wasn't my fault at all . . . I . . ." She stopped warily, but Gilpin pounced.

"Whose fault was it?"

"It wasn't mine! What did that cop say about me?"

Mr. Gilpin examined his fingernails carefully. "He said nothing about you. He wanted to know if I thought you are a respectable person."

Brigid's face flamed, and Gilpin watched her interestedly. She had a number of things to say about the policeman, and she wanted to know what Gilpin had said about her. She could think of no reasonable way to put them, and she fought them back. Gilpin looked disappointed.

"I told him," he said mildly, "that as far as I know you are."

Brigid stared at him, openmouthed. Mr. Gilpin had stood up for her? She was so relieved that she forgot all caution.

"Oh, thank you, sir! Thank you, Mr. Gilpin. It was all a mistake. It wasn't my fault at all . . ."

Funny little Mr. Gilpin had taken her side and sent that nosy cop packing. He deserved an explanation.

"You see, we were in a restaurant . . . Me an' my friend Maria . . . There were two men . . . One of 'em was a soldier, an' he said somethin' awful to Maria, an' she ran outside, an' I went to help her . . ."

Mr. Gilpin no longer looked pleasant. He looked as if he had tasted something repellent.

"A soldier?" The way he said "soldier" made it sound dirty.

"Well . . . one of 'em was. The one that made the trouble, but . . ."

"You allowed a soldier to accost you in a restaurant?"

"No, sir! I wouldn't ever do that! The other one wasn't wearing a uniform."

Gilpin shook his head. "They don't have to in the city, O'Donnel. If they didn't accost you in the restaurant, just where did you meet them?"

"Uh . . . well, you see, Mr. Gilpin . . ."

He shut his eyes momentarily. "In the street!"

Oh, God! Brigid prayed silently. Get me out of this.

Mr. Gilpin drew a deep breath. "I shall have to discharge you, O'Donnel."

"But it wasn't my fault! I told you . . ."

He raised a small, offended hand. "Whose fault has nothing to do with it. You allowed a common soldier to pick you up . . . in the street! There was some sort of altercation in front of a number of people. Just suppose one of them came to Lord and Taylor's to make a purchase and found you in our employ! Why, that's appalling!"

Brigid gathered her wits and pled urgently. Gilpin simply looked more shocked. When she ran out of words he repeated coldly that she was discharged.

Obviously he was not to be moved. "Will you give me a reference?" she asked despondently. "I've worked here almost a year an' I've never given any trouble."

"Not a line! The fewer people who know that Lord and Taylor's made the mistake of employing you the better."

Brigid's eyes burned, but she fought back the tears. He would not have that pleasure.

"I've money due me," she said desperately.

He handed her an envelope. "Three days. Count it."

She opened the envelope numbly. One dollar and

46

ninety-nine cents. The miserable little bastard hadn't even the heart to make it an even two. She put it in her pocket and found her way blindly out of his office.

In the corridor she dried her eyes, counted the money again, and swore luridly. Street waifs in an orphanage acquired a vocabulary not even guessed at by the good Sisters, and Brigid used it all. Gilpin, the policeman, and the two soldiers drew the brunt of her fury, but she had some for herself.

He trapped you, O'Donnel. All that damned cop did was ask about you, and you had to shoot off your big Irish mouth and tell that dirty little Nancy Boy all about it. You thought he was standing up for you, and he was just tolling you on. Had your money all ready . . . just waiting for you to blab it all out so he could fire you.

Rage expended, she confronted a grim prospect. No reference, no job. No job, no room. The day she could not pay Mrs. Pfalz, the widow would put her out. She had to find some kind of work before that happened.

She went to Stewart's, hoping Maria could help her get a place there, but she should have known better.

"Doesn't work here any more," said the timekeeper. "I don't know where she is."

No need to ask why. God, that cop must hate women. She ate little in the following days. A dollar and fifteen cents of the three days' pay from Lord and Taylor's had to be saved for Mrs. Pfalz. That was a week's rent, payable in advance by noon Sunday without fail. She had to keep the room as long as she could, even if it meant nothing to eat, because once she was locked out the chance of finding a decent job all but disappeared. Thursday, Friday, and Saturday she walked uncounted miles looking for work.

Once she found it—in a basement where a dozen women worked buttonholes in a mountain of garments. They were paid by the buttonhole, and they worked in grim silence like machines. Brigid was so slow at it the manager gave her a few coins at the end of the day and told her not to come back.

She lived on soup, bologna-ends, and stale bread,

grudging the pennies spent on this miserable fare. On Sunday she went to Saint Bernard's despondently. Gloved and hatted, she arrived before Mass, blessed herself with a finger dipped in the font by the door, and made her way to the side altar of the Blessed Virgin behind its bank of winking candles. There were some pennies in the box with the fresh candles, and they tempted her sorely. She had so little money left. She compromised guiltily by relighting a candle that had gone out, without putting anything in the box.

"Hail, Mary, full of grace . . ." the familiar words tumbled from her lips, ". . . pray for us sinners now . . ."

Prayers I need surely, she thought, but I need help quick. I don't want to be what my ma was. Her room rent was due and she did not have it.

Mass began, and she followed it automatically, staring up at Saint Bernard in his big stained-glass window. The great, soothing words of the priest came to her distantly, and for the moment she forgot her empty, complaining stomach and remembered Reverend Mother Felicitas in Boston, extolling the powers of Saint Bernard. *"Rem-murrer,"* her young charges called her, and they listened wide-eyed as she told how the good saint had come to the monastery he had built in Italy to find it besieged by flies that tormented the monks.

Flies, I excommunicate thee, Saint Bernard had said, and on the morrow they lay dead in windrows, every one of them.

If he could do that to flies, Brigid wondered, why couldn't he help me a little? Just a word with Mrs. Pfalz, maybe?

The widow Pfalz must have been tougher than the flies. She listened to Brigid's plea and shook her head.

"You owe me for a week already. You promised to pay it and you haven't, and now you've lost your job."

It was true. Three weeks ago Brigid had begged a delay so she could use the rent money to buy a coveted pair of new shoes. In the anguish of losing her place at Lord and Taylor's she had forgotten it. Mrs. Pfalz held out her hand for the key.

48

"Two dollars and thirty cents and you can have it back. I'll give you a week before I put the room up to let and sell your things."

"Oh, no! My clothes?"

"Everything. If there's any money left over besides what's owing, I'll give it to you."

Brigid stared at her in silent misery until she shut the door. Her mother's last resort loomed before her, but she would put it off as long as she could.

She knew how to trip the latch on the gate in the alley opening into the back court of the tailor shop, and after dark she did so, to spend the night in Mrs. Pfalz's woodshed. When she slipped out in the morning, though, she saw the children watching her from the second floor window, and she knew the widow would fix the gate latch before another night.

3

The only activity visible from the window of the Fort
Columbus library was a small dog digging excitedly in a
new flower bed. Michael Brennan watched him glumly.
From a distance came the harsh, monotonous commands of the man who had taken over recruit drill
when the headquarters orderly had summoned Michael
from that dull task.

Michael preferred boredom to what confronted him.
He had been half-expecting this summons since Mon-
day, and there was no use speculating that Captain
Dennett might have something pleasant to say to him.

The other occupant of the room dabbed at a corner
with a broom. He was a recruit whose blistered feet had
earned him a job as barracks orderly in lieu of drill.
There was no dirt in the corner, but the presence of a
corporal demanded activity. The recruit knew that not
even a corporal ought to be in the library at this time of
day, and was puzzled, but that was because he did not
yet understand the requirements of good military order.
A noncommissioned officer could not join common sinners waiting for judgment on the bench outside the detachment commander's office.

Michael ignored the recruit and leafed irritably
through the newspapers on the table. The *Evening Post,*
Hoarce Greeley's *Tribune,* and the weekly *Ledger* were

beyond his ken. He found them dull. The *Ledger* had dropped the Reverend Henry Ward Beecher's serials simply because he had been tried for adultery, but Michael found a stimulating tidbit on an inside page. A correspondent speculated that the woman involved with President Grant's secretary, General Orville Babcock, in the Whiskey Ring scandal was actually a beautiful Saint Louis courtesan known as "Sylph."

"Sylph," wrote the *Ledger*'s man, "is the essence of grace, distilled from the buds of perfection, with a tongue on which the oil of vivacity and seduction never ceased running. . . ."

It was hard to picture the woman in language like that. Michael tried the *Post*. William Tweed, from his prison cell, offered his remaining property, and testimony against his partners in sin, for early release. Governor Tilden rejected the offer. A great European engineer declared the half-completed Brooklyn bridge "arrogantly ugly." Michael found another man with whom he could sympathize. Despite his resignation, the Congress was determined to impeach ex–Secretary of War Belknap. A full trial might reveal the extent of his conspiracy with his first and second wives to defraud the government.

Michael watched the dog, up to his elbows in dirt now, and swore silently. Women are the devil's limbs, he told himself. The orderly, grown used to Michael's presence, hummed tunelessly a hymn brought out of church and onto the street by Moody and Sankey's ten-week revival meeting at the Hippodrome.

"Soldier," said Michael.

"Yes, Corporal?"

"Shut up!"

The headquarters orderly appeared in the door. "Corporal Brennan?" he said cautiously. "You're to go in now."

Michael tugged his blouse down over his hips and knocked twice at Captain Dennett's door—crisply but not too hard.

Dennett commanded the entire recruit detachment on

Governors Island. He was a lean, swarthy man, a brevet colonel at the war's end, reduced in 1869 to his present rank. He regarded Brennan sourly.

"You know why I sent for you, Corporal?"

Clearly, pussyfooting around Captain Dennett would be useless, and Michael abandoned any pretense of innocence.

"Yes, sir."

Dennett flicked a paper across his desk as if it smelled bad, and Michael needed only a glance to identify it. The policeman's scrawl across the weekend pass was unmistakable. But the damned cop had not stopped there.

"Patrolman George Schultz of the metropolitan force was here yesterday." Dennett bared his teeth in what might have been a smile. "Sergeant Schultz, he used to be. Two hitches in the Fifth Cavalry. Good man. Damned few make sergeant in two hitches."

May the devil take his black soul, thought Michael fervently. It seemed that women and the United States cavalry were his nemesis. But none of this showed on his face. Ramrod straight, he kept his eyes fixed at a point on the wall several feet above the captain's head. Dennett sighed unconvincingly.

"You've been a good soldier, Brennan . . . until this." He touched the defaced pass delicately.

Dennett's reputation was an evil one. No one had ever even suspected him of leniency, much less caught him at it. If minor sins like this one were properly handled by the two elderly lieutenants commanding the companies of the detachment, Michael could have counted on a reprimand and another chance. But Dennett knew his lieutenants, and selected cases at random for his own rulings.

"Sergeant Schultz," he continued, "tells me he has made inquiries about the women involved in this." His eyes glittered and he leaned forward. "They are respectable! Damn it, Brennan, I'm not surprised that fool Smigocki can't tell a decent woman from a whore, but you . . . you ought to know better!"

There was a silence that lengthened until Michael's nerve broke.

"Yes, sir," he said woodenly.

Dennett fixed him with a reptilian eye. "Come down off that wall and look at me, Corporal."

The idea was repellent, but Michael obeyed.

"The men of this detachment are more than just soldiers. They represent the United States Army in New York City. Brennan, you have disgraced the whole outfit. Have you got anything to say for yourself?"

Michael considered a number of things he had planned to offer in defense, studied Dennett's furious face, and abandoned them. Nothing in the captain's expression or posture—crouch would best describe it—offered the slightest hope for what he had in mind.

"No, sir. I made a mistake, sir."

"Well, by God! That's honest, at least. All right, Brennan, I'll give you a break. Report to the adjutant within twenty-four hours with a request to be transferred back to your regiment, or I'll have you before a court-martial for disorderly conduct in a week."

A break. Well, yes. To Dennett's way of thinking, Michael decided, this bordered on coddling. He had heard about Dennett's courts.

"Well?"

"Sir, I will report to the adjutant right away."

"Good. And, Brennan . . ."

"Yes, sir?"

"If he wants to know why you're making such a fool's request, you can tell him you need to soldier a while with your company to get your stripes back."

Michael digested that slowly, and Dennett gave him a questioning look.

"Yes?"

"Nothing, sir."

"All right, Private Brennan. That's all. Tell the orderly to send in the next one."

Michael saluted, faced about precisely, and marched out. At the moment he had no very great anger at Dennett. But he could not decide which he would rather have in his hands at the moment—a spiteful little red-head or Patrolman George Schultz.

"Throw him another one," he told the orderly. "He ain't full yet."

Recruit drill continued on the parade ground, but that was no longer his concern. Before he went to see the adjutant, he had an unhappy job to perform. He walked back to his barracks to find Smigocki transferring the contents of his wall locker to a canvas bag.

"What the hell are you doing?"

"What d'you think? I'm going back to Fort-damn-Barrancas!"

4

A night on the kindling in the widow Pfalz's woodshed
had not improved Brigid's appearance, and on Monday
afternoon the heavens burst with a cold rain that completed her ruin. There was no use asking for work the
way she looked now.

She headed for the Bowery in search of a dry stoop
under which to spend the night. The Bowery was no
place to look for decent work, but the cops were more
tolerant of poor folk who slept under other people's
steps. A heavy gust of rain drove her to cover in the
doorway of a restaurant on Houston Street, and a few
minutes later a man stepped in with her. He was muttering at the weather and did not notice her.

Whenever the door of the restaurant opened it emit-
ted wonderful odors of food, and Brigid breathed them
in, swallowing hard. On Friday a mission on Fourteenth
Street had given her a bowl of soup and four stale rolls,
the last of which had been her Sunday meal. She was
surprised the man standing in the doorway with her did
not hear the complaints of her empty stomach.

A couple left the restaurant, squeezing Brigid behind
the door, and her unknown companion stepped into the
rain to let them pass. In the watery light of the street
lamp, his big mustache looked familiar, but she had
spoken to so many men in her search for work that he

could be any of them. When he returned to shelter, his heel came down hard on her foot and she squeaked in protest.

"I beg pardon, miss," he said, peering at her in surprise. "I didn't see you come out."

"I didn't," she said inanely. "I've been here all the time."

The restaurant door opened again, and instead of stepping out to make room, the stranger crowded closer to Brigid. A lady would have protested, but Brigid was not thinking of that. She was too hungry. She slipped her hand into his and gave it a squeeze.

"Ah!" he said. "Well . . ." Replacing his hat, he pushed the door inward to let the light fall on her face. "All right. Where shall we go?"

Brigid had trouble with her voice, and he could not hear her reply.

"Where?"

"I said . . . will you give me supper . . . first?"

He looked dubious, and she managed a tremulous smile.

I must look like a drowned sparrow, she thought. I don't know how to do this. Oh, Ma, if you'd only lasted long enough to teach me. She expected that now he had seen her he would change his mind.

But he didn't. "All right," he said again. "This will do. No use getting any wetter."

She nodded and gripped his hand.

"You'll have to let go so we can go in," he chuckled. "I'll buy you supper."

He led the way to a table and she followed, her skirt leaving a wet track on the floor. Seated, she preened herself, looking at the bar mirror. Like a wet sparrow for sure, she saw. Taking off her hat, she tucked up wet strands of hair.

"A drink?" he asked.

She shook her head. She wanted nothing to delay the arrival of food. He was studying her curiously and she dropped her eyes. Good grief, she thought, I have surely seen that mustache before.

56

"Beer and a shot of rye for me," he told the waiter, then looked at her. "You want to order now?"

"Oh, yes, please!"

The waiter extended a wooden paddle with the menu tacked to it.

"Soup," she told him without looking at it. "You can bring that straightaway, and I'll decide on the rest by the time you get back."

Brigid looked at her escort shyly and found him frowning. At the same moment she remembered where she had seen the mustache, he remembered her.

"I'll be damned!" he exclaimed. *"You! . . ."*

She couldn't help it. She was rocking with laughter. She should have been furious, haughty, anything but squealing with laughter, but she couldn't stop it. She pointed a shaking finger at him.

"The cop! God in his holy Heaven . . . you're the cop!"

"O'Donnel," he said in astonishment. "Brigid O'Donnel . . . one-six-three West Twelfth Street."

"Not any more," she giggled. "That was when I was rich. Do I have to call you Officer?"

He was laughing, himself, now. Half rising, he made her a mock bow. "George Schultz, and I'm pleased to see you again, Brigid."

"Where's your uniform? And that fearful great stick?"

"It's my day off." He frowned again. "What are you doing . . . ?" he jerked a thumb toward the street.

She was going to enjoy this. There was no other way. And she was going to have all the supper she could hold. He owed her that.

"Well you may ask, George Schultz. It's you that brought me to it."

"How, for God's sake?"

"You took your busy self to Lord and Taylor's and told that Mary Ann of a Super some awful story about me."

"I did not! He fired you?"

She nodded.

57

"But I never told him anything. I just asked . . . well, I asked about you."

She giggled again. "That was enough. That little maggot had me up an' got the story out of me. Ah, he's the clever one, he is! Oh . . . good!"

The waiter had put a bowl before her, and George Schultz watched, grinning, as she ordered her supper between mouthfuls of soup.

"I'll have the ham hocks and cabbage with a side order of potatoes an' some bean salad, and you can bring some rolls an' butter right away."

Schultz laughed. It was impossible not to enjoy her frank anticipation. "That sounds fine. I'll have the same, and bring me another beer . . . a schooner this time."

Brigid gave him a wicked look. "I've changed my mind. Can I have a glass of beer, too?"

"Sure."

He watched in growing amusement as she finished the soup and attacked the heaping plate of meat and cabbage the waiter brought her.

"How long since you ate, Brigid?"

"I can't remember. Can I have some cheese and a big cracker?"

"Surely. My God, you eat like a dock-walloper, girl!"

She pointed to the door as she spread butter on the last roll. "Good Saint Christopher brought you there to make up for the evil you've done. You can't back out now."

"I won't, but . . . I don't understand. Would no one else give you supper?"

Brigid found and ate the last crumb, and looked at him seriously. Even if he was a cop and the cause of all her trouble, he seemed a nice man.

"Would you believe me, George, if I said you're the first man I asked?"

"Well . . . if you say so."

"It's true." She finished the cheese and cracker and sighed. "Oh, that was good. You see, George, I was

58

that low, I'd decided the next man I saw I'd ask him. That's when you stepped on my foot."

"What if I'd said no?"

"No what?"

"No supper."

She frowned. "I don't know. I was so hungry I didn't think about that."

"Are you still hungry?"

She saw where that question led. "Can I have some dessert?"

He sighed and beckoned the waiter.

"Pie," she said. "What kind is there?"

"Apple's good, miss."

"That's all right," said George, "bring two big pieces and coffee. You want coffee, Brigid?"

"Oh, yes!"

When she had cleaned her plate and was watching him over the rim of her coffee cup, he tried again.

"Still hungry?"

"No, thank you. It was a grand supper." But that wasn't what he was asking at all. She bit her lip.

"What's the matter?"

"It's just . . . ah, George, I'm thinkin' that if I have to be a whore . . . I don't want to start with you." She watched him apprehensively. "Are you real mad?"

He thought a moment. "No. I guess I had it coming. I got you in this fix, didn't I?"

She nodded and he put his hand over hers. "I'm sorry. I was a soldier once, and these coffee-coolers here in the city give me a pain. I had to find out what kind of girls you and your friend are. I wouldn't have made them trouble if you'd been . . ." He shrugged.

"What I am now?" she finished softly for him.

He said nothing, and she picked at her napkin.

"I guess you're thinkin' I've had my supper an' now it's time I paid for it, aren't you?"

"No. I didn't mean that. I'm sorry I made you so much trouble, and you don't have to give me anything. What are you going to do now?"

"I don't know. Maybe I'll go somewhere else and look for a decent job."

"I don't mean that. I mean tonight. You've been locked out, haven't you?"

"Oh . . ." With that supper inside her, she felt more courageous. "I'll make out."

"But it's raining like hell out there. Where can you find a place? Have you got any money at all?"

"No! And I'm not askin' for any!"

"I wasn't offering it. You want a place to sleep?"

She eyed him doubtfully.

"Dammit! You can stay at my place and I'll not bother you. I told you I'm sorry for what I did."

She considered his offer warily. Maybe he means it, she decided, and it's got to be better than a leaky stoop somewhere. She smiled at him.

"I guess I've got to learn to take all I can get, haven't I, George? You're a good man. I'll take your word . . . an' a bit of your room if you mean it."

His rooming house was not far—on Saint Luke's Place just below Bedford—and she clung to his arm as they jumped the overflowing gutters. He had a second-floor room, as shabby as her own, but it was dry and warm after he lit a kerosene stove sitting in a sand box in the corner.

5

Smigocki's bitter announcement that he was being sent back to his artillery company at Fort Barrancas was no surprise to Michael. Ex-sergeant George Schultz of the Fifth Cavalry was obviously a very thorough policeman. Pulling his uniform blouses from his locker, Michael threw them on the bed and set to work.

Keeping a curious eye on his roommate, Smigocki prodded the red spot on his shoulder left by Brigid's hatpin and muttered a sulfurous Polish oath. The extent of the disaster created by that redheaded spitfire overwhelmed him. His case had been dealt with summarily—he was not a real corporal. The company first sergeant had tossed his cherished acting-corporal's stripes in a drawer and told him curtly to take the cars back to Florida on Monday with a draft of recruits for the Fifth Artillery.

Having escaped from Fort Barrancas to the paradise of New York only eight months past, the prospect of return to that dank hellhole appalled Smigocki. Watching Brennan, he understood that he was not alone in his misery. Michael was carefully stripping the corporal's chevrons from his blouse with the point of a knife.

"You too?"

Michael ignored him. He folded the chevrons, put

them away, and donned a stripped coat. Settling his forage cap on his head, he made for the door.

"Where you going?" Smigocki demanded.

"I don't know it's any of your business, Smig," said Michael mildly, "but I'm goin' to the adjutant's office to make some arrangements." He checked the set of his cap in the mirror. "I don't like it here anymore."

Smigocki stared at him in astonishment. Brennan had obviously just been reduced from corporal to private. A visit to the adjutant's office probably meant he was being sent away from New York. He should have been furious, but instead he grinned and departed whistling.

In the past few months Smigocki had begun to think of himself as an old soldier—a successful one just like Brennan. But the way Brennan was taking this catastrophe made it clear they were not at all alike.

Their backgrounds seemed to be similar. Each had left his native land for America in search of something. Each had tried civilian life in this new country, and in the end, both had come to the army. But there were considerable differences in their paths.

Reaching America after the war, Smigocki had no contact with the military until the great depression of 1873 drove him into the army for shelter. Enlisting in the artillery, he had served in sleepy coast-defense posts and had seen no fighting. Brigid O'Donnel had given him his first wound. Michael Brennan, on the contrary, had seen fighting in and out of the army, and he had not joined the regulars as a refugee from anything.

Born in Cork in the last year of the terrible Irish famine, Michael had escaped starvation because his father's employment on the docks was sustained by thousands of desperate men and women abandoning the country. At seventeen, Michael had become a roustabout too, but unlike the elder Brennan, he enjoyed the political turmoil disrupting the port city of Cork.

As a matter of course, he had joined the Fenian movement, intrigued by the Byzantine complexity of secret cells, agents, and activity brewed by the Irish Republican Brotherhood. Some of these he enjoyed too openly. Identified by the police in one too many dock-side brawls, he faced a choice of prison or flight, and he chose the latter. His membership in the Brotherhood had been neither informed nor passionate. Conspiracy and brawling were fun, but the larger issues bored him. He had not the foggiest notion who Karl Marx might be—only that the Irish Catholic clergy decried that strange ally of the Fenians as the source of a heresy called Communism and did its effective best to destroy both movements. In the process they lost Michael, because he distrusted a church whose priests talked to the police about their parishioners.

Reaching New York in the summer of 1864, he had been drafted from the dock into the Union army and a month later found himself in the trenches outside Richmond in Virginia. The Confederacy was dying, but General Robert Lee's hungry veterans in the thirty-seven miles of earthworks defending their capital did not seem to realize it.

South of Petersburg where the Federals probed for Lee's flank, there was a war of movement, but not in the Army of the James holding the center of the siege lines. Here there was nothing but cold, miserable trench warfare, which left Michael no impression greater than his survival of it. His outstanding memory of the war was a stinging little defeat of no importance at all, inflicted on his regiment after Richmond had fallen.

Michael's regiment of draftees had followed the retreating rebels as they marched toward Appomattox Courthouse and the war's end. Overtaking a graycoat column, the Union brigade commander ordered his drafted unit onto the forward slope of a ridge overlooking the Confederate line of retreat to slow the southerners with musket fire until he could encircle and mop them up. It seemed a safe job for a doubtful regiment.

The Confederates were moving along a muddy road which was still, surprisingly, hedged by cross-rail fences not yet taken for firewood. No one expected trouble from the shabby little column of defeated men, and Michael's regiment had opened fire at a comfortable range with a feeling of security. The result was shocking.

Above the bark of their muskets the northerners heard a thin yelling of Confederate officers, and without even breaking step the rebels had wheeled and erupted from the road. They did not even pause to throw down the fence. They simply burst through it, the rails flying into the air. Nor did they pause to return fire. Bowing their heads, they came across the field at a fast, purposeful walk, eating up the distance at a surprising rate.

"Shit—oh, dear!" Michael's corporal had muttered, scrambling to his feet. "Them bastards ain't gonna stop!"

Michael had been seized by the same conviction. Nobody—nothing—was going to stop those Confederates. They came swinging through the smoke of Yankee muskets, bearded men and beardless boys, and suddenly they were running, making a shrill terrible noise.

A winter in the trenches before Richmond had developed one thing in the regiment of draftees—a keen sense of self-preservation. The bluecoat line dissolved into clusters of fleeing men. Greener officers would have yelled and used the flat of their swords on the fugitives—real veterans would have used their revolvers. Michael's officers did neither. They went with their men.

On the next rise of ground there were derisive yells and a waving of black hats. A part of the encircling force had stopped to watch the show, and Michael's regiment made for them in a scrambling run. Rebel slugs cracked overhead and tore up chunks of muddy grass, and Michael never forgot that last despairing sprint, greeted by laughter and cheerful insults from the regulars on the crest. The roar of their rifles as the draftees stumbled through them was a wonderful sound.

One of those veterans, ducking to reload in safety, had grinned at Michael. "You fellers sure can move when you want to!"

"Hell! We had to get outta there!"

"You're right about that. Them Rebs was goin' to eat you up."

"What in hell got into 'em?" Michael had wondered aloud.

"Shoo!" said the regular. "They was just plain mad. What'd you fellers do to 'em?"

He slammed a careful shot down the slope and slid back into cover once more. "Hope they don't take it in their head to come on up here. Ain't seen Rebs that mad in a year now."

Four days later the war in Virginia had ended. Michael Brennan never saw Appomattox Courthouse, nor even the great victory parade up Pennsylvania Avenue in Washington. His regiment was mustered out of service quickly, and he drifted back to New York and the only trade he knew—stevedoring on the docks. It proved dull until one day a voice from the past whispered in his ear.

"Michael Brennan, is it not? The Brothers are wantin' a word with you, lad."

That was in December of 1865, and Michael had found himself once more embroiled in Fenian plots. The American branch of the movement was launched on a strange, mad enterprise. Godfrey Massey, ex-Confederate officer, was gathering rebel and Yankee veterans and wild-eyed Irish immigrant boys to invade Canada. Incredibly, in May of 1866, some six hundred men—including Michael Brennan—actually crossed the Niagara River near Buffalo, New York, under command of a wild man named John O'Neill.

Before dawn on the first of June the Irish tricolor flew for the first time over English soil, and by seven o'clock the Queen's Own Volunteers of Toronto had dressed ranks and marched into the Fenian muskets lining Limestone Ridge by Fort Erie. Veterans among the Irish picked off a dozen and wounded thirty of these brave amateur soldiers, driving off the rest, but next day British regulars appeared and O'Neill's little army scrambled back into the United States.

From his nine months of static war and three days of

comic-opera skirmishing in Canada, Michael Brennan had distilled one sure thing. If ever again he had to do with the military, it would be with the regulars. He wanted no more of conscripts, volunteers, or militia.

But then he had no intention of joining the army. For four years he had drifted happily from job to job. New York, Buffalo, Cleveland, Saint Louis—he tried them all. In Buffalo he laid street-railway tracks, and in Cleveland he worked in a buggy factory. In Saint Louis he had a run of luck at poker and worked at nothing at all, until he encountered an army recruiting corporal who lost money gracefully at poker, agreed that soldiering was a dog's life, and suggested dice as an alternative to cards.

Michael lost all his poker money at craps and wagered his own enlistment against ten dollars. High dice won him first roll, but it was a pair of sixes and he was back in the army. The recruiting corporal was a big man—as big as Michael—so there had been no discussion of the honesty of his dice.

"Hell," the corporal had laughed, "it was your ten dollars. So what if I lost it? That was a good bet. Now I got you an' the ten dollars an' your enlistment bounty to boot."

Michael paused on the stoop of the barracks and looked at the quadrangle gloomily. Cards and dice had always made him trouble, but not women—not until Brigid. But then he remembered another woman and a chill ran up his back.

That game of craps in Saint Louis had sent him to the Nineteenth Infantry in Louisiana. It was on "reconstruction duty," an elegant name for federal occupation of the defeated Confederacy, but that ended abruptly in 1874 when the regiment transferred to Fort Wallace in Kansas.

Like many trans-Mississippi posts, Wallace had been left behind by the frontier. It had seen considerable fighting while it guarded Smoky Hill wagon trail and the construction crews of the Kansas Pacific railroad, but by 1874 the trail was a memory and the railroad had reached Colorado.

But because it had good barracks and eight fine sets of officers' quarters, the army clung to Fort Wallace though its garrison had little to do. Not until nine months after Michael's arrival had his company seen any action, and then it was dignified by that name only because a man was wounded.

The company had been hurried sixty miles east by rail to defend the citizens of Grinnell Station against "hostile" Cheyenne Indians—who turned out to be a little band trying to exchange buffalo skins with a store-keeper for flour and salt. The storekeeper had cheated them and they protested, and the telegrapher at the railway depot had heated the wires demanding army protection.

The whole affair would have amounted to nothing but a shouting match except that the trader's wife had discharged a shotgun from the store window. The lieutenant had restrained his troops and the Cheyennes had taken to their heels, but at extreme range some sorehead among them had arched an arrow at the troops. It clanged off the tin roof of an outhouse and opened a spectacular gash in Private Michael Brennan's cheek.

The wound had healed nicely, leaving a very satisfactory scar, and Michael had not heard another shot fired until the last act of the Red River War in Texas spilled northward.

During the winter of 1874–75, General Phil Sheridan had deployed most of the forces of the Military Division of the Missouri to round up the Comanches, Kiowas, and Cheyennes who had been terrorizing Texas. When he had them all back on their reservations he ordered "ringleaders" and "Indians guilty of crime" sorted out for transportation to the ancient Spanish fortress of Castillo de San Marcos in Florida. They were put in the charge of Lieutenant Richard Pratt, whose experience with them at Fort Marion—as the army named its Florida prison—led him later to found the Carlisle Indian School in Pennsylvania.

During this sorting-out, in April of 1875, a black-smith at the Cheyenne and Arapaho Agency in the Indian Territory was fitting leg-irons on a Cheyenne named Black Horse when the taunts of his women moved the Indian to bolt. He was shot down, but the fracas set a hundred and fifty nervous Cheyennes in motion. They had hidden their weapons on a nearby sandhill, and from this elevation they stood off three troops of cavalry reinforced by a Gatling gun. Subsequently most of them drifted back to the agency, but a party of sixty struck north to escape. In a burst of ingenious speed, cavalry went in pursuit.

Lieutenant Austin Henely's troop of the Sixth Cavalry loaded forty troopers and their horses onto rail cars, and by a circuitous route reached Fort Wallace, where they should have been ahead of the fleeing Indians. Henely borrowed a lieutenant, two wagons, and four doughboys from Major Hambright, commanding Fort Wallace, and went after the Indians.

Riding south, he found the Cheyenne trail and realized they were far ahead of him, already across the Kansas Pacific tracks and headed for Nebraska. Henely turned north and caught his quarry on Sappa Creek, only thirty miles south of the Kansas-Nebraska line, where he surprised them with a dawn attack. Michael Brennan, on loan from his infantry company, had joined in that assault.

It was Michael's introduction to the dirty fighting that was the reality of Indian warfare. The army tried to dignify its engagements with Indians as war in conventional terms, but its opponents were not a military force. They were a people in arms forced to fight with no recourse but guerrilla warfare. Under those conditions, killing was not confined to men.

When Indians killed white women and children it was reported as savagery. When the army killed Indian women and children it was preferably not reported at all—a clue to the feeling of combat soldiers about it. Inevitably there were some who enjoyed indiscriminate killing, but most of the regular army had strict Victorian ideas about killing civilians—particularly women and children. Officers who encouraged it were considered deviants of an unattractive sort. They might win renown as great Indian fighters, but their soldiers never forgot how they gained it.

Austin Henely, however, was a very correct young lieutenant. When he had surrounded his quarry he invited the startled Indians to surrender, but they responded with a blast of gunfire. Some escaped but the remainder, dismounted and trapped, dug in and fought. From a dry stream bed they knocked over an alarming number of cavalry horses, so Henely dismounted to attack on foot. Michael had gone into the attack with the cavalrymen.

Sprinting for a rock in front of the Indian position, he had been knocked sprawling by an Indian bullet that plowed diagonally across his back just under his shoulder blades. He knew it was a bad wound when he put his hand into the hot, wet mess of his coat in the small of his back, but Henely was up and yelling for a final rush and Michael had gone with him.

He never understood what had become of all the Indians who had been shooting at him. Other men boasted later of clubbing or shooting Indians when they broke into the dry wash, but where Michael entered it there was only one, and she was dead.

He never forgot her. Whenever he was sleeping off a bit of whiskey, she haunted him.

She had scratched out a hollow in the sand where she had fought and died, her head pillowed on a pile of spent cartridges and a carbine beneath her. At a distance she had seemed just a heap of faded cloth with a mop of black hair, but close up she was human, female, and shocking.

She must have raised up too high, trying for a difficult shot, for she had been hit in the throat. She had thrashed over onto her back to die, her face no longer brown but a pale orange in death. Before it had frozen in agony she might have been handsome, for she was certainly young.

Michael had knelt beside her, fighting his nausea. His back felt as if it had been drilled by a hot poker, but he could think of nothing but the dead girl.

I didn't kill her, he had told himself desperately. I couldn't have. I didn't even know she was here. Jesus, Mary, and Joseph, why did she stay?

No one else seemed worried about the dead woman. Lieutenant Henely had said Michael was a good soldier and would have a medal for his bravery, but that had gotten lost somewhere in the cracks of the army. All he got from the fight at Sappa Creek was a recurrent nightmare about a girl he might have killed.

He shook off this memory and clattered down the iron steps to the ground-floor stoop of the barracks. It was not true that that was all he had from Sappa Creek. When it was known that eight of Henely's troopers and none of the infantry would receive the Medal of Honor, Major Hambright had exploded. All his inquiries produced nothing, so he had rewarded Michael in his own way. Somehow he had him transferred into the Twenty-first Infantry with promotion to corporal and even more surprisingly detailed to a house-cat job in New York City. It was, in Michael's opinion, better than any medal, and now a redheaded, green-eyed little witch had blown it all away.

6

George Schultz sighed. Brigid, tugging at the ribbon holding her wet hair, paused with her arms uplifted to look at him.

"What's the matter?"

"Nothing. Why?"

She had stripped off her wet dress and hung it on the door of the cupboard by the stove. That left only her chemise and a petticoat with limp, smudged flounces. She followed George's bemused eyes and laughed. The damp chemise clung to her with fidelity, and with her arms raised, her small, full breasts taxed its capacity.

"Shut your mouth, George," she told him cheerfully. "You'll catch a fly."

He looked sheepish and she gave him a smile. "Have you a spare blanket I can wrap around me till my clothes dry a bit?"

"I've only the one on the bed, and it's rough enough to take the hide from you. Why don't you just get under it for a while? There's a sheet, top and bottom."

Her green eyes snapped at him. "No, thank you, George. I'll take your word for it. Come on, now . . . find me something to cover myself with, will you not?"

He sighed again and rummaged in the cupboard until he found a gray woolen shirt, a collarless pullover relic of his army days, washed almost white and soft as vel-

71

vet. Brigid held it to her shoulders, measuring its length judiciously. It fell to an inch above her knees, and she looked doubtful.

"Ah, well. Needs must when the Devil drives. I'd thank you, George, if you'd just go and see how the rain is doing while I get into this thing. Have you a towel for me?"

"You want me to leave?" he asked plaintively.

"Ah, no! Just look out the window, man."

The soft, abrasive sound of her towelling sent tingles up his back, but he kept his eyes on the drenched street until she asked if he could lend her a comb or a brush.

"It's a currycomb I'll be needing for this mop if I don't treat it to a little soap and water soon. That devil's dam of a landlady won't even let me in to wash myself."

George turned to find her sitting crosslegged on his bed, the shirttails tucked under her knees, frowning as she worked a hairpin through the thin wool to close the neck of the shirt.

"This thing hasn't a button to its name, George. Have you no girl to sew them on for you?"

"What for? I've no girl and no need for that shirt anyway. Haven't worn it since I joined the force."

He handed her his hairbrush. The shirt enveloped her small body, shoulders drooping to meet the rolled sleeves pushed up her arms. He wished it were not so big.

There was a long silence while she pulled the brush through the damp tangle of her hair, the gaslight striking warm glints in its depths as it began to dry. George studied his visitor with interest.

A small girl, maybe an inch over five feet, but just barely. Her face was pensive at the moment, and he tried to guess her age. There were a lot of contradictions in that face.

The nose was small, very cleanly modeled, the bridge inset beneath the smooth curve of the forehead, the tip pertly upturned. Her mouth was wide with full lips, a little flattened in repose, but when she smiled or spoke or gave her attention to something that interested her it

72

moved and curled provocatively. The small round chin flaunted a minute dimple at its center. But these were the conventional features of a pretty young Irish girl. The contradictions were more interesting.

The green eyes could change from ingenuousness to deviltry in a flash, and sometimes to a startling hardness. The fine lines bracketing her eyes and mouth seemed born of laughter until the eyes turned hard. Then they bespoke a toughness, hard-learned. She hadn't seemed tough enough at supper to make her living soliciting men on the street, but maybe she was cleverer than he thought.

Suddenly conscious of his scrutiny, she peered at him beneath her arm and frowned.

"Sure and when you watch me like that, I'm minded you're Officer Schultz an' not just a kind man with a shirt to spare. What is it now, George?"

She was still working the brush through her waist-length hair, and George's eyes made her aware of the movement of her breasts under the loose shirt. She sighed and put the brush down.

"I was only wonderin' how old you are, Brigid," he said hastily. "I've been tryin' to guess but I cannot."

"I thought policemen were good at that," she said tartly. "I don't really know myself. I'm thinking I must be twenty-one or -two . . . Maybe more."

He leaned forward and touched the corner of her mouth with a finger. "I didn't think you got those lines in fewer years. Have you no family at all to tell you how old you are?"

"None that I know of. My ma died when I was a little thing, and I never saw my da. The good Sisters in Boston raised me and they said my name is O'Donnel, but that's not certain."

"You've reason for a few lines, then."

She rapped the brush on his knee. "Away with you! A wrinkled hag, am I? Ah, well, it's a comfort you took me in for kindness' sake an' not just to see my pretty legs."

"Are they? You've had 'em shrouded like the dead ever since you got here."

She rapped him again, harder. "Shame on you, George Schultz! You said you'd not devil me if I came here."

He got up from the chair and bent to adjust the stove. "I'm not botherin' you," he muttered irritably. "I was only talkin'."

Brigid was instantly contrite. "I'm the one should be shamed. I ask your pardon, George." She watched the rain drumming on the window for a moment and shook her head.

"I'm in one hell of a fix, ain't I?"

She looked so forlorn he was sorry for her all over again, but there was mixed with his sorrow a less lofty urge to put his hands on the shapely body that moved so disturbingly under his old shirt. He wanted to comfort her, but not by talking to her.

"That prissy little bastard at Lord and Taylor's!" she said harshly. "If he'd only given me just a line that I'd worked there a year with nothin' about my character, I could have found me a decent job."

"I doubt it, Brigid," said George softly.

"What d'you mean? Why not?"

"Don't you know one of those soldiers laid a charge against you? It's on the book at the station house."

"Oh, my God! No! You mean the cops are lookin' for me?"

The idiocy of that question dawned on her as she asked it. The man whose bed she was sitting on could arrest her on the soldier's charge—or, for that matter, on the more serious one of accosting him in the doorway of the restaurant if he wanted to.

She stared at him apprehensively. "I only asked you for supper! I didn't . . ."

He laughed. "I'll not take you in, Brigid . . . for that nor anything that babyfaced Polack came cryin' to us about."

She clutched the gaping neck of the shirt and watched him suspiciously.

74

"I mean it. Nobody's looking for you. The book's full of men's mistakes they want somebody to pay for. We don't have time for that stuff."

"Then why can't I find a job?"

"Any good store would check with us before they hired you, even if you had a reference. You'd get no decent job with a charge against your name. There's lots of places don't check, though."

"Concert halls? No, thank you. I've no mind to go to hell in a short skirt an' belled boots. And I want no part of those Bowery dance halls either."

"That's no worse than pickin' up men on the street, is it?"

Her face flamed and she seemed about to burst out at him, but instead she dropped her eyes and sniffed miserably.

"What about a job as kitchen maid . . . Or parlor maid? Lots of families don't check before they take on help."

"Fat chance! Listen to these." She dumped a pile of pink *Police Gazette*s from George's washstand shelf and snatched out a copy of the *Herald*. Jerking the newspaper open to the pages of microscopic print listing women seeking work, she read angrily:

" 'One-six-two West Twenty-eighth, ring third bell, respectable Protestant girl as chambermaid. . . . Three-six-seven West Twenty-first, top floor, good Scotch Protestant girl as plain cook. . . .' " She threw the paper on the floor.

"Look at me, George Schultz! Do I look Scotch . . . or Protestant either? What the hell's wrong with a good Irish Catholic girl, I'm askin' you?" She added something under her breath that made him laugh.

"So what are you going to do?"

She shrugged. "Go back to Boston, I guess. The Sisters'll find me servant's work somewhere. Plenty of their girls come back with dirtier cards than mine."

"You'll take a servant's job, then?"

"What are you tryin' to get out of me?" she burst out. "I told you I won't go to a dance hall an' . . . I

75

don't want to do what I tried to do this night . . .
There's nothin' else for me."

"Would you leave the city?"

"And do what?" she demanded in astonishment.

"Work for an army family. I know a lieutenant who's
looking for a girl."

"I don't have to leave New York to find that kind of
work!"

"Ah, you idiot! He's got a wife an' two children.
They want a girl to look after the kids. The thing is . . .
they've got to find one who won't marry the first man
who crooks a finger at her when she gets out west."

Brigid's face was a study in disbelief. "Marry a soldier? Good Saint Joseph an' sweet Saint Anne! What
kind of a girl would do that?"

"Now watch your mouth! I was a soldier before I
was a cop, and I'm proud of it."

"Yes, but you quit! You were smart enough to do
that."

He groaned and ran his hand through his hair.
"You're a hard case, Biddy. I doubt you'd do for the
Carters anyway."

"George, don't call me Biddy . . . An' what makes
you so sure I wouldn't do? If I won't marry a soldier, I
might be just what they're lookin' for. Tell me about
them."

"They're good people. I've only just talked to her,
but I know she's a real lady and he's a damn fine soldier."

Brigid looked puzzled. "Then why does he have to
leave New York and go somewhere out west?"

"He's been here for three years," George explained.
"He's going back to his regiment, that's all."

"Why doesn't he get himself sent to Boston or
Philadelphia instead of going out there with all those
Indians?"

"Damn it, girl . . . he wants to go. He wants to get
promoted, and he can't do that pushin' papers in a staff
job in the city."

Brigid sniffed. "Sounds dumb to me. Now wait . . .

76

Wait!" Schultz's scowl was angry. "I don't know anything about your old army, but I can learn . . . if it would get me a job. Would they be good to me? I'm not scared to go west, but I'd not want to live in a . . . a tent or whatever soldiers live in."

"They'd be good to you if you give 'em no trouble. And you'd live in a tent if that's all they got. If they took you on an' paid your way out there, you'd have to swear not to quit for at least a year. Can you do that?"

"Sure. I told you I'd not marry a soldier, and a year's time enough to find me a better job in a city. There's got to be some cities out there."

"There's more than soldiers will be after you to marry. Plenty of civilians looking for a wife. And with that head of hair, there might be some Indians after you as well."

"You don't scare me, George. I'm not afraid of Indians." Her eyes sparkled and he saw she was intrigued. "How much would they pay me, d'you think?"

"I don't know. Ten, maybe fifteen dollars a month. That's with board and room and travel thrown in."

"Ooh! That's a lot. D'you think they'd have me?"

He shrugged. "Who knows? I'll put in a word for you, that's all I can do. They're packed up and staying at a hotel now. When I get off duty tomorrow I'll ask if you can come talk to 'em about the job. If you look sharp and mind your manners, you might get it."

"Look sharp?" she wailed, "Oh, God, what'll I do? Look at me!" She pounded her fists into the bed. "Oh, if only that fiddler's bitch would let me into my room to get another dress!"

"How much do you owe?"

"Two dollars an' thirty cents . . . an' no way to get it save lookin' at the ceiling over a man's shoulder!"

"Didn't you save any money at all?"

"Save!" she glared at him. "You crazy man, how could I save? I made four dollars a week if they didn't stop any of it for fines. I paid a dollar fifteen for the room, and you want to know why I didn't eat, buy my clothes, *and* save money on the rest?"

77

He chuckled at her anger, and she shook a small fist at him. "Funny, is it? I'd like to see how much you saved out of that, George Schultz! Sure an' I put a few pennies by, but what d'you think I've been eating since you got me fired from my job?"

"Not a hell of a lot, from the size of that supper you put away." He looked at her calculatingly. "I might lend it to you."

"Ah, George . . . don't torment me! That's wicked."

He began to count money from his wallet onto the bed, and she watched wide-eyed.

"You mean it?" she whispered. "You'd really lend it to me? But . . ."

"I mean it," he said grimly, "and no strings. You can pay me back if you get the job."

"Ooh . . . George!" What he had been wanting all evening hit him so hard he almost lost his feet. Brigid's arms were locked about his neck, her entrancing breasts flattened against his chest. She pulled his head down and kissed him excitedly, but when he regained his balance enough to grab for her, she fended him off, kissing him lightly on the tip of his nose.

"You're no cop, George! You're a great man, an' I swear I'll go to Mass an' pray for your soul. What time tomorrow can I go see the whatsisnames?"

"Carters. Lieutenant and Missus Carter. And I don't know if they'll see you until I talk to them. Maybe they've already found a girl."

"No! They ought to see me even if they have! I'll be better than anything they've found."

Looking at her sparking eyes and mane of red hair, he doubted the Carters had found a girl who looked like this one, but they weren't looking for that. He was less sure of her qualifications as a nursemaid, and he said so.

She brushed that aside. "In the home in Boston I had to do for the little kids—we all did. I know all about kids, an' worse ones than the Carters have . . . I hope!"

"All right. I'll stop at their hotel when I get off duty, and then I'll come back here. That'll be around noon."

"I'll be here," she promised. "I'll wash my hair and get my best dress and be back here long before then." She clutched the money and looked at it happily. "I'd go now, but that old devil wouldn't unlock the door this time of night."

"No need for that," said George hastily. "Plenty of time in the morning."

"Can I come back here . . . to the room, I mean? Or would you rather I wait outside?"

"I'll give you a key. My landlady's not that particular."

"Thanks. For the key and the compliment."

He laughed at her again. "Well, then . . . Maybe we'd better hit the hay. You got to get your beauty sleep if you're goin' to look like a proper nursemaid tomorrow."

Brigid's eyes narrowed. "Where," she asked, "do I sleep?" She eyed the ancient chair and prodded its peeling leather. "Does it have bugs?"

"Name of God, why would you want to sleep in that thing? Here's a perfectly good bed, big enough for two."

"No. I won't sleep with you, George."

"Why not? What's wrong with me?"

"I doubt there's anything wrong with you in the way you're thinkin'. That's the trouble."

"What? What's the trouble?"

"Tomorrow morning," she told him sweetly, "you're goin' to see your friends an' tell 'em what a grand girl you've found to work for 'em. You're goin' to say, just as serious as you can, she's a strong Irish girl, God-fearin' an' honest as the day is long . . . gentle with kids, clean-mouthed an' convent-reared. Doesn't give a fig for any man alive an' ready to stay unwed for years." She pushed him away gently with a twinkle in her eyes. "If you have to roll off the girl to go an' tell that great story, the devil would have your soul before dark. The only character I'll have, George Schultz, is

79

the one you're goin' to give me, an' I don't want you all worn by a hard night's work."

"I'll be damned!"

"Ah, no! Not at all, at all. It's that I'm savin' you from, don't you see? Now give me that great blue coat you wear when you're persecutin' poor girls on the street, and I'll use it to keep me from the cold and your wicked eyes."

Swearing softly, he brought the coat and had for reward one more kiss, warm enough, but with two small fists doubled against his chest to spring the trap if he tried to close it. She bid him good night and showed him her legs for the first time as she swung them into the chair and tucked his police overcoat about them.

7

Brennan and Smigocki lived in the south barracks of Fort Columbus, the quadrangular stone-and-brick structure that gave its name to the army post on Governors Island. Four large two-story buildings, slate-roofed with double-tiered porticos on their fronts, formed the quadrangle. Three of these housed soldiers—members of the permanent party of the recruit depot and music boys, who were bandsmen in training. The fourth, on the western side, had been converted to officers' quarters. At each corner of the quadrangle were two small pentagonal buildings in whose upper floors were company tailors and married soldiers, the lower levels given over to sculleries and privies.

Michael Brennan's destination—the adjutant's office—lay outside the quadrangle to the north, and to reach it he took the walk in front of the officers' building. Midway, he encountered a dark-haired young woman pushing a perambulator. She propelled this with the gentle jiggling motion employed by nursemaids to keep their small charges disinterested in outside affairs, and when she saw Michael she smiled at him brightly.

"Morning, Miss Norah," he said, tipping his cap, but when he did not stop to talk, Norah Brannigan pouted.

"My," she murmured, "aren't we formal this morning."

She was employed by Lieutenant and Mrs. Coursey, who lived in one of the separate officers' houses on the northeast point of the island, and Michael was a frequent visitor to the Courseys' vine-covered back porch, his appearances occurring whenever the Courseys were in the city for the evening and Norah on duty with their infant son.

"I'm for the adjutant's office, Norah," Michael explained. "Another time, maybe?"

Norah's bright eyes were fixed on his sleeves. She had worked on the island for more than two years, and small military subtleties did not escape her. The fresh tracks left by Michael's departed chevrons were eloquent.

"Oh, Michael!"

"Yes. Well . . . it's a pleasure to see you, Norah." Another tip of his cap and he was gone, leaving her to stare curiously at his departing back.

Might as well have been busted at evening parade in front of the whole post, Michael thought sourly. Every servant and orderly in the officers' quarters will have the word by dark. A memory of red hair and snapping green eyes clouded his brow. Irish women, he muttered. They're the ruin of a good man.

It was an unusual thought for Michael Brennan. He had always considered an Irish girl as good as any other for his purposes, though he could not abide them when they gathered with their own kind. If they were not gabbing about their mighty sacrifices to support the family they were whispering about somebody's illness—preferably terminal. But they could be so warm and loving by themselves. That was the rub. Ah, women are fire and men are tow, and the Devil he comes and begins to blow. His mother used to say that, so he probably had it backward, but it certainly fitted his case. He climbed the steps to the adjutant's office and put Irish girls resolutely from his mind.

The Acting Assistant Adjutant General of Fort Columbus was another elderly lieutenant. Even the war had not brought him a brevet promotion, and he was fairly certain to retire or die as a lieutenant.

He listened silently to Michael's formal request to be returned to his regiment, his eyes—like Norah's—on the big Irish soldier's newly bare sleeves.

"Captain Dennett?" he asked.

"Yes, sir."

The lieutenant sighed. "You're in the Twenty-first, aren't you, Brennan? What company?"

"K Company . . . I think, sir."

"You think? What do you mean?"

"I never served in it, sir. I was transferred out of the Nineteenth when I was promoted, and I never joined the Twenty-first."

The adjutant nodded. Every company in the army was short one or two noncommissioned officers who had been detailed to the administrative overhead of the force. Somewhere on the frontier an acting corporal did the work in K Company for which Michael Brennan had worn the stripes and drawn the pay. When trouble in heaven drove one of these absentee birds home to roost, his regiment welcomed the return of its chevrons if not the bearer. Michael's homecoming would be less painful because he would be preceded by a telegram announcing that his corporal's chevrons were available for reassignment.

"Let's see . . ." The lieutenant thumbed a fat, well-worn volume of general orders. "Regimental headquarters of the Twenty-first is in Fort Vancouver, Washington. I'll have to send a telegram about the stripes and ask where they want you. Have you any furlough coming to you, Brennan?"

"I've not had any since I've been here, sir."

"I can give you a couple of weeks, then. Where d'you want to spend it?"

"In the city, sir?"

"New York? Absolutely not! I thought you were trying to get away from a court-martial."

"Yes, sir."

"Why don't you go to Philadelphia and see the Cen-

83

tennial? I'll give you fourteen days' furlough en route to the Twenty-first, and you can go as soon as they tell me where you'll be assigned."

Officially the Centennial Exhibition, the nation's celebration of its hundredth year of independence, would open in Philadelphia on the tenth of May. To the adjutant and several million other Americans, this exposition was known simply as "the Centennial."

"That'll be fine, sir."

"All right. See the Sergeant Major and he'll give you your orders as soon as they come in. Have a good time in Philadelphia, Brennan, but don't report late to your company. Have you got enough money to take care of yourself?"

"Oh, yes, sir. I've enough for that."

It was a bald-faced lie, but Michael saw no reason to trouble the adjutant with facts. How he would manage a furlough in Philadelphia on the remains of his last month's pay was a problem he would have to solve himself.

Departing the headquarters building, he gave the matter some thought. A drink would help. It would make heavy thinking easier. There was no saloon nearer than the city, but if he were caught off the island without a pass Captain Dennett would scalp him this time. There was one place at Fort Columbus where a man might find a little whiskey.

Up by the officers' houses on the north point was a stable and blacksmith shop where they kept their private horses. This establishment was managed by a genial civilian named Gustavus Moestaert—known to his friends as Gus Mustard. In addition to saddles, bridles, and harness, Gus's tack room often housed a very private poker game—five-card draw for purists, Red Dog for less particular gamesters—and Gus usually had some bad whiskey for sale to club members.

Michael strolled casually into the odorous gloom of the passage between stalls and tack room. There was no sound except the stamping of horses and a rustle of mice in the hay loft overhead. The door to the tack room was shut tight, and that was a good sign. He knocked, and after a moment Gus Mustard opened the door cautiously.

"Good day to you, Corporal Brennan."

"Let me in, Gus."

The farrier shook his head. "Not now, Mike. I've a few friends here."

"Hell, I won't bother them."

Gus did not open the door. "No rank in the game, Mike. You can't gamble with privates—you know the rules."

"No problem," Michael told him, displaying a bare sleeve. Gus whistled softly.

"When did that happen?"

"Dammit, Gus, you goin' to stand there jawin' till somebody sees me? Let me in!"

There were five men sitting crosslegged around a blanket on the floor, and they eyed Michael coldly. He knew them all—permanent privates of the Columbus Barracks garrison—Gilooly, Martin, Reeves, and two Smiths, identified by size as Big and Little Smith. They considered his intrusion unwarranted, for the army was adamant against noncommissioned officers gambling with private soldiers. Gus jerked a thumb at Michael's arm and they relaxed.

No one ventured a joke about the missing stripes. Brennan was too big and too ready with his fists for that, but demotion entitled him to join the game if he wanted.

"You gonna sit in?" asked Little Smith.

"No, I want a drink. You got any, Gus?"

"Sure. Dollar a pint."

"Why, you damned old robber! A dollar for a pint of your rotgut?"

"If you can't pay for it, don't bad-mouth it."

"I can pay for it, but I'll be damned if I pay that much for a pint of forty-rod booze."

"If you got money, Brennan," said Little Smith,

85

"why don't you take a hand? You ought to have some luck comin' your way."

The reference to his loss of rank was too mild to provoke Michael's anger, and after a moment he nodded.

"All right. You playin', Gus?"

"Nope."

"He never plays," grumbled Reeves. "Just gets rich draggin' a nickel a pot for lettin' us use his damn room."

Michael shed his blouse and dropped two dollar bills and some coins on the blanket. The players shifted to give him room, impressed by this show of affluence.

Little Smith was right. Red dog is an outrageous card game, but it favors a bold man with some poker skill, and Michael had a run of good fortune.

An hour later Martin threw down his cards with a grunt of disgust. "You're too hot for me. I'm clean."

Big Smith nodded agreement. "I'm out, too. Can't stand this."

Michael bought a pint of whiskey from his winnings and soothed the remaining players by passing his bottle around. He needed them.

A little after dark, Gilooly and Reeves were stripped, and watched glumly as Michael and Little Smith, the winners, dealt each other cold hands for a couple of sizeable pots. Michael took both, and Little Smith grinned at him.

"Man, you can't lose! I want out before you skin me too. All right?"

"Sure, I'll call it quits. You want to split another bottle?"

In seven hours Michael had won seventeen dollars and some change—more than a month's pay as a corporal. He felt expansive. He and Little Smith shared the bottle, and Michael listened to the soldiers' salacious gossip about affairs in the laundresses' quarters.

This long, ramshackle building at the south end of the island housed sixteen married soldiers whose wives had the archaic and prized status of Laundress on the army's rolls. Suds Row it was called, and social relations there were always interesting—so interesting, the way Smith described them, that Michael decided he would pay a call on a married friend who lived there.

The shortest path from Gus Mustard's poker club to the south end of the island led behind a line of houses called Officers' Row. One of these was a big, single house for the post commander; the other two were double houses, each accommodating two captains or lieutenants and their families. About a pint of Gus Mustard's whiskey was enough to make most men tipsy, but not Michael Brennan. He was humming softly to himself, however, as he negotiated the brick walk, being careful of its edges.

"Psst! Michael?"

The whispered summons startled him until he realized where he was. Lieutenant Coursey's back porch, shaggy in its vine cover, loomed beside him.

Well. No need to walk all the way to Suds Row, he told himself happily. Pushing open the screen door, he groped in the darkness until his hands found Norah Brannigan. She pushed them away.

"Leave me go! And be quiet now."

The house was as silent and dark as the porch, but Norah put a finger on his lips. "No, they've gone to the city, but you'll wake the babe. Stop it now!"

She was objecting to his searching hands, and he silenced her with a kiss.

"Whew!" she gasped when she escaped. "What have you been drinkin'?"

"Terrible. Fearful stuff. Norah, love, the lieutenant didn't happen to leave a drop of the friendly creature handy, did he?"

"I doubt you need it!"

She held him off, peering at his face and he sighed deeply.

"You do look bad, Mike. Are you in real trouble?"

"Ah, Norah, wimmen are divvils an' men are fools, are they not?"

"I always heard it the other way 'round. What did you do? Who is she?"

87

He swallowed noisily. "Name of God, Norah, give me a drink. I'm that destroyed by trouble I can't talk."

Norah sniffed. "Hell will freeze over an' the Devil go on skates before that day comes. All right, but be quiet!"

She led the way into the kitchen and found a candle. Shielding its glow with her hand when she had it alight, she produced a decanter from a cupboard.

"What is it?" whispered Michael hoarsely.

"It's Mister Coursey's good rye whiskey . . . not that you'd know good from bad."

He sniffed appreciatively as Norah poured a generous measure into a cup. He tasted it and groaned.

"Ah, God! That's elegant rye!" He sipped again, then gasped.

Norah had measured into another cup an amount of water equal to the whiskey she had just given him, and was pouring it carefully into the decanter.

"Jesus, Mary, an' Joseph, girl! What are you doin'?"

"Don't jiggle me!" she snapped.

"But you're puttin' *water* in that grand whiskey! You'll spoil it entirely!"

Norah completed her infusion and glared at him. "You think he doesn't measure it? I don't want him after me for nippin' his old whiskey." She blew out the candle and gave him a push. "Back to the porch with you now."

"But I thought—"

"I know what you thought. You can just forget it. I'll not have you wakin' that innocent babe with your carryin' on. Out with you now!"

He comforted himself with a swallow of Lieutenant Coursey's whiskey, and felt his way back to the porch. The black-haired nursemaid did not follow.

"Norah?"

"I'm right here." He could just make her out, leaning against the door jamb with her arms crossed. "And you're not goin' back in there either."

"Ah, Norah, love . . ."

"Don't blarney me! Who is she?"

"Who?"

"The one that got you busted. Who else?"

Michael finished his whiskey regretfully. The decanter could stand a little more water, but first things first. He put the cup on the floor, out of the way, and felt carefully for Norah. She slapped his hand.

"What happened?"

He groaned. "Norah, I'm a great fool, I am."

"I know that. Tell me what happened."

"Well, it was last week . . . when we got our pay. I had a drop or two an' went into the city a bit to see the sights. This little redheaded piece came along, an' Norah . . ." He sighed noisily and hung his head.

"Ah, come off it!" she snapped, "And you went chasin' after her, didn't you?"

"I did," he replied in a muffled voice. "But, Norah, she was such a pretty thing. A little bit of a girl with a great head of red hair an' big green eyes. How was I to know she was so wicked?"

"Oh, hell, Michael Brennan! You're a grown man. You'd ought to know better than foolin' with a New York slut."

"I guess I lost my wits, Norah."

"Small loss. What happened to make Captain Dennett so mad? Cassie Burke said he gave you hell."

"What does that silly idle woman know about it?"

"Her friend Dolan works in the headquarters. He told her."

"Well, damn Dolan an' Cassie Burke too!"

"No use swearing at them. It's you that made the trouble."

He tried to edge her through the door, but she put her hands behind her and clung to it.

"No! I'll not. Let me go!"

"Ah, Norah . . ." He tried to kiss her but she evaded him. "If only you'd gone with me that night."

"I swear," she giggled, "you're the biggest fool unhung, Michael Brennan. You never asked me."

89

He quit trying to push her through the door, caught her face in both hands, and kissed her. It was a long, thorough kiss, and when he released her she was panting.

"Stop it now!"

But while she clutched the door she left herself defenseless, and her blouse, he discovered, buttoned up the front.

"Ooh . . . Michael!"

Her full breasts gleamed palely in his hands, and Norah arched her back, offering them up. He kissed them in turn and she moaned.

"Come on, Norah, darlin' . . . come in now."

"No . . . no! We can't!"

He bent his head again to her breasts, and Norah bolted against him. She was a big girl and she drove him back a full pace. He collided with the porch swing.

It was a big wicker thing, long enough to hold four persons seated, suspended from the porch roof by chains. Michael groped for it with one hand, keeping a grip on Norah with the other. She let go of the door and grabbed his hand, protesting. Capturing the swing, he dumped her into it and it creaked alarmingly as his weight followed.

As soon as he gave up trying to get her into the house, Norah became cooperative. It was still difficult. Her blouse and chemise had ceased to be a problem, but by the time he gathered up her voluminous skirt she had a roll of clothing about her waist as big as the fender on the ferry boat—and about as handy.

The wicker creaked and the chains jangled and Michael had to keep one foot on the floor to keep the swing from dumping them both out. Norah began to squeal breathlessly until he was certain they would have a sentry peering in at them. There was a guard post at the commanding officer's house.

But perhaps the sentry thought it was only cats quarreling, and Norah's plaints ended in a soft cry of delight. After that she laughed and gasped and babbled something about the poor innocent babe.

If it slept through that, Michael thought cheerfully, the creature will sleep through the final trumpet.

He rocked her in the swing and kissed her until she recovered her breath and became restive. Michael caught her hands and held them.

"Norah, love," he whispered, "let's have just one more sup of Mr. Coursey's whiskey. Taps'll blow any minute now, an' I've got no pass to be abroad."

"Ooh!" she moaned, cupping her swollen breasts in her hands. "Brennan, you're naught but an animal! Holy Mother, look at me!" She tugged at the wad of clothing about her waist.

"I am, darlin', an' it's enough to drive a man wild. I wish I could see the whole of you now."

"Oh, aye! But you're wishin' more for another drink, aren't you?"

She pushed him away and did what she could to clothe herself. Michael interfered, and she put her arms about his neck and kissed him long and lovingly.

"Are you still thinkin' of that redheaded slut?" she whispered.

It was a good thing she could not see his face, for he was at that moment wondering how it would feel to hold that green-eyed hellion as he was holding Norah.

"How could you think it, love?" He kissed her again and set about buttoning himself into his coat while she slipped into the kitchen. She was back in a minute with an inch of whiskey in the cup.

"I dassen't give you much, Mike. He'll know if I put more water in."

"Ah!" he breathed happily, "that's enough. I'd not want you in trouble because of me."

Across the parade ground the door of the adjutant's office slammed and they heard the bugler's heels on the steps as he came out to sound taps. Michael gave Norah the cup and a final loving pat on her bottom as he stepped off the porch.

The sentry at the end of Officers' Row grinned at him in the light of the lantern at the head of the steps from the boat landing.

"The bugler's out, friend, an' the launch just got in with some officers on it. Best get a move on."

"I'll make it," Michael told him. "Just give 'em 'Halt, who goes?' when they get to the top, will you?"

8

"They want to talk to you."

George Schultz's brief report of his visit to the Carters brought a shout of joy from Brigid. She had spent the morning getting ready for this. Her room unlocked by George's loan, she had washed herself and her hair, brushed, pressed, and donned her best clothes, and hurried back to wait his return impatiently.

"You've got a chance. I don't think they've found anyone yet. Let's have a look at you."

She revolved for his inspection. Her gray wool dress, buttoned to the throat to hide the rust spot on her best lace collar, even had a pretense of a bustle. She had gathered back the fullness of the skirt and fastened it with a big black ribbon bow. Her shoes were worn, but she had blacked and rubbed the toes until they gleamed. With care they were all that would show. Her red hair was pinned in a thick bun at the nape of her neck, surmounted by a small plain hat set decorously level.

"You'll do," George told her with a grin. "How're you going to get there?"

"I'll walk."

"To the Buckingham? It's on Fiftieth Street!"

"I'll walk fast."

"And you'll not be there by dark. Here . . ." He

produced a coin from his pocket. "I want you to have the job so you can pay all this back."

So she set forth for the Carters in style—fifty cents was enough to pay her way uptown and back with some to spare. In willful celebration of this largesse, she climbed aboard one of the special drawing-room cars of the Sixth Avenue elevated railway, casually handing the conductor the additional dime required of passengers who desired—and could afford—a guaranteed seat on an upholstered wicker bench.

At Fiftieth she left the elevated and walked east to Fifth Avenue, where the staid Buckingham shared the intersection with the bare ribs of the new Roman Catholic cathedral under construction.

The small lobby of the hotel was elegantly furnished, and a portly gentleman, seated by the registration desk, watched her approach with interest. House detective, Brigid's experienced eye told her. Two bellboys in scarlet livery with pillbox caps also watched admiringly.

"I'm to see Lieutenant and Missus Carter," she told the clerk firmly.

"And your name, miss?"

"Brigid O'Donnel. I'm expected."

Whatever he was thinking did not show on his well-trained face. He indicated a sitting room just off the lobby and told Brigid she could wait there. She had the room to herself, and settled primly on an ornate settle facing the fireplace, which sported in this season a thicket of potted plants behind glistening brass fenders. As she took her seat she noted that the man by the desk had changed chairs to keep her in view. The Devil fly off with him, she thought. Does he think I'm going to pinch something?

Shortly there was whispering behind her, and she turned to find two children peering at her curiously. The older was a boy of seven or eight, she guessed, a handsome young fellow with a shock of unruly blonde hair falling over one eye. His companion was a small girl, equally blonde but younger and plumper. The boy

94

detached his hand from her grip when Brigid looked at them.

"You're the lady who wants to go with us." It was not a question but a statement of fact. Brigid smiled.

"If you're the Carters . . . yes. But if you aren't . . ." She spread her hands palms up, then reversed them with a motion as if brushing something away. It was not at all what he expected, and his eyes widened in surprise. In his experience, prospective servants were more serious and deferential. He studied Brigid with interest.

"I'm William and she's Amanda. She's only six and I'm lots older."

Brigid nodded gravely and smiled at the little girl. "I'll bet you don't let anybody call you Mandy, though, do you?"

"How did you know that?" demanded William in surprise.

Brigid had just stated the first and foremost of the laws of Louise Carter. In her presence, no one twice addressed her daughter as "Mandy."

"Easy. My name's Brigid, and I won't let anybody call me Biddy. If it was Amanda I wouldn't let 'em call me Mandy."

Amanda had no strong feelings about nicknames, but this pretty young woman seemed to be taking her side in something. She climbed onto the settle and slipped her hand companionably into Brigid's.

William held out. "We're goin' way out west," he said forebodingly. "Aren't you scared of Injuns? You got a lot of hair. If they scalped you they could get two horses for it, I bet."

"Pooh! I'm not scared. Your da wouldn't let an Injun hurt me. You wouldn't either, I'll bet."

That was more persuasive, and William brightened. "I guess I wouldn't," he said calculatingly, "if you weren't all the time fussing about taking a bath an' goin' to bed an' doin' lessons."

Brigid nodded. "I know. Everybody has to do all

95

that, but I don't like anybody to nag me about it either."

William was reluctant to give up his bargaining. "But what if Papa an' me weren't there? You'd be scared then."

There was a rustle of skirts and a tall young woman appeared beside the settle.

"For shame, William," she said softly. "You must not try to frighten Miss O'Donnel." She held out a slim hand. "I'm Louise Carter."

"Brigid O'Donnel, ma'am," Brigid responded, bouncing off the settle.

"And this is Lieutenant Carter."

He was so tall Brigid had to tip her head back to look at him, and he smiled at her. His face was strong, square-jawed with a neatly trimmed mustache, and his gray eyes twinkled. Because George said he was in the army, Brigid had expected a uniform of some sort, but Lieutenant Carter's brown wool Norfolk jacket and trousers were far from that. The children's blonde hair was understandable. His was sandy brown and Louise Carter's a golden honey-blonde, piled high and elegantly on her small, aristocratic head.

The Carters seated themselves and Brigid resumed her place on the settle beside Amanda, taking care that her skirt showed no more of her worn shoes than necessary.

"Sergeant Schultz spoke to us about you," said Mrs. Carter in a soft, clear voice. Brigid was puzzled by George's promotion until Mrs. Carter added that they had known him when he was in the army.

"He said you are seeking employment as a nursemaid and he recommended you highly."

God's blessing on him, thought Brigid. "Yes, ma'am, I am that." It seemed wise to face the problem of her present unemployment quickly.

"You see, ma'am, I've been working in a big store but I quit that and I'm wanting to quit the city as well."

"Oh? Why did you leave your job?" No dancing about the point with this one, Brigid saw. Louise Carter's blue eyes were kind, but the question was plainly direct.

"I'll tell you, ma'am, straight out. Decent work for girls like me is hard to find in this city. The pay is terrible small but there's so many of us looking for it that a wicked man thinks a girl will do anything to keep her job. The manager where I worked . . . well, he said I must do what he wants or . . ."

She stopped there and watched Mrs. Carter cautiously. God forgive me for that lie and do not let the lady ask the name of the store, she prayed silently. Half-successfully at any rate, for Louise Carter did not ask. Indeed, she swept away Brigid's next hurdle with her reply.

"Ah! I see. Obviously in those circumstances you had no reference from him. Have you ever cared for young children?"

"Oh, yes, ma'am! Not in a family, but at the convent I did."

The Sisters of Charity would have been pleased at the promotion of their home for foundlings but they would have chastised her for untruthfulness. Mrs. Carter looked impressed and Brigid hedged.

"My ma and my da died when I was little, ma'am, and I was raised by the good sisters in Boston. The older girls had to look after the little ones."

"In a convent?"

Brigid blushed. "Well . . . it was really just a home for kids like me. We called it a convent sometimes."

The admitted falsehood was small and appealing and Louise Carter smiled. Brigid congratulated herself, but Lieutenant Carter was frowning. He had been watching this exchange between his wife and the pretty red-headed girl.

"If we employed you, Brigid," he said, "we would be at considerable expense to take you with us to our new post. We couldn't have you leaving us to be married as soon as we arrive."

"Oh, sir, I've no mind to marry. I'd sign a paper that I'd not if you want that."

He chuckled. "That would be more like indenture than a job, Brigid. It would mean nothing even if you did. No, I meant we would have to have an understanding between us that we are sure you would keep."

"I'll take my oath, sir, and I would keep it."

He shook his head. "Have you thought about that carefully, Brigid? You're a pretty girl and every man for miles will pay you court."

She was about to affirm her determination not to marry a soldier but thought better of it. The Carters might take offense.

"I'll not have any man for as long as you say. You set the time and I'll abide by it, sir."

They looked at her curiously, and Brigid realized that sounded odd. They would wonder what had happened to her in New York to make her say such a thing.

"I want to marry, sure," she plowed on, "but not soon. When my time with you is done, I'm thinking I'd like to find me a job in some great city out west . . . San Francisco, maybe. They say it's a grand town."

"Ah, Brigid," said Mrs. Carter, "it is a big city, but a bad one for a young girl all alone."

Lieutenant Carter still looked dubious. Brigid addressed him with all the sincerity she could muster.

"I tell you truly, sir, I want to work for you but I'd not want to be a servant girl all my life. When my time is out I'd want to look for better, an' they say a girl like me can find that out west. I can't get there by myself, an' I'd work hard for the chance to go with you. I know it costs a lot an' I'll work for you till you say I can go."

Carter grinned. "That's more honest than any we've heard yet. What do you think, Louise?"

Mrs. Carter did not think very long. "Very well," she said. "I will make a proposition, Brigid. We leave the day after tomorrow to visit my parents in Philadelphia for a month or more. You shall come with us and we will see how we get along. When it is time for us to go west I will tell you if we want you to come with us, and you will say what you want to do. If you do not come we will pay your way back to New York. If you do, it must be for at least a year. Your pay will be ten dollars a month, with your meals and lodging of course. If you stay with us beyond a year, your pay will be increased. How is that?"

Brigid squeezed Amanda's hand and beamed. "I could ask no better, ma'am. I'd like to try."

"All right. I think you should come tomorrow with your trunk and stay the night with us, for we leave early the next day. Is that time enough for you to pack your things?"

Brigid suppressed a giggle. "Surely, ma'am." Where in the world, she wondered, will I find a trunk?

"You will need a hackney cab to bring your luggage," continued Louise Carter. "How much is that?"

Brigid looked blank. She wanted to name a stiff figure so she could buy George Schultz a handsome present, but she had never been in a cab in her life and she had no idea what they cost and dared not name a sum.

"Can't be more than two and a half," said Lieutenant Carter. "I paid that for a cab from the Battery. Here . . ." He gave Brigid two bills and a fifty cent piece. She looked awed.

"Oh, that's a lot, sir!"

"It may cost more. If it does, you must tell me and I will repay you."

If it costs more than that, thought Brigid, I'll have to walk. But I've enough now to buy George something and get myself here too. It simply could not cost two dollars and a half to get from Twelfth to Fiftieth Street by any means.

"All right, Brigid," said Louise Carter, rising and extending her hand, "we shall expect you tomorrow, and you will stay the night with us here."

"Thank you, ma'am," said Brigid, taking her hand joyfully. "I'll be here surely, as early as I can."

She hugged Amanda and swept out through the lobby with all the dignity a girl an inch over five feet could muster. The house detective and the bellboys watched her exit with interest.

Brigid took the horsecar downtown because it cost three cents less than the elevated railway, and she wanted every penny she could save. If she quit her room on the morrow maybe she could get something back from the widow Pfalz, but that was doubtful. What could she buy for George Schultz? She put that off. First she must tell him what had happened.

Her radiant face when he admitted her to his room gave him no need to ask.

"George," she told him happily, "you're a good man an' I'll pray God to hold you in the hollow of His hand. I got the job!"

"Is that all I'll have?" he asked grinning.

She gave him a kiss and knew he longed for more. "Nah, then . . ." she said softly, "it's all I can give till I've had something to eat. I've not had a bite since you fed me last night."

"You're a costly girl, Brigid," he sighed. "I should be glad you're not mine to keep for long. When do you go?"

"Tomorrow I must take myself an' all my things to their hotel. They're off to Philadelphia the day after, an' I'm to go with them. She said I'm to bring my trunk an' he gave me money to pay for a hackney cab all the way to Fiftieth Street." She frowned. "George . . . ? Where can I get a trunk?"

"What for?"

"She said bring a trunk! You want me to look like a gypsy with my things in a paper poke?"

"Have you nothing? Not even a carpetbag?"

"No. I've got to get a trunk."

He looked thoughtful. "Wait a bit. I've got an idea."

He was gone for a good half an hour and she prowled his room impatiently, wondering what he was doing. When he returned he brought a small leather-covered trunk, battered and peeling. Brigid eyed it suspiciously.

"Wherever did you find that?"

"I guess some poor soul left it here. I saw it in the hall closet a while back, and the landlady sold it to me for a dollar." He dropped it on the floor and glared at her. "You want it or don't you?"

"Oh, yes! They're goin' to pay me ten dollars a month an' I'll pay you back for everything, George . . . I promise I will." She counted on her fingers. "I owe you two dollars an' thirty cents you gave me to pay that damned widow . . . fifty cents to get me to the Carters . . . an' a dollar for the trunk. That's . . . umm . . . three dollars and thirty cents?"

"Three dollars and eighty cents, and interest on the loan if it's a long while coming back," he told her, grinning.

"Ah, George . . . you wouldn't! An' me a poor orphan girl."

"Hah!"

She stopped his scoffing with another kiss, but cautiously. Each one lasted longer than the one before, and George was pressing.

"You can forget the interest," he told her when he let her go. "I'll take it this way."

"Not unless you feed me!"

"All right. You're a wicked little thing but I can't deny that pretty face."

She stuck out her tongue at him gleefully and he took her to a restaurant just off Broadway. They dined grandly and she knew it cost him a lot. She had two glasses of wine and another meal that made him stare in astonishment. But the wine made her gay and affectionate and she clung to his arm when they left the restaurant.

"You want to go all the way back to Twelfth Street?" he asked glumly on the sidewalk. It was cold and Brigid shivered.

"It's a long way," she said in a muffled voice. "Can I have your chair again?"

101

George looked hopeful and led the way. His room seemed colder even than the street, and Brigid wrapped her arms about her and shivered again. She was thinking hard as he groped for the gas jet.

George Schultz had been kinder to her than anybody in New York. He had cost her a job at Lord and Taylor's, but he had found her another. Fed her and given her a place to stay when she had none. And what had she given him? No Bowery hooker could have given less, and what she could save from her cab fare to the Carters' hotel would hardly make amends.

"George?" she said softly.

He was searching through his pockets for matches. "Yes?" he said irritably.

Brigid tugged at his coat, and when he turned she walked into his arms and kissed him, long and warmly.

His lips moved from hers over her chin and into the warm hollow of her throat, his hands searching the slim back arched against him.

"George!"

"Mnnn?"

She wanted more attention than that. He straightened with a gasp. She had pulled out his shirt and pressed small, icy hands against his bare back.

"I'm freezing, George! Can't we go to bed?"

"God, yes! Come on."

He let her go and she slipped under his arm. By the time he had got out of his clothes and reached the bed she had spread his coat over the blanket and was already in it, waiting for him, curled beneath the covers.

He crawled in, uncoiled her, and settled happily atop her small figure. She gave an anguished squeal.

"What's the matter?"

"Saint Euphemia and all the angels! You'll squeeze the life out of me, man . . . you weigh a ton!"

"I'm sorry . . . I didn't think!"

"That's all right," she whispered, giggling. "Just get off me, will you?"

She put her hands on his chest and pushed him onto his back. "There," she said, "that's better."

102

"But . . ."

"Shh!" She clambered onto him, laughing softly.

"Easy . . . Oooh, George, be easy now!" she gasped as his hands cupped her breasts. Her warning was only temporary though, and the impression grew upon George Schultz that he had somehow caught in his arms a small, explosive bolt of chain-lightning.

A long time later, in the lovely warmth of his bed, he remembered something that puzzled him.

"Brigid?"

"Shh!"

"No . . . tell me. Who is Saint Euphemia? I thought I knew 'em all."

She snuggled against him happily. "She was a great lady in Rome long an' long ago."

"How did she get to be a saint?"

"You talk too much, George! She defied the wicked pagans an' they tried every way to break her great heart."

"Did they?"

"Never! First they gave her to some evil men but the blessed angels saved her. Then they hung her up by her long hair an' she prayed 'em to shame. In the end they had to squash her betwixt two great rocks."

"Ah!" He rose on an elbow to look down fondly at the small happy face shrouded in the mass of red hair. "So you felt like her when I lay upon you?"

"Oh, I'd never! Let me go to sleep, George."

"Why not?"

"Ah, George . . ." She kissed him wearily. "She died a Virgin Martyr, that's why. Now hush, will you not?"

103

9

Only twelve days after the adjutant at Fort Columbus asked for them, the Twenty-first Infantry responded with orders for Private Michael Brennan. K Company, Camp Belknap, Oregon, said the telegram. Report not later than May 31.

It was a quick reply, considering the distances involved. Nobody knew where Camp Belknap was until the quartermaster's clerk looked it up. He said it would take at least five days to get there from Philadelphia, and Michael swore. That left only ten days of his furlough for the Centennial. He was in a hurry to leave. He had hoarded his money, spending none on Norah, who was furious with him about that. Nevertheless, when he bid her good-bye she wept bitterly, and he departed Governors Island and Fort Columbus with a sense of relief.

His journey began auspiciously. On reaching Jersey City he discovered that the Pennsylvania Central Railroad had just lowered its excursion fare to the Centennial to two dollars and sixty-five cents—an unexpected windfall. The swarming grounds of the exposition in Philadelphia tempted him on arrival, but he put off visiting them. His poker winnings would have to be supplemented in some fashion, and that could best be arranged in the city. Leaving his carpetbag in the baggage room of the depot, he took the street railway into town, pausing only long enough to buy a copy of the *Public Ledger,* which he opened to the theater advertisements as soon as he boarded the horsecar.

A number of theaters offered drama or comedy, but the legitimate stage was not what Michael was looking for. He consulted the announcements of the variety theaters and concluded that the best for his purpose was the Grand Central Variety Theater, with its mixed bill that included a "thrilling frontier drama" featuring Julian Kent as Wild Bill in a desperate encounter with a ferocious Rocky Mountain bear, as well as John and Maggie Fielding, Irish impersonation artists, presenting a short comedy, *Irish Domestics,* plus an infant musical prodigy, popular singers and danseuses, and the "Imperial Ballet Troupe."

A five-minute walk from the car stop on Market Street brought him there just after the Wednesday afternoon matinee had begun. That was no loss. He wanted the last show of the evening, and it began at eight o'clock. General admission was twenty-five cents, but Michael wanted to be close to the stage. After a study of the seating plan, he bought a parquet seat for seventy-five cents. He whiled away the afternoon looking into the neighborhood saloons until he found one with a free lunch good enough to justify the exorbitant price to which the Centennial had raised a schooner of beer in Philadelphia. Promptly at eight he returned to the theater.

Wild Bill did his best to put life into his wrestling match with the bear, but the tame animal was obviously bored; she rested her head on the actor's shoulder and surveyed the audience with mild curiosity. The infant prodigy was terrible, but the "Imperial Ballet" had Michael's close attention. They were followed by the Fieldings with their farce-comedy, and he found what he was seeking.

The skit was ridiculous—one man and six women, all determinedly Irish, played the servants of a wealthy house, donning the costumes and wigs left behind on the morning after a masquerade party with appropriate jigs, songs, and jokes. Michael fixed his eyes on a plump blonde, clapping loudly at every line she uttered until her curiosity was aroused and she looked for her noisy admirer.

She had a grand figure, generously displayed by her tights, and a round, pretty face. Her dark, sparkling eyes searched the front row of the parquet. When they reached him, Michael applauded silently and saluted her with a wink. She grinned impishly, and he wondered how such dark eyes came with that blonde head. The longer he looked, the more pleased he was with his choice.

After a musical uproar of song and dance, the curtain fell with a thump behind the cast and they took their bows, blowing kisses to a thunderous ovation, pranced offstage, and were four times recalled before the audience reluctantly began to leave.

Michael found the stage entrance up the alley off Walnut Street. It was guarded by a fat, flint-eyed man, who accepted a quarter disdainfully as the price of a message to Miss Sarah that a gentleman wanted a word with her.

Sarah took her time. Three quarters of an hour elapsed before she bounced out, elegantly dressed, gloved, and hatted.

"Oh!" she said pertly. "It's you, is it?"

"Michael Brennan, at your service, ma'am." He made her a flourishing bow, doffing his new straw hat with a sweep.

"Well?"

"I've just come from New York . . ." He paused to see if she looked impressed, but she did not. "I don't know a soul in Philadelphia, an' a strange town is a poor place without a pretty girl to keep you company. You're the prettiest in the show, Miss Sarah, an' I'd hoped you'd let me give you supper. You'd know the best places, of course."

It was a proven opening, and he saw her eyes sparkle.

"You're a bold one, aren't you, Mr. Brennan? Don't you think I've already got an engagement for supper?"

He looked rueful. "I feared that. I could have asked another and made sure of company, but I'm not a man for second-best."

"Get on with you now. Your Irish is showing. Have you silver in your pocket to match that tongue?"

"Ah, yes! I have indeed."

She considered him a long moment, a forefinger on her chin, and then she smiled.

"Well . . . it just happens I don't have an engagement this night, Michael Brennan, so . . ." She held out her hand. "Come on, then. I'm that hungry I could eat a horse."

"Ah, we'll find better than that, Miss . . . ?"

"Delmar. Call me Sarah. And for God's sake buy me a pretzel before I die of hunger! I've not had a bite since breakfast."

"A what?" Michael's acquaintance with pretzels was limited to the kind he found in saloons in a bowl on the bar.

"A soft pretzel, silly! Haven't you ever had one?"

A peddler with a cart, in the mouth of the alley, plucked something from his tin oven that looked like a bagel to Michael. He watched astonished as Sarah juggled it, smearing it with mustard from the peddler's pot.

"It's good," she told him, her mouth full. "Here!" she thrust a morsel of the hot, crusty bread into his own. The mustard was sharp and the combination delicious.

"You're right," he said, paying the grinning carter. "I never saw one of those before." He offered his arm and she pulled it close against her.

"Now!" she chortled, blowing crumbs from the gloved fingers of her other hand. "Let's go."

"A drink before supper maybe?" he asked.

"Whiskey? Never! I'm afeared of that. I want a beer." She laughed at his expression. She had surprised him, and it amused her.

107

"Sarah," he told her gravely, "you're not only the prettiest . . . you're the best. Lead on."

Again she surprised him. Instead of making a beeline for the most expensive restaurant she could find, she led him to a roaring, smoky cavern of a saloon. She called it McGerrity's place though it bore a big green-and-gold sign proclaiming it the Hibernian Club. She was obviously a favored customer. The owner himself seated them, and men crowded around their table to banter with Sarah. She managed them well, never turning her attention from Michael for long.

It was a promising beginning, and Michael congratulated himself. She was not only a handsome piece but she knew her way around. She was bold and her language a little raw, but she was no wanton, and he discovered she had a fierce pride in her shabby profession which he was careful not to damage. Sarah was exactly what he hoped to find, and he exerted himself to please her. She responded with interest.

They had supper and more beer, and danced repeatedly to McGerrity's small, brassy band. Sarah was as light in his arms as the lively feathers on her hat, which eventually made him sneeze explosively. She laughed at him and scaled the hat onto their table.

"That's better," he whispered, kissing her lightly on her ear. She squeezed his hand in response.

"How long will your company be in Philadelphia?" he wanted to know, and she was pleased by his promotion of the Fieldings' little troupe.

"Oh, I don't know," she responded casually. "We've a booking in Baltimore in July . . . maybe. Of course if Bernie gets us into New York, we'd cancel everything for that."

That was less likely even than the distant Baltimore engagement, Michael thought. A Bowery dance hall maybe, but hardly a New York theater.

"Who's Bernie?"

"Our agent. He got us the place at the Grand Central. What with the Centennial and all, it's better than Chicago."

"You didn't like Chicago? What theater were you in?"

She grinned and tugged at his hand. "Come on . . . last dance! The band's goin' to quit."

"How do you know?"

"Listen to 'em! They're playin' 'Good Night, Ladies' . . . Come on, now."

There was no room to waltz on McGerrity's crowded floor. Michael just held her close and swayed to the music, and she was warm and soft and clinging. When the music stopped she stood on tiptoe to kiss his cheek.

"Oh," she sighed, "that was grand, Michael Brennan. You're a nice man."

"Have we got to go?" he asked in alarm. "What time is it?"

"Two o'clock, silly! Can't you see that great thing over the bar?"

"Sure . . . but they won't close now, will they?"

"I've had all the beer I can hold, an' the band's quit . . . an' I'm a workin' girl, remember?"

Except for an occasional night car plodding along Tenth Street, the city seemed silent and deserted. Michael put his arm around Sarah's waist and after a moment she rested her head on his shoulder as they walked away from McGerrity's. It was pleasant and aimless, and before long it would lead to kissing and squeezing, but Michael was thinking of more than that.

In a little while one of two things would happen. She would take him home or she would want to go with him. The latter was out of the question. The price of a hotel room at this time of night would be ruinous. The girl had to have a room somewhere, and once he got her there he meant to stay. With luck and the right kind of attention, she might let him stay the rest of his furlough, and his money would go twice as far. Perhaps not in innocence, Sarah gave him his opening.

"Where are you staying?" she murmured.

He stopped abruptly and looked stricken. "Would you believe," he asked her, "I forgot to find me a place?" He laughed. "When you said you'd come out with me, it went right out of my daft head."

Sarah eyed him suspiciously. "So what are you goin' to do?"

"First," he said firmly, "I'm goin' to walk you to your door. I'd not have you wanderin' these streets alone. Then I'll find me a place."

They walked on for a bit and her head returned to his shoulder. When they stopped for a curb, Michael kissed her, cautiously at first and then more thoroughly. Sarah responded happily. Then she pushed him away and gave him a quizzical look.

"You're a funny man, Michael Brennan. Most I know would want to see me farther than my door."

"Ah, Sarah," he replied softly, "you think I'd not? It's just that I was afraid you'd send me packin' if I spoke my mind so soon. I want to see lots more of you, love."

She lifted her face and fitted herself warmly against his long body, offering him her lips. When he let her up for breath she giggled.

"Come on, then. I can manage that."

She had a basement room at the end of a malodorous hall. Her candle showed him little of it, but he was not curious to see more. It was all he needed, and with pretty Sarah leading the way he did not even need the candle.

She was as direct about her loving as everything else. When he had unhooked, unbuttoned, and unlaced her plump, shapely body she gave it as freely as she had given her lips—no romping or coy teasing, just a generous giving that made his heart near burst with happiness.

10

The journey from New York to Philadelphia was more exciting for Brigid than for the Carter children. They were experienced travelers—as William was quick to point out—amused by her worry about the extravagance of a hackney cab all the way from the hotel to the ferry slip at the foot of Desbrosses Street.

Across the Hudson, at the new terminal of the Pennsylvania Railroad, they took the cars south at a breathless forty miles an hour, and not until they reached Trenton did Brigid recover a measure of authority. A young conductor entered the car there and paused to answer the children's eager questions and admire their pretty custodian. After a whispered conversation with her, he led them all forward through the swaying, clacking cars.

When they returned with sooty faces, Mrs. Carter sighed and applied a damp towel to her daughter, who chattered happily as she was scrubbed. Lieutenant Carter put down his paper to look at her curiously.

"Where in the world have you been?"

"To the engine!"

"Really? How did you get up there?"

Amanda pointed to Brigid, who was smiling at the conductor as she toweled her own flushed face.

"She took you? I thought they wouldn't let anyone into the locomotive."

"Do you think," his wife murmured tartly, "conductors are any less susceptible to red hair and green eyes than the rest of you?"

"Ah!" Carter chuckled. Brigid and the children were listening respectfully to the conductor explain about air brakes. "I see. Well, they seem quite fond of her already."

"Certainly. Everybody is. She's having as much fun as they are."

Shortly before noon William flattened his nose against a window and shouted, "I see it! I see the fair!"

The train slowed to cross the new bridge over the Schuylkill River just above the Girard Avenue bridge, which was jammed with carriages and pedestrians.

"Good heavens!" exclaimed Louise Carter. The exposition had been open for eight days now, but every visible part of it was packed with eager visitors. Across the river, the train turned south and picked its way through a maze of tracks toward the main station. Only excursion trains went into the new depot at the fair. The children gazed longingly at the disappearing fair.

"Grandmother and Grandfather are waiting for us," their mother explained. "We'll come back and see it soon."

The Brunings' greeting of their daughter and her family seemed very restrained to Brigid. Not until Amanda was swept up to be hugged and kissed was there any crack in their dignified reserve. A little awed, Brigid resurrected the curtsy required by the Boston Sisters of their wards in the presence of important folk.

A cab took them back across the Schuylkill over the Market Street bridge, and from her perch on the jump seat Brigid studied the Brunings covertly.

George Schultz had said Mrs. Carter was thirty, so her parents ought to be nearing sixty. They didn't look it. That, Brigid decided, was probably because they had never had to work very hard. Their clothing was expensive, elegant, and conservative, and their conversation was the same. If Louise Carter's father had a first name it was never used. She called him Papa and the children called him Grandpapa—all of them stressing the last syllable in a way Brigid had never heard. His wife addressed him invariably as Mr. Bruning.

There was more to their conversation than formality, however, and after a little Brigid understood that these were not cold people—they simply communicated more subtly than any of her acquaintances.

The cab turned off the main thoroughfare into a quiet street lined by tall, close-ranked brick homes, and Mr. Bruning leaned to tap William on the knee.

"Where are we, my boy?"

"Pine Street!"

"That's correct, William," said his grandmother. "Do you remember the little rhyme I taught you?"

"Market, Arch, Race, and Vine . . ." William chanted, and Amanda joined in chorus for the rest: ". . . Chestnut, Walnut, Spruce, and Pine!"

"Those are street names," Louise Carter explained to a puzzled Brigid. "It helps to remember them."

In the second block of Pine they turned right, into a narrow street only a block long, identified as Albion by a board high on the front of the corner house. Brick sidewalks accommodated numerous large maple trees and an occasional sycamore, whose foliage arched completely over the street. On both sides brick houses presented a continuous front, and Mrs. Bruning rapped with her parasol on the glass partition between them and the driver, indicating one of these as their destination.

The Bruning home was of ochre brick with a graceful stone arch framing a fanlight over the door. The latter was flanked by brass lamps and reached by four white marble steps. The house front was severely plain except for a pair of bronze fire-company plaques centered between the second-story windows. Brigid had to tip her head far back to count three stories plus an at-

113

tic identified by wooden dormers with fancy trim projecting from the slate roof.

An elderly black woman opened the door, to be greeted joyously by the children and with obvious affection by Louise Carter. The lieutenant gave her a wink and a grin.

"Do, Lord! Cap'n Carter, you shore look graceful!"

"Still just a lieutenant, Martha."

"Shoo! Oughtta be a ginnul by now."

"I agree, Martha, but the army's slow."

Mrs. Bruning gave instructions about the baggage-wagon when it arrived. "Have you something for the children, Martha?" she concluded.

"You know I got samwitches foh everybody, Miz Bruning, an' a pitcher lemminade foh them chirren."

"Shall I help Martha, ma'am?" Brigid asked of Mrs. Carter. Martha rolled her eyes and looked disgusted, and Louise Carter sighed.

"Martha, this is Miss O'Donnel, who will help me with the children while we are here and perhaps when we go to the West."

"Humph!" sniffed Martha, and disappeared down the hall muttering something about poor-white-trash help. Brigid's face reddened.

"It will take a little while," Louise Carter said softly. "Martha's been in command here since before I was born. Come, I will show you the children's room and your own. Which is it, Mama?"

"We aired the top floor room at the right of the stairs for Miss O'Donnel when we had your telegram, Louise. Martha has put linen in it."

Brigid followed Mrs. Carter upstairs, understanding the need for four floors when she realized how narrow the house was. A parlor occupied the entire second-floor front, and the third floor was entirely given over to bedrooms. When she had bathed Amanda's hands and face and supervised William's hasty performance of the same chore, the children fled downstairs and she climbed to the attic to inspect her own accommodation. It was a small room, comfortably furnished, with a

114

blaze of afternoon sun at the single dormer window. Martha had brought linen—blanket, sheets, and towels—but they were piled at the foot of the unmade bed. Obviously Martha was doing no favors for this white girl of ill-defined status.

Brigid considered that status as she descended the stairs. She could cope with William and Amanda and she would find a way around Martha, but how to deal with the Brunings baffled her. Louise Carter apparently expected her to know how, and the only way to preserve that illusion was to guess at the right move— and be right the first time, she concluded apprehensively.

She and the children had their supper in the big pantry behind the dining room and the meal came up from the basement kitchen in a dumbwaiter—the first Brigid had ever seen. Martha served the Brunings and the Carters in the dining room from this device, and by the time supper was over, Brigid had learned to operate it. Her assistance was not welcomed by Martha, but when the dessert came up, she gained a point.

"You never bought that ice cream!" she told Martha, cleaning her bowl as enthusiastically as the children. "You made it, didn't you?"

"Of coss! Ain't no boughten ice cream in this house."

"I knew it. What are the little stringy black things in it?"

"Fanilla beans. You ain't seen them in Noo Yawk?"

Brigid shook her head. "Never had ice cream that good anywhere before."

After supper the children were permitted to join their elders in the sitting room and Brigid accompanied them, awed by the room and its occupants. The furniture was dark and heavy and there was a lot of it. There was a lot of everything—tables, chairs, cabinets, piano, paintings, and wall-brackets—and every flat surface was occupied by something: vases, figurines, ornately framed miniature portraits, dried flowers, and other oddities whose nature escaped Brigid. Most of

115

the floor was covered by an India carpet whose faded colors of rust, honey, and cream proclaimed great age and cost.

Mr. and Mrs. Bruning occupied armchairs, surrounded by the materials of their present occupation—newspapers and journals for him, a riot of colored yarns for her. She was stitching these onto a piece of canvas stretched over a wooden hoop. Louise Carter searched the unused portions of her father's newspapers and extracted names and fragments of events which she and her mother discussed in a baffling way. Other than this sporadic feminine review of local gossip, the room was silent. Cass Carter and his father-in-law did not exchange comments on their own reading.

William pulled a heavy book from the shelves and put it in Brigid's lap. "Come on, Amanda," he urged.

"What is it?" Brigid asked.

"We always look at it, don't we, Amanda?"

His sister squeaked and put her hands over her eyes. "It scares me," she said happily as she joined Brigid and William on the settle.

Louise Carter gave them an amused look. "Not too much, now. You'll have bad dreams."

Brigid opened the book cautiously and gasped. It was her first glimpse of Dante's *Inferno*, illustrated by Gustav Doré's graphic notions of the fate of the damned. Good Saint Michael and all the archangels! she thought. If the sisters in Boston had one of these, there'd be fewer of us gone astray. She and Amanda held hands tightly while William turned the pages.

After a while, Mrs. Bruning addressed a question to Lieutenant Carter. "I gather, Cassius, that you must go again to the frontier. Has the government told you where?" Her voice indicated a deep disapproval of the prospect.

Carter put down his journal and Brigid tried to follow his reply and keep an eye on Doré's painful underworld simultaneously.

"Camp Belknap is the name of the post, ma'am. It lies in the southeastern corner of Oregon."

116

Mrs. Bruning looked as though she had scented something offensive. Her needle stabbed into the canvas with a loud pop. "I must say I have never heard of it. How does one go there?"

"I expect we shall take the railroad to Winnemucca, in Nevada. From there to Camp Belknap we will travel by stage or army wagon."

"Winne-mucca?"

Lieutenant Carter winced and Brigid stared open-mouthed at Mrs. Bruning. It sounded as though she had just said something indecent. Cass shot his wife a pleading look, but she was suddenly interested in something in her newspaper.

"Yes, ma'am," he said softly. "I understand it is the nearest railroad station to the post."

"And that is called Belknap?" Mrs. Bruning resumed her attack.

"Yes, ma'am."

The pop of punctured canvas was accompanied by an audible sniff. "I understand, Cassius, that the military is by nature a coarse organization, but I cannot fathom why it would name one of its establishments after that odious man, Belknap."

To Carter's intense relief, that comment caught the attention of Mr. Bruning. He lowered his paper and peered at his wife.

"Are you well-informed about Mr. Belknap, Sybille?"

"Of course. The rascal connived with his wife to sell a lucrative government post." Another and louder pop of speared canvas. "He shall not escape, however. The Congress has moved to impeach him despite the unseemly haste with which Mr. Grant has accepted his resignation and appointed another Secretary of War."

"Well, my dear, that is the popular view of the matter, but I have it from Judge Kronmeyer that the foolish man knew nothing of the transaction and is guilty only of trying to shield his wife from the consequences of her natural folly."

"Indeed, Mr. Bruning, that only confirms my im-

117

pression of his own folly. The man has married in succession two sisters of doubtful background and breeding. Why, their brothers were in the Rebel army."

Dante forgotten, Brigid listened admiringly to this exchange. The abrupt switch from Camp Belknap to the misfortunes of the late Secretary of War for whom it was named was bewildering but fascinating.

"Curious!" snorted Mr. Bruning. "I should have thought, Sybille, that with your advanced notions about women you would have had more sympathy for the Tomlinson sisters. Carrie, I believe the first one was. I cannot recall the name of the other."

"Amanda," said Mrs. Bruning tartly, "who has been known all her wasted life as 'Puss.' That is all one needs to know of her character."

Brigid noted that Lieutenant Carter looked both relieved and amused. She could guess at the reason. It seemed that the Brunings had accepted him as a son-in-law, but not his profession. What had begun as criticism of the army had been happily diverted to a pursuit of Mister Belknap's wives. Sensing a lull in this debate, Mrs. Carter took advantage of it.

"Amanda," she said firmly, "that is quite enough of that fearful book. You children have had a long day and it is time you were in bed. Will you take them up, please, Brigid?"

11

A little morning light seeped into the basement through a grimy window and awakened Michael Brennan. He looked about the room without moving.

Nothing more or less than he had expected. How many, he wondered, had he seen for the first time this way—from a strange bed with a girl of one night's acquaintance. He glanced cautiously at Sarah.

She had kicked off the covers and was deeply asleep on her back, arms and legs widespread. Her arm rested heavily across his chest, and he shifted it carefully. He was right, he saw, about the hair. That blonde head came from a druggist's shop, but it was clean and smelled faintly of perfume. He pushed his nose into it and breathed deeply and happily.

"Umnh?" murmured Sarah. She opened one eye and looked at him. Michael stopped his nuzzling and waited. Sometimes they were grouchy when they first awakened.

Not Sarah. She smiled and traced the line of his jaw with a warm finger, the smile turning to a frown when she encountered the long scar ending in his scalloped ear. He drew his forearm up slowly across her big, firm breasts and she gasped, squirming until she had flattened them against his chest. He kissed her into breathless silence, but suddenly she stiffened and pushed herself up to peer over his shoulder. Her busy fingers had found the welted scar across his back.

"God above us! How did you get that?"

He tried to draw her head down but she evaded him. "No! Tell me."

He sighed. "Indian. Shot me. Come here, will you not?"

"No! Why did he shoot you?"

"God! You do ask a lot of questions."

"I want to know!" She was on her knees now, looking down at him round-eyed. "And what happened to your face?"

Apparently the only way he could get her back was to answer her. "That was an Indian too, only he used an arrow."

"An arrow!" she gasped. "Jesus, Mary, and Joseph! The same Indian?"

He laughed. "No, silly. Two Indians in two different places."

"How did you get mixed up with so many Indians? What did you do to make them mad at you?"

"Sarah, love," he sighed. "I'm a soldier. That makes most Indians mad."

He waited for her reaction. No matter if she made her living showing her legs on the stage—she probably felt the same way about soldiers as most girls.

She surprised him, burying her face in his neck and holding him tight. "I thought soldiers had to wear a blue suit," she murmured.

"You don't mind?"

"What?"

"My being a soldier?"

"Oh, hell no! Why should I?"

Obviously she did not mind at all. The idea of his fighting Indians seemed to excite her. She demonstrated this enthusiastically, and Michael encouraged her until she squealed in delight. Disentangling an arm, he clapped a hand over her mouth.

"You'll wake the house!" he cautioned her.

"Who cares?" she gasped. "Oh, God, Michael . . . you're a grand man, you are."

Gently he shifted her considerable weight into the crook of his arm and held her fast while he stroked her glowing body.

"Michael?" she breathed into his ear.

"Um?"

"I'm not Sarah Delmar. I'm . . ."

He hushed her gently. "I didn't think so, love, but it makes no difference."

"That's fake too," she whispered, tugging at a lock of her blonde hair.

"I can see that," he answered dryly, "but I like it. Stop telling secrets now."

"You told me yours." She looked at him worriedly. "I'm just plain Mary Margaret Foley . . . not Delmar. Little Maggie who ran off with the actors to get away from a damned mop and bucket. I've never been in Chicago, either. I had a job holding rabbits in Noonan's Varieties until Bernie came with his show. One of his girls quit and I got her place."

"It doesn't matter," he assured her, and he kissed her until she stopped frowning. But there was one thing that puzzled him.

"Sarah?"

"Yes?"

"What kind of a job is 'holding rabbits'?"

"Giovanni . . . the World's Greatest Magician. He pulled rabbits out of a hat and I had to hold them. It was easy except when he forgot to give 'em their booze."

"Good God! What do you mean by that?"

"He gave 'em stale bread dipped in rye whiskey before the act . . . when he remembered. That way they got sleepy and they didn't kick when he pulled them out of the hat."

"Well . . ." He patted her comfortingly. "Maggie or Sarah, I don't give a damn. And I wouldn't call you *little* Maggie, either." His hand cupped her solid backside lovingly and she pinched him, hard. He had to capture her hands to stop her, and that led to more excitement.

After a long while, Sarah groaned. "God, I'm hungry. I want some breakfast!"

"Have you anything here?"

"Lord, no! There's mice as big as elephants in this basement. I can't keep anything in the room. Come on, let's go get something to eat."

"All right. But Sarah . . . ?"

"What?" She was splashing water on her face from the big basin, and her voice was muffled.

"Can I stay a while, Sarah?"

"Why not? You'll scare the mice away." She gave him a dazzling smile. "Get your clothes on, will you? I'll not have time for breakfast if you don't hurry. I have to be at rehearsal by noon."

He paid for their breakfast though it pained him. Clearly he was going to have to persuade Sarah to take up cooking in her room if his money was to last as long as his leave. She sensed his distress and grinned at him wickedly.

"I thought you had a pocket full of silver?"

"Well, I've a bit, but did you ever see a rich soldier?"

She laughed and tucked her arm through his. "I'll not let you go hungry, Michael. What will you do until tonight? You can't come to rehearsal—Bernie would have a fit."

"I must go back to the depot and get my bag."

"All right. Here's my key so's you can put it in the room. I'll leave a ticket for you with old Fatso at the stage entrance, and I'll see you there after the show tonight."

Her objection to home cooking was apparent when he returned to the room with his carpetbag. A big gray rat, picking its way across her bedside table, paused to watch him coolly.

Mice, he thought. No wonder she says they're big as elephants. He put down the bag and took her hairbrush from the wash stand. The rat ambled to the edge of the table but paused again to look at Michael before he jumped. The thrown brush dropped him, stunned, against the wall, and Michael's boot heel crushed the life from him with a squeal. Holding his trophy by its long tail, he forced open the window and slung it into the alley.

Surveying the dingy room, he grinned happily. It would do fine despite the livestock. It was only a place to sleep, and with Sarah to keep him company nights, there'd be no time to think about the rats. Only about all the money he would save by not having to rent a room for himself.

12

"Mercy!" exclaimed Louise Carter. "I had forgotten how hot it can be in Philadelphia." A group of people pushed between her and her husband, and she wrinkled her nose in distaste. "This used to be such a quiet, beautiful park."

Brigid steadied Amanda on the wooden step provided by the Pennsylvania Sons of Temperance for small patrons of their drinking fountain. The Catholic Total Abstinence Fountain was grander—surmounted by a statue of Moses—but the thirteen-sided wooden replica of a Greek temple contributed by the Sons of Temperance had a special attraction. Its twenty-six spigots produced iced water.

"Don't gulp," cautioned Brigid. "Just sip."

"Can't. Goes up my nose."

"I think," said Mrs. Carter, "we have had enough for today."

It was only midafternoon, but it had been a long day for the Carters. They had risen with the sun for a visit to the Centennial and had reached the fair before nine via the excursion steamer up the Schuylkill River.

It was not much of a ride, but the children begged for it. They had walked from the Bruning house to the streetcar terminal on Twenty-third Street, riding from there up to the landing at the city waterworks on the

124

Schuylkill. Crossing the river under the massive iron trusses of the Girard Street bridge, the steamboat landed its passengers on a pretty little island below the Centennial grounds.

"You've got it turned too high, Amanda. Here . . ." Brigid moved to help, but she was distracted by a familiar voice addressing Lieutenant Carter. Amanda gulped water and exploded in choking coughs.

"Pat her on the back," Mrs. Carter urged, and Brigid complied, still trying to identify the voice.

"Yes, I'm Carter," she heard the lieutenant reply.

"Brennan, sir. Private Michael Brennan. I was with the lieutenant that time we went out of Camp Robinson to get the wagon train."

"Brennan! I remember . . . You brought in the wounded teamster."

"Ouch!" squeaked Amanda. "Don't hit me so hard, Brigid. Let me down." She lifted an accusing face to Brigid, who blotted it with her handkerchief.

Brennan! In the name of God, where had he sprung from? Her mind raced. What'll happen when he sees me?

Amanda escaped the handkerchief and skipped off to see who her father was talking to. If I could only hide somewhere, Brigid thought desperately. I could stay until he's gone and say I felt faint.

She felt anything but faint. When he recognized her, the story of that brawl in New York would come out somehow. The Carters would discharge her on the spot. There was no place to hide. Plunging her face into the sparkling jet of water, she pretended to drink and almost strangled herself.

"We are going now, Brigid," Mrs. Carter called. She relinquished the fountain and joined the others as slowly as possible. Mrs. Carter gave her a curious glance, but her husband and Brennan were deep in a discussion of Indians.

When Michael Brennan saw her, he blinked and looked mildly curious—nothing more. Lieutenant Carter glanced at her.

"Ah! Brigid. This is Private Brennan. We shared a hot fight with the Indians once. Brennan, this is our children's nurse, Miss O'Donnel."

Brennan studied her with interest. After a barely perceptible pause he nodded politely.

"Pleased to meet you, Miss O'Donnel."

Brigid's throat refused to yield a single word. She could only stare at him. It was impossible he didn't know her, yet he acted as if he had never seen her before.

Lieutenant Carter turned back to him. "You're out of the army now, Brennan?"

Michael was wearing the same gray suit he had worn that memorable evening in New York, with a single addition—a stiff-brimmed straw boater hat with a big red, white, and blue Centennial ribbon. He had taken it off to greet the Carters, and now he replaced it with a jaunty tap on its flat crown.

"No, sir. I've been on duty with the recruit depot, but I'm going back to my regiment now. I just stopped off for a bit to have a look at the Centennial."

"Precisely what we are doing," said Carter heartily. "You were in the Nineteenth, weren't you?"

"I was, sir, but I'm transferred to the Twenty-first."

"But that's my regiment!"

"Yes, sir," Michael grinned. "I know."

Carter frowned. "Private, you said? I'd have thought you'd be corporal by now."

Brennan looked sheepish. "Ah, well, sir . . . I did make corporal, but . . ." He lowered his voice confidentially. 'The lieutenant knows how it is. New York's a wicked place for a field soldier like me."

Carter laughed. "No court-martial, I hope."

"Ah, no, sir! Nothing like that. I got a bit crosswise of my captain an' I had to leave my stripes with him. That's all."

This exchange meant nothing to Brigid. Her ignorance of the army made it impossible for her to connect his presence in Philadelphia with his loss of

126

"stripes" and that donnybrook in New York. She was far too busy wondering what he was doing here and why he pretended not to know her.

"Well," said Carter, "you'll have 'em back soon enough with the regiment. Just keep your nose clean and look for action."

Michael listened to this advice with an expression of exaggerated respect that sickened Brigid. She could not imagine what he was up to.

"I'll probably see you in Oregon," Carter continued. "I'm going back to command K Company, and when you've been assigned you must let me know where you are."

"Now that's a bit of luck, sir," said Brennan. "I've got my orders, and I'm assigned to the lieutenant's company at Belknap."

Brigid shut her eyes. This she understood. I've been bad, she thought grimly, but not enough to deserve this. Brennan's words penetrated her anguish dimly.

"Sir, I'd—uh—like to ask the lieutenant something."

"What's that?" Carter foresaw a request for a loan, and his reply was cautious.

"I was just thinkin', sir . . . it's no easy thing takin' the family all the way to Oregon on the cars, an' me bein' in the lieutenant's company an' goin' the same way an' all . . . Maybe the lieutenant would be wantin' an orderly for the trip?"

The military jargon baffled Brigid. She had no idea what an orderly was, and she watched Carter's face for a clue.

"By Joe!" he exclaimed. "Not a bad idea at all. Louise?" He turned to his wife who was waiting patiently for this conversation to end. "My dear, Brennan has asked if we need an orderly and offered himself for the job. Can you use some help with your packing and moving?"

Louise Carter was no recruit. In twelve years of army life she had shared with her husband the service of numerous soldier servants, and in her experience their selection required more deliberation than this.

"You know best about that, Cassius. I would welcome Brennan's help if you think it proper to accept his offer, but . . . did you not say you are on leave, Brennan?"

Her response was in what Lieutenant Carter called her Old Philadelphia tone. Brennan countered adroitly.

"Yes, ma'am, I did. But you see, ma'am, I'd be honored to work for you an' the company commander, an' besides . . ." His smile was ingenuous. "I'd be on duty if I was the lieutenant's orderly, an' I could save my leave an' maybe see a bit of the fair too."

You criminal, Brigid seethed. Now she understood what an orderly was, and the prospect was appalling.

Louise Carter smiled. They always had a trick in mind. At least he was honest about it.

"Well, in that case I suppose it's all right. I can certainly use some help. There is a great deal to do before we go."

"That's settled then," Carter said. "I'll get a telegram off to regiment at once. When were you due at Belknap, Brennan?"

"Last day of May, Sir. I was plannin' to leave Friday next."

"I'll have your orders changed so you go when I do. Where are you staying in Philadelphia?"

"I found a place in town, sir," Brennan replied blandly.

"Must be damned expensive. Louise, couldn't we find something for him at the house?"

Brigid decided she would not faint, but she might be sick, if Mrs. Carter said he could have the other room on the Brunings' attic floor. The prompt reply was a small comfort.

"Not in the house. It's full from top to bottom." Louise Carter thought a moment. "There is a room over the stable, though. It hasn't been used since Papa let the carriage go, and I've no idea what it's like now."

"Ah, it would do fine, Missus Carter," Brennan assured her. "I'd not care what it's like, an' I'd be near to hand when you or the lieutenant are wantin' any little thing done."

Brigid stared at Mrs. Carter in amazement. How could she be so mesmerized by this grinning Irish serpent? The family started for the street-railway depot at the main gate of the exposition and she followed numbly, racking her brain for understanding of Brennan's behavior. He knew her. Why pretend he didn't?

She found a clue in something he had said to Carter. He was going back to his regiment because he had "gotten crosswise" of his captain. Maybe George Schultz had talked to the captain? And Brennan had lost his job in New York because of that? But the army didn't fire people—it just sent them to Oregon. She stopped abruptly, and Amanda, whose hand she was holding, looked at her in surprise.

Of course. If he told the Carters why she had lost her job, they might find out why he had lost his. He had lied to them just like she had.

"Come on, Brigid!" Amanda urged. "They're waiting for us."

It was an even match. The winner would be the one who found a way to get the other fired without losing his own place. That, she saw, was going to require some really artistic lying.

They took a yellow horsecar with a big maroon lamp at the front—one of the City Passenger Company's specials shuttling between downtown and the fair along Chestnut, Lancaster, and Belmont streets. The Chestnut Street bridge was jammed as usual, and the car moved an inch at a time.

Brigid explored her problem. Being a servant girl was a comedown from Lord and Taylor's, but the alternatives were worse. She liked the Carters, and the prospect of going to the frontier was exciting. Now that her job was threatened, she realized how much she wanted to keep it.

Brennan, she thought. I'm cursed with the man. He

129

was sitting with Lieutenant Carter in the seat in front of her, and she stared at the back of his head with such loathing it was a wonder he didn't feel it.

Next day he moved into the carriage house, and Brigid avoided him like the plague. Much as it galled her, however, she had to admit the skill with which he won over the Bruning establishment. He began at the top. Under his practiced hands Mr. Bruning's shoes began to gleam like Lieutenant Carter's, and Martha watched admiringly in the kitchen as he applied blacking, brush, spit, and a rag to bring them to a mirror finish.

"Do, Lord!" she muttered, "you better'n that boy at th' U-nited Stase Ho-tel what used to do them shoes."

Louise Carter had only to look distracted and Brennan was there, asking what was to be done. Mrs. Bruning was more difficult, but he captured her by spading, raking, and rolling the fallow garden in the back court. The family gardener of forty years had died the year before, and with him Mrs. Bruning's interest in her plants.

"I could find no sheep manure, ma'am," Michael told her gravely, "though I know that's best. That's horse manure, but I sieved it real good before I spread it."

"I declare," pronounced Mrs. Bruning, "it hasn't looked like that since poor old Julius went."

"Ah, ma'am, an Irishman's born with a spade in his hand."

Horse manure is right, thought Brigid sourly, overhearing this exchange. Martha had succumbed because he kept the big coal hod by the kitchen range full and praised her cooking fulsomely. The children were fascinated by him, and only Brigid held out. Inevitably he succeeded in catching her alone in the back hall and stopped her with a wink and a grin.

"How did you come by this place, Bridey?" he asked. "What kind of a fairy tale did you spin 'em?"

130

"Nothing more than you," she snapped. "An' don't be callin' me Bridey either. I'd not want them thinkin' I'd ever seen you before."

"I'm sure of that, love," he chuckled. "Why, they might ask about you, an' what could I say? That I saw you taken up by the cops for stabbin' a poor man in the street?"

She gave him a look of such cold fury that he drew back in mock alarm. "And I . . ." she hissed, "would have to tell 'em you an' that Polack bum were run in by the same cop for molestin' decent girls!"

"True," he nodded gravely, "that's what any girl in your fix would say. Which one of us d'you think the lieutenant will be believin'?"

"You . . . you bastard!" she choked. He could do it. He could pull that old-soldier bit and Carter would believe him . . . not her. Brennan eyed her small clenched fists and shook his head.

"Now, Bridey . . . You know I'd not do a thing like that. Not to a friend. An' you an' I are goin' to be friends . . . Aren't we?"

She put her face in her hands. Even match, hell! A word here, a hint there . . . he would keep this threat hanging over her until she paid for his silence. I'll not do it, she swore to herself. So help me God, I'll find a way to get him before he gets me.

Michael watched her storm into the pantry and grinned to himself. This was going to be a lot better than Sarah and her basement room. All he could eat for nothing plus eight dollars a month from Lieutenant Carter on top of his army pay. His stay in Philadelphia prolonged at no cost to his leave. Now that he had scrubbed it clean, his room over the stable was fine, and the bed—a Bruning castoff—was big enough for two.

And we'll take care of that soon enough, he gloated, his eyes on Brigid's trim little figure. She had cost him the best job he ever had. Cost him his corporal's stripes and delivered him into the hands of that evil

131

man, Dennett. Now she had to stop his tongue if she wanted to keep her job. It was a happy prospect.

But Brigid O'Donnel would not come begging his silence. Ah, no. It would take time and cunning and that was a game to delight an Irishman's heart. He rubbed his hands in anticipation.

13

In a house as full of people as the Brunings', Brigid's caution made it hard for Brennan to find her alone. She dodged him expertly, at the same time praying he would not give up his chase and get her fired by telling Lieutenant Carter the truth about her lost job in New York. Despite all her precautions, within a week he stumbled upon another and more dangerous bit of information.

In the children's room one morning she found Mrs. Carter circling the big four-poster bed with a field-hockey stick in her hand.

"Whatever are you doing with that, ma'am?"

"Bats!"

"Ooh!"

"It happens all the time. I cannot remember a summer that the wretched little things didn't get in. Is the window open?"

"Yes, ma'am."

"All right. I'll hold the chair and you stand on it and poke them. They'll go right out the window."

Brigid gulped. "They'll go right into your hair!"

"Nonsense! That's an old wives' tale. Take the stick and poke them."

"Poke them where?" Brigid whispered.

"In the canopy of the tester bed, silly! Come on."

Gingerly, Brigid mounted the chair, shut her eyes, and jabbed at the sagging middle of the canopy.

"Not there, Brigid! Around the edges."

Brigid shifted her attack and was rewarded by a chorus of squeaks. She dropped the stick and wrapped her arms about her head as two small black creatures rocketed around the room and out the window.

"Good!" said Mrs. Carter triumphantly. Brigid hiked up her skirt and climbed down, to find her employer looking at her with a frown.

"Are those the only stockings you have, Brigid?"

"No, ma'am, but my other pair's for good." She lifted her skirt and looked at her ankles. "Is something wrong?"

Mrs. Carter smiled. "I didn't know you could darn stockings so many times. I've been thoughtless, Brigid. You shall have half your month's pay at once so you can buy yourself a new pair."

It was this unexpected wealth that led to Brennan's discovery. Brigid bought sturdy black lisle stockings and displayed them happily to Mrs. Carter and Martha in the kitchen.

"That's better," said Louise Carter, grateful there were no male members of the family present to admire this glimpse of Brigid's shapely legs. "I should have thought to give you some money sooner."

But there was a good deal remaining after the purchase of stockings, and Brigid felt guilty about George Schultz. How to get the money to him baffled her so she appealed to Mrs. Carter.

"I—uh—owe some money in New York, ma'am, and I thought to send some of what you gave me, but I don't know how. I'm afraid if I just put it in an envelope someone will steal it."

"You are quite right about that, Brigid. It would never even get out of Philadelphia that way. But I gave you only five dollars. Are you certain you should send it away?"

"I must, ma'am. I promised. I'll only send a little now, and some more later."

134

"Well, that's very commendable. I will ask Mr. Bruning to purchase a postal money order for you, and you can send that quite safely through the mails. For how much do you wish it?"

"Two dollars and a half, ma'am?"

"So much? You will have little left for yourself."

"Ah, I don't need much, ma'am."

She offered the money and Mrs. Carter accepted it without further protest. Next day the money order was brought and she showed Brigid where to enter the name of the recipient.

"Use pen and ink. That way no one can change it."

Brigid filled in the blank and lifted a pleased face with a bright blue streak at the corner of her mouth. "I borrowed William's indelible pencil. Is that all right?"

Mrs. Carter smiled. "Of course. If you hurry, Brennan will mail it for you. He is taking some letters to the post office for me."

To her dismay, Brigid discovered Michael waiting at the kitchen door. She hesitated, but could think of no reasonable excuse for not giving her letter to him. Reluctantly she addressed and sealed the envelope and handed it over.

"I gave him money for stamps," said Mrs. Carter as she left the kitchen. "You needn't bother about that."

Michael was studying the letter. "Officer George Schultz?" he asked softly. "Now why would you be sendin' money to him?"

"Will you get out of here?" snapped Brigid. "And mind your own business!"

"Strange," he grinned. "What can you be payin' that cop for?"

Brigid glanced desperately at Martha and pushed him through the door. "Go, will you? Just go on an' leave me be."

It was a stroke of unbelievable bad luck, and she awaited its result anxiously. Mrs. Carter was a kind woman, but she was not likely to listen to an involved explanation of why her nursemaid had a police warrant

135

against her and was sending money to the policeman involved.

Michael made no immediate use of his discovery. Beyond a knowing smirk when he encountered her, he gave her no more trouble than usual. But he had not forgotten the incident. Before the week was out he stopped her in the upstairs hall.

"I was wonderin' if you'd care to visit the city this evenin'," he said. Brigid stared at him in astonishment.

"With you?"

"Surely. Who else?"

"Why, I'd . . . You . . ." she sputtered into horrified silence.

Michael said nothing. He just waited, and Brigid's anger turned to worry. He had her in a corner.

Given a chance, she might be able to explain her situation to Louise Carter, but if Michael spoke to the lieutenant first, there might be no chance. Mrs. Carter would be so angry at what she heard from her husband that she would never listen. Brigid evaded.

"Why?"

"Why what?"

"Go into the city with you."

"Just for a bit of fun." He grinned ingratiatingly. "You've not had much since you got here. Go on now an' ask her. She'll let you go."

Numbly Brigid approached Mrs. Carter, hoping for refusal, but Michael was right.

"You really haven't had any time for yourself, have you, Brigid? All right, you may go, but you must be back by twelve. Tell Brennan I said so."

So Brigid walked out with Michael into the warm summer evening and was excited by the prospect of an evening on the town despite her worry.

"Where are we going?" she demanded happily when they descended from the horse car.

Michael pointed at the Chestnut Street Theater.

"A bite of supper and then maybe a show? That's good, but there's lots more. We'll look at some and you can choose."

"Good! Where shall we have supper?"

Michael hesitated so long she gave him a puzzled look. It was just as well she could not hear his silent thoughts. He wanted to show off his pretty redhead at McGerrity's, and he was weighing the chances that Sarah would be there. His parting from that sprightly young woman had been amicable enough—she had accepted his explanation that his services were required by a high-ranking army officer and made their last night together a memorable one. But how she would react to Brigid was something else.

"What's the matter with you?" Brigid demanded.

To hell with it, he decided. "Come on. I know a grand place."

The Hibernian Club was as crowded as ever, but McGerrity remembered Michael and found them a table. He grinned when he was introduced to Brigid.

"O'Donnel is it? Welcome to this house, miss. For Brennan and O'Donnel the first drink is on me. What's your pleasure?"

"Thank you, Mr. McGerrity," Brigid replied demurely. "I'll have a glass of beer, if you please."

"Good lass! A pitcher is it then, Mr. Brennan?"

"It's a good way to start," Michael beamed. Magically a waiter appeared to crash a pitcher of foaming lager on the table with a schooner for Brennan and a glass for his girl. McGerrity observed all the amenities. Michael poured both full and lifted his schooner to the proprietor.

"May you be in heaven before the Devil knows ye're dead, Mr. McGerrity."

"Same to you, Brennan. You and your Brigid enjoy yourselves here."

Brigid gave Michael a surprised look. "Sure and you're a favored guest in this place. You've been here before?"

"A time or two," he replied casually, handing her the menu. "What will you have for your supper?"

Brigid studied it and her eyes sparkled. "I'll have the codfish and potatoes with a dish of boiled greens."

"That's poorhouse fare! Don't worry about the cost, lass."

"I'm not. That's what I want. I was raised on it and it's been a long time since I had it. I want a big piece of rye bread and butter with the fish and I'll have the rice pudding after."

"God save us, girl! Were you raised in a workhouse?"

"Close to it. D'you mind, then?"

"Not at all. I only thought you'd be wanting something finer."

"Ah, no. Missus Bruning sets a grand table, an' I'd welcome a plain dish for a change."

She was well into her codfish when a minor disturbance behind Michael drew her attention. A pretty blonde girl, impressively corseted, whispered urgently in the ear of the biggest man she had ever seen. He pushed her away and peered at Michael.

An orange-and-gray plaid suit strained over his giant form, and his face was fascinating. From Brigid's point of view it was wedge-shaped, sloping from a broad jaw to a point—she supposed—somewhere in his crest of curly black hair. Bushy eyebrows formed a solid dark bar across his forehead, sheltering bright black eyes and a magnificent nose, thickly furred at the nostrils. Catching her look, he gave her a huge smile.

The blonde gave Brigid a hostile look and whispered to him again. He shook his head. "I want to meet your sojer. That is him?"

He rested an awesome hand on Michael's shoulder, and Brennan looked up in surprise. Catching sight of the girl, he got to his feet warily. Brigid was intrigued by his expression.

"Ah . . . good evening, Sarah. I don't believe . . ."

The blonde giggled. "Nick Tomchik. Nick, meet Michael Brennan."

The giant accepted Michael's hand and crushed it happily. Stepping back, he measured the Irishman with his eyes, and again his face split in a huge grin. "Pretty good! But not so good as Nikolai, eh, Zarah?"

The blonde pursed her bright lips and blew in his ear. Michael's face reddened and she gave him a wicked look.

"Aren't you goin' to introduce your lady, Michael?"

"Ah . . . yes . . . of course. Brigid, this is Miss Sarah Delmar and—uh—Nick?"

The big man bowed, and to Brigid's astonishment seized her hand and kissed it. "Nikolai Tomchik." He shook Michael's shoulder gently. "By God, sojer, you got an eye for pretty girls! We drink a glass of beer with you, hey?"

It was not an invitation to be debated. He stretched out both hands and they came back with a chair in each. Seated, he trapped a waiter in the same fashion.

"Beer!" he rumbled, and Michael's pitcher was replaced by a full one.

Brigid was studying the gaudy blonde calculatingly, but Tomchik suddenly reached a hamlike hand to tug at a strand of her hair, and her eyes widened apprehensively.

"Like fire," he rumbled admiringly. "Like warm fire when the weather it is cold. Ah, sojer, she is beautiful lady."

Brigid blushed and he put his arm around Sarah, teasing a blonde curl with his finger. "Is wonderful. In my country every girl got black hair."

Brigid glanced at Michael, but he evaded her eyes and concentrated on his supper. Tomchik's admiring stare finally moved her to speak.

"And where are you from, Mr. Tomchik?"

"Servia, Miss Brigid. I was best blacksmith in Lovtcha. Now I am best in this place."

That's clear, Michael thought sourly. No horse would be fool enough to give him an argument. He looked up incautiously and Sarah gave him a sly smile.

"I guess you found yourself a better room, then, Michael?"

"Why, yes, I did, Miss Delmar. I've no complaints."

"Miss Delmar, is it? Lah-di-dah, aren't we formal!"

Jesus, Mary, and Joseph, save me from my great

139

folly, Michael prayed silently. How could I have done this? Tomchik chuckled at his bristling girl.

"What's the matter with you, Zarah? Drink now, an' be good."

He took a gulp of beer and scowled ferociously. "Ugh! Terrible. We got to have some thing better."

He caught a passing waiter. "You bring some little glasses an' my bottle slivovitz, hah?"

"Bottle o' what?"

"My bottle slivovitz. Mr. Shawn he knows where it is. You ask him."

"Jeez, mister, I can't even say it! You want some whiskey?"

"No!" Tomchik pushed back his chair and swept the waiter aside. "Come on, sojer. I give you something good."

"What's that?" demanded Brennan warily.

"In my country," explained Tomchik, "we don' eat plums. We make 'em better." He rolled his eyes delightedly and dragged Michael away. It was a mistake to leave those two women together, but Michael had no choice.

The chilly silence at the table was broken by Brigid, watching the two men make their way to the bar.

"My, he is a big one, isn't he?"

"You want him too?" Sarah demanded truculently.

"What do you mean? Why would I want him?"

"You got Michael. You can't have them both!"

Brigid's face flamed. "I haven't got him and I don't want him! I don't want your monster either. What are you talking about?"

Sarah sniffed. "I was Nick's girl before Michael came, but he moved out of my room into yours, so I took Nick back. I be damned if you're goin' to steal him too!"

Brigid exploded. "That damn soldier's never been near my room! Can't you get it through that fake yellow head I don't want either of them?"

"Don't you talk to me like that, you redheaded slut!"

140

Brigid was around the table with her fingers in Sarah's hair before the blonde girl realized what was happening.

"Slut yourself!" she panted.

"Ow!" squealed Sarah. "Leggo my hair, damn you!"

Brigid pushed her head to the table with one hand while the other plucked a generous hank of blonde hair. Sarah screamed.

Twisting free, she became dangerous. She rapped the rim of Brigid's glass on the table edge, shattering it to leave a jagged, razor-edged weapon, with which she lunged at Brigid.

It was a wild swing and Brigid dodged, struggling to draw her own weapon—the hatpin. She absorbed a roundhouse clout in the eye from Sarah's free hand, but then she had the hatpin. Using it like a rapier, she drove the squalling blonde girl into a nearby table whose occupants clutched for their dancing glasses.

"Come ahn—knock it off!" growled a disgruntled man, but then he saw the jagged glass in Sarah's hand. "Jaysus! Look at that!"

"Leave 'em fight!" shouted his companion. "I say four bits on the blonde!"

There was a scramble to give the girls room, and McGerrity roared at Tomchik:

"Look at yer woman, you big bohunk!"

Michael shook his head furiously. He was trying to dominate two straight shots of Serbian plum brandy and was having trouble.

"Holy Mother!" gasped Tomchik. "Look at that frog-sticker! She put that in Zarah we got a dead girl!"

That damned hatpin again, Michael groaned. He pushed himself off the bar to look at the circling, spitting women. In his opinion the shattered beer glass was more dangerous than Brigid's hatpin. He shoved Tomchik forward.

"Grab Sarah! I'll get the redhead."

They burst between the two girls and Michael flattened Brigid against the wall. "Stop it!" he growled, fending off the hatpin. "Stop now, will ye?"

"She tried to stab me!" Sarah yelled, squirming in Tomchik's grip. "Lookit that friggin' stiletto! Lemme at her!"

"Nah!" rumbled her captor. "You don' wanna fight. The sojer's my friend."

"Screw the soldier! I don't want him—I want that redhead bitch! Lemme go, you goddamn bohunk!"

Brigid got through Michael's defense with the hatpin and he swore explosively.

"You stick me with that thing again, Bridey, an' I'll belt you silly! Come on, let's get outta here!"

She lunged at him, hissing, and he trapped her, wrapping his arms around hers and pinning them to her sides.

"Out, damn it!" Lifting her bodily from the floor, he carried her, kicking and swearing, toward the door.

"Hold what you got, Nick!" he encouraged the big Serb as he brushed past him.

"I got her, sojer! When you get rid of that devil, you come back. We finish my bottle, hey?"

Brigid's flying feet cleared a path, and McGerrity pursued them to the door. "Soldier! Wait . . ." he yelled excitedly. "Will they mix it in the ring? I can make a helluva purse on them two! Winner'll take fifty dollars, easy!"

"Great God, McGerrity . . ." Michael panted. "Get yerself a pair of alley cats and shove 'em in a crocus sack if you want that kind o' fight. Stand aside, man!"

On the sidewalk he set Brigid down hard and shook her. "That's enough, now! What if the Carters hear you been street-fightin' again?"

"You bastard!" she panted. "You're the one to tell 'em, too, aren't you?"

"Nah . . . nah! Nobody's goin' to tell 'em if you'll just simmer down now."

Surprisingly, she did. She tugged her jacket straight and felt her disordered hair.

"My hat!" She wheeled and headed for the door of the saloon, and almost made it before Michael caught her.

142

"No, you don't! You're not goin' back in there. McGerrity'll save it an' I'll get it for you. Give me that damned hatpin."

Again she surprised him by handing it over. Her fingers had found something more serious than a lost hat. She probed her eye gently.

"That slut of yours hit me!"

"Let me see." He tipped up her face and whistled softly.

"Is it bad?"

"That's goin' to be the mother and father of all shiners."

"What'll I do?" she wailed. "What'll I say when Missus Carter sees it? You . . . !" she hissed. "It's all your fault, Michael Brennan! You were sleeping with that bitch, weren't you?"

"Whatever gave you that notion?" He backed away from her, grinning.

"She said so!" Brigid shrilled. "That's what she's so mad about. You had her an' then you left her!"

"I was only improvin' myself," said Michael smugly.

"You great fool! D'you think I'd have you? D'you think I got in a fight with that whore over you? Oooh, God!" she moaned, cupping her swollen eye.

She was so little and so appealing, Michael felt contrite. "I'm sorry, Bridey. I swear I am. I'd ought never have taken you in there."

"Much good that does me now!" She glared at him with one eye. "I want a piece of meat!"

"What?"

"Meat, damn it! I've got to put something on this eye. You got me into this—you get me a piece of raw meat."

He smothered his laughter, and when they came to the door of another saloon he pushed her into a dark corner by the door.

"Stay there an' don't get in trouble till I get back."

"Where are you going?"

"To see if they'll sell me a piece of meat in here."

143

He returned with a dark wet lump of something in a scrap of paper, and Brigid sniffed it suspiciously.

"What is it?"

"Liver. That's all they had, an' it cost me two bits."

"That won't do any good! I want a piece of beef."

"I can't help that. Just clap the thing on your eye an' maybe it'll help."

Muttering darkly, Brigid applied the liver, cupping a hand to catch the blood that dripped from it. Under the next street light she removed it and held up her face.

"How is it now?"

"Lord, Bridey, it's hardly been on a minute." He turned her face to the light and sighed. "Well . . . I guess it helped a little."

"You're lying!"

"I'll not fool you, love. It'll be bad tomorrow."

"Oh, what can I tell her?" she wailed. A tear spilled from her good eye. "She'll put me out, surely!"

"You want the job so much?" he asked, surprised at her anguish.

She sniffled. "What will I do? I can't get a decent job in New York. You fixed that, damn you!"

Michael frowned. He wanted this girl in his bed any way he could get her, and he had devoted a lot of thought to her. But only as a problem to be solved. He had never seen her cry, and suddenly his lust was complicated by sympathy. She looked so forlorn his heart went out to her. Also, if Mrs. Carter put her out, he would never get her to his room over the stable. Clearly, something would have to be found to explain that eye.

In a vacant lot a carnival made the night hideous with its steam calliope. He studied it, still frowning. Freaks, mediums, and Fatimah, the World's Greatest Exponent of Egyptian Dance, proclaimed the sleezy signs. No help there. But the squeal of machinery caught his ear and he identified its origin—a steam-driven carrousel with little cars affixed to spokes revolving on a track about a central axle.

144

"There!" he exclaimed. "Come on."

"I don't want to go in there!"

"Whisht now and come. I'll get you an excuse for your eye."

He hustled her, protesting and still clutching her liver, into one of the cars and paid the fifty cents demanded without protest. She sat glumly beside him while the thing made a dozen revolutions before slowing to a halt.

"You just wasted your money," she grumbled. "I don't like those things an' I don't feel any better."

"You will tomorrow. Now listen to me." She was sniffling again. "Stop crying, Bridey. I'm goin' to tell you what to say when they ask what happened. You tell her I took you on that fool thing an' when it stopped—all of a sudden—you banged your head on the pole an' hurt your eye. Lost your hat, too."

Brigid stared at him suspiciously. "An' what'll you say?"

"I'll be that sorry she'll know it's the truth. I'll ask about your poor eye an' I'll damn meself for takin' you on that merry-go-round."

"You'd do that? Truly?"

"I will."

"I don't believe you. You want to make trouble for me. Why would you help me like that?"

"I don't want to make you trouble, Bridey. That's not what I want at all."

She said something shocking and glared at him. "I know what you want. And if I don't give it you'll get me fired."

"I'd never do that to you!"

"Would you not? I can see what you're up to. Holdin' it over my head. You'll tell Mister Carter some awful story if I don't give you what you want."

"Ah, come on, now . . ." He pulled her hand from her face and flung the liver into the darkness. "I'd never do a thing like that to a girl," he lied glibly. "I'm not denyin' I've thought about you. Lots. But t'was only what any man would think."

145

"And what's that, for God's sake?"

"That you're a pretty girl an' I'd give my soul to put my two hands around you an' give or take a kiss or two. Is that so bad?"

She sighed, a little mollified but still unbelieving. "Brennan, you're a good-for-nothing creature. It's by the likes of you the sins of the world are made. Mind you, I'll be grateful if you'd tell her one of your fearful lies about how I blacked my eye . . . but not so far as you want, I'm thinkin'."

"I'll do it an' gladly!" he assured her.

They caught a night car on Chestnut Street, and after a long five minutes' silence she turned on him again.

"I still don't understand. I can't tell when you're lyin' an' when you're tellin' the truth."

He shrugged. "What difference? If you get in trouble about your eye, like as not I'd be in it too. Look, Bridey," he said seriously, "it's a good place for both of us. If we keep our mouths shut about each other we can both keep our jobs. What d'you say?"

She watched him suspiciously, but when he took her hand she let him hold it. "And you'll leave me be?"

He nodded, smiling. "Truce. Until your eye's all well again."

"And then . . . ?"

"Then I'll get you."

14

Brigid's appearance at breakfast next morning was greeted by awestruck silence. Her left eye was swollen shut, yellow and purple, with an iridescent green crescent beneath it.

"Ooooh!" gasped Amanda. "How did—?"

"I went on a merry-go-round thing," snapped Brigid, "and I bumped my eye when it stopped."

"Hoo-ee!" chortled Martha. "I thought that no-account soljer done hit you. Do it hurt?"

William opened his mouth to comment, but Brigid glared him to silence. Breakfast—oatmeal, scrapple, potatoes, and biscuit—was eaten in careful silence, everyone trying not to look at Brigid. Only Martha was irrepressible.

"I gone fix you a napkin wif ice in it to draw that swellin'. Cain't do nuthin' 'bout them pritty colors, though."

Louise Carter appeared, carrying hat and gloves, and gasped. Her face was a study. She tried not to look at the eye, but it was hard.

"The children . . . the children are to visit Mister Bruning's office this morning, and I . . . was going shopping . . ." She gave up and stared appalled at Brigid.

147

"What in the world . . . ?"

"At the carnival, ma'am," replied Brigid in a muffled voice. "I went on a merry-go-round and it stopped all of a sudden and I bumped my head."

"Oh, dear! Does . . . does it hurt?"

"No, ma'am. But I'm that embarrassed I can't think."

She put a hand over her battered eye and watched Mrs. Carter mournfully with the other.

"That's awful, Brigid! How could Brennan have let such a thing happen to you?"

"He couldn't help it, ma'am. It . . . it was just an accident."

Mrs. Carter was trying hard to look sympathetic, but she was having difficulty. Brigid squinted at her hopelessly and she gave up the struggle. Clapping a hand over her mouth, she turned her head away.

"Oh, do forgive me, Brigid!" she gasped. "I know it must be awful."

She's trying not to laugh, Brigid realized with a rush of relief. The blessed woman's not mad at me at all.

They were interrupted by Brennan, who came up from the basement, his hands full of polished shoes. His eyes shifted from Brigid to Mrs. Carter and back to Brigid.

"Oh, my!" he said solicitously. "They ought to be sued, that's what."

"What are you talking about, Brennan?" Mrs. Carter demanded. "How could you let this happen to poor Brigid?"

Brigid watched him suspiciously, but his act of contrition was superb. He actually hung his head and blushed.

"I'm that sorry it happened, Missus Carter, I don't know what to say. It was only a little bit of a merry-go-round, but they stopped it too quick an' Brigid was flung against the pipe you hold onto."

Brigid let her breath out cautiously. "You can be sure, ma'am," Michael added righteously, "I gave 'em a piece of my mind."

Louise Carter eyed him doubtfully and he looked even more contrite. "It was all my fault, ma'am. She didn't want to go, but I said it would be all right. She couldn't help it happenin'."

Brigid's undamaged eye twinkled at him. He had kept his word and handsomely. He scowled and clenched a fist.

"I've a good mind to go back there an' whip that booger that was runnin' the engine."

"You will do nothing of the sort!" exclaimed Louise Carter. "It was an accident, and you are not to make more trouble about it. I certainly expect you to be more careful in the future though, Brennan."

"Ah, yes, ma'am . . . I will that, you can be sure!"

It was a flawless performance, and Brigid was proud of him. She knew he was an accomplished liar but she had never thought he would do this well.

Mrs. Carter looked mollified. "Well, the children shall go with their father. Papa likes to show him through the offices. I'm sure, Brigid, you would prefer to remain indoors today and do something for that eye."

"Perhaps a piece of raw meat?" Michael asked innocently.

"Go on, now," Martha snapped. "I gone fix her a ice bag an' we gonna draw that risin' right out."

June, hot and humid in Philadelphia, neared its end before Brigid's eye was respectable again. The swelling soon disappeared, but, as Martha had said, there was nothing to do about the pretty colors.

Her affliction had an advantage—as a defense against Michael. As long as her eye remained multi-colored she had a legitimate objection to walking out with him, but when he managed to catch her alone she had trouble.

Cornered in hall or stairway she became all sharp elbows and busy hands fending him off, but they were only delaying tactics. She escaped from these encoun-

149

ters squeezed, kissed, and panting, praying she had paid enough for his silence.

On the Fourth of July the entire family attended the celebration in Independence Square. Mr. Bruning obtained tickets of entry to the square but—delayed by the grand parade down Chestnut Street of former Union and Confederate troops—they found this a farcical honor, shared by almost fifty thousand other ticket-holders.

By the time the ceremonies began at ten o'clock, the mercury had topped ninety degrees. Crushed in the crowd, they would have considered the affair an uncomfortable failure had it not been for the spectacular intervention of five representatives of the National American Woman Suffrage Association.

The stand and speaker's platform, backed against the old State House on the north of the square, provided seats for the great—Republican Presidential candidate Rutherford Hayes, Emperor Dom Pedro of Brazil, Generals Sherman and Sheridan, and President Grant's representative, Thomas Ferry, president *pro tempore* of the United States Senate. Grant had decided not to attend, and since Vice-President Henry Wilson had died the preceding November, representation of the executive descended upon Senator Ferry.

Susan B. Anthony, leader of the suffragist movement, had campaigned strenuously and unsuccessfully for a place among the seats of the mighty. She had something to say and she saw the Centennial Fourth of July in Philadelphia as a splendid occasion to say it. General Joseph Hawley, head of the Centennial Commission in Philadelphia, turned her down. Senator Ferry in Washington refused her appeal, and it seemed that the feminine threat had been repelled, but that was wishful thinking. The resourceful suffragists simply displayed legitimate press passes and took seats in the section reserved for journalists.

General Hawley called for order and the Bishop of Pennsylvania delivered a prayer to the restless crowd, followed by a chorus singing the Independence Day hymn composed by Oliver Wendell Holmes. The mayor of Philadelphia displayed an original manuscript of the Declaration of Independence and handed it to Richard Henry Lee of Virginia, who read it aloud in a reverent, sonorous voice. As he concluded, the five ladies made their way down the aisle to him—Susan Anthony, Sara Spencer, Phoebe Couzins, Matilda Gage, and Lillie Blake.

Confronting a baffled Senator Ferry, Miss Anthony presented him with her Declaration of Independence for Women, then led her troops off the platform and into the crowd, distributing copies of the declaration as they went. A forest of hands sought these broadsides, and General Hawley's shouts for order went unheeded.

Making her way to the bandstand in front of Independence Hall, Miss Anthony mounted it and faced the throng, shielded from the sun by an umbrella held by Matilda Gage. On either side stood Sara Spencer and Phoebe Couzins, formidable freedom fighters and veterans of the Republican and Democratic national conventions respectively, where they had pled unsuccessfully for a woman's suffrage plank in the party platforms.

While Bayard Taylor read his National Ode from the speaker's platform, Miss Anthony from the bandstand declaimed her Declaration of Independence for Women, who, ". . . no longer bound to obey laws in whose making they had no choice . . . demand justice for the women of this land!"

The Bruning-Carter family made its way home, perspiring mightily. It was blocks before they found a horsecar with room for all. Mr. Bruning's face was grim but his lady smiled quietly, clutching her copy of the women's declaration.

Mister Bruning's repeated view that Susan Anthony and her ladies should have been taken in charge for public disturbance provoked from his wife only smug

151

looks and discreet silence. These might have become intolerable had the house on Albion Street not soon been rocked by an event of greater personal significance to its members.

15

Thursday morning—July sixth—the children's breakfast was disturbed by a commotion belowstairs. Martha's distant shout was followed by hurrying feet on the kitchen stairs, and Brennan burst into the pantry.

"Where's the lieutenant?"

"Having his breakfast. Why?"

He made for the dining room and Brigid scrambled to intercept him. The variety of trouble he could make was endless.

"Don't go in there! What do you want?"

He brushed her aside and she clung to him protesting, "You big dumb Mick . . . you're not supposed to go in there! What do you want?"

The Brunings and Carters stared at them in surprise. "Yes, Brennan?" Carter said. "What is it?"

Michael held out a slim newspaper with towering black headlines, and all eyes turned to Lieutenant Carter as he looked at it.

"Good God!" he said in a hushed voice.

"Cass!" exclaimed Louise. "What's the matter?"

"Custer and five companies of cavalry dead in Montana," he read tonelessly. There was instant shocked silence.

"How?" whispered his wife.

Carter squinted at the smeared print. " 'On June

153

25th, Custer found the Indian camp of two thousand lodges on the Little Horn River . . . He attacked with five companies of the Seventh Cavalry . . . Indians poured a murderous fire from all directions and General Custer, his two brothers, his nephew and brother-in-law were all killed . . . Not one of his detachment of more than two hundred and fifteen officers and men escaped.' "

At intervals throughout Friday and Saturday, the Philadelphia newspapers issued fresh bulletins as details of the disaster arrived by telegraph from the West. Michael bought copies as they appeared, and a deepening pall settled on the house in Albion Street. The Brunings waited for their daughter to broach the inevitable.

"I must go at once," Cass told her.

"But your leave's not up!"

"I'll not wait to be sent for, Louise. It will distress your parents, but I've got to go."

"We'll all go," she said quietly. "I'll not be left behind."

"But I may have to go into the field the minute I arrive."

"I've waited before while you went to fight. I can do it in Oregon better than here. And closer to you."

Her announcement broke the tension. Trunks stood open for packing in the upstairs hall, and Lieutenant Carter paid a long visit to Horstmann Brothers, Philadelphia's famous military outfitter. His long-unused field equipment required refurbishing.

Sunday the ninth the Carters and the Brunings were to dine at the home of old friends, and Cass donned dress uniform for the first time since his arrival. He saw no harm in advertising his imminent departure for the scene of conflict, and it impressed the Brunings. He glittered satisfactorily in consequence of Michael's skilled attention to brass and leather, and for the first time in three years proper vertical creases were pressed into the long skirts of his dress coat.

William and Amanda were fed and put protesting to

bed before their parents departed, a little awed by their mother in an elegant evening gown with her hair piled high.

Brigid closed the bedroom door on their whispering and found Mrs. Carter before the big hall mirror. She had paused and turned up the gas jet to make final adjustments to her costume and hair.

"Missus Carter?" Brigid said tentatively.

"Yes, Brigid?"

"You're going soon . . . aren't you?"

"Next week, I should think."

"Am . . . am I to go with you, ma'am?"

Louise Carter gave her a searching look. "D'you still want to go?"

"Oh, yes, ma'am! I'm not afeared."

Louise Carter's eyes sparkled. "Good for you! If Mr. Carter must go at once to the war, I shall need you very much. Of course you may come if you want to, though . . ." She smiled impishly. "I doubt there'll be any merry-go-rounds there."

Brigid blushed, and Mrs. Carter laughed gently.

"I'm ever so glad you want to come, Brigid, and that's all settled then. Monday you and I will visit the shops and see you have all that you need."

She started downstairs, but paused. "You will stay close enough to hear the children if they misbehave? They're so excited they'll be an hour getting to sleep."

"I'll be right here, ma'am." Brigid pointed at the end of the hall. "I can hear everything, an' I'll stay up till I'm sure they're asleep."

The second-floor hall opened onto a small porch overlooking the back courtyard, and Brigid had slept there for several weeks. The attic floor was intolerably hot even at night, and with the Brunings' approval Brennan had set up a folding cot on the porch for her. She slipped downstairs to this retreat after everyone else had retired, and was up and away in the morning before anyone. A big maple in the yard screened her impromptu bedroom from outside view, including that of Brennan's domain in the carriage house.

With the departure of the Brunings and Carters the house fell silent. Martha finished her kitchen chores and took herself off with a soft "Good night" to Brigid, who sighed happily, taking down her hair to brush it, intrigued by the sparkle of electricity in the gathering dusk as she pulled the brush through it. When she had finished she gathered it up and held it high to feel the slight breeze on her neck, then tied it in a luxuriant ponytail on top of her head.

I won, she told herself happily. I've beat him. If I can keep him dancing till we go, I'm safe. She fanned herself with one of the bulletins on Custer's unhappy fate and happily contemplated Monday's promised shopping expedition.

Michael's voice rumbled softly in the dark hall. He was bidding William and Amanda good night, and she held her breath, hoping he would not come looking for her. Oh, Lord, she wondered, what can I say to him? If he finds out I'm going he'll make trouble.

It was a futile hope. He came onto the porch and leaned on the railing, looking into the court. He was smoking a thin cigar that lit up his big nose and strong face each time he drew upon it, and for a moment she thought he might not know she was there. That was foolish.

"Hot, ain't it?" he inquired pleasantly.

"Umn. You been smoking that thing in the house? Missus Bruning will know."

"Keeps the skeeters off. I don't see how you sleep out here with them."

"Missus Carter gave me a bottle of citronella. And there's worse company," she added tartly.

He chuckled and seated himself uninvited on the cot beside her. It groaned under his weight, and Brigid shifted away warily.

"I'm thinkin' the Lieutenant will be goin' soon," Michael said. "Are Missus Carter an' the kids goin' with him?"

Brigid shrugged. "She's packing her trunks. I guess she will."

156

"She hasn't told you?"

Brigid evaded. "She hasn't come right out and said it."

"What about you?"

"What about me?"

"Ah, come on, Bridey! You know what I mean. Are you to go with her?"

There was no way out of that one so she lied bravely. "I don't know for certain."

He snorted and flicked a shower of sparks over the rail. "Silly idle women! You think you might—you think you won't—you don't know. When will you make up your minds?"

"What difference to you? If she doesn't take me, I'll go to Boston and find work." After a moment she added slyly, "An' you'll never see me again." It was too dark to see his reaction to that.

"Boston? What about your cop in New York?"

"I'll not go back there, an' you can just keep your bad mouth off of him. He was good to me. After you and your Polack friend got me fired from my job, he helped me. He sent me to the Carters and he lent me money to get my clothes from the old bitch that locked me out when I couldn't pay my rent. I'm bound to give him back his money, but that's all."

"Is it, now?" he asked teasingly.

"It is, an' I don't care what you're thinkin'! Why d'you keep picking at me about him?"

"I'm not. I only wanted to know if you're goin' with the Carters."

"Sure! An' I know why, too. Well . . . if you run to the lieutenant with some awful story about me, you're probably wastin' your breath."

"Ah, Brigid," he groaned, "don't start that again. I told you I wouldn't do that."

Like hell you wouldn't, she thought, if you don't get what you want. Ah, if I can just keep him sniffin' around till we're away. Once we're gone from here, they'll think twice before they fire me, no matter what he says.

157

He flicked the cigar into the court, where it exploded in a glow that excited the drifting fireflies, and she could feel his frustration. It was time to give a little. She leaned against his shoulder and sighed loudly.

"Ah, Brennan," she murmured, "you're a cruel, hard man, you are."

His arm was around her at once. "You're wrong, Bridey. I could never be hard with you."

She relaxed against him, and that was a mistake. His hand slipped off her shoulder and cupped her breast. She squirmed, protesting.

"Don't, now! You've made me trouble enough, God knows. Can't you leave me be?"

"I never meant to make you trouble. And I'll never leave you be, Bridey." She was trapped in his arm and he tipped up her face with his other hand to kiss her. She submitted without response.

He was not discouraged. His hand fumbled at her breast and she squirmed vigorously.

"No! Please, Michael . . . don't!"

"Why not?"

"I'm scared. S'pose they come back an' find us here?"

"We'd hear 'em comin', silly. If you're afeared, let's go to my room."

"I can't do that! I promised I'd stay here an' listen for the kids."

"To hell with the kids," he muttered. Both his big hands were at her now, and when they became more than she could bear she flattened herself against him and tucked her head beneath his chin.

"Come out of there," he urged, "and give us a kiss."

"No . . . I'm afeared!"

"Of what, for God's sake?"

"You!" Her response was so muffled he could scarcely hear it, but he was delighted. He returned to the attack and Brigid resisted skillfully. She let him fondle her breasts, but when he began unbuttoning her blouse she distracted him by offering her mouth to be kissed. While he was busy at that she rebuttoned the

158

blouse. Her breath shortened, but she was in no danger of losing control.

"I'd swear," he groaned, "if I didn't know better, I'd think you had four hands . . . all busy. Come here!"

He lifted her bodily from the cot and dropped her in his lap. He was no novice at this game, she found. He was skilled and patient, and in minutes he reduced her to pleading.

"Don't . . . Please, Michael! Don't do that to me!"

Only the return of the family saved her. A carriage clattered in Albion Street and there were voices at the front door. Brigid exploded gratefully from his arms.

"Get out of here, man! Quick, now!"

"Ah, damn it to hell!"

"Don't be mad," she giggled breathlessly.

He was frustrated and furious. She lifted a flushed face and locked her arms about his waist.

"Michael?"

He swore under his breath, but her offered lips were not to be ignored. Her tongue, warm and searching, turned his swearing to a groan of delight.

"There'll be another time," she whispered. "Now will you get out of here?"

Book Two

A Report on Camp Belknap, Oregon, to the Surgeon General, War Department, U.S. Army, by Assistant Surgeon Josef Brenner, U.S. Army, August 31, 1875

Camp Belknap is located near the mouth of Sweet-water Cañon where it opens into the great Harney Lake Valley of Grant County, Oregon; the cañon penetrating some three miles east to west into a spur of the Blue Mountains which terminates not far to the south. Its walls are precipitous, of dark volcanic rock, four to five hundred feet in height at some places; its breadth at the post not over six hundred yards.

The nearby portion of Harney Lake Valley, known locally as Big Meadows, contains two lakes of considerable size called Malheur and Harney. Sweetwater Creek, rising in the head of the cañon, flows past the post to its confluence with the Silvies River; its water is clear and sparkling, fed by numerous springs higher up in the cañon.

North of Camp Belknap the country is steeply mountainous, the post lying almost on the line at which the mountains give place to the vast flats or plateau, stretching away to the south. This plateau is, except for sagebrush and stunted junipers, destitute of growth other than a few patches of marshland. The mountains to the north are thickly forested with juniper, fir, and pine.

Wild animals and birds of countless species abound in the neighborhood, principally in the mountains, though some of them venture onto the great plateau, particularly those attracted by the opportunity to prey upon the numberless wildfowl and their nests, which can be found in season among the marshlands about the lakes.

Camp Belknap can be reached only by military, hired, or private conveyance, there being no line of public stages approaching nearer than Canyon City, a mining town and county seat, 72 miles distant, due north. Portland, Oregon, nearest city of any magnitude, is 375 miles north and west, via a weekly stage from Canyon City to The Dalles on the Columbia River and thence by steamboat and railroad downriver. The nearest railroad station is Winnemucca on the Pacific lines in Nevada, distant 442 miles via weekly stage from Canyon City to Boise City, Idaho, connecting there with a daily line of stages to Winnemucca. Directly overland the distance is 280 miles. The nearest military post is Fort Boise, Idaho, 255 miles via Canyon City, but only 170 miles over the new route through the Malheur Mountains, passable winter and summer. The nearest telegraph station is at Baker City, Oregon, distant 180 miles northeast. Boise City and Baker City are on the main line of daily stages from Kelton on the Union Pacific Railroad in Utah to The Dalles aforementioned.

The only obstacle to travel during the year is occasioned by snow, which falls in winter to such depth as to preclude passage north from the post except by horse trail, kept open by the mail-rider. Roads south are usually passable in all seasons. During winter there is great irregularity in the transmission of mails, but when there is no interruption, the usual time occupied in transit from Department Headquarters in Portland is ten to fourteen days; from Washington, thirty. The only inhabitants near the post are some small bands of Paiute or Snake Indians, quite peaceable since their defeat in 1868.

The post was established in 1867 as a base of operations against these Paiutes, was first called Cantonment on Sweetwater Creek, then was known as Camp Sherman, and in 1869 was designated Camp Belknap. When completed in 1868 it was designed to accommodate two companies of cavalry, two of infantry, and a considerable quantity of stores and supplies.

Quarters for the enlisted men consisted originally of four buildings along the east end of the parade, each thirty by one hundred feet, of unhewn logs with shingled roofs. One of the infantry barracks was completely destroyed by fire in 1872. Mess rooms and kitchens are in four buildings on a line in the rear of the barracks, and at a greater distance there are two sinks for enlisted men. Two bathhouses are located on Sweetwater Creek where it crosses the cañon immediately below the post, one of them furnished with a bathtub and wash-sink.

Laundresses and married soldiers occupy two wood-framed and planked buildings, each sixty by thirty feet with verandas eight feet wide, front and rear. Each building is divided into four sets of quarters with two rooms to a set. These buildings are situated across Sweetwater Creek northeast of the main post, and about a hundred yards downstream on the same side are two log houses, each nineteen by thirty feet, divided into two rooms each, now occupied by the Post Ordance and Commissary Sergeants.

A line of officers' quarters extends along the north side of the parade, facing south. There were originally seven buildings in this line, but the second from the east burned to the ground in 1874 and has not been replaced. The commanding officer's house, in the center of the line, is larger than the rest, built of hewn logs. It has two large rooms on each side of a central hall, each warmed by a stone fireplace. A planked addition in rear provides a bathroom, earth-closet, and servant's room.

The remaining five company officers' quarters are each twenty-nine by forty feet, built on the pattern called "four pens and a passage," each with an eight-foot veranda, front and rear. They are framed of wood

165

and covered with one-inch boards, upright, joints battened, walls and floors of double thickness. A hall runs from front to rear, with two rooms on each side. Each building was intended to house two families, one on either side the central passageway, but the presently reduced garrison happily makes that unnecessary. Successive occupants have gradually enclosed the halls and rear verandas to provide kitchens, servants' rooms, and other necessaries. When these houses were built there were no government-issue cooking ranges available for them, and the Department Quartermaster granted a temporary authorization for kitchen fireplaces constructed by unskilled labor; however, when ranges were subsequently available, the Quartermaster denied their issue on the grounds that fireplaces had been provided. In view of this, subsequent occupants have purchased and imported cooking stoves at personal expense, leaving them behind for their successors, who are, of course, expected to remunerate the previous owner for this personal property.

At the western end of the officers' row, somewhat removed, is a large log structure intended to house bachelor officers. A second story, framed and planked with wood, has been added to this, and the ground floor is no longer employed as living quarters but given over to a variety of uses: library, theater, and chapel in one room, school and courts-martial in another. The library contains forty-three volumes, some of interesting antiquity.

Along the west side of the parade, from north to south, are the hospital and the storehouses for quartermaster and commissary supplies. The central structure of the hospital is a duplicate of the company officers' quarters, expanded by additions to both sides and rear. It contains a dispensary, office, steward's room, kitchen, mess room, wash room, and two small wards with five beds each. An earth-closet commode is attached. Though rambling and unsightly, the entire structure is well-sealed, with adequate ventilation.

The commissary and quartermaster storehouses are

log buildings, thirty-four by seventy-five feet, twelve feet to the eaves, containing necessary offices as well as storage spaces. The shingled roofs leak badly and continuously, to the detriment of the large quantity of stores housed here since the post was completed. The loss to the government occasioned by this wholly inadequate shelter is enormous. Funds should be allocated to effect needed repairs or transport the stores elsewhere. This recommendation has been submitted annually since 1872 without effect. Behind the Quartermaster storehouse is a log stable and extensive corral, dating back to the period when this post maintained a numerous train of pack mules.

On the south side of the parade are two log cavalry stables with corrals behind, the guardhouse, and, sufficiently removed from it for safety, a magazine. Both the latter buildings are of unhewn logs, well chinked and mortared. Only one of the cavalry stables is now in use, the other constituting an eyesore since it has been robbed of all useful fixtures such as doors, window frames, shutters, metal appurtenances, et cetera.

Behind the officers' quarters and across the creek to the north is a large U-shaped log structure housing the post trader's establishment and his family. In an annex to this he operates an adequate restaurant with a room set aside for an officer's mess and billiard room. He generally keeps on hand a small stock of general merchandise. Numerous small buildings scattered about the post house a variety of functions. At the northeast corner of the parade is the Adjutant's Office. Behind the hospital on the creek bank is a stone building providing a bakery adequate to post needs, and in the vicinity of the stables are wheelwright, farrier, and blacksmith's shops. The water supply for the post is obtained from Sweetwater Creek, distributed about the garrison by a water wagon once or twice daily. There is at the post one Babcock's fire extinguisher, but with insufficient hose to be of effect more than fifty yards from the banks of the stream.

The present contract price of beef at the post is 8½

167

cents a pound, mutton being supplied at any time in lieu of beef at the same price. In consequence of severe frosts during each month of the year, vegetable gardens can scarcely be maintained. The few vegetables that survive the frost are devoured by wild creatures, large and small, which invade the post nightly, or, ultimately, by swarms of crickets and grasshoppers. Chickens survive only if brought indoors at night; predatorproof shelters for them are impossible with locally available materials. Attempts by married officers with infants to keep a cow have proved fruitless since the animal is so threatened at night by wild felines as to give bad or no milk.

Owing to its isolation, the necessities of frontier life are difficult and expensive to obtain at Camp Belknap, and officers, particularly those with families, coming here for a tour of service are well advised to provide themselves accordingly. Common items essential for housekeeping are only accidentally to be found for sale by the post trader. If needed, and if possible, officers with families should bring servants.

There is no society outside the garrison, and a tour of service at Camp Belknap provides an admirable opportunity for all officers to avoid living beyond their means for the duration of their assignment here.

1

The last car of the Union Pacific Express inched out of Council Bluffs onto the bridge spanning the Missouri River. The locomotive, already in Nebraska, hooted distantly.

The observation platform was crowded. Michael and William leaned over the railing and Brigid hugged Amanda to her knees as they peered at the turbulent river fifty feet below, spinning coffee-colored webs of foam against the iron piers.

In the course of their excited journey through the cars to the platform, they had acquired a conductor who boasted about the bridge and admired Brigid covertly.

"See those piers?" he pointed to the bridge supports. "Twenty-two of 'em, eight an' a half feet across. Sunk 'em to the bottom an' then the crews went in an' dug till they hit bedrock. One of 'em is eighty feet below water level."

"Gee!" exclaimed William, "how'd they breathe in there?"

The trainman was not listening. The wind whipped Brigid's skirt tight against her legs as she bent to show Amanda the piers, and he forgot about the bridge until Michael nudged him.

"The kid's askin' you something."

"Oh . . . sorry! What was it?"

William repeated his query.

"Sealed 'em and pumped air in. When they hit bedrock they filled 'em with concrete. No matter how much ice comes downriver it can't shake those piers."

The train was rolling through Omaha now, and the conductor was silent, concentrating his attention on Brigid. Michael scowled at him.

"Missus Carter know where you are?" he demanded of William.

Brigid sniffed. "Sure. I told her where we were goin'. I guess we better go back, though."

"Good. I'll go with you. I got to see a feller in the baggage car."

"About a place to sleep?" she asked.

He grinned at her. "You still worryin' about where I'll sleep?"

Where he slept was of no concern to Brigid so long as it was far from her, but she was puzzled by the travel arrangements. As an officer, Lieutenant Carter had an army travel warrant covering tickets and Pullman accommodations for himself and his family. Brennan's ticket, paid for by a similar warrant, did not include the Pullman. The army considered that luxury unnecessary for an enlisted man, and if Lieutenant Carter thought his orderly should have a berth he could pay for it himself.

He had paid entirely for Brigid's travel, and when she found out what that cost she guessed he simply couldn't afford to take care of Brennan in the same way.

Carter finances had been a mystery to her until just before they left Philadelphia. She had earlier extracted from Michael that an infantry first lieutenant was paid a hundred and fifty dollars a month by the army, and she could not understand how the Carters lived so comfortably on that amount. The Brunings were obviously well-to-do, so she guessed they provided a little quiet assistance. This was confirmed when Mrs. Carter took

170

her to Wanamaker's the Monday before their departure.

A clerk had greeted them with a deference Brigid recognized from experience was accorded only to valued customers.

"Good day, Mr. Adams," Louise Carter had replied. "This is Miss O'Donnel, who is going with us to Oregon to care for William and Amanda. We must outfit her for the journey."

Brigid had foreseen black-and-white uniforms, but she was happily incorrect. Mrs. Carter selected plain clothing, but not uniforms, and she selected lavishly. There were two beige cretonne dresses for warm weather and two of black bengaline for cold, plus blouses, underwear, stockings, and even a pair of sturdy shoes. Brigid's small figure required no alteration of the garments, and they were boxed and tied as fast as selected. These necessities out of the way, Mr. Adams won himself a commendation to Brigid's favorite saints.

"It will be difficult, Miss Louise, to obtain anything stylish on the frontier. Will the young lady not require a costume for special occasions?"

Mrs. Carter looked thoughtful. "I suppose you are right, Mr. Adams. What have you in mind?"

He offered first a dress of dark green corded silk, and when Mrs. Carter saw it topped by Brigid's flaming hair and green eyes she gasped.

"Oh, my! That is grand, but . . . perhaps something just a bit simpler?"

Mr. Adams's second choice was more acceptable. It was a skirt and cuirass bodice of lustrous silk and cotton with one of the new self-bustles. It had a wicked effect on Brigid's shapely figure, but its cocoa color was less spectacular than the green.

"D'you like it?" asked Louise Carter.

"Sweet Saint Anne!" breathed Brigid, staring round-eyed in the long mirror. "I never saw anything like it before!"

Her enchantment was irresistible, and Mrs. Carter

laughed. "You shall have it, then. Mr. Adams, will you send all these things to the house as soon as possible?"

"Of course, Miss Louise."

"And . . ." Louise Carter eyed the pile of boxes calculatingly. "Put them on Mrs. Bruning's account." She smiled at the clerk. "At decent intervals, please, Mr. Adams."

Brigid was jarred from this pleasant reverie by a nudge from Michael.

"I thought you were going back to the Carters," he said.

"I was. Come on, Amanda." She gave the conductor a smile. He might be useful before the trip was over.

"Where are you going to sleep, Michael?" William demanded, remembering that problem.

"There's a soldier in the baggage car with some stuff for the engineer officer in Arizona. Something he calls a dumpy level that's worth a hundred dollars, an' they'll let him sleep there to see nobody fools with it. Maybe I can make myself a place with him."

"Can I see it—the dumpy thing?"

"Sure. Come on."

They all followed Michael through the Pullmans to a passenger coach, the second-class car to which his travel warrant consigned him. Between that and the baggage car was another coach, what the railroad called a third-class special, carrying immigrant families bound west. It was packed with men, women, and children surrounded by their bundles and boxes. The women and girls wore short vests of braided velvet over embroidered blouses and big colorful skirts, and they noted Brigid's passage in a soft unintelligible language.

"Russkis . . . Polacks, maybe," Michael explained.

In the baggage car they found a young man in army uniform with the crimson-and-white-piped chevrons of an engineer corporal on his sleeves.

"This is Corporal Baker," Brennan introduced him, and Brigid held out her hand with a smile that made the corporal blush.

"I'm pleased to meet you," she told him. "These are Lieutenant Carter's children and they want to see this great thing you're guardin'."

Baker indicated a long, metal-strapped box on the floor of the car behind which he had made himself a blanket-lined bed.

"Can't open it, miss. Very valuable instrument. Got to watch it all the time."

There was certainly no room for two in the cubicle he had fashioned for himself, Brigid decided, but Michael would find a way to enlarge it. He would not spend much time in his second-class coach seat. Maybe in someone else's, she thought, remembering the pretty dark-eyed girls in the immigrant car.

Forty-five miles out of Omaha the train stopped at Fremont, county seat and flourishing little town, and they were introduced to the railroad meal system. West of Omaha there were no dining cars, and the express would make three stops a day to allow the passengers to dine. Meals were gulped in haste, for a stop was never more than half an hour and often less if they were behind schedule.

The food varied from good to awful. Some stops boasted a comfortable hotel with adequate service, but many had only a shabby restaurant existing on captive diners. The one constant was the price—extortionate by Brigid's standards—never less than a dollar for any meal.

By labored calculation she reckoned up the cost of her meals for the trip and gasped. Added to her ticket and Pullman berth the sum was almost a hundred and seventy-five dollars. There was one comfort. Nothing in her past could persuade the Carters to part with her after they had laid out that much money.

Twilight lingered after the supper stop at Grand Isle. William and Amanda were absorbed in a toy bought at the Centennial Fair—a cast-iron barn into which a farmer tossed a penny when his spring was cocked and the coin balanced on his fork. Brigid studied the limit-

173

less graying vista of prairie until a soft voice interrupted her.

"Miss O'Donnel?"

It was Corporal Baker, his blouse buttoned neatly to the collar and his sandy hair dampened and brushed to careful order.

"Why, good evening, Corporal," she greeted him in surprise. "Did you want something?"

It seemed he only wanted to talk to her. Brigid's acquaintance with soldiers was limited to Brennan and colored by her distrust of him, but Baker seemed different—shy and very polite. Intrigued, she made room for him and explored this oddity.

It was not easy. Once seated he lost his tongue. He admired the children's toy bank and the prairie and then he admired Brigid—but silently. She extracted from him that he was a technician of some kind in the army Engineer Corps, that he had never fought any Indians, and that he never wanted to. After that he simply sat. The porter, noting this decorous situation, skipped their section and made up a berth for Lieutenant and Mrs. Carter. Displaced by this, Louise Carter came to check on her children.

"Why haven't your beds been made up?" she exclaimed. "Brennan, what are you . . . ?" She broke off, looking puzzled. "But you're not Brennan!"

"This is Corporal Baker, ma'am," Brigid explained hastily. "He's a friend of Brennan's."

"Well," said Louise Carter crisply. "You must go now, Corporal. The children should be in bed. Brigid, call the porter at once."

Her face flaming, Brigid pointed in the direction of the baggage car. "Go on!" she hissed at Baker. "You heard her."

Baker took a few steps and looked back. "Who's she?"

"That's Missus Lieutenant Carter. Now scat!"

She sought the porter, swearing under her breath. Damn all soldiers anyway. She thinks I asked that fool to sit with me.

The berths were made up, marvelous secretive compartments closed by heavy curtains. Brigid had never seen one before this trip, and she usually looked forward to bedtime, but not this night. Her pleasure was spoiled. She hurried Amanda into a nightgown and popped her unceremoniously into the lower berth. William she prodded into the upper with threats.

"I'll be right back," she assured Amanda, "soon's I wash my face."

There was someone in the aisle, and she flattened herself against the berths to let him pass, but he did not move. She looked over her shoulder to discover Corporal Baker, watching her expectantly.

"What are you doing here?" she gasped. "I told you to go away!"

He looked at the curtained berth. "Isn't that Brennan's seat?"

"Of course not! What gave you that fool notion?"

The answer was in his transparent face, and she did not know whether to laugh or swear.

"You crazy thing! He told you that?"

"Well . . . not exactly."

"But you traded him your bed for his seat, didn't you?"

There was no need to explore what Baker thought went with the seat he had obtained for his bed. That was obvious as he puzzled out what had happened to him.

"You deserve it!" Brigid whispered. "Don't you know where his seat is?"

"I guess not."

She pointed. "In the car next to the Russkis." She shook her head wonderingly. "You're a nice young man, Baker, but the fool-killer will get you if you don't stay away from criminals like Brennan."

The night passed with no further disturbance, but Brigid slept poorly. Amanda was an active bedmate, kicking hard when crowded, and William was up with the dawn, shouting for them to see the fat prairie dogs sitting on their mounds to watch the train roll by.

The breakfast stop was at Sidney, and Brigid's appetite was chilled by the thought of what Mrs. Carter might say about Corporal Baker. She hoped they had not heard that altercation in the aisle after the berths were made up. But the Carters breakfasted with friends at the nearby army post, Sidney Barracks, and she was spared the problem. Lieutenant Carter gave her money to pay for breakfast for the children and herself at the railroad hotel.

On the platform afterward they encountered Michael with several soldiers from the post. They all looked alike to Brigid, but William pointed out the "23" above the crossed rifles on the forage caps of the local soldiers.

"That's how you tell what regiment they're in," he explained proudly. "The rifles mean they're infantry just like Papa an' Michael."

"Good mornin', all!" Michael greeted them cheerfully. Brigid ignored him, and towed Amanda toward the Pullman car.

"What's the matter now?" he asked William.

"I dunno. Whyn't you ask her?"

Michael caught up with her as she handed Amanda up to the conductor, and she glared at him.

"What's the matter, Bridey?" He was struggling with laughter, and that made her angrier.

"I told you not to call me that, an' you know damn well what's the matter! You flimflammed that dumb soldier into trying to sit with me, an' Missus Carter thought I asked him to. Why, that fool wanted to stay all night!" she exploded in fury.

"Did he really? He must have made a mistake about the seat."

"Brennan," she snarled, "you're the worst liar unhung . . . an' that's got to be the dumbest man alive!"

She scrambled unaided into the car, showing her ankles as she climbed, and one of the soldiers whistled softly.

176

"Oh, boy!" he said admiringly. "Who does she belong to?"

"Me," said Brennan smugly. "She's a little grouchy in the morning, but it don't last."

Past Sidney, the train entered Wyoming Territory and began a long climb toward the roof of the continent. At the dinner stop in Cheyenne, Brigid saw her first buffalo—only a shaggy head on the wall of the railroad hotel dining room, but awesome to her. William was scornful because he had seen real live buffalo.

Up they climbed to a straggling hamlet named Sherman, with a big sign proclaiming it "The Summit of the Rockey Mountains," and the conductor eyed it nostalgically.

"Eight thousand feet up," he told them. "When we laid the line, this was the highest piece of track in the whole world."

Amanda felt queasy and curled up beside her mother, leaving William free to indulge in some illicit reading. The day before in Grand Isle, Michael had found him looking wistfully at a shelf of Ned Buntline's paperback novels, and one of them had been smuggled into the train. Not even Brigid knew of its presence. It fitted nicely inside Rand McNally's new *Business Atlas of the Great Mississippi Valley and Pacific Slope*, which had been purchased in Philadelphia in the vain hope that it would show the location of Camp Belknap.

Unaware of the contraband contents of the atlas, Brigid deemed William safely occupied and started for the observation platform at the rear of the train. Her journey ended in the next car, where she found Michael sprawled comfortably in a Pullman seat.

"What are you doing here?" she demanded suspiciously.

He lowered his newspaper to inspect the numbered metal tag on the arm of the seat. "It's my place."

"It is not! I know where your seat is."

He shook his head. "I didn't like that one. Neither

177

did Baker. He took his bed back, so I got me a seat an' a bed."

Brigid's suspicion deepened. "You never paid for this. How did you get it? What'd you tell that conductor?"

"I didn't tell him anything." He produced a deck of cards and thumbed their worn edges fondly. "My friends here did the talking."

Brigid tried to look disapproving but gave it up. She giggled and sat beside him.

"God pity the priest who has to hear your sins, Michael."

"Aw, that conductor's a Mormon. The priest wouldn't mind a poor Irish lad takin' a seat off him in a friendly game."

"Poor Irish my foot! It's a good thing you're in the army. The cops can't catch up with you."

"The army likes the Irish . . . an' I like the army. Don't have to take a bad mouth from any man whilst I'm wearin' the uniform."

"Pooh! If you'd find yourself a job you wouldn't need that blue suit."

"*If* I could find a job! Sure an' didn't you look for work in the city before your friend George Schultz took you in?"

She bristled but he would not let her interrupt. "Couldn't find anything, could you? Unless you put on a short skirt an' red boots to hustle suckers in the Bowery. And why not? Remember those ads in the newspapers? 'Honest Protestant girl wants work . . . Good Scotch woman to cook an' sew.' You couldn't lie your way into a job any more'n I could, with the map of Ireland all over your pretty face. Those New York swells don't want Irish in their town . . . savin' cops an' whores an' tracklayers."

That was too close to the truth for comfort, but she would not admit it. "That's just talk. You'd rather loaf an' gamble in that blue suit than work for a livin'."

"I work for my livin', Bridey, and never you doubt it! Those swells back east get their money's worth out

178

of me every time they want some Indian kicked off his land . . . or his butt whipped when he gets fed up with it." He leveled a warning finger at her. "You'll see when you get where you're goin', an' I want to hear what you've got to say about us soldiers then."

Brigid bounced up indignantly. He was right about being poor and Irish, but his language was too strong for her and she still saw no good in soldiers. "That's as may be, but I doubt it—unless they're a sight different from you, Michael Brennan."

With that she left him, so angry she failed to notice William's sleight of hand with his atlas when she plumped down beside him.

During their second night on the train they crossed the Continental Divide, and about noon the next day—just short of the Utah border—stopped briefly at a little station named Bryan where there were soldiers waiting for mail and newspapers.

"Cavalry!" exclaimed William. "See the yellow stripes, Brigid?"

Michael peered over her shoulder and snorted scornfully. "Coffee-coolers!"

"What's that?"

"See their caps? Second Cavalry from Camp Stambaugh. Their regiment's been out fightin' Indians all summer, Will, an' these are what they left behind to pick up the mail—too worthless to take along. That's why they call 'em coffee-coolers." He grinned at Brigid. "Your cop friend in New York had a good name for 'em—loafers, ghosters, coasters, an' floaters."

"He was speakin' of you an' your Polack friend, wasn't he?"

Michael laughed. "And right he was, Bridey. I'll not deny it."

Crossing from Wyoming to Utah, the train plunged into Echo and Weber Canyons, awesome slots in the earth whose walls towered five to eight hundred feet above. So deeply embedded were the cars that it was often impossible to see the sky. In the late afternoon

179

Brigid's devoted conductor paused to point at a lone tree to the right of the track.

"See the sign?" he asked.

William spelled out its weathered message: "One Thousand Miles from Omaha."

"Thousand-mile Tree," said the trainman. "Thirty-four miles an' you'll be in Ogden an' that's the end of the Union Pacific."

They reached Ogden a little after six o'clock, and learned to their astonishment they would depart at exactly that time but one hour later. The railroads seemed to set the time-changes as they pursued the sun across the continent, and Central Pacific time in Ogden was an hour and seventeen minutes earlier than that of the arriving Union Pacific train. All passengers going farther west had to change at Ogden, and while the Carters had their supper Michael supervised the transfer of baggage, praised by Mrs. Carter for his devotion to duty.

"What about your supper?" she wanted to know.

"Ah, I'll get a bite in the station, ma'am," he told her, and Brigid made a face at him. Like a cat licking its whiskers, he looked. She had no doubt that he had fed himself while he was supposed to be counting trunks.

"Did you get your bed transferred too?" she whispered slyly.

"I hadn't time to arrange that, but seein' as there's only one more night I thought you'd find me a place."

"Never! I'd not have you near these innocent kids with your evil ways!"

"Oh, my! You found the book, then?"

"I did, an' I threw it out the window!" she said virtuously.

"So she wouldn't think it was yours, hey?"

Saving their exterior color, the famed Silver Palace sleeping cars of the Central Pacific seemed much like the Pullmans of the Union Pacific. The Carters boarded, and Michael handed up Amanda to the porter, giving Brigid an arm up next. He stifled an impulse

180

to give her a complimentary pat on her trim bottom as she climbed to the door. She was still pretty mad about the dime novel.

Brigid did not see him again until breakfast next morning at Elko in Nevada, and she was too fascinated by the Indians on the platform to remember her irritation or ask where he had slept. Some of the Indian women begged, but the men stared impassively at the passengers flocking to the hotel.

"They let them go wherever they want?" she asked Michael in a hushed voice.

"Those? They're tame Indians, Bridey. They'll not hurt you."

She shuddered. "They look awful mean to me!"

The morning dragged after that. The track followed the canyon of the Humboldt River, once more five hundred feet below stone-turreted crests on either side, and not until Beowawe did the hills fall away. The cars picked up speed across the rolling flats, bare of all vegetation except the ubiquitous sagebrush that covered everything now. The Carter family fell silent as the end of this seemingly endless journey drew nearer.

"How much farther?" demanded William.

Brigid relayed the question to the porter, who looked blank.

"Where to, miss?"

"Winnemucca."

He looked at his watch. "Ninety, maybe a hundred miles. Be there before you know it. We're makin' thirty miles an hour easy."

But it was not that quick. Brigid counted the slow hours as they passed—ten, eleven o'clock, noon. She tried to imagine what Oregon would look like, but it seemed as distant and unknown as the moon and she felt small and lonely. The porter came back and paused by the Carters' seat.

"Winnemucca in ten minutes, Lieutenant. Don't stop there long. You want me to tell your soldier to get the baggage ready?"

2

WINNEMUCCA, said the sign on the railway station, with a few statistics stenciled below: "Humboldt County, Nev. Elev. 4,332 ft. Pop. 1,200. San Francisco 413 mi. Ogden 420 mi." Some wag had drawn a pencil through the population count and scrawled beside it: "900 not counten chinks & injuns."

The westbound train from Ogden was awaited by an army lieutenant with four soldiers, and a few civilian idlers drawn by the excitement of the arrival of anything in Winnemucca. Except for his shoulder straps, a civilian would have difficulty telling the officer from his men. His uniform fitted his short, stocky body with the same weathered ease as theirs, and his features were undistinguished except for the air of tough competence shared by all five. Second Lieutenant Benjamin MacKeever would never be called handsome, and particularly not with the monumental scowl he was wearing now. He looked at his watch repeatedly.

Until the train arrived he was the commanding officer of Company K, Twenty-first U.S. Infantry, Camp Belknap, Oregon. If it brought what he expected, he would revert to company junior officer, and the prospect irritated him.

As were all infantry companies, his was entitled to a captain, a first lieutenant, and a second lieutenant. Like

182

most, it rarely had all three present for duty. When he graduated from West Point in the summer of 1875, Ben MacKeever had been assigned to K Company as its second lieutenant. The first lieutenant was absent on detached service, and before the end of the year the captain found a staff job in Louisiana. As the only officer with the company, Second Lieutenant MacKeever assumed command.

After six months of this high status, Ben had begun to hope the situation would continue indefinitely, but command—even of an under-strength company three hundred miles from the nearest railroad—was too great a prize for so junior an officer. The regimental commander began to ask questions of the War Department.

Washington queried the Military Division of the Atlantic, where K Company's captain and first lieutenant were on detached service, and was told Captain Dariah was "indispensable" but First Lieutenant Carter could be retrieved. In January the Adjutant General issued orders transferring Carter back to line duty as soon as he could be released from his staff post in New York City.

K Company's First Sergeant Magruder was pleased because he knew Carter well. It was obvious that somebody would rank young MacKeever out of his command, and as Magruder's wife Molly put it: "Better the divil ye know than the divil ye don't."

MacKeever decided to greet his new commander at the railroad in person, so when the Carters were due, he left the company in Magruder's capable hands and went to Winnemucca with four soldiers. The first sergeant said both the Carters were great people, but Ben was apprehensive about Mrs. Carter. His experience of company commanders' wives was limited to plump, irascible Mrs. Dariah, who had had a tendency to meddle in company business.

The rails hummed and the distant hoot of an engine signaled the imminent arrival of the Central Pacific Express. Within minutes the thirty-five-ton Rogers locomotive trundled past, its six-foot driving wheels

183

shrieking as the engineer braked to a stop, spotting the lead Silver Palace car precisely beside the platform. The first passenger to alight was an army first lieutenant, and Ben saluted him smartly.

"MacKeever, sir. Second Lieutenant, K Company, Twenty-first Infantry."

"Hallo, MacKeever," Carter greeted him. "Good of you to meet us."

The porter was helping a tall, fair-haired young woman descend from the car, and Ben, braced for another Ada Dariah, was startled. This had to be Mrs. Carter, and he made her a formal bow.

"Ma'am, the ladies of the post asked me to say they are eager to see you and they hope you had a comfortable journey."

"That's most kind of you and the ladies, Mr. MacKeever," Louise Carter replied, offering a slim gloved hand and a dazzling smile. Ben's solemn expression came unwrapped. There was more to his carefully rehearsed greeting, but he was distracted by what was happening at the door of the sleeping car. A pretty young woman with flaming red hair and other disturbing attributes was reaching up on tiptoe to help a little girl on the step. A small boy followed and all three joined the Carters.

"These are our children, William and Amanda," said Mrs. Carter. William shook hands and Amanda curtsied, at which her mother looked surprised.

"We've been practicing," said the redhead. "Isn't that good?"

"It's certainly unexpected. Mister MacKeever, this is Brigid O'Donnel, our children's nurse."

"It's a pleasure, Miss O'Donnel," said Ben sincerely. He was trying to think of more to say, but a strange soldier appeared, his arms full of luggage, accompanied by the porter with more.

"That's all the hand-bags, ma'am," he told Mrs. Carter. "They're taking the rest off the baggage car now."

Noting MacKeever's puzzled look, Lieutenant Carter explained, "This is Private Brennan, my orderly. He joined us in Philadelphia."

For a moment MacKeever ceased to be a welcoming junior officer and reverted to his lost status of company commander.

"Brennan, eh?" he said curtly. "We wondered where you had got to. We picked you up on the morning report quite a while ago."

"Didn't regiment tell you I took him as orderly?" asked Carter.

"No, sir. We thought he'd got lost."

"I sent a telegram. You didn't have a copy?"

MacKeever shook his head. He looked at Mrs. Carter and decided there was no need to explain now that Camp Belknap was not on the telegraph line.

"How do we travel from here?" asked Carter.

"Ambulance, sir. I brought one from the post and a couple of wagons."

"Why so many?"

"I expect we'll need them, sir."

"How long," asked Mrs. Carter softly, "does it take to reach Camp Belknap, Mr. MacKeever?"

"Five, maybe six days, ma'am. It's two hundred and sixty miles by road."

"Are there some towns along the way?"

"Well, ma'am . . . there are some," he replied cautiously, "but I don't think you'd want to stop in them. I brought tents and camp gear. That's why the extra wagon."

"Oh, boy!" exclaimed William.

Whatever his mother thought of a camping trip through southeast Oregon did not show on her face.

"I suggest," continued MacKeever, "we stay the night in Winnemucca. The Central Pacific House is a good hotel, and we can start early tomorrow." He indicated the four soldiers waiting nearby. "The men will bring whatever you want to the hotel and load the rest of your baggage on the wagons."

"Good idea," said Carter. "Are they all from the company?"

"Yes, sir. There's one more at the stable, keeping an eye on our mules."

"Don't recognize a one of them. If you'll excuse me a moment, Louise, I'll just have a word with them."

Brennan cleared his throat softly, and Mrs. Carter looked at him.

"Will you be wanting anything from the baggage car at the hotel, ma'am?"

"Since we shall be camping," replied Louise Carter, "I will need the old canvas valise that's done up with rope. Do you know the one I mean?"

"Yes, ma'am." Michael looked at MacKeever. "With the lieutenant's permission, sir, I'll make sure the men get the right one."

The young officer scowled. He had brought four men to take care of these things, and he wanted no help from Brennan. Before he could say so, Mrs. Carter intervened.

"That would be helpful. Brennan knows all our baggage, Mr. MacKeever. I hope you don't mind."

The lieutenant swallowed his irritation. There would be time enough to straighten out the company commander's orderly when they got back to Camp Belknap.

"Not at all, ma'am. May I show you to the hotel, then? We can inspect Winnemucca on the way."

Louise Carter took his arm and looked at the town, all of it visible from the station platform. Ben MacKeever could have sworn she shuddered slightly.

Winnemucca was built on two levels separated by a wide sandy river bed with a trickle of water wandering through it. The older and more distant section was considerably lower than the newer, which occupied an immense sand bank beside the Central Pacific track, and the two were linked by a wooden bridge spanning the Humboldt River bed. Most of the houses were of frame and plank construction, inexpertly built, for they leaned companionably on one another. There were a few solid adobe structures and one large brick building that caught Mrs. Carter's attention.

186

"That's impressive, though it seems out of place, doesn't it?"

"County courthouse, ma'am. I understand they built it to get the county government to move here from Unionville. It must have cost a fortune."

The streets were wide and sandy, bordered by a surprising number of trees, which took precedence over plank sidewalks. These either encircled a tree or simply stopped on one side and began again on the other.

"It seems so dry," remarked Louise Carter. "How in the world do they keep the trees alive?"

MacKeever pointed to ditches on either side of the streets. "When the river's up they turn water into them. That keeps 'em going."

The Central Pacific hotel was large and comfortable, with a central portion of adobe and a wooden wing on each side. The Carters had one of these to themselves, and it included a bathroom provided with running water from an iron tank on the roof. Heated by the day's sun, the water was comfortably lukewarm, and everyone had a bath before an early supper, at which they were joined by Lieutenant MacKeever. He explained that he had spent the preceding night at the hotel.

"What about the men?" asked Carter. "Where are they staying?"

"In the wagons, I expect, sir. I told them they could pitch a tent, but I doubt they need it." He grinned. "They won't do much sleeping. I guess Winnemucca looks pretty bad to you, but not to us. They'll take care of Brennan."

"Tell us about Camp Belknap, Mr. MacKeever," Louise Carter asked when the hotel dessert had been served. It was a glutinous tapioca pudding which even the children gave up, though Ben and Brigid finished their portions happily.

He responded enthusiastically. He described the country surrounding the post in detail—high mountains on the north and endless flats to the south, with two big lakes not far distant. For William and Amanda he

187

told amusing stories of the wildlife which was abundant.

"Major Suter—the post commander—won't let anybody shoot game on the post, so the deer come right down to the houses at night. You'll see them in your yard."

He answered Lieutenant Carter's questions about the company explicitly and in detail, but when pressed about the officers' quarters he became a little vague. Ben MacKeever had his own theory about women—don't worry them with unpleasant details and they will be happier—but the expression on Mrs. Carter's face as he glossed over the condition of her future home made him wonder if it applied to her.

Eight o'clock the next morning found the entire party breakfasted, packed, and assembled at the stable behind the hotel. The wagons were loaded, teams hitched in, and the soldiers standing ready though a little pale and puffy eyed. An army ambulance had been refitted for the trip, its litter racks stripped out and replaced by three transverse seats, one facing rearward just behind the driver's seat and two more facing forward. The first was just a bench, but the other two had backs and armrests with canvas padding. There were in addition a light spring-wagon loaded with baggage and camp gear, and a big blue-painted army wagon drawn by six mules, its canvas cover lashed tight over the bows to protect the Carters' trunks and boxes.

Lieutenant MacKeever inspected this assembly and nodded. "Good. Noonan, you and I will take turns driving the ambulance. Moses and Schurtz on the spring-wagon . . . Steiger and Taylor on the baggage wagon. Steiger, are you alive, man?"

"Sir, can I tell the lieutenant this afternoon?"

His plaintive response brought a snicker from his comrades. The preceding night had obviously been a happy one for all of them.

"You'd better be alive by then," MacKeever told him. "There's no way you can keep up with us, and I don't want you trying. You'll be on your own by to-morrow but I want you at the post no more than three days after I get there. You understand?"

"Yes, sir."

MacKeever considered Brennan sourly. He had not planned on an extra man, particularly a city soldier who would only be in the way.

"I expect you'll want your orderly with you, sir. He can ride the light wagon, I guess."

Carter sensed his junior officer's irritation. He was trying to think of a way to ease the problem when Michael provided it.

"Sir, the spring-wagon's heavy loaded. If the lieu-tenant doesn't need me, maybe I'd be more use on the baggage wagon."

Lieutenant Carter studied the clumsy vehicle and nodded. "Good idea. The more strong backs with that thing the better." He glanced at his wife. "We wouldn't want anything to happen to that wagon, would we?"

Louise smiled. "I suspect Mr. MacKeever has planned this trip very thoroughly. If Brennan can help with our trunks, I should think we can spare him for that."

Well, thought MacKeever. That takes care of that, all right. But after a moment he began to wonder who had settled it. He looked a little puzzled, and Louise Carter held out her hand for assistance into the ambu-lance.

"Shall we go?" she asked mildly.

Ben handed her up and took the reins himself, shar-ing the driver's seat with the Carters. Brigid, the chil-dren, and Private Noonan climbed into the back of the vehicle. MacKeever released the brake, slapped the long reins on the backs of the four-mule team, and shouted explosively. It was a wordless shout, and Mrs. Carter gave him a smiling look.

"I thought they wouldn't go unless you swore at them."

"We've been practicing, ma'am. I don't think they care what you say as long as you sound mad. May

189

have to slip in a word or two when we get to the mountains."

"That's all right. Just let me know when you feel it coming and I'll hold my ears."

Ben guided the team across the bridge and up the slope beyond, and they topped it to find nothing left of the town except a dreary little cemetery. Winnemucca Peak loomed to the west, and on the east a line of low hills reached into the distance, the Little Humboldt River at their feet marked by clumps of green trees and brush.

Louise Carter's understanding about the mules was encouraging, and Ben gave his elegant seat-mate a cautious grin.

"Look back, ma'am," he said softly.

Finding nothing out of the ordinary, she seemed puzzled.

"It'll look a lot better the next time you see it."

Her laugh was genuine and infectious. "I wondered when you'd find the courage to say that, Mr. MacKeever."

The only remaining signs of habitation in the valley were a few clusters of Indian huts—"wick-ee-ups," MacKeever called them.

"Snake Indians. Paiutes, the Agent says. Ten years ago they were big trouble, but since General Crook whipped 'em they've been quiet. Their chief is called Winnemucca and he lives on a reservation by Camp Belknap."

"Aren't they all supposed to be on it?"

Ben shrugged. "Some of them wander back and forth. No one bothers as long as they stay out of trouble."

The valley floor was flat, and MacKeever made good time with his ambulance as long as he kept out of the deep ruts left by heavy-loaded freight wagons in the road. The baggage wagon was out of sight behind them by the time he pulled into a grove of trees for a lunch of sandwiches provided by the hotel. While they were eating, a Concord coach bowled past along the road, rocking and swaying behind four running horses.

"What's that?" Brigid asked Private Noonan.

"Stagecoach, miss. Goin' to Boise City."

"Does it always go that fast?"

"Sure. They change teams every twelve or fifteen miles. You'll see the stations. They go like that day an' night, an' they'll be in Boise in four days."

"Why didn't we go in one of those?"

Noonan looked flustered, and Mrs. Carter smiled. "I expect it doesn't go to Camp Belknap. Isn't that correct, Mr. MacKeever?"

Ben sighed. "Yes, ma'am. Nearest station to the post is about seventy miles. They're fast all right, but it's no joyride. How many passengers do you think they're carrying?" he asked Brigid.

"Four?" she ventured.

He chuckled. "More likely eight, miss."

"God above us!" exclaimed Brigid. "However do they all fit in there?"

"Like spoons."

MacKeever studied the astonished girl and smiled as he thought how much the coach passengers would admire having her on board.

Late in the afternoon they left the road again at a long, low building built of logs with an earth roof sprouting weeds in clumps. A sign identified it as Willow Point stage station, and Mrs. Carter examined it closely. Catching MacKeever's eye, she smiled.

"I think a tent will be better than that. Are we going to make camp now?"

He pointed. "Yes, ma'am. On the river . . . just over there."

The Little Humboldt was a quarter of a mile distant via a track through the station hay field. The ambulance and the light wagon were driven into a pleasant grove of willows, and in a remarkably short time the soldiers pitched camp—two small "A" tents for the Carters and a tarpaulin stretched between trees to shelter the baggage and the rest of the party. Coffee-

191

colored and scarcely a yard in width, the river ran among the willows and beyond it the gullied slopes of the hills rose, multicolored in the slant rays of the setting sun.

"Would you ladies like to wash?" MacKeever asked them. Mrs. Carter eyed the sluggish stream doubtfully.

"Not here," he said. "Bring your towels and I'll show you."

They crossed the Little Humboldt on a fallen log and he led them up a rocky gully to an unattractive orifice in the ground. It looked as though someone had boiled something in it repeatedly, leaving the residue to harden around the rim. There was no water in it when they arrived, but after a moment it drew a deep breath and gurgled. The basin filled with a steaming liquid, yellowish in color. Mrs. Carter sniffed suspiciously.

"It looks awful and it doesn't smell too good," MacKeever said, "but it's hot. If you'd like to bathe, I'll see nobody disturbs you."

The hot spring belched softly and both women shrank from it.

"I think we'll just wash our faces," said Louise Carter firmly. "Brigid, will you help Amanda, please?"

By the time they returned to the tents, dusk was gathering and Private Schurtz had pots and pans set about a cooking fire. The other two soldiers were grooming the mules, haltered to a picket line and rummaging happily for grain in their nose-bags. Brigid and Amanda paused to watch and one of the animals rested its head companionably on Brigid's shoulder. MacKeever expected a squeal of protest, but she surprised him.

"Get on with you now," she told the beast cheerfully, pushing its head away.

Schurtz's supper was plain but good, and before they finished it the creak and jingle of the baggage wagon announced its approach through the hay field. Lieutenant MacKeever chuckled.

"Steiger made good time. I guess he doesn't want to eat his own cooking."

It was not an idle comment. As soon as Steiger,

192

Taylor, and Brennan had put up their mules they closed around Schurtz's cook fire and emptied his pot. Noonan had brought out a banjo and picked at it softly until Schurtz recognized a tune and won a round of applause for a solo rendition in German of "There Is a Land of Pure Delight." After that there were more hymns—familiar Moody and Sankey favorites—and everyone hummed or sang them as Noonan picked out the melodies.

"It's a pity," said Lieutenant MacKeever, "you didn't do this last night instead of trying all the saloons in town."

The soldiers grinned sheepishly, and Noonan shifted to a less uplifting though equally familiar tune—one the postwar army on the frontier had made peculiarly its own. Michael Brennan suddenly lifted his voice in a rich, clear baritone:

> "Oh, the dames of France are fond and free,
>   And Flemish lips are willing;
> And soft the maids of Italy,
>   While Spanish eyes are thrilling;
> Still, I'll not fall prey to all their wiles—
>   Their charms shall not ensnare me . . ."

He caught Brigid's eye across the fire and winked at her as he sang the last two lines:

> " . . . For my heart turns back to Erin's Isle,
>   And the girl I left behind me."

There was a moment of appreciative silence, broken by Mrs. Carter. "I declare, Brennan, I didn't know you could sing like that. That's very good."

"Ah, Missus Carter," he replied, smiling, "every soldier knows that tune . . . whether he's a Paddy or not."

MacKeever watched this exchange curiously. A smart dog-robber, he thought, applying to Brennan the army's scornful name for an officer's soldier servant.

193

Mrs. Carter's obvious approval of the big Irish private meant he would be lost to the company at Camp Belknap.

The War Department officially forbade the ancient practice of an officer employing one of his soldiers as a servant, but if the officer could not find or afford a civilian and the soldier was willing, the rule was generally overlooked. There were plenty of willing privates. An orderly escaped most company duties and had a little extra pay from his officer for the job—ample compensation for the envious scorn of his comrades and vengeful pursuit by the company first sergeant. A dog-robber's best defense against that was the satisfaction of his employer. If he could also ingratiate himself with the officer's family, he improved his chances of escaping recapture by his company, and MacKeever saw that Private Michael Brennan understood that.

Amanda, snuggled against Brigid, was nodding sleepily, and Mrs. Carter smiled at her. "Bedtime for that one . . . and for me as well."

"You too, William," said Lieutenant Carter. "I think we'd all better turn in."

The circle about the fire broke up slowly and Schurtz banked his fire in a mound of ashes.

"How much guard do we need?" Carter asked MacKeever.

"Just a man on the picket line, sir."

"Only one?"

"That's all we need this close to town, sir. We'll double up when we get farther north."

MacKeever's estimate was accurate and the camp slept undisturbed until dawn, when the picket line guard awakened the young lieutenant. Ben brushed ashes from the fire and put a can of water in the coals. When it bubbled he sat cross-legged with a scrap of mirror on his knee to shave, stropping his razor softly so as not to disturb the Carters. He did rouse a few birds in the willows, and they greeted each other sleepily, but the rest of the camp was silent until the mules caught sight of the rising sun. Their salute brought Brigid scrambling from her tent in alarm.

"Jesus, Mary, and Joseph!" she gasped to MacKeever. "What is it?"

He stopped shaving to admire this apparition—big green eyes and a tangle of red hair above the old quilt wrapped about her, showing her bare ankles and feet as well. She stared, appalled, at the mules, their heads back, eyes closed, pumping out the cracked organ notes of their ritual greeting to the day.

"God above us, Mr. MacKeever! What ails the poor things?"

"I don't know," he chuckled. "They've been doing that ever since God made mules. If He can hear 'em I bet He's sorry he did it."

"You mean there's nothing wrong with them?" she shouted above the uproar.

"Absolutely nothing. There'd be something wrong if they didn't do it."

He could hear her explaining the noise to Amanda in the tent, and after a little she reappeared. Again MacKeever suspended his shaving. The fitted costume she had worn the first day was gone, replaced by an ancient corduroy skirt and a thick-knitted sweater, its bulky turtleneck high under her chin. Settling gracefully on the other side of the fire from him, she began brushing her tousled hair, unconscious of his admiring eyes. Schurtz appeared, snorting and scrubbing his head with his knuckles, to build up his fire. He too paused from time to time to watch the red hair snapping under Brigid's brush. Noonan put a stop to this pleasant show. He stared at Brigid openmouthed until she stopped brushing, parted her thick mane of hair and gave him a questioning look.

"What's the matter with you?"

Noonan blushed. "You look just like my little sis, Mary Margaret, when she gets up of a mornin'."

Brigid sniffed. "I'll bet! An' after she's done her hair, I s'pose she gets to make up the fire, too. Don't just stand there gawkin', man. Find Schurtz some wood so's we can have some coffee."

"*Ja!*" rumbled Schurtz, "go find some dry sticks, Noonan, and I make the lady a cup of coffee."

MacKeever finished his interrupted shaving, wiped his razor, and grinned to himself. This one, he decided, is going to shake up old Camp Belknap. Tucking the razor into its sheath, he replaced it in his saddlebag and pulled out a bottle of bay rum he had bought from the barber at the hotel. He splashed some on his face, luxuriating in the sharp, pleasant sting of it.

"Oh," said Brigid, "that smells good!"

It was a casual remark but it struck Ben MacKeever as startlingly intimate. He was not used to shaving in the company of a girl. Blushing like Noonan, he got to his feet, but Brigid had not noticed his reaction. She braided her hair quickly around her head and pulled on a green woolen knit cap that covered her ears and made her rosy face look not much older than Amanda's. Squatting on her heels, she leaned to watch as Schurtz raked the coals from the lid of his dutch oven to inspect the biscuits baking inside. He gave her one and waited while she sniffed, broke off a piece, and tasted it.

"Beautiful!" she told him gravely, and the big German beamed with pride.

The quick shift of her interest from his bay rum to Schurtz's biscuits amused Ben. How long, he wondered, do the Carters expect to keep this redheaded prize for a nursemaid at a post full of lonely soldiers.

Breakfast finished and the camp packed up, they took to the road again. MacKeever introduced his charges cautiously to the rigors of frontier travel, but he kept them moving, and three days later they reached Camp McDermit on the Nevada-Oregon line. It belonged to the Department of California, but all the military bound for Fort Boise or Camp Belknap in the Oregon Department passed through it and knew it well. Captain Wagner, commanding the single troop of cavalry stationed there, welcomed all visitors.

The welcome was not without another bit of initiation, watched with amusement by Ben MacKeever. The two troop officers and the post surgeon with their wives gathered at the Wagners' quarters to meet the Carters, and Louise asked for a drink of water. The orderly brought it promptly. It was the color of strong tea, but Mrs. Carter drank thirstily until near the bottom of her glass she encountered a small lively object. She watched it for a horrified moment, then put down the glass unfinished. The doctor's wife noticed this.

"The river's awfully low," she whispered to Louise, "but it's the only water we have. It's full of those things, and we strain the water into a barrel, but they get in anyway. Doctor says they'll give you the remittent fever if you swallow them, so I always pick them out right away."

3

At dawn on the twenty-fourth of July, Ben MacKeever led his little party out of Camp McDermit and up the long, slow climb from Quinn's River Valley across the Nevada boundary and onto the vast, undulating plateau of southeast Oregon. Here they left the stage road and bore west on a rutted track, the freighters' route to the mining camps of the Pueblo and Steen's Mountains. The second day out of McDermit was spent working around the northern shoulder of the Steen's Mountains into an even more desolate tableland that seemed to have no limits, but as dusk fell, MacKeever pointed to a distant mountain range just disappearing into the purple haze to the north.

"Blue Mountains," he told them. "Belknap's right at this end of them."

"You plan to get there tomorrow?" asked Lieutenant Carter doubtfully.

"If there's been no rain, sir. There's two lakes and a lot of swampy ground between us and those mountains. If the water's up we'll have to circle wide to get around them."

Bored by discussion of something he could hardly see, William wandered away to drop pebbles in a clear spring bubbling up nearby. Ben MacKeever joined him.

"You know something, Will? If you whittled yourself

a boat and threw it in there, it could go all the way to China."

"Why, Mr. MacKeever!" exclaimed Louise Carter.

William peered into the spring excitedly. "You mean it goes right through and comes out the other side?"

"Well . . ." Ben glanced at Mrs. Carter. "What I meant was, it just might get to China. You see," he explained, "this spring is the beginning of the Malheur River, and it runs that way—" He pointed east. "Until it empties into the Snake River. The Snake's the boundary between Oregon and Idaho, and it runs north till it meets the Columbia. Now the Columbia River . . ."

William was looking at him blankly, and William's mother was trying not to laugh.

"Yes," said Ben. "Well . . . the Columbia separates Oregon from Washington, and it runs west right into the Pacific Ocean. If your boat made it down all those rivers and across the ocean . . ." He grinned triumphantly. "It would land in China."

Both the elder Carters were chuckling now. "Mister MacKeever," said Cass, "you must have stood pretty high in geography at the Point."

"I shouldn't like to have any money invested in your boat, William," Louise Carter laughed.

William was persuaded that it was too late to whittle a boat and they compromised on a notched stick as a substitute. He and Ben dropped it into the spring, but when they started back toward Schurtz's fire it was still bobbing in an eddy less than a dozen feet downstream. MacKeever grinned ruefully at Mrs. Carter.

"I guess it might take a long time."

Next morning the road across the flats proved dry, and MacKeever whipped his mules into a lope a part of every hour, rolling north at a fast clip. The only vegetation to be seen was sagebrush and stunted junipers until they came in sight of the lush green smears marking the swampy ground around the lakes. Enormous flocks of ducks rose complaining at their ap-

199

proach, followed by less attractive clouds of mosquitoes. Everyone slapped and swore at this invasion.

"Would it help to put the curtains down?" Louise Carter shouted to her husband, who was on the driver's seat with MacKeever.

"I doubt that would keep them out," he replied, "and you'd surely smother in there."

"Wrap up in a blanket, ma'am," advised MacKeever, and Mrs. Carter enveloped herself and the children in one, huddling together so that only their faces showed. Brigid, sharing the back seat with Private Noonan, had no blanket, but she improvised. She thrust her feet and skirt into a grain sack and pulled down her knit cap and sweater sleeves as far as they would go, flapping the latter at her exposed face.

"Are they like this at the camp?" she demanded irritably of Noonan.

"Not when the wind's from the north."

"And when it isn't?"

"You make a smudge with wet juniper bark an' sit in the smoke till you turn black, an' nothin' will bite you."

"Ugh!" snapped Brigid.

Lieutenant Carter took their minds off the mosquitoes with a shout. "Looks like a welcoming party ahead."

Everyone craned to look. There were five soldiers gathered about a smoky fire in a clump of wind-blasted junipers just ahead, and one of them stepped into the road to wave and shout.

"That's John Randell from the cavalry troop," said MacKeever. He braked to a stop and Randell hurried to the ambulance, pulling off his forage cap as he came. He was a tall, good-looking young man, towheaded with a magnificent handlebar mustache. Dusty second lieutenant's straps on his shoulders identified his rank.

"Welcome, ma'am," he said to Mrs. Carter. "We're glad you're here."

"This is Mr. Randell, ma'am," MacKeever said.

200

"He's post adjutant, catcher on the cavalry baseball team, and he used to be my roommate in the bachelor quarters till he ran off last spring and took himself a bride."

The troopers had smothered their fire and were tightening girths on their horses. One of them led Randell's mount to him and another swung into his saddle and galloped away from the ambulance.

"You're going to announce us, I see," said MacKeever.

Randell beamed at Mrs. Carter. "The ladies have been waiting since noon. They'll want to know you're here."

She beat dust from her skirt and looked at her husband pleadingly. "We look like gypsies, Cass! Can't we stop long enough to change?"

Randell rolled his eyes dramatically. "Don't stop, ma'am. They'll skin me alive. You look fine, honest you do!"

Louise Carter surrendered, laughing, and he ran for his horse. Mounted, he swung alongside the ambulance and pointed to the mouth of a canyon opening into the mountains a mile distant.

"Belknap's just inside that. We'll be there before you know it."

The remaining troopers fell in behind the vehicle, riding close to look at Brigid. Her snub nose was fiery from the sun, and the knit cap gave her a rakish air, but that was no matter. They had heard her introduction to Mr. Randell and they knew this was a girl who was not off limits for a soldier's admiring look.

The two wagons rumbled across a stream on a plank bridge and into the mouth of the canyon whose walls of dark volcanic rock rose almost vertically on either side. It was a startling slot in the mountains, barely six hundred yards wide, and part of that was taken up by a brawling creek that spilled into the stream they had just crossed.

The change from the desolate flat was abrupt and delightful. The floor of the valley was covered with

201

lush grass and—as Randell pointed out—it ran east and west, so the sun flooded it all day. Their road circled a thick stand of poplars beside the creek, and suddenly Camp Belknap was spread before them, filling the canyon from wall to wall.

It was not impressive. The creek cut across the canyon here, and beyond it were the backsides of a row of log barracks with shingle roofs. MacKeever drove his team between them and a wooden structure identified by a sign as the adjutant's office, and they were in a long quadrangle of buildings, all facing inward.

Drawn up in front of the nearest barracks in full-dress uniform were twenty-eight infantrymen—the present-for-duty strength of K Company, Twenty-first Infantry. A bantam-sized first sergeant bawled them to attention and faced the ambulance to give his new company commander a flourishing salute.

"Stop!" said Lieutenant Carter. "Pull up here."

MacKeever groaned. "But, sir . . . look!" He pointed at the row of officers' quarters lining the north side of the parade ground. On the veranda of a big log house in the center of the row a group of officers and ladies was obviously awaiting the Carters.

"I can't help it. I've got to say something to them. Didn't you know he was going to turn the company out?"

"I told him not to, sir. He knows the post commander's waiting for you."

Carter jumped down and returned the sergeant's salute then pumped the old soldier's hand heartily.

"By God, Sergeant Mac . . . it's good to see you again. Give 'em 'order arms,' will you?"

He stepped in front of the short double rank of soldiers as the long Springfields clashed to rest, and nodded approvingly.

"You look good, men. I'm glad to be back."

"Sir . . ." MacKeever tugged at his sleeve. A short, portly officer with luxuriant gray sidewhiskers was striding toward them.

"Post commander's coming, sir," said Magruder with
202

a straight face. "I thank the Lieutenant for stopping to speak to the men. They'll be proud to be the first to welcome the lieutenant."

Carter turned away, and MacKeever glared at his first sergeant. "I thought I told you . . ."

"Couldn't help it, sir," said Magruder stoutly. "Adjutant's orders."

"I'll bet," growled Ben. "Magruder, I know how you get around lieutenants. All right, dismiss the company now."

Carter handed Louise down from the ambulance to meet the portly officer, and MacKeever arrived, panting, just in time to introduce him.

"Major Suter, may I present Lieutenant and Mrs. Carter," he gasped. "Ma'am, this is Major Suter, the post commander."

The Major made a courtly, old-fashioned bow to Louise Carter.

"Byron Suter, at your service, Mrs. Carter. Welcome to the post."

He shook hands with Carter and William, acknowledged Amanda's curtsy gravely, and offered his arm to Louise to lead her along the planked walk to the waiting group on his veranda.

"I suspect, my dear," he told her with a twinkle in his eye, "you would rather wash and change before you meet us all, but this is a big day for us, and I'm afraid we can wait no longer."

She hugged his arm in recognition of the kind welcome and made graceful small talk as she eyed the row of houses with a sinking heart. The Suters' house looked comfortable enough—it had a first floor of hewn logs with a planked half-story addition above—but the rest were depressing: small framed houses with upright battened planks and a steep shingled roof extending to cover a front veranda. Untouched by paint, they had weathered to a uniform gray relieved only by the striated red stone of their chimneys. She noted two doors opening onto the veranda of each, and repressed a shudder. Each of these shanties was obviously meant to house two families.

Between the first and the second house in the row was a gap marked by charred log foundations. Fire, the familiar disaster of isolated posts, had robbed this garrison of one of its sets of quarters. There remained five more in addition to the big log structure, and Louise Carter tried to guess at the number of ladies waiting on its veranda. A complicated equation involving the number of families present and her husband's exact date of rank would determine if the Carters fitted themselves into half of one of the company officers' houses or luxuriated in a whole one—not quite as large as her father's carriage house in Philadelphia.

At the Suters' gate, she was wondering what to do with Brigid, for Major Suter insisted the children must come in. First Sergeant Magruder appeared and solved the problem.

"I an' Missus Magruder will look after her, ma'am. Molly's waitin' at your quarters."

"Our quarters?" gasped Louise. "We've already been assigned them?"

"The best, ma'am."

"But . . ."

"Come on, Weezie," her husband whispered urgently. "They're waiting for you."

The Suters' parlor was overfull. Besides Major and Mrs. Suter, there were Surgeon Brenner and his wife, Mathilde, the cavalry troop commander, Captain Smith, with his wife and nineteen-year-old daughter, young Randell and his bride, and the two bachelor officers of the post—First Lieutenant Slade of the cavalry and Ben MacKeever. Louise Carter tried hard to put names and faces together, but her task was complicated by a young girl who evaded introduction. An explanation was offered by Mathilde Brenner, plump, friendly wife of the post doctor.

"That one," she whispered, "is Prudence Morton, the daughter of the post trader. She is dodging Abigail Smith."

204

"Oh?"

"Yes. You met Abigail. Her husband commands the cavalry troop, and she sent the invitations to this party. She left out the Mortons, and her daughter Susanne—bless her heart—she slipped Prudence in anyway, so both of them are dodging Susanne's mother."

"I see," murmured Louise. She had forgotten about the rigidity of society on small army posts.

There were refreshments in the Suters' dining room—tea, coffee, and a big sheet cake sent by Lieutenant Carter's company. It was armored in clay-colored icing with "Welcome to Camp Belknap" spelled out across its top in letters made of powdered hard candies. A pretty young woman sawed pieces from this masterpiece with difficulty.

"This is our new bride, Arabella Randell," Mrs. Suter said, introducing the cake cutter. "She and Mr. Randell were married only this spring. He came to meet you on the road, I believe."

The bride smiled a little nervously and hacked off a piece of cake for Mrs. Carter.

"You must taste it," warned Adelaide Suter. "They've been working on it for days. I doubt," she whispered, "that you can damage it. I think your company cook bakes a very permanent cake."

Louise chewed determinedly. "It's very kind of them. I must thank them tomorrow, just as soon as we are settled a bit."

Adelaide Suter patted her hand comfortingly. "You are settled, my dear. There are two empty sets of quarters and you have the best of them. One is just beside us here, but Byron put his foot right through the floor when he inspected it, so you have the other, which is next to Doctor Brenner."

"With whom do we share it?" asked Louise apprehensively.

"Share it? My dear, you have it all . . . such as it is. They're supposed to hold two families, but we are so few now that there is no need for that."

205

She laughed at Louise Carter's obvious look of relief.

"We've put in some tables and chairs and cots to tide you over until you have all your own things. It's not like back home, but . . ." She winked engagingly. "It's damned well clean. I saw to that myself."

Darkness was falling before the assembly at Suter's broke up. The close-knit family of Belknap's officers' row had welcomed the newcomers with open arms, and the Carters were grateful if a little weary.

Dr. Brenner offered Louise his arm. "I'll walk you to your new home, Miss Louise. I'll wager you're ready to put your feet up for a little rest. Mathilde will give you supper when you're ready."

"Oh, Doctor, that's too much! We can't impose on you like that. Mrs. Suter said the post trader has a good restaurant, and we will—"

The doctor rolled his eyes in mock despair. "If I let you eat beans and bacon at Morton's place, Mathilde will kill me. She's gone ahead to see that everything is ready, and you're to come whenever you wish." He stopped and swung open a gate with a flourish.

"Your house, Miss Louise. I expect Sergeant Magruder is waiting to show you about. He's very proud of what they have done to it. You all come over now just as soon as you are ready."

There was light inside the house, and Magruder, with a lean woman a head taller than himself, appeared on the veranda to greet them.

"Ye'll remember my Mary, Missus Carter?"

"Molly Magruder!" Louise hugged her. "Of course I do . . . I hope you're well, Molly?"

"Never better, ma'am," replied Molly, launching at once into a list of preparations made. "Bacon an' eggs an' a bit of milk in the cold room, an' there's coffee, fresh bread, potatoes, sugar, salt . . ."

"Whisht, now, Molly!" interrupted her husband. "Sure an' there's a bit of all that's needed, Missus Carter."

But Molly was not to be shushed. "An' there's wood

for the stoves, an' enough biscuits for your breakfast that I made myself this day, an' ye've only to warm 'em a bit . . . unless I can come an' do breakfast for ye tomorrow, ma'am."

Laughing, Louise Carter embraced her again. "Oh, Lord, Molly, you're the best woman in the world. Brigid and I can manage breakfast." She looked about, seeking Brigid.

"She's inside with the kids," said Molly. "Ah, Missus Carter," she added with a twinkle, "ye'll never lack for hands to split kindlin', with that grand head of red hair in yer kitchen. Every bold young buck in barricks will be at yer door."

"Oh, no!" said Louise firmly. "You and Sergeant Mac are going to help me see that doesn't happen. She's a good girl, Molly, and I want no nonsense in my kitchen. Come, now . . . let's have a look at the house."

In this house there were three instead of two doors opening onto the veranda, and Mrs. Carter looked puzzled. The center one was a weathered door, but it was set in a section of raw new planks.

"This one still had a dog-run through the middle," explained Magruder. "Hasn't been used since there was two families in it. When the Major said t'would be yours, we closed up the dog-run to make you a hallway."

He ushered them into this, bare except for a pile of luggage and a big stove at the back.

"This side," he indicated the left, "ye've got a parlor and a dinin' room. There's two bedrooms on the other side, an' we covered in the back porch to make an inside kitchen an' a room for yer girl. The old kitchen is a storeroom an' a fine new necessary."

"New what?"

"Doctor Brenner calls it a inside earth-closet, ma'am," Molly explained. "He showed 'em how to make it, an' he says it's first-rate."

Louise peered into the room identified as a parlor, and Sergeant Magruder lifted his lantern so she could see. The interior was freshly whitewashed and the smell of lime was overpowering. The dining room was the same, but the new kitchen smelled pleasantly of fresh-cut planks. There was a cooking range set in a tin box, and even a sink made of wood, with a zinc lining and a pipe to drain off water.

Back in the central hallway, Louise called the children and was answered by a warning hiss from the rear bedroom.

"Shhh, Mama! Go on, Brigid . . . get 'im!"

"What in the world?"

She looked into the room to find the children crouched by the door, William holding up a lantern to illuminate the far corners. Brigid, in one shoe, the other gripped tightly in her hand, stalked something cautiously.

"Shh!" warned William.

"Aha!" exclaimed Brigid, hurling her shoe. A small animal darted into the front room with a chorus of squeaks, its feet scrabbling on the plank floor.

"What was that?" demanded Lieutenant Carter.

Magruder looked embarrassed. "I'd swear we got all them little boogers out. One of 'em must of slipped back."

"One what, for the Lord's sake?" gasped Mrs. Carter.

"It's a rat!" announced Brigid angrily.

"It's naught but a chipmunk, miss," Magruder assured her. "T'will do ye no harm."

Brigid glared at him. "No harm? D'ye mean we're to have that great beast gallopin' through the house when it pleases?"

The sergeant sighed. "We stopped all the holes we could find, but I guess we missed one."

"Well, we'll not hunt the poor thing down tonight," said Louise Carter. "Tomorrow we can find the hole and close it up."

"I hope it lets itself out before then," Brigid muttered, retrieving her shoe. Mrs. Carter gave her a warning look.

"It's a splendid house, Sergeant Mac. I declare, you

have done wonders with it." Her praise banished Magruder's glum look, and Molly beamed too.

"Now . . ." Louise assumed command firmly. "Brigid, you and I will make up some beds, and Sergeant Mac, will you be kind enough to step next door to Brenner's and say we shall be there for supper in an hour?"

"I will, ma'am, an' if there's aught ye're wantin' ye've only to let me or Molly know."

"I shall, and I thank you both for everything you've done. Molly, I hope you will let me come soon to meet the rest of the company wives?"

"Whenever ye wish, ma'am. There's four of us, an' I doubt ye know the others. They've joined since you was last with us."

The Magruders ushered out, Mrs. Carter and Brigid found bedding in the luggage to make up the iron army-issue cots, each of which was already furnished with a freshly filled straw tick. Before they finished, Lieutenant MacKeever arrived, scrubbed and freshly uniformed.

"I'm to take supper with you at Brenner's, ma'am, and they sent me to say Miss O'Donnel should come too. She and Angelina will look after the children."

"Angelina?"

"Sergeant Couza's daughter, ma'am. She works for the Brenners."

"Oh. Well, that's fine. However I shall go nowhere until I change clothes and get rid of some of this dust. Cass, would you be good enough to bring a pitcher of water to our room?"

"I'll get it, ma'am," offered Ben.

"No, Mr. MacKeever, there's something else I'd like you to do if you will."

From a valise she produced a cylindrical object wrapped in a towel. Unwrapped, it proved to be a tightly stoppered decanter of dark liquid.

"What's that?" asked her husband.

"Some of Papa's excellent Pennsylvania bourbon. Mister MacKeever . . ." She broke off to look at him severely. "May I ask what you would prefer to be called by your friends?"

"Why . . . Ben, ma'am. It's Benjamin, but nobody calls me that."

"Good. Ben it shall be. I trust you know how to make a whiskey toddy?"

"Surely, ma'am."

"Splendid. Molly said there is sugar in the kitchen. If you will find some cups and make us each a toddy, we will christen the Carters' new home."

Ben looked astonished, and she completed his confusion by reaching to kiss him on the cheek.

"You're a good man, Ben. You brought this circus all the way from Winnemucca without losing your temper once. I'm awfully glad you're in our company."

The young officer blushed and grinned at her. "I'm glad too. And the trip wasn't near as bad as I thought it would be."

Josef and Mathilde Brenner proved delightful hosts. They seemed to be in their mid-forties, and both retained strong traces of their native German accent. Between visits to the kitchen, where Angelina, Brigid, and the four children had their supper, Mathilde explained this.

"We are not so long in this country. When my Josef finished at the university in Bavaria there was war again . . . always fighting. So after we are married we came from München to Charleston, but . . ." She clucked deprecatingly. "We are there only three years and there is more war."

Cass looked puzzled. Charleston? The army was chronically short of doctors, but it seemed unlikely that an ex-Confederate surgeon would be an officer in the regulars so soon after the war. Doctor Brenner was an Assistant Surgeon in the Army Medical Department with the rank and pay of a first lieutenant of the line. Mathilde must have noted his wonder, for she shook her head, smiling.

"Rebellion we have seen in Bavaria, and we do not like it. We went to Lancaster in Pennsylvania, where there is a cousin of mine, and Josef wanted to fight for our new country against the rebellion. They needed doctors more than fighters, thanks God, and he is four years in the war but never hurt. Now there is no more rebellion, but . . ." She smiled at her husband. "We are still by the army."

The men withdrew for cigars and brandy, Louise remaining with Mathilde to help with the coffee. It was not a prolonged separation. In a few minutes Mathilde Brenner brought her tray into the parlor.

"We want our coffee, Louise and I, but not by ourselves. No, Mr. MacKeever," she said firmly, "there is no need to put away your cigar. I like it."

The sitting room was comfortable and cheerful, lined with bookshelves on either side of the fireplace. There must have been a hundred volumes, and Louise Carter admired them openly.

"How ever did you manage to bring them all with you?" she asked.

"Without my books," chuckled Mathilde, "I do not go."

"What can you tell us of the history of Camp Belknap?" Cass asked the doctor, and Mathilde groaned.

"*Herr Gott!* You should not ask him that. Everything he knows . . . and he will tell you."

Cass looked surprised. "Are you an historian too, Doctor?"

"Historian, archeologist, architect, doctor . . . everything!" replied Brenner grimly. "Because the Surgeon General of the Army says I am. A medical report once every year . . . that is all right. But not for him. He wants to know what is the temperature, how much it rains, where do the houses leak, how old are the rocks, how many animals, how many Indians . . . everything!"

"What in the world does he do with it all?" asked MacKeever.

"He puts it in a book he calls a medical circular. Medical! It would make Francis Parkman bite his hands for jealousy. It is a history book with enough medical things so he can make the army print it for him. Hah! A colleague of mine says a doctor in the army has nothing to do but confine laundresses and dose the clap—"

"Josef!" murmured his wife, "There is company here."

The doctor chuckled. "You think Miss Louise does not know about these things? She is in the army as long as you, Mathilde. He lies, that colleague of mine. If he writes in his report everything the Surgeon General wants, he has plenty to keep him busy."

He poured more brandy, urging Louise to take a little, which she did when Mathilde winked at her and asked for some.

"This place, this Camp Belknap," Brenner continued, "there is no need for it, you know. It is an antique that is kept because of the antiques that are here."

His guests looked puzzled, and he laughed. "I do not mean us. Not all of us, anyway." Mathilde gave him a reproving look.

"What I mean is the stuff that is rotting in those storehouses by my hospital. *Mensch*! You would not believe what is there—uniforms and shoddy blankets and tents like Mathilde's lace curtains—all from the war. When General Crook, who was a lieutenant colonel then, came here to beat the Indians, someone has hauled all that trash up here from the railroad and left it."

"It's been here for ten years?" asked Carter in astonishment.

"What is left of it, yes. Here the mice live in boots with pasteboard soles and have babies in those funny black hats we had when the war began. You remember those hats?"

"Oh, Lord, yes!"

"Well, General Crook made his base here while he whipped Chief Pauline and his Paiute Indians after the

212

war. It was a big post then—two troops cavalry, two companies infantry, and six pack trains with eighty mules in each one. In those storehouses is enough things for all those soldiers, but when Crook is gone so are the soldiers and they leave all that stuff behind."

"Why don't they condemn it and sell it . . . or give it to the Indians?"

"The Indians are not that crazy, and there is no one to buy it. The white settlers? They don't come here. They go to the gold mines or to that beautiful land by the coast that is so rich even a Prussian can grow potatoes in it. No, my friend, we cannot sell it or give it away, and in Washington they do not know what to do, so they do nothing. I think maybe we stay here and watch that stuff until a thousand generations of mice have eaten it all. The army does not need Camp Belknap but it does not know how to get rid of it."

"What about the Indians?" asked MacKeever quietly. "Someone has to watch them."

"Not if we leave them alone on the reservations where we have put them." Doctor Brenner jerked his arm toward the east. "Crook put the Paiutes on a reservation over there, and they are quiet. There is no gold on the Malheur River and it does not make good farmland, so the whites don't bother them." He studied the young officer gloomily.

"Up north, yes. If they moved Camp Belknap to the Wallowa Valley it would be useful. Soon now we will drive the Nez Percé Indians from that land we gave them, and they will fight. They will lose but they will fight, because we leave them no choice."

Carter was intrigued by the doctor's bitter view of the situation, but his wife was stifling a yawn and Mathilde Brenner frowned at her husband.

"Enough, Josef. It is no time for your lecture on how bad we are. These good people have been traveling since the sun was up and they are tired."

In the veranda she gave Cass a lantern to light his way home. "Soon," she said, smiling, "you will not
213

need it to find the way, because I hope you come every day to this house."

They thanked her and bid Ben MacKeever good night. Brigid and the children had long since gone to bed. As he opened the door to their new home, Cass looked at his sleepy wife.

"They're an odd pair, and the doctor seems to have unusual notions about Indians, but they're very kind."

"More than kind," Louise replied. "Thank the Lord for such neighbors. Mathilde and I shall be great friends, and the doctor will be good for you. I think he has no great itch to fight Indians."

4

Steiger made better time with the baggage wagon than Lieutenant MacKeever had reckoned. Nightfall of the twenty-eighth of July found him two days behind the Carters and only fifteen miles from Camp Belknap. Had he pressed on, he could have reached the post a day ahead of schedule, but he stopped where dusk found him.

"Why don't we go on in?" Brennan asked. Steiger gave him a hard look.

"I'm in no hurry to get back to that damn place." He pulled a whiskey bottle from his bedroll and held it up to see how much was left. "Just enough for one more night an' no freeloaders bummin' me for a snort."

They broke camp early next morning and reached Belknap before noon, greeted wistfully by the sentry at the bridge.

"How was it, Steig?"

"Beautiful!"

"Did you bring us a little somethin'?"

Steiger looked disgusted. "They don't give it away, Nathan."

At the barracks he pulled up his team and glanced at Brennan on the seat beside him.

"I got a word for you, friend, if you've a mind to listen."

"What's that?"

"Get off this wagon an' go find Sergeant Magruder. He's been waitin' for you since May, an' puttin' it off ain't goin' to help."

"What about the Carters?"

"You talk like a recruit! You ain't goin' to dog-rob for Carter without the first sergeant says so. Try to get around him an' he'll have your ass. Go an' get it over with, man."

Michael grinned. "You got somethin' there, Steig. I'll do it."

He pulled his bag and bedroll off the wagon and dragged them onto the stoop of the barracks. A young soldier watched from the door of the orderly room.

"You'd be Brennan?"

"That's right. Is the First Sergeant here?"

"Gone to dinner. He'll see you when he gets back. You want to draw your bedding?"

"I guess so. Where do I put it?"

"You're in Corporal Wortman's squad. I'll show you."

The log barracks had a long dormitory at each end, with orderly and supply room plus a few cubicles for unmarried sergeants in the middle. The company clerk led Michael to the west end of the building.

"Plenty of room. Only thirty-four men in the company now. Pick you a spot and I'll give you a bunk."

From the supply room he produced a folding iron cot, two blankets, a cotton bed-sack, and a bundle of wooden slats for the cot. Michael initialed the property sheet as proof he had received them.

"You can get straw for your bed-tick at the cavalry stables," the orderly told him. "I can't issue you a rifle till the First Sergeant comes back."

Michael studied the long barracks room. Walls, ceiling, and floor were sheathed with unpainted planks, the floor scrubbed soft and white. There were fourteen cots, seven to a side, with a wide aisle between. One end of the room was heated by a cast-iron stove, the other by a fireplace big enough to accept four-foot logs. Michael knew that whoever slept by that alternately broiled and froze unless he spent the night tending the fire. The stove would make a better neighbor in winter.

But of course there was no empty space there. At the foot of each bunk was a blue-painted wooden box with the owner's name and rank stenciled on the lid, and Michael sought clues to the pecking order around the stove. Two of the four nearest bunks belonged to corporals, and the other two were occupied by privates. That did not automatically make them vulnerable, and Michael turned to the wall at the head of the bunks for more information.

Above the row of cots a plank shelf ran the length of the room, each man's field equipment folded and stacked above his bunk, with his dress shako topping the pile. On pegs beneath the shelf hung overcoat, dress coat, and a spare fatigue blouse. The coat sleeves displayed even a private's status.

Light blue service-chevrons above the cuffs of one pair of coats indicated their owner had two previous five-year enlistments; one of the chevrons was edged in red to show wartime service. An old soldier with more than ten years' service could not be evicted by Michael. The fourth place might be available. The coats bore no service stripe, and Michael, in his second enlistment, could preempt it if the occupant could not defend it with his fists. He dropped his carpetbag on the bare slats of the cot. During the day a soldier's bedding had to be folded and piled at the head of his bunk for neatness' sake and to discourage napping.

Dispossession of the owner had to await confrontation, but that would not be long delayed. A bugler on the veranda of the adjutant's office sounded recall from the morning's fatigue duty, and within minutes the occupants of the barrack room began trooping in. The first was a big red-faced corporal who stopped short on seeing Michael.

"Who are you?" he demanded.

217

"Michael Brennan, Corporal. The clerk says I'm in your squad."

"Ah, yes. I'm Wortman. We've been waitin' for you."

"I heard that."

The corporal grinned. "So I got your stripes an' now I got you. You seen the First Sergeant yet?"

"Clerk said he'd gone to dinner. I'll see him when he gets back."

"You'd better. He's got the red-ass for you, Brennan."

"I'll be go to hell!" exploded a lanky, tow-headed soldier, staring at Michael's carpetbag in disgust. "You gonna let him take my bunk, Corp?"

"He ranks your ass, Tobin. He can if he wants . . . unless you stop him."

Tobin's pale blue eyes measured Brennan thoughtfully. He shook his head. The big Irishman had six inches and thirty pounds on him.

"There's plenty of room," said Wortman. "You can find a place close enough to that damn stove. Let's eat an' then you can play house."

The mess hall was a framed wood building behind the barracks, about a third of its interior occupied by the kitchen and the remainder by a long trestle table with backless benches on either side. There was also a smaller table with chairs. K Company lined up at the kitchen counter to get its dinner, commenting obscenely on the cook and his food.

The latter was no surprise to Michael—a thick chunk of good bread, a slice of stringy beef roasted until it was crumbly, boiled potatoes, and coffee. A tin plate and cup with iron knife, fork, and spoon were the available tableware, each item closely accounted for because the army issued nothing for its soldiers' mess tables. These things were bought from the company fund, which was raised by skimping on rations and converting the savings to cash, supplemented by a levy on the profits of the post trader's store.

218

Wortman, the company's junior corporal, presided over the long table while the rest of the noncommissioned officers sat at the smaller one, their status reflected by a tray of jarred and bottled condiments bought from their own pockets and jealously guarded.

When his meal was finished, each man rinsed his utensils in a pot of lukewarm water and returned them to a rack on the kitchen counter. Once a week, by Lieutenant MacKeever's repeated order, the cook dumped everything in a stock pot and boiled it for ten minutes, but the tinware still turned black and unappetizing and the most detested extra duty to be had was its periodic scouring with wood-ashes and lye.

The company drifted back to barracks, and at one o'clock the bugler summoned most of them to make-work of some sort. Michael helped Tobin move his bunk, set up his own in the vacant spot, and drew field equipment from the supply room. The clerk gave him a chit authorizing him to draw a rifle from the magazine by the guardhouse, and Michael gave him a hard look.

"The First Sergeant's here, then?"

"He is. He'll send for you when he's ready."

The rifle was a brand new Model 1873 Springfield, the .45 caliber infantry "Long Tom" with a trowel bayonet—an odd looking thing that resembled an oversize pie-server. The rifle was encased in acrid-smelling grease so old it had set like varnish. Michael swore feelingly, and Corporal Wortman laughed.

"I catch you drainin' coal oil outta the lamps to clean that thing an' you're on report, Brennan."

"What in hell am I supposed to clean it with then?"

"Buy your own kerosene at the trader's store."

"I'll be damned! They give us scrub brushes to clean this place, don't they?"

"Sure, but you can't get that crap off with a brush."

"I can if I dip the son-of-a-bitch in boiling water."

"Jeez! I never heard of such a thing. It'll rust."

"No, Corporal," said Michael dryly. "Not if I oil it good."

"Yeah! An' what about the stock?"

"The cavalry's got linseed oil."

"Brennan?" called the orderly from the door. "First Sarn't wants you now."

First Sergeant Patrick Magruder was a little man with a big chest and broad shoulders that made him look top-heavy. His well-tailored uniform was fitted to exaggerate that. He had a luxuriant mustache, piercing blue eyes, and a close-cut ruff of gray hair around his bald head. He studied Michael coldly for a moment, then looked at the pay book on his table.

"Brennan, Michael Timothy," he read softly. "First hitch in the Nineteenth Infantry. Wounded in action twice. Conduct excellent, character good. Discharged an' reenlisted in the Twenty-first an' got a pair of corporal's stripes off my company. Never worked a day for 'em. That was in . . . let's see . . . June, eighteen hundred an' seventy-five. May, eighteen an' seventy-six, the stripes came home, an' now you're here . . . two months late." He frowned at the pay book. "Hell of a note, ain't it?"

The answer to that would be a matter of opinion, and it seemed to Michael that Magruder was not seeking opinion. He said nothing.

"You served in the war?" asked Magruder.

"Yes, Sergeant. Just short of a year."

A stubby finger searched the record. "Right. Eleven months. Why aren't you wearin' red trim on your hash-mark?"

"I was in a drafted regiment, Sergeant. I thought the regulars wouldn't count that."

"Thinkin' gets privates in trouble, Brennan. You were in the war, you wear the red trim . . . whether you earned it or not. Now tell me how you got my stripes."

"When my hitch in the Nineteenth was up, Major Hambright said if I re-upped he'd get me the stripes and a job with the recruiters in New York. I signed up, Sergeant."

"Who the hell is Major Hambright?"

"He was post commander at Fort Wallace in Kansas, Sergeant."

"Ah! Thought a lot of you, didn't he?"

"I don't know, Sergeant. I think he was just mad. I volunteered to go after some hostiles with a troop of the Sixth Cavalry. We caught 'em, an' after the fight their lieutenant told the Major he'd put me in for a medal. I never got it and the major was mad."

"He got you my stripes an' a candy-ass job in the city just for that?"

"I got hit pretty bad in that fight. The Major said if the cavalry wouldn't do anything about it, he would."

Magruder made a disgusted noise. "I see. Now tell me why you turned in the stripes an' came back to work."

"I was advised to, Sergeant."

"Oh? Who gave you that grand idea?"

"Captain Dennett, Sergeant. Recruit Detachment commander."

A grin spread across Magruder's face. "Cap'n Felix Dennett. Advice, was it? More like: 'Turn in your stripes an' go back to your company . . . or stand a court-martial.' Right?"

"Yes, Sergeant."

"Well . . . he put nothin' in your book about it, so I'll not be askin' what you did to provoke that great man. You'll start clean with me, Brennan."

That, thought Michael, was damned doubtful, but maybe he meant it. From the looks of the company, Magruder could use a real soldier. But the sergeant was not finished.

"You're dog-robbin' for the new company commander, I take it."

It was a statement, not a question so Michael studied the wall above Magruder's head and said nothing.

"Well?"

"If the company commander says so, Sergeant."

"The company commander hasn't said a damn thing

about it. Mister MacKeever says you was detained in Philadelphia to be Lieutenant Carter's orderly."

"I was, Sergeant, but I thought it was just for the trip out here."

Magruder looked interested. "Are you tellin' me you want to pull duty with the company?"

Michael took a deep breath and looked the little man squarely in the eyes.

"I'm not likely to get my stripes back unless I do, am I, Sergeant?"

The first sergeant smiled again. "I'm thinkin' you've seen the light, Private Brennan. Whose stripes you goin' to lift this time?"

"You'll pick the man, Sergeant."

"Will I now, by God! And when will I do this thing?"

"When you're satisfied I'm the better man, Sergeant."

"Well, I'll be damned! You got the gall for it, I'd say. Have you told the Lieutenant you'll not be workin' for him any more?"

"Not yet, Sergeant. I'll ask your leave to do that."

Magruder stood up, grinning. "You got it. I'll be waitin' to know what he says."

"Yes, Sergeant."

"Good. You're dismissed, Private Brennan."

Michael found the baggage wagon, half unloaded, behind the Carters' house, and Steiger peered at him from under the rolled back cover.

"You see him?"

"I did that."

"I don't see any tooth-marks. You still workin' for the Carters?"

"For the time bein'."

"All right. Here's a pinch-bar an' yonder's a box you can open. The missus said be extra careful with it."

Michael prized off the lid and found Mrs. Carter's glassware, wrapped in newspaper and bedded in straw.

"Where's the redhead?" he asked Steiger.

"She was out here a while back, raisin' hell about

some oilcloth. She took it inside when I found it for her."

Michael looked into the kitchen and heard an erratic pounding in the pantry. Brigid was on her knees folding and tacking oilcloth on the shelves. She was using a hatchet, clumsy and ineffective in the cramped space, and Michael watched her with amusement until she hit her finger and exploded angrily. She thrust the finger in her mouth and swore indistinctly.

"Can't you find a hammer?" he asked. "Won't hurt as much when you miss the tack."

She turned a red, angry face to him and blew a straggling lock of hair aside. "It's about time you got here. You finish this."

"I'm unpacking glasses outside. I'll want you to bring them in."

"She said cover these shelves before you put anything on them."

"There won't be anything to put on 'em if that bunch brings it in. Come on, now."

He dug out and unwrapped the glasses and Brigid carried them into the house, fending off offers of help from the other soldiers. As soon as she appeared they had all found something to do around the packing box. Before it was empty Mrs. Carter appeared, her hair bound in a bandanna kerchief.

"Brigid, I thought I said . . . Oh, Brennan! Thank goodness you're here."

"I asked her to help me bring the glasses in, ma'am. They're less likely broken that way. I'll cover the shelves."

"You're right. That's a good idea, Brennan."

When she went into the house Brigid stuck out her tongue at him. "You're bad enough, God knows, when you're wrong, Michael Brennan, but you're a real cross to bear when you're right. Stop grinnin' an' get on with it, will you?"

The contents of the box transferred safely to the kitchen, Michael finished covering the shelves and then went looking for Mrs. Carter. He found her in the central hallway where she and Brigid were putting china in a cupboard.

"Is the Lieutenant here, ma'am?" he asked.

"I think he's with Major Suter. Did you want to speak to him?"

"Yes, ma'am."

Louise Carter frowned at the sugar bowl she was holding. She knew from Steiger where Brennan had been, and she suspected what had happened.

"Can I be of help, Brennan?" she asked softly.

"No, ma'am, but I'd like to thank you, Missus Carter, for all your kindness."

"Oh, dear!" she sighed and put the sugar bowl carefully in place. "What happened?"

"Nothing, ma'am. Only . . . if the Lieutenant don't mind, I'll be goin' to duty with the company now."

"That," said Mrs. Carter grimly, "is something you will have to discuss with Lieutenant Carter. I expect he will be here shortly."

"Yes, ma'am. I'll just help finish the wagon an' keep an eye out for him. Thank you, ma'am."

He returned to the wagon and Louise Carter shut the cupboard door with a bang. "Damn all first sergeants," she muttered, and Brigid looked surprised.

Finding Michael in the kitchen a little later, she gave him a wicked grin. "So they caught you. Now you'll have to go to work, won't you?"

"You'll not be sorry to see me gone, Bridey?"

"It'll be like the sins of the world off my back to have you out of this house. But I thought you were too smart to get caught."

"What makes you think I'm caught?"

"Ah, come on, Michael! You'd never quit this soft job if you had the choice. I know what you're up to . . . you an' your sweet talk for the missus. You want her to tell Mister Carter he mustn't let you go."

He shook his head, grinning. "I liked workin' for 'em well enough, but I've no mind to keep it up. I'll not get what I want dog-robbin' for Mister Carter."

"What do you want, for heaven's sake?"

224

"My corporal's stripes. What you cost me with your temper an' that damn hatpin. I'll not have 'em unless I go back to the company."

"Oh? And what makes you think you'll have 'em if you do?"

"I will. I'm a better man than any corporal in this route-step outfit, and good as any sergeant I've yet seen."

"Ooh—la! Aren't you the modest one."

"Not at all, at all. I know what I'm worth, an' so does the Lieutenant, only he can't promote me for hangin' around his kitchen."

Brigid sniffed. She had learned to respect Michael's ability to get what he wanted, but this was too intricate for her. Nevertheless she hated to let him have the last word. She looked smug.

"That's as may be, but you aren't as smart as you think you are."

"Oh?"

"That's right. With all your connivin' you didn't get me fired, did you?"

He took her chin between his thumb and forefinger and held her despite her squirming protest.

"Did you ever think, Bridey, I might not have wanted to get you fired?"

"Let me go! I don't believe you."

He shook her gently, smiling at her flushed face. "Think on it, luv . . . Just look about you. If I wanted a girl to listen to the sweet things I'll whisper in her ear, could I find a better place? You've nowhere to run now, Bridey . . . an' naught better to run to than Michael Brennan."

She was so surprised she stopped squirming and stared at him. His eyes twinkled.

"No doubt I'll be gone a bit . . . fightin' Indians an' all . . . but you'll be right here when I get back."

"Ooh! Let me go, you big—"

He stopped her sputtering explosion with a kiss and was out the door, laughing, before she could retaliate.

In the orderly room next morning, when Lieutenant

Carter had examined and signed the morning report, Sergeant Magruder gave his company commander a sidelong look.

"Private Brennan asked leave to speak to the Lieutenant, sir. I told him he could."

Carter frowned. His wife had said Brennan was looking for him, and from her expression he gathered there was more she would like to say.

"I've not seen him yet, Sergeant. You have?"

"Yes, sir."

"Well, before I send for him you'd better tell me what's on his mind."

"Well, sir . . . I think he wants to pull duty with the company for a time."

"Ah! You gave him some advice, Sergeant?"

"Ah, no, Lieutenant. I'd not do that. I understood from Mr. MacKeever he'd be your orderly, but he says to me himself he wants to stay with the comp'ny an' buck to get his stripes back . . . if the Lieutenant will let him try."

"Has he got a chance?"

"For his stripes, sir?" Magruder looked thoughtful. "He's got more service than Wortman, an' those are Brennan's stripes Wortman is wearin'."

"What do you know about that?"

"Does the Lieutenant know Captain Dennett? He was Brennan's commander at Fort Columbus."

"I've heard of him," Carter grinned. "Who hasn't?"

"Well, sir, it's my guess that Brennan got crosswise of Cap'n Dennett—which God knows is not hard to do—an' the Cap'n gave him the usual choice—take a bust to private an' join the comp'ny, or take a chance on a court."

"I thought that might be it. What was the trouble?"

"I've not asked him, sir, an' he didn't tell me. Brennan's no recruit. He told me straight out he wants his stripes back an' he's willin' to work for 'em. He's seen some fightin', sir, which is more than Wortman has. If the Lieutenant asks me, I'd say give him the chance."

Carter considered a moment then nodded. "All

226

right. I'll do it. He's a damned good orderly, though. Can you find me another?"

"I've three in mind, sir."

"Three! I only need one, Sergeant."

Magruder grinned. "Missus Carter will pick one of 'em, sir. If he satisfies her, I'll see that he satisfies the Lieutenant."

5

Dr. Brenner's annual report to the army's Surgeon General in 1875 pretty accurately summed up life at Camp Belknap. "There is," he wrote, "no society outside the garrison, and a tour of service here provides an admirable opportunity for all officers to avoid living beyond their means for the duration of their assignment to this post."

Belknap lacked more than society. Because there was no civilian community within miles of the place, there was of course no routine mail delivery. The army contracted with a firm in Canyon City to fill this need. Their rider met the weekly stage from The Dalles on the Columbia River, collected letters and newspapers addressed to Belknap, and rode seventy miles south to deliver them. If he stayed sober and the weather was good, a letter came by this means from Portland in ten to fourteen days, or from Washington in thirty. Parcels arrived on a contractor's freight wagon hauling supplies to the post whenever the Canyon City post office made such arrangements.

Adjustment to this remote existence was difficult for newcomers, but the Carters handled it well. Louise was no stranger to the frontier and she was prepared for most problems. Her chief concern was the children's education. Herself a graduate of an elegant Philadelphia female academy, she was determined that William and Amanda should achieve an equal or higher level of schooling. This required that they not fall too far behind through the lack of good schools in southeast Oregon.

William's somewhat erratic instruction at the post school was supplemented by his mother's tutoring, and Amanda—deemed too young for classes in the post library—was instructed regularly at home. Her lessons were largely reading from Louise Carter's small library of classics, and Brigid was welcomed at these sessions. She found Emerson, Hawthorne, and Thoreau either over her head or intolerably dull. Reading at the Boston orphanage had been confined to the lives of the saints, which was poor preparation for New England philosophy.

Searching for something less weighty, Brigid found tucked behind the set of Thoreau's books a novel entitled *The Maiden Widow*. She read it with delight, unaware that she had stumbled upon Louise Carter's secret addiction to the melodramas of Emma Southworth.

Louise Carter had been reading the domestic-sentimental thrillers of Emma Dorothy Eliza Nevitte—E.D.E.N. for short—Southworth since her first tour on the frontier as a bride. Their titles were revealing—*The Hidden Hand, The Missing Bride, The Fatal Marriage*—and it was no surprise that Mrs. Carter took pains to hide her Southworths. She had a standing order for them with her Walnut Street bookshop in Philadelphia, but it was very confidential and her husband never saw the invoices.

Cass Carter had no interest in romantic novels, but he had long since discovered his wife's secret passion for them. He viewed it with amusement as another proof that Louise Bruning Carter was not entirely the proper Philadelphia lady most people thought her, and now and again he teased her about it.

"By the way," he remarked one evening, "have you

received another of those racy books you read when you're supposed to be having an afternoon nap?"

Louise blushed furiously. "They are not racy books! What a thing to say, Cass Carter!" After a moment she giggled. "How did you find out?"

"Brigid."

"Brigid! What has she to do with it?"

"Oh, I heard her reading to Brennan in the kitchen. I thought he'd brought in some trashy dime novel, but she hid the book behind the sugar can and I found it."

Louise bit her lip. "Which one was it?"

"You mean there's more than one hidden around?"

"Oh, Cass, don't be mean. Which was it?"

"I don't know. Something about a man walking up and down with his head on his breast and all his fingers in his teeth . . . gnawing away like a wild beast."

"Oh, dear! However did she find it? That must be the latest one—*The Deserted Wife*, I think. What did you do with it?"

Before Cass could answer, there was a crash from the kitchen and he looked startled. Louise frowned.

"That's just Brigid letting me know how she feels about doing the dishes."

"What happened to the cook—Benedette?"

"Why, he went to the hospital. Didn't you know?"

"Good Lord, no! What happened?"

"I'm not certain but I suspect Brigid knows."

Private Mario Benedette was the third of Sergeant Magruder's candidates for the job of cook at the Carter house. Advertised as a master of Italian cuisine, he fell short of that capability, but at least he did not fry eggs in deep fat. In addition, his great Italian passion was directed more at Brigid than at cooking.

After his first day in the kitchen Mrs. Carter sensed the difficulty. "What do you think of Benedette?" she asked Brigid cautiously.

"If you can stand his cooking, ma'am," Brigid replied grimly, "I can handle him."

Louise Carter suspected Brigid of carrying out that threat. She had found Benedette that morning sitting

230

by the stove with a lump on his balding head. His response to her questions was confused and rambling.

"Of course I sent for Dr. Brenner," Louise explained, "and he said the man had a concussion. He took him to the hospital, so Brigid has to do the dishes."

What happened to Mario was never explained directly to the Carters. Two days later he sent word that he did not feel he could handle the job, and Mrs. Carter gave up soldier cooks. The resources of K Company were obviously exhausted, so she searched elsewhere.

But the essentials of the story drifted back piecemeal. Brigid asked Michael circumspectly if he would take a frying pan to the post blacksmith for repair. Its bottom was so bulged it would not sit upright on the stove. Naturally Michael teased the truth out of Brigid and repeated it gleefully in the barracks, whence it made its way back to the Carters. Benedette, returned to duty as an infantryman, added to his lust for Brigid an abiding hatred of Brennan.

He was not the only one in the company who found Michael Brennan a little hard to take. Soldiers normally put their own evaluation on a new arrival, who accepted it and lived with it. The difficulty with Brennan was that he expected them to adjust to him. His preemption of a choice bunk in the squadroom won him no friends, but it took a week for him to provoke real trouble. Surprisingly, it occurred on the parade ground.

Officers rarely attended morning drill—that was the province of the sergeants—but Cass Carter was feeling his way back into troop duty and one day he appeared. Sixteen soldiers, all that remained after detailed and special duty men were subtracted, were going through the motions of close-order drill. Carter watched for a while and then called on First Sergeant Magruder in the orderly room.

"Something wrong, sir?"

"The drill is lousy, Sergeant. And there aren't enough men out there. Let's buck it up."

Next day K Company marched out to drill call with six sets of fours. Only eleven men had escaped Magruder. For two hours he whipped the company through its evolutions, his harsh, rasping bark driving even the laggards into smart step. For the third hour he called on the junior noncommissioned officers to take over in turn. Wortman, the newest corporal, was last.

Wortman knew his drill but the men were tired and bored and he gave his commands in a hurried singsong voice that was more annoying than commanding. He got by until he attempted a complex movement involving several rapid changes of direction, followed by a too-quick order to reverse march. Chaos ensued and Private Michael Brennan stepped out of the confusion to lean on his grounded rifle, watching the shambles in disgust.

"Comp'ny . . . *HALT!*" bellowed Wortman. "What the hell are you doin', Brennan? Get in ranks!"

"Just as soon as it's safe, Corporal."

Wortman's face turned crimson and he started for Brennan, but Magruder intervened.

"That'll do, Wortman. You . . . Brennan! You learned all about drilling in the city?"

"Before then, First Sergeant."

"Show me."

Shouldering his rifle, Michael marched in front of the scrambled company and waited for the men to sort themselves out. The parade ground fell silent. He said nothing, just stared at the infantrymen until they realigned themselves sheepishly. Then he nodded.

"Right by fours," he said quietly, waiting until every man's eye was on him. "Fours right . . . *HARCH!*"

Wortman had tried to maneuver in too small a space, and Michael knew better than that. He shook the little column out on a long traverse of the parade ground, and when it had settled into stride he gave them a cadence count, thrice repeated in quick succession. By the end of the third count the company was marching and bellowing in unison. At the far end of the parade he turned his column left and left again. Walking backward at its head, he grinned at the sweating doughboys.

"Nah, then . . ." His voice was low and confidential, but it carried to every man. "Pop yer chests up an' show the bastards what ye can do when ye've a mind to it."

The little group of sergeants watched in silence as K Company came to life. It was no magic—only the comfortable, competent feeling of moving in lock-step with a body of men.

"Hahnt . . . two . . . three . . . *HOAR*!" Brennan's clipped count swept them forward. Precise as a hundred-dollar watch, the company returned, made a column right, left, and left again; wheeled on right into line and halted before Sergeant Magruder to present arms with a crash that raised the birds from the trees along the creek. Brennan gave them a solemn wink and the command to ground their rifles; faced about and grounded his own. He did not give Sergeant Magruder a rifle salute—that was due only an officer.

The First Sergeant's wrinkled face showed nothing. "All right, Brennan," he said quietly, "dismiss the company."

Wortman pulled at Brennan's arm as they crossed the road in front of the barracks. His face was white and set.

"You tried to show me up, you son of a bitch!"

"I guess I did, Corporal. And watch your mouth."

"God damn you, Brennan . . . you can't talk to me like that!"

Michael stopped and waited for the rest of the men to go into the barracks. A few hung back, curiosity aroused by Wortman's fury.

"Get along with you," Michael told them. "I an' Corporal Wortman will have a private word or two."

"You lissen to me, Brennan . . ." Wortman exploded.

233

Michael's raised hand startled him into silence. "You better listen to me, you dumb Dutchy. I told you I'd have my stripes back, an' if you can't find your ass with both hands in broad daylight, I'll have 'em off of you."

"Why, you friggin' Mick! You want to settle this right now?"

"With pleasure, Corp. Take off that coat an' lead the way. An' you don't want nobody to back you up neither."

"Why not?"

"Because I mean to whip your ass, Wortman, an' I'd think you'd not want a crowd to watch."

Speechless with rage, Wortman pulled off his blouse and threw it onto the barracks stoop.

"Come on . . . I'll show you who's goin' to whip whose ass!"

He led the way behind the bathhouse, out of sight of the curious faces crowding the barracks windows, and squared off stiffly, his fists held high in a boxer's stance.

"What kinda rules?"

Brennan looked pained. "Rules, shit! Come to the party, man!"

It was over in four minutes. Wortman was big and strong, but he had no real understanding of a free-for-all fight. He landed a dozen blows on the big Irishman, who only laughed at him, and then he closed in frustration. That finished him. He tried to butt, and Michael's big hands closed lovingly on his ears. Three times his head rose and fell, each time connecting solidly with Michael's knee. After the third, Michael let go and Wortman sat down with a dazed look.

"Would ye care for more now?"

Wortman could only shake his head. He was having trouble getting words through his smashed mouth.

"That's all right, then. Wash yer face an' let's go eat dinner."

"Gaah!" said Wortman indistinctly. "I can't eat."

"Makes no difference if you eat or not, but you got

234

to walk into that mess hall like nothin's happened. You're the corporal, remember?"

"They'll know," mumbled Wortman.

"Not unless you tell 'em. I'll not."

"You won't?"

"Hell, no! This was betwixt you an' me. Long's you're wearin' those stripes you got to act like they belong to you. Now wash your face an' let's go." He held out his hand, grinning through swollen lips. "Are we quits?"

"We are for now, I guess. Next time I'll be ready for you."

Michael clapped him on the back. "Don't press yer luck, lad."

Their faces were lurid proof of what had happened, but no amount of chaffing got the story from either of them. Sergeant Magruder stopped Wortman after drill next day and studied him impassively.

"What happened to you?"

"Fell off the stoop, Sergeant."

"All by yourself?"

"T'was my own fault, First Sergeant. I've no complaints."

"I take it then I'll hear no idle chatter about it?"

"Not from my squad, Sergeant."

From the looks of the two men, Wortman had taken the worst of the punishment, but there was no change in Brennan's demeanor. He was as respectful to Wortman as to any other corporal, and Sergeant Magruder was puzzled. He kept a wary eye on Brennan, for the Irishman had clearly whipped his corporal and it was unlike a soldier to take no advantage of that.

November brought snow to Camp Belknap with in-
creasing frequency. Some nights the mercury fell to ten
degrees above zero, and the ice on the banks of Sweetwater Creek thickened daily. These were signs that
time was running out on the garrison's annual last-
minute race to cut, split, and stack enough firewood for
the winter. Major Suter's rigorous schedule for com-
pletion of this task might have succeeded but for an
unexpected distraction. Late one afternoon, with no
warning, half the cavalry troop from Camp McDermit
rode into Belknap.

Lieutenant Seth Hunter, commanding this detachment, declared he was simply carrying out Division orders to conduct a "tour of instruction"—an explanation
accepted by no one. It was far too late in the year for a
routine training exercise, and he brought with him two
oddities that deepened the mystery—a brand-new Gatling gun and a brigadier general of the Connecticut militia. Ominous reasons for the gun could be speculated
but the appearance in Camp Belknap of an Eastern militia general was absolutely without precedent.

Seth Hunter was a West Point classmate of John
Randell, so it was Randell's task to get the truth out of
him. Pretty Arabella gave him a grand supper and her
most charming smiles, but the results were poor.

Hunter's private explanation was no better than the one he gave Major Suter.

"A month ago," he told Randell, "we got orders to send half the troop to Winnemucca and back on a tour of instruction. Didn't make any sense, but Captain Wagner said General McDowell's a new commander and there's no telling what he'll do. I got the job. When I got to the railroad there was a telegram from Division: 'Wait for a train with equipment for your post.'"

He paused to roll a cigarette, and Arabella wanted to try one, so he had to make another, which came apart when she licked the paper to seal it. After some delay he continued.

"That was the gun. I took it off the train and the general came with it."

Randell looked puzzled. "You mean it's his gun?"

"No connection. He got off with a whole squad of aides and said he wanted to come with us. I didn't argue with him. Took him to McDermit, and when I got there Captain Wagner had another telegram from San Francisco. 'Take the gun to Belknap.'" Hunter grinned and spread his hands. "So help me, Jack . . . that's why I'm here."

"But the general? What does he want?"

"To shoot ducks."

"Ah, come off it, Seth!"

"That's right. Somebody told him there's more ducks here than anywhere in the world."

"I wonder," muttered Randell, "who told him that?"

"I can't imagine. Why don't you ask his aides? He's got three of 'em."

That was another part of the puzzle. Brigadier General John Quinn had indeed three *aides-de-camp*: a major from the Adjutant General's office in Washington, a Connecticut militia captain, and a second lieutenant from General McDowell's staff in San Francisco. Division had also provided him two enlisted orderlies, a corporal and a private. No regular-army one-star general traveled with such a retinue.

237

"I hate aides," said Randell bitterly. "They're more trouble than generals."

Arabella smiled sweetly, which was remarkable. There had been a difficulty about housing General Quinn's aides.

The militia captain and Lieutenant Shelby from San Francisco were given a room to share in the bachelor officers' quarters, but the Washington major balked. He wanted private quarters befitting his rank. The entire house next to the Suters was empty but in such bad condition it would not serve. There remained only one alternative.

When John Randell had brought his bride to Belknap in the spring he had been assigned the double set of quarters at the east end of Officers' Row. He should have warned Arabella that since he was the junior married officer on the post, he could be ranked out of half of the house by anybody senior to him who wanted it. But that was not the sort of thing you told your bride. Arabella had a lot of handsome furniture and she naturally distributed it throughout both sides of the house. When her husband announced that Major Gregg was moving in, there was a bad half hour. John Randell explained what he should have made clear months before, and she surrendered angrily.

"He can have my guest bed but I will be damned if I feed him," she conceded.

Nevertheless, when Gregg arrived she greeted him politely, and the ladies of the post were relieved. Breeding will always tell, they said, but Arabella nursed a fine Bostonian grudge against the usurper. There was no evidence of this in her amusement at her husband's remark about aides.

"Ah, well," said Seth Hunter. "They liven up the post, and God knows you can use that. Are you going to give them a party?"

"Oh, yes," replied Randell. "The mother and father of all parties." He brightened a little. "That'll take some time though, and maybe we'll get snowed in. Then you can spend the winter with us."

His classmate shuddered. "Not on your life! I'll put the horses on snowshoes if I have to."

Lieutenant Randell reported the gist of this conversation to the post commander next day. Presumably Division would eventually send some instructions concerning the Gatling gun, but General Quinn remained a mystery. The junior aide from San Francisco could shed no light on the matter, and the Washington major stuck to the story about ducks. No one wanted to question the militia captain, so Belknap's officers were left to draw their own conclusions. Only Private Michael Brennan found an explanation for General Quinn's presence, but since no one asked, he did not share it.

To Michael the best source of information was obvious and the means of extracting it equally so. He invited General Quinn's senior enlisted orderly to have a beer at the post trader's store.

"The gun?" said the corporal. "Hell, man, there's goin' to be a war next year. You got Indians around here, haven't you?"

"Paiutes. They been quiet for ten years."

"What the hell are Paiutes? I'm talkin' about Nez Purses. Come spring you gotta put 'em off their land an' they're gonna fight sure as God made little fishes. That's what the gun's for. One of them new ones. Kills folks at eight hundred yards."

"If it don't jam up. What about the general?"

"Plain as the nose on your face. He's no general. Just a fat-cat Irish ward-boss buckin' for election. Gov'ner or senator or somethin'." He winked confidentially at Michael. "But he's a real gent. You ever see a reg'lar gen'ral buy a soldier a beer?"

"God save us, no!"

"He did. Night we got to Winnemucca, he give me an' Kimball a beer right in the ho-tel bar. That Washin'ton major liked to had a fit."

"So what's he doin' up here?"

"Buckin' for election, I told you. Watch that prissy militia captain he's got with him. He spends a month's

239

pay ever time he gets to a telegraph station sendin' a bunch of crap back East to the newspapers. Make the home folks think the old man's a real soldier—roughin' it out here with the reg'lars."

"McDermit's bad enough, an' it's on the telegraph line. Why didn't he stay there?"

The corporal chuckled. "You ain't goin' to believe this, but it's a fact. He wants to shoot ducks."

That was so unreasonable it was probably true, Michael decided. He nodded gravely. "Ducks we got. I can show him more in one day than he'll see back east in a year."

"Is that a fact?" The corporal flicked his beer bottle with a fingernail and it rang empty.

"Another?" asked Michael.

"Sure, I'll have one more. I got to tell the Old Man you know where he can get some good shootin'. He'll like that."

"I'm your man. Any time," Michael assured him. But the corporal had several more beers and he decided it would be wise to provide a reminder.

The next day was Sunday, and Michael obtained a pass, borrowed the company shotgun, and spent the day exploring the marshes around Malheur Lake. The gun was an ancient Springfield musket converted to breech-load brass shotgun shells, but by noon he had killed as many ducks as he could carry. Marking half a dozen good stands in the head-high reeds, he trudged back to the post with his bag of waterfowl. There were enough to make a meal for the company with a dozen left over, and these found their way via the soldier cook to Mrs. Suter's table, where General Quinn dined nightly. As a matter of course the visiting general occupied the Suters' guest room.

Michael's gift of fat mallards raised a quick response. The following day Lieutenant Carter received a note from Major Suter asking the name of the donor. His cook had forgotten the man's name but remembered he was in the infantry company.

"Ducks? Who's been shooting ducks?" Carter demanded of Sergeant Magruder.

The first sergeant looked blank, but the company clerk spoke up. "Private Brennan used the comp'ny shotgun Sunday, Sergeant."

"Ah!" said Carter. "Where is he?"

"Wood-cutting detail, sir," Magruder replied. "They'll not be back before dark."

"Why? They can't cut wood at night."

Magruder sighed. "Brennan's in charge. He'll get back too late for retreat but just in time for supper."

The Lieutenant chuckled. "All right. Send him to my quarters as soon as he's eaten. I'm for supper at Major Suter's tonight, and I want to know about these ducks before I go."

At seven o'clock Michael rapped on the Carters' kitchen door and was admitted by the new custodian of that establishment. Benedette had been replaced as cook by a young Chinese named Mah Kim, recruited by Mrs. Carter from the family that managed the post trader's restaurant.

"Hello, John," Michael greeted him. His address was not contemptuous. By western custom all Chinese males were called "John." As a matter of fact, Michael approved heartily of Mah Kim. He was the first Carter cook to display no letch for Brigid, and he made superlative pie.

"Hallo, Mist' Brennan. You wan' Missy Bridge?"

"No, the Lieutenant sent for me."

"Lootenan' an' Missy Cahtah get ready go Maj' Sootee house for suppah."

"I know. I'll wait. Where's Brigid?"

"Put kids in bed. You want cup coffee?"

"You bet! You make good coffee, John."

"Li'l bit pie? I make lem-men custah pie."

"Come on! Where'd you get the eggs?" He bit into a wedge of the pie and looked surprised.

"I'll be damned! How'd you do it?"

241

Mah Kim looked smug. "Missy Cahtah got stuff make any kind pie." He displayed a tin with a pry-off lid and Michael took it curiously. The label displayed a swollen and prideful hen proclaiming the contents to be crystallized eggs. In smaller print there was assurance that these were whole eggs, dried and powdered in the most healthful fashion. Michael pried off the lid and sniffed.

"What do you know! It is eggs. Can I have another piece?"

He was working on that when Brigid rustled in, an empty mug in each hand. She had obviously just tucked the Carter children into bed with their late-evening cup of warm milk.

"Bless us!" she exclaimed. "The champion fighter of Company K, is it not?"

"God bless all here," responded Michael gravely.

"Don't give me that Irish nonsense!" Brigid saw the second piece of pie in his hand and sniffed. "How'd you know there was pie?"

"That isn't why I came. Lieutenant Carter sent for me."

"Oh? What's the matter now? You in trouble for bashing Corporal Wortman?"

Michael winked at the Chinese cook. "She talk mean like that to you, John?"

"His name's not John!" exploded Brigid. "You call him right, Michael Brennan. What would you do if he called you Paddy?"

"I've been called worse."

Mah Kim smiled and put the last piece of pie into his hand.

"You've given him all of it!" Brigid protested.

"You can have halfers," Michael soothed.

"I don't want it, but the kids will!"

"Don' fuss, Missy Bridge. I make nothah one."

"You're too good to him, Mah Kim," she sighed, settling wearily into a chair. "You ought never to let him know you've made pie. He'll eat anything that don't eat him first."

Michael shook his head in mock despair. "Hide the fryin' pan, John. She'll bend it over my head like she did Mario."

"Nah, nah!" said Brigid. "I'm that tired I couldn't raise it. Can I have a cup of tea, Mah Kim?"

Michael watched with interest. There was coffee on the stove but she wanted tea, and Mah Kim made it for her. He put the pot, sugar bowl, and a valuable tin of milk before her, and it was obvious that these two were getting along well.

The new orderly, Schroeter, grumbled in barracks about his status in this kitchen. He complained he got nothing to eat out of the Chinaman unless Mrs. Carter intervened for him. Brigid was clearly on a different footing.

A cupboard door slammed in the hallway, and they heard Lieutenant Carter grumbling about his clothes brush. Distantly his wife's voice was raised in denial.

"Oh!" gasped Brigid. "I've got it."

Carter appeared in the kitchen door, plucking threads of lint from his dark-blue uniform frock coat. The twin rows of brass buttons winked satisfactorily, but Schroeter had been careless with his polishing rag.

"I'll get it, sir," Brigid skipped around him. "I know just where it is."

"Thank you, Brigid. Ah! Brennan. What's this about you shooting ducks for Major Suter?"

Michael jumped to his feet and beamed. "Ah, it's grand sport, sir. I bagged a few last Sunday at the lakes."

"Enough to send the post commander a dozen?"

Brigid was back with the brush, dabbing cautiously at Lieutenant Carter's coat until Michael took it from her. Deftly he lifted the lint from the garment, working carefully around the two double stripes of gold braid on the cuffs. There was a small button at the top of each of these, and he clucked deprecatingly when he examined them.

"What's the matter?"

"That Schroeter. With the Lieutenant's leave, I'll just

243

be showin' him how to use a button-board so's he don't get polish on the braid."

"All right. Now, what about those ducks?"

"Well, sir . . . knowin' the post commander has important guests, I took the liberty of givin' his cook a few of 'em. God knows there's plenty in the marsh around those lakes. Would the Lieutenant be wantin' a few, now?"

Carter gave him a quizzical look. "I didn't know you were a hunter, Brennan. Where'd you learn wing-shooting?"

"Ah, Lieutenant, 'tis no great thing for a natural shot like myself."

Brigid groaned, and Carter smiled at her. "Well, you get yourself and your great talent into a clean uniform and report to Major Suter at fatigue call tomorrow morning. He wants to discuss ducks with you."

"Yes, sir."

Louise Carter put her elegantly coiffed head in at the door. "Good evening, Brennan. Cass, we shall be late if we don't go."

They departed, and Michael pushed a piece of wood into the stove, setting aside the kettle so it would not boil out. Sleet pecked at the windows and a cold wind searched beneath the outside door. Mah Kim put away the last of his pots, turned up his jacket collar, and nodded to Brigid.

"I go now."

"Where's your coat, you crazy pagan?"

"Got no coat. Don' need coat."

"Yes, you do!" She took her own ankle-length sheepskin from behind the pantry door and thrust it at him. "Put it on. You get sick an' I'll have to wash dishes again."

Mah Kim shrugged and pulled on the bulky garment. He and Brigid were very nearly the same size. He ducked his head with a soft hissing sound and went out.

Perhaps it was thanks. Communication with Mah Kim was difficult. He said little and worked hard, but he had won Brigid's admiration the day he arrived.

244

Finding her swearing at a sad-iron that had scorched the ruffles of a blouse, he took it from her, reheated it, and pressed out the ruffles with ease. She would have turned over all of Mrs. Carter's blouses to him, but he dampened his work by spraying water on it through his teeth, and Louise Carter objected violently to that.

"Poor old Mah Kim," said Brigid, refilling her tea mug. "I feel sorry for him."

"Why? He's not old nor poor either."

"Who does he talk to? He doesn't say ten words a day to us."

"He lives with that Chink family at the trader's restaurant. They talk to each other."

"Yes, but what about a girl? I bet there isn't a China girl in a hundred miles of here."

"He's workin' on that."

"What do you mean?"

"He saves every penny he makes, an' I'll bet he's got five hundred dollars in the trader's safe. As soon's he—"

"Five hundred!" gasped Brigid. "That's more money than I ever saw. What's he goin' to do with it?"

"When he's got six hundred he'll buy himself a girl in Frisco."

Brigid looked suspicious. "You tryin' to tell me they sell China girls in San Francisco? Where? In the market?"

Michael laughed. "Nope. Wish they did."

"Then who does he buy her from? Her family?"

"Not likely." Michael poured himself more coffee and searched among the condiments on the table. "Where's the milk?"

"You can't have any more. That canned milk is hard to get an' we have to save it for the kids. Now tell me where he'd get a girl for six hundred dollars."

He sighed and stirred sugar into his mug. "From a Chinese whorehouse."

Brigid glared at him, and he shrugged. "Well, you had to know. You think I made it up?"

"Never that!" she replied grimly. "I've no doubt you

245

know all about it. But who'd want a girl from a place like that?"

"It's not an ordinary house. A white man can't even get in one of those places."

"So how do you know about it?"

"Ah Quong at the trader's store told me. That's where he got his wife."

"I don't believe you! She doesn't look like any whore I ever saw."

"I told you these are high-class whores—only for rich Chinks. The pigtail that owns one of those places buys girls from their families in China an' pays their way to the States. They stay maybe a year an' then he's got to get some new ones. For six hundred dollars he'll sell Mah Kim one that's hardly used at all."

"That's disgusting!"

"Not at all. The girl wouldn't go with him unless she wanted to. And besides, soon's he buys her he'll take her to the nearest justice of the peace an' marry her."

"Why would he do that if he bought her?"

Michael grinned. "So's he can bring her back here without you nosy females raisin' hell."

"Oh. Well . . . it sounds dirty to me, but I s'pose if he marries her it's all right. That's better than whoring for a living."

"God save us, woman! Is that all you think of getting married?"

"Depends on who you marry. What time is it?"

"Nine-thirty," he replied, looking at his watch. "Why?"

"You've got to go. I don't want you here when the Carters get back."

"Well! Now I know where I stand." He stood up and tugged playfully on one of her braids.

"Ouch . . . don't!"

"I hear the ladies are gettin' up a grand ball for the visitin' general. If you're good, maybe I'll take you over an' let you peek in at 'em."

She tossed her chin scornfully. "I'll not need your help, thank you. I'll be there an' I won't have to peek."

246

"I declare! You're goin' dancin' with the officers?"

"Of course not, stupid! Angelina an' I are to help in the ladies' retiring room. Missus Carter told me. Now get your big self out of here, Michael, please."

She prodded him to the door, but relented enough there to let him kiss her. When his hands grew bold she squirmed free.

"Maybe you better get Mah Kim to buy you a girl too."

"Can't. I haven't got six hundred dollars."

"Nor ever will, you dumb Mick . . . so long's you stay a soldier."

He opened the door and grimaced at the gust of sleety rain that blew in. Then, very quietly, he shut it again.

"Turn out the lamp," he told her softly.

"I'll do no such thing! What's the matter with you?"

"Turn it out, I said. There's somebody out there."

The quiet intensity of his voice moved Brigid. The kitchen lamp was a big nickel-plated one suspended by a chain from the ceiling, and she had to climb on a chair to reach it.

"Where's the Lieutenant's pistol?" Michael asked, his eye to the crack of the door.

"I don't know. There's a shotgun in the hall."

"Bring it . . . an' all the shells you can find."

"The what?"

"Shells. What you shoot in it. They're brass things."

"Oh . . . I know. They're in a bag on the hatrack."

She was back in a moment with Carter's double-barreled shotgun and a canvas haversack of shells. Michael toed open the stove door, broke the gun, and looked through the barrels at the glowing coals. An orderly as dumb as Schroeter might have left a rag in one of them. He loaded the gun, wishing he knew what kind of shot he had. There was no way to tell in the dark.

"What is it? What's out there?" Brigid demanded in a whisper.

247

"I don't know. That's what I want to find out. There's someone by the woodshed."

"The sentry maybe?"

"Oh, hell, no! He's under cover somewhere." He slid the bar on the door into its iron hasp. "Now, you don't open this until you hear me knock on it . . . an' you know it's me."

"Wh—where are you going?"

"Out front. You think I'm just goin' to stroll out an' ask him the time of night? Stay here an' be quiet, now."

She swallowed hard and nodded, a futile gesture in the dark, but her voice had abandoned her. Michael's hand found her braid and gave it another light tug. Then he was gone through the hall.

Brigid leaned against the door and watched the fire-light from the stove make orange arabesques on the floor. She waited until she was sure the pounding of her heart could be heard outside, and when there was a light double tap on the door she squeaked in alarm.

"It's me—Michael. Open up."

She forced the bar back and opened the door a crack. Sleet stung her face, but she could see nothing.

"Open the damned door, Bridey! It's wet out here."

She swung it wide and Michael entered towing a reluctant figure behind him.

"Who is it?" gasped Brigid.

"Only a squaw. Light the lamp."

She searched in the dark for matches, puzzled by a faint mewing sound.

"What's that?"

"I guess she's got a baby with her. Will you light the lamp?"

"I'm trying, damn it!" Climbing on the chair, she tripped, and sprawled across the table, spraying matches in all directions.

"Glory be to God, Bridey! What are you doin'?"

She had rapped her chin painfully, and the hurt combined with her recent fright made her swear atrociously. Michael chuckled. Finding a match, he flicked it alight with his thumbnail and set the lamp burning.

248

"You in one piece?"

Brigid nodded, rubbing her chin and staring at the Indian woman.

"Who is she?"

"I've seen her hangin' around the store," Michael replied. "Must belong to one of the scouts."

Whoever she belongs to, Brigid thought, he doesn't take much care of her. She was wrapped in a threadbare blanket, soaked and dripping on the floor. Her face was so thin it seemed composed of nothing but cheekbones, big black eyes, and a hawk's beak of a nose. The eyes never left Michael, and she began to shiver violently.

"The poor thing's half frozen," exclaimed Brigid. "Put some wood to the stove, Michael. Here . . ." She tugged at the sodden blanket. "Take that thing off." The woman clutched it tighter.

"I won't hurt you," Brigid urged, pointing to a chair by the stove. "Sit now and take that wet blanket off. Shake the grate down, Michael, and blow up the fire, will you not?"

"I doubt she knows what you want," he responded. "Take it slow and show her."

The woman would not sit, but after a little the warmth of the stove persuaded her to give up the blanket. Brigid spread it over a chair to warm a little. It would take hours to dry.

"Sure an' she's naught but a girl. She needs something hot in her—will she drink coffee?"

"I don't know. Show it to her and see."

Brigid poured a mug full and offered it, and the woman's response was heartbreaking. She shook her head and lifted the small, buckskin-wrapped bundle toward the white girl.

"Ah, Mary Mother . . . the poor little thing! What can we give it?"

"From the size of that one," Michael answered dryly, "I'd think she's the only one can feed it. Maybe you'd better feed her first."

"You're right! There's soup in that pot. Put it on the eye to warm whilst I get some bread. Maybe she'll take the coffee if I sweeten it good."

She spooned sugar into the mug until it brimmed. This time the girl took it and sipped, clutching her baby in one arm. Brigid got a loaf of bread from the pantry and cut thick slices, the Indian watching her hungrily over the rim of the mug. Michael had the fire roaring now, the eye under the soup beginning to glow.

It was good, thick soup. Mah Kim had coaxed army-issue dessicated vegetables into a tasty brew with seasoning and a beef bone. Brigid filled a bowl, set it on the table, and piled bread beside it.

"Eat now," she coaxed, holding out an iron spoon. The Indian girl ignored her. Crouching on her heels, she held the baby in her lap and dug with a grimy finger in her coffee mug for the sugar in the bottom. Brigid shrugged and put the bread and soup on the floor beside her.

When the mug was clean, the girl dipped the same finger in the soup, tested it, uncovered her baby's face and pushed her finger into its mouth. The tiny brown face wrinkled like a walnut. Bright shoe-button eyes popped open and it sucked eagerly, then ejected the finger with a yell of rage.

"It's too hot!" Brigid protested. "That's for you. Here . . ." She held out the spoon again. Taking it in a clenched fist, the girl gulped a mouthful of soup. The baby howled and she tried again to feed it with a finger.

"Can't you do something for the babe?" Michael asked.

"What, for God's sake? You're right . . . it's too little for anything but milk. She's got to feed it."

Cupping her breast in her hand, Brigid pointed to it and then at the baby. The Indian looked puzzled.

"Not me, you crazy thing! You feed it." Brigid put a finger on the girl's breast. The Indian made a harsh sound and raised her hand to Brigid, palm up and empty.

"No good," said Michael. "She's dry."

Brigid jumped to her feet and ran to the pantry, returning with a small tin which she thrust at Michael.

"Make a hole in that for me. Missus Carter will take on, but I can't help it. I cannot listen to that poor babe cry."

It was condensed milk, a genuine rarity, and Michael opened it carefully with Mah Kim's cleaver. Brigid spooned half the contents into a cup and stirred hot water into it.

"Cut me a strip from one of those towels." She pointed at the dishcloths above the sink. "The cleanest one."

When Michael gave her the cloth she rolled it into a tube and soaked it in the sweet milk. Pushing aside the Indian girl's protective hand, she popped the dripping cloth into the baby's mouth. Again the bright eyes opened wide, but this time there was no yell—only a happy smacking sound.

"I'll be damned!" said Michael softly.

The Indian girl watched suspiciously, and Brigid gestured for her to try the milk herself. Gingerly she dipped a finger in the mixture and tasted it. Her tense mouth relaxed a little.

"Now then . . ." gently, Brigid eased the infant from its mother's arms. "Go on," she urged, pointing at the soup, "you eat now."

Watching Brigid anxiously, the girl wolfed down her bread and soup. In a minute the baby's smacking grew louder, mixed with querulous sounds. Brigid extracted the rolled cloth to soak it again in the milk and the baby howled. Its mother clucked soothingly as she scraped up the last of the soup.

"Give her some more, man!" Brigid told Michael. "Give her all she wants."

Brigid fed the baby until it could hold no more. Its eyes closed and milk dribbled from its mouth. Not so its mother. She finished all the soup and looked at Michael hungrily. Brigid gave her the sleeping infant, cut more bread and covered it with brown sugar.

251

"She'll be sick," warned Michael.

"That's all right so long's she's full first. Have you never been hungry, then?"

"Why sure, but . . ." He looked at Brigid curiously. "What do you know about it?"

Brigid looked grim. "I know, all right."

There was a knock at the front door and the Indian girl snatched for her blanket. She tried to break away, but Brigid held her.

"That'll be the Carters. Let 'em in."

"The door's open. I went out that way."

"They don't know that. Let 'em in."

"What about her?" Michael indicated the frightened Indian.

"They'd just as well see her. I can never clean up this mess before they get here."

At the sound of voices in the hall, the Indian girl struggled to get away, but Brigid would not let her. Louise Carter took in the scene at a glance.

"What is this, Brigid?"

"She came to the door, ma'am . . . begging. She's starved."

"But Brigid . . ." Louise Carter was appalled. "You can't take in people like this when you're alone with the children!"

"I wasn't alone, ma'am. I . . ." She looked at Michael appealingly.

There was a momentary silence, broken by a muffled belch from the baby.

Mrs. Carter stared at the Indian girl, who had wrapped herself and the infant again in the damp blanket.

"What was that?"

Brigid turned back a corner of the blanket to reveal the baby's happy face. As Louise Carter stared in astonishment, it blew a milky bubble and belched again.

Lieutenant Carter had noticed the shotgun against the wall, and he looked at Brennan questioningly.

"I was leavin', sir, maybe an hour past, an' I saw someone standin' by the woodshed. Brigid doused the

252

lamp and brought your gun. I went out the front way an' scouted the yard an' found this squaw. I guess she was tryin' to get up nerve to beg for food, sir."

"They were both of 'em starvin', ma'am," Brigid broke in. "Had you been here, you'd have done the same."

"Who is she, Brennan? Do you know?" Carter asked.

"I've seen her around, sir. I thought she might belong to one of the Indian scouts, but they're drawin' pay. Their women got no reason to be as hungry as this one."

Louise Carter was not mollified. "Nevertheless . . ." she began, but the baby's black eyes were fixed on her in wonder, and her anger came unraveled. "Oh, damn!" she said softly. "I can't really blame you, Brigid. The poor little thing."

The baby blew another bubble, a big one. Mrs. Carter studied it curiously for a moment, glanced at the Indian and then at Brennan.

"Did she . . . I mean . . . ?"

Brigid understood what was troubling her. "No, ma'am. She hasn't any milk. I guess she's been hungry too long. I . . . I took a can of the condensed milk, ma'am." She looked so worried Louise Carter was abashed.

"That's all right. I think I would have done the same. But you mustn't do it again, Brigid. We'll have a whole troop of them at the door every day."

The Indian girl edged away, watching the Carters anxiously. Mrs. Carter sighed.

"I think she wants to go. Did you give her something to take with her?"

"No, ma'am."

"Won't do any good," said Lieutenant Carter. "They'll just take it away from her."

"Surely she has sense enough to hide it. Give her a loaf of bread, Brigid, and some of those dried beans."

Brigid filled the ruined dishcloth with beans from the big crocus sack in the storeroom and put it with a loaf

253

of bread in the girl's arms. The Indian wrapped the food and her baby in her blanket, and when Brennan opened the door she faded like a wraith into the darkness. The Carters went to bed and Brigid attacked the soup pot gloomily.

"I'll do that," Michael told her. "You mop up that water."

"No. You'd best go now."

"What's eating you, Bridey? I'm only tryin' to help you."

She gave him an angry look. "You'll help me to more trouble, you will! You saw she's put out with me."

"So how's my scourin' the pot to raise her temper?"

"It's not the damn pot, Michael! I promised I'd pay no heed to any man, an' when she hears you hangin' around she'll think I'm makin' up to you."

"That I doubt," he replied, holding the pot beyond her reach, "unless she's gone out of her mind entirely. Nobody hearin' the way you talk could think you're sweet on me."

"Oh, give me that an' get out of here, damn it!"

But there was more than anger in her green eyes, and when he trapped her arms and held her close she sniffed forlornly against his chest.

"Ah, Michael, don't trifle with me. I'm that lonesome I might get foolish."

"You need a man, Bridey . . . an' a little lovin', I'm thinkin'."

She pushed him away, not ungently. "Not from any soldier, I don't. I'm not that daft. Now get you gone, Michael . . . please."

"Give me a kiss?"

"No!"

"All right. I'm goin', but never you doubt I'll be back, Bridey."

"I'm not likely to, you big *gommach*," she told him with a smile, but she pushed him toward the door as she said it.

254

7

Michael Brennan's interview with the post commander was mutually satisfactory. Major Suter wanted someone to take General Quinn duck hunting, and he had found his man.

An hour before dawn next morning Michael knocked on the Suters' kitchen door and found the general ready to go. James Quinn might look comical in his brigadier general's uniform, but not in his hunting clothes. The canvas jacket and pants tucked into knee-high rubber boots were plain and hard-worn, not something donned like the uniform just for a tour of the frontier. Michael studied this outfit approvingly as the general ordered a last cup of coffee for both of them before they departed.

Most men off for the duck marshes at this early hour would not trouble to shave, but Quinn had. His red face glowed with health, blue eyes sparkling beneath a thatch of white hair. He was portly but he moved easily and he was no swell sport, Michael noted—insisting on carrying his own gun and rucksack despite offers by both Michael and the Suters' orderly to help.

A light spring-wagon with a pair of sleepy mules accommodated the party with room to spare. Of General Quinn's three *aides-de-camp*, only Lieutenant Shelby, the officer from Division Headquarters in San Francisco, accompanied them. Major Gregg of the Army Staff had no interest in duck shooting, and it appeared from the general's humorous comments that his Connecticut-militia aide had no interest in anything cold and wet. Captain Riordan was a serious, bespectacled young man who made no pretense of being a soldier. Michael gathered that back east he served as General Quinn's personal secretary—blue-suited now solely as protective coloration for this trip. Apparently Riordan's functions had to do principally with Connecticut politics.

It was going to be a perfect day for duck hunting—beginning with cold rain that would shortly turn to sleet and probably snow before noon. The general accepted this with enthusiasm. On the marsh he shot well and retrieved his downed birds even when that required wading into icy water over the tops of his boots. He proved a serious and expert hunter but not a grim one. When Lieutenant Shelby had to wade after a crippled duck, swearing luridly as the bird drew him deeper into the clattering reeds, Quinn roared with laughter and chaffed the young man merrily.

John Shelby was a keen hunter too, and as good a shot as the general. Complimented on his eye by the older man, he told them he had been born and raised in Savannah and had hunted duck and marsh hens in Georgia rice marshes since he was big enough to carry a gun. The weather grew fouler by the hour, and when the birds were put to flight by the shooting they circled and returned at once. By noon Quinn called a halt. The three of them had shot well over a hundred ducks.

They would have gone home then, except that the general pined for a chance at geese. When those wary birds were put up, they circled high and came down on the far side of the lake in open water where they could not be surprised. Michael volunteered to walk around and start them up, but before he went he offered Quinn the long converted Springfield. The general's English Needham was a beautiful weapon, but its twenty-six-inch barrels would never touch geese.

256

"They'll come this way, sir, but high an' fast. 'Tis a clumsy old beast but it'll outreach your own."

Lieutenant Shelby worked the other shore, and in an hour the General had six fat Canadian honkers. When they had piled their bag in the back of the wagon Quinn produced a large silver flask. His shivering companions eyed it enviously.

"Never drink while I'm shootin', an' I never shoot with men that do," the general told them, "but we're finished shootin' for this day." He handed the flask to the lieutenant, who took a long gulp and passed it back. Quinn looked surprised.

"Give it to Brennan, man."

Michael beamed and let a long swallow of mellow brandy warm his throat. "Dear God an' that's a lovely thing, sir."

The general chuckled and took his own drink. "From what part of Ireland do you come, Brennan?"

"County Cork, sir, an' the town itself."

"Was it politics or an empty belly brought you here?"

"I had a bit to do with the Brotherhood on the docks, sir. Mayhap a bit too much."

"And have you kept in touch with the movement since you came?"

"I went to Canada with O'Neill in sixty-six, sir."

"No, by God! Did you so? Do you correspond with the Fenians yet?"

Michael shook his head. "No, sir! If I'm goin' to soldier, General, I'll have the real thing, not that variety show!"

Quinn laughed. "My sentiments exactly! Though a better name for that foolish thing would be farce comedy."

The flask went around once more and was returned empty, and General Quinn sighed. "It's been a grand day indeed. You've done us proud, Private Brennan."

Michael acknowledged the compliment with a nod, but Quinn had not finished with him.

"We're not all comedians like O'Neill and his lot,

257

my boy. The Irish vote in Connecticut is big and growing bigger. The Yankees are gettin' soft, and we'll take the state from them soon. How much time have you left to do here?"

"I've only just signed on for my second hitch, sir. I've four and a butt years to go on it."

"Have you never thought of doing them where's there's more people than ducks?"

Michael grinned. "I was at Fort Columbus in New York until May this year, sir."

"And you left that to come here?" General Quinn sounded incredulous.

"Well, sir, it was a bit like leavin' Cork. I needed a change of air, sir, and this is a grand, healthy place for a man."

Quinn laughed. "I'll wager it was a woman then, if you've left off foolin' with the Brotherhood. Am I right?"

Michael managed to look abashed. "You are, sir."

"Serious?"

"Ah, no, sir. My book's clean."

"Would you like another job back east?"

Michael considered that carefully. It seemed unlikely General Quinn had that much influence with the regular army, but you could never tell about a politician. His reply, after a moment, was surprising.

"I'd like it a lot, sir, but I've a mind to get my stripes back first."

"Hell, man!" exclaimed Quinn, "that's a small thing, unless . . ." His blue eyes twinkled. "You're tellin' me you want 'em the hard way."

"That's about the size of it, sir."

"All right," the general chuckled, "I've no quarrel with that." He winked at Michael. "I think the better of a man who knows what he wants an' how he means to get it."

The weather had worsened, gray clouds dropping lower and snow threatening. Quinn stood up and returned the empty flask to his rucksack.

"We'd best be gettin' back, I'm thinkin." But as he

climbed into the wagon he paused to speak again to Michael. "Captain Riordan will tell you where to write. When you're ready, I've a job waitin' for you, Brennan."

Shelby's reaction to this exchange was mixed. He had won his own brand-new lieutenant's bars the hard way, and he was trying to decide whether Brennan meant what he said or was just an accomplished rogue making sure of a good thing.

John Shelby's father had died fighting for the Confederacy in Cobb's Georgia Legion. A prosperous merchant before the war, he had left his widow and son something far more valuable than his good name—a few priceless European investments to tide them over the hard postwar years. The widow's good looks and Captain Shelby's forethought drew a number of ambitious gentlemen to her stately Savannah home, but she rebuffed all suitors and devoted her comfortable income to the defense of a little island of times past.

Ten years old when the war ended, Shelby had grown up in this atmosphere of carefully preserved comfort, and he had shaken it badly when he sought and obtained one of the first appointments to West Point from Georgia following its reestablishment in the Union. His four years at the academy had been difficult. The class of 1876 was predominately northern and a Georgian, son of a Confederate officer, did not have an easy time of it.

Graduation and a commission in the cavalry had not ended Shelby's difficulties. He was assigned to the Sixth Cavalry in Arizona, but when the orders were published, the regimental commander expressed doubts to General McDowell. Colonel Oakes was a tolerant man, but he was concerned about the reception Shelby might find in a regiment that had fought through the entire war and was still largely officered by combat veterans.

McDowell had a solution. He would keep Shelby on the Division staff in San Francisco and put him to work on the extension of the military telegraph line from

California through Arizona. The Sixth Cavalry would have a chance to look their new lieutenant over before he joined him.

Because he had bucked all opposition to make himself a place in the army, John Shelby was attracted to any man who chose the hard road. Brennan's choice was intriguing, but nothing in Shelby's brief experience of soldiers made it credible, and he was curious to see if Michael's rejection of Quinn's offer would outlast the general's stay at Belknap.

For a week the Suters and K Company ate duck daily, and so many were delivered to the Carter house that the family could not eat them all. The surfeit reminded Brigid of the hungry Indian girl and her baby.

Mrs. Carter made it clear that she did not want them at her door again, but there had to be some way to get around this. Brigid had paid off her debt to George Schultz and had a little money of her own. She spent some of this at the post trader's store on flour and canned milk, and went looking for help in getting it to the Indian girl. Peter Hanst, one of the quartermaster's civilian wood-cutters, was her first target.

"I heard about that gal," said Hanst. "She's Petoe's woman. Squis-Squis."

"That's her name?" Brigid asked, astonished.

"Yep. Means some kind of little partridge. She's a Salish Injun from up north. I heard tell the Crow Injuns took her off her people in a raid, an' when they couldn't find none of 'em willin' to buy her back they sold her to Petoe. What you want with her, missy?"

Brigid showed her purchases and explained, but Hanst shook his head. "Ain't right smart. When Petoe found out she'd been down to your place, he whupped the hell outa her."

"Why doesn't he take care of her, then? If she's his wife and that's his baby, he ought to feed them."

"Well, now . . . I dunno whose kid that is, an' only an Injun would know if she's his wife. He's got another woman in his tepee, an' could be he jest bought Squis-Squis to help out with the heavy work."

"Well, damn him then! How can I give her these things?"

"You sure don't want to do it where anybody kin see you—least of all Petoe. He ketches her takin' that stuff from you, an' he'll jest whup her again."

"If he won't feed her, why can't I?"

" 'Cause he's jest plain Injun. Too proud to work an' damned if he'll let his women beg."

Brigid's angry face told him he was getting nowhere, and he sighed heavily.

"Tell you what. I ain't about to give them groceries to that gal, but if you wrap 'em up good an' leave 'em in that old com-mode by the crick—the one y'all don't use no more—I'll see she gits the word."

It was not very satisfactory, but Brigid accepted it as the best she could do. She added a pair of ducks to her purchases and left them in the abandoned outhouse as Hanst had directed. Next day they were gone and she wondered if the raccoons, or some other hungry Indian, had taken them, but when she repeated the process a week later she found the food replaced in the night by a pair of soft, knee-high buckskin moccasins.

After that, there was always something left where the food had been. Trifling things, heartbreaking in their poverty: dried berries and acorns polished and strung to make a colorful necklace, or perhaps only a tawny buckeye, rubbed to a soft gleam. When her money was gone, Brigid was reduced to snitching food from the Carter pantry, but she tried to leave something every week. Mah Kim knew, of course, but he thought she was giving it to Michael, and he made no complaint.

8

Camp Belknap meant to give General Quinn a memorable party, and as the day of this affair drew nearer Brigid had little time to think of Squis-Squis and her baby. Servants, orderlies, and borrowed soldiers were deployed by the ladies of Officers' Row in the rush of final preparation.

The entire ground floor of the bachelor officers' quarters were requisitioned and scrubbed and polished until it gleamed. The walls were decorated with company guidons and martial trophies—sabers and bayoneted rifles. Intricate chandeliers and wall-brackets were carved from wooden cracker boxes and filled with candles. The floor of the schoolroom was covered with bleached canvas, stretched tight and tacked down. For dancing, it would be sprinkled lightly with corn meal. Over the mantel of the big stone fireplace was hung a tinted lithograph of President Grant trimmed with bunting, and a wreath of evergreens.

The library would serve as the ladies' retiring room, with Brigid and Angelina in attendance, and the wide hallway, lavishly decorated with greens and illuminated by countless candles, would be the buffet room. Every house on Officers' Row contributed to the table— long-hoarded tinned and bottled delicacies, linens and precious crystal, silverware to surround the big pewter punch bowl, loaned by Major Suter.

This bowl had been presented to him at the end of the war by the officers of the volunteer regiment he commanded, and around its ample girth it bore the names of all the regiment's battles interspersed with elegant quotations from martial classics. It had always been the most imposing item on Camp Belknap's party tables, but now it had competition.

Belknap's most recent bride, Arabella Randell, contributed from her trove of wedding gifts a magnificent pair of silver Queen Anne–style Rayo lamps. How she had transported these monumental treasures with their etched glass globes and chimneys intact all the way from Boston was a wonder, and jealous ladies whispered that "the Cavalry Beauty" was trying to outshine the post commander.

The duties assigned to Brigid and Angelina were not very demanding. They had only to help the ladies with their cloaks and dancing shoes and see that the dressing tables were neat and well-supplied with all essentials. Brigid had entertained a hope that she might finally wear her beautiful brown dress, but Mrs. Carter, in consultation with Mathilde Brenner, put an end to that.

The ladies shared a concern about the impact of Brigid and Angelina on the young bachelors, of whom there would be three—Ben MacKeever, Win Slade of the cavalry troop, and General Quinn's junior aide, John Shelby. Brigid's green eyes and flaming hair matched by Angelina's dark Italianate good looks could be destructive of good order. Plain black dresses, suggested Mathilde Brenner, with white aprons as a badge of office, would clearly identify their status. It was so decreed.

The girls accepted the ruling sadly, but this was Brigid's first formal ball in any status, and she wanted to do it justice even in plain black. She took her problem to her friend, Prudence Morton, the trader's daughter, and Prudence had an idea.

She found an ancient but still authoritative corset that had a comprehensively distracting effect on Brigid's small, shapely figure when she was laced into it. The plain black dress developed a good deal of slack, but this was effaced by judicious alterations. As added attractions, Prudence loaned a pair of her own black silk stockings and, surreptitiously from her father's small stock, a pair of black patent leather pumps, low-cut with steel buckles at the toe and elegant spool heels two inches high. Brigid gladly agreed to the condition that if they suffered visible damage she would have to buy them.

On the day of the party she washed and brushed her hair until it shone, and braided it into a thick, gleaming coil on top of her head. To this would be added at the last moment a black grosgrain ribbon bow, also loaned by Prudence. Not until the children's early supper had been finished was she free to make final preparations.

Mah Kim would stay until after the party to keep an eye on William and Amanda and guard against fire— the dreaded and ever-present threat in a lamplit house with wood-burning stoves. But Mah Kim could not help with the corset, which required assistance if it was to be laced properly, so Brigid applied next door to Angelina for help. She returned to the Carter kitchen just as Mrs. Carter rustled in to give final instructions, wearing a Worth ball gown purchased in New York not a year past. High fashion even by New York's sophisticated standards, it was going to send the less fortunate ladies of the garrison into seizures of envy.

"Oooh . . . Missus Carter!" gasped Brigid. "You're beautiful!" Distracted by this sincere compliment, Louise Carter failed to look closely at her maid, but Cass followed her into the kitchen and it dawned on her that his expression of amused surprise was not for her. He had already commented flatteringly on her appearance. She looked at Brigid.

Angie had applied herself energetically to the corset laces, and Brigid's normally bright face was rosier than ever. Louise Carter wondered fleetingly if the girl had

264

found a rouge pot somewhere, but that was a minor concern. Brigid's pretty face would be the second stop on the itinerary of any male scrutiny.

"Oh, my!" she said softly.

Brigid looked worried. "Is something wrong, ma'am?"

"No. That is . . . no. You look splendid, Brigid."

Her husband grinned at that cautious response, and, confidence restored, Brigid happily plucked up her skirt to display silk-sheathed ankles and the gleaming pumps.

"See what Prudence lent me? Aren't they beautiful?"

She meant of course the shoes, but it was the black silk hose that held Cass Carter's admiring eyes.

"Yes, indeed!" he murmured.

His wife gave him a hard look. "Brigid," she said hastily, "I think you had better get into your coat and go along at once, so you will be there before any of the guests arrive. Remember . . . you and Angelina are to stay in the cloakroom. You must be there any time anyone requires your help."

"Oh, yes, ma'am. We will."

There was a more generous display of shapely legs as she exchanged the pumps for Squis-Squis's moccasins and skipped out, shoes in hand, bundled in her shapeless overcoat. Lieutenant Carter heaved a noisy sigh.

"Cass," said Louise grimly, "if I see that lecherous smirk on your face again I shall leave the party."

"Yes, ma'am."

"Where in the world do you suppose she found that . . . that thing she's got on under her dress?"

"Isn't it one of yours?" he asked innocently.

"Oh, Cass, you're incorrigible! You know damned well I never had such a thing in my life."

"I suppose it would be gilding the lily, wouldn't it?"

He caught the fist she shook under his nose and kissed it until they both burst into laughter.

"My God!" gasped Louise, "wait till Abigail Smith sees her. She'll have a fit!"

265

"No. If she felt a fit coming on she'd go home and take a physic."

Cass's remark reflected the general opinion of the wife of the cavalry-troop commander. Mrs. Smith was a chilly woman, bedeviled by exaggerated notions of propriety.

Her husband was several years past sixty, half-crippled by a vague back ailment and frankly marking time until a vacancy on the retired list would permit him to quit active service. Many an officer with worse physical limitations was well loved by his associates, but Gideon Smith had an even more maddening deficiency. His power of decision had declined to near zero, and he approached any problem with so many suppositions, fears, and cautions that it was gone before he could solve it. The captain and his quirks were tolerated humorously by his associates, but officers and ladies walked softly around Mrs. Smith. The Carters had found but one chink in the armor of this formidable woman—her son who was a cadet at West Point. Him alone she viewed with unwavering fondness.

Louise giggled. She remembered the Smiths' welcoming call upon them, when this son become the sole topic of conversation. When they had gone, Cass had muttered darkly that he supposed Abigail Smith had hatched the boy. He could not imagine her lowering herself to achieve a child by normal means.

"You think she'll make a fuss about Brigid?" he demanded as they started for the ball.

"Probably, unless something worse distracts her."

"You aren't worried?"

"Not in the least. Brigid's a good girl. After all the hurrah we've made about this silly party, do you expect her to go without dressing up as best she can? That's all there is to it. Good Lord! Even Abigail Smith cannot make a seductress out of Brigid."

Mathilde Brenner was giving the buffet table a last-minute inspection when Brigid and Angelina arrived, so she did not see them until she looked into the cloak-room later. Brigid greeted her with a curtsy, not quite up to her usual style because her freedom of movement was limited.

"Good evening, Missus Brenner," she said breathlessly.

Mathilde swallowed hard. Looking at the two serious, pretty faces confronting her, she wondered again about the wisdom of this arrangement.

"Good evening, Brigid. My, you both look nice."

"Thank you, ma'am," they chorused together.

"Now, you know what you're to do, don't you?"

"Yes, ma'am."

"I know you'll want to watch the dancing, and when there is no one here you may peep through the door . . . but you must not wander away."

Mathilde Brenner had a dismaying picture of what would happen if these two appeared in the ballroom. No young lieutenant on the outside of a quantity of Major Suter's renowned whiskey punch should be exposed to that temptation.

She disappeared, and booted heels scuffed on the taut canvas. Brigid and Angie peeked through the curtains screening the cloakroom door at the two soldiers who had posted themselves on either side of it.

"What ever are they for?" Brigid whispered.

"I don't know," replied Angie. "They always do that. Just for show, I guess. Who is it?"

Brigid looked again and giggled. On one side was a cavalry trooper, resplendent in yellow-plumed helmet and full-dress uniform, with a gleaming saber hooked to his belt. On the other was Michael Brennan, equally elegant if not so gaudy.

"What are you tittering about, Bridey?" he asked.

"That fearful hat! I never saw you in that funny thing before." She was staring at his infantry dress shako with its stubby white pompon.

"Never you mind the hat. I'm here to see that you don't take that empty red head into the hall and distract the gentry."

"Pooh! You've naught to do with me, Michael Bren-

267

nan. All you're for is to stand straight an' keep your beady eyes off the ladies."

"Ooh, it's Michael," breathed Angie. She hooked a finger in his polished belt and tugged gently.

"Don't be tormentin' the guard, Angie," he told her. He had the old soldier's trick of speaking without change of expression or visible movement of his lips as he stood at rigid attention, and Brigid was fascinated. It was like watching a ventriloquist.

"Come out a bit," he urged, "an' give us a look."

"We dassen't," Angie whispered.

"Don't listen to him," warned Brigid. "He'll only get you in trouble."

Angie gave Michael's belt a last teasing pull and withdrew her head. After a moment Brigid followed, frowning.

"Why does everybody say we mustn't go into the hall?"

Adjusting her lustrous black hair at the mirror, Angie grinned wickedly. " 'Cause we're better-lookin' than anything they'll see out there."

The band had taken its place, with strange sounds as it tuned up—not surprising in view of its composition. A cavalry bugler with a borrowed trumpet and a drummer from the infantry company were fairly proficient but the remaining four were amateur and part-time musicians. One of them did his best with the antique and weather-ravaged piano, the violinist was noted for his repertoire of hymns, the banjo player was fairly good, but the fourth had learned his music from a lesson book purchased from a mail-order house with his unusual instrument. It was a Sarrus-o-phone, a distant relative of a bassoon advertised as well suited for the frontier because it was made of metal instead of wood. Brigid winked at Private Noonan, the banjo player, and he gave her a shy smile in response.

The guests began to arrive, and the ladies made for the cloakroom. Like Brigid, they saved their dancing shoes from the mud by wearing everything from their husbands' boots to army galoshes—the clumsy rubber and canvas footgear called snow-excluders by the Quartermaster Department. Angie and Brigid helped them out of their coats and into their shoes and they preened before the mirror, complimenting each other's gowns with calculating eyes. When the last of them was gone Angie whistled softly.

"Did you see the diamonds on the Cav'ry Beauty?"

Brigid sniffed. "I did, but she's not as elegant as Missus Carter."

General Quinn, filling his resplendent dress uniform to bursting, led off the first dance with Adelaide Suter, and he proved as keen a dancer as a hunter. He danced with every lady present in strict order of rank, and he charmed them all. Soldier he might not be, but he was courtly, entertaining, and a splendid dancer. He flattered his partners shamelessly and they loved it.

The Washington staff aide, Major Gregg, performed his duty dances then applied himself to the punch bowl. He was joined there by Lieutenant Slade, and they watched General Quinn's genial pursuit of the ladies.

"Don't be fooled by that fancy militia uniform," said Gregg. "He's a big man in Connecticut politics and a good friend of the army. He helped stop the Congress when they tried to cut our pay this year."

Slade looked impressed. Mr. Banning of Ohio had led the annual attack on army pay in the first session of the forty-fourth Congress with a comment remembered bitterly by every lieutenant drawing less than fifteen hundred dollars a year in pay. Smaller salaries, said Banning, would be better for them because they don't know the value of money. A pay cut would teach them to avoid extravagance and practice economy.

"You people are wise to make a fuss over him," Gregg continued. "We expect to see him in the Senate next year."

"I didn't know he was running for election."

"He's not. But Senator Millard's a very sick man. He'll resign and Quinn'll be appointed to the seat. He's sure to hold it when they vote on a replacement, and this trip won't hurt him a bit. Lots of militia officers in the Connecticut legislature, and they're damn proud of Quinn for roughing it with us like this."

Slade grinned to himself. Quinn's presence at Belknap suddenly made sense and he chuckled as he watched the General whirling Louise Carter in a waltz, the tasselled ends of his buff sash standing out behind him. Roughing it with the regulars, was he?

Major Gregg suddenly spied Mrs. Randell fanning her flushed face and catching her breath between dances. Abandoning the punch bowl, he begged a turn with her, and though she had just fended off an offer she accepted him graciously.

Arabella Randell was young and pretty and new to the army, and perhaps Gregg thought her too dazzled by the attention of a lofty staff major to remember that he had ranked her out of half her home. More likely he gave it no thought at all. Her smile was distracting as he led her onto the dance floor.

She was a statuesque young woman and her gown was new and daring. She danced gaily, head back to smile at her partner, and no ordinary man could ignore the splendor of Arabella's decolletage. Major Gregg was quite ordinary. He stared at Arabella until half the company was smilingly aware of his fascination. So intent was his study that he finally tangled his feet and, to the amusement of the watchers, lurched forward to embrace his bewitching partner clumsily. In her most elegant and penetrating Bostonian accent Arabella gaffed her catch.

"Oh, dear, Major Gregg! I do hope you have not hurt yourself. Should we not rest a bit and take a glass of punch?"

Gregg's face flamed. He was saved from further embarrassment by Quinn, who descended upon the couple with a jovial remark that no man deserved such beauty if he preferred talking to dancing. Gregg surrendered Arabella with frosty dignity.

Slade watched with amusement. It wasn't wise of Arabella, but he admired her for it. He sighed regretfully. He wanted to dance with Susanne Smith, but he had already had one and her card bore another reserved for him. Her mother's formidable eyes would turn cold if he danced too often with Susanne, for Abigail Smith aimed higher than a cavalry lieutenant for her daughter.

So Win Slade sipped his punch and waited for his assigned dance. John Shelby joined him and Slade made conversation. He had learned from Gregg a much better explanation for Quinn's visit than the duck-shooting theory, and it occurred to him that Shelby, on the staff of the Military Division headquarters, might cast more light on the appearance of the Gatling gun. It was not difficult to raise the subject.

"The gun? That's plain. You'll need it next summer if not before. I hope I can get in on the fight."

"You think we'll have fighting here?"

"Sure of it. Everybody at Division thinks so. You know the commission they sent to talk the Nez Percés out of the Wallowa Valley has broken up?"

"Sure, but they haven't published their report yet."

"Colonel Wood is in San Francisco writing the report now." He lowered his voice confidentially. "General McDowell sent the gun on Wood's recommendation."

Slade saw nothing unusual in that. Since Wood was Adjutant General of the Department of the Columbia, he could be expected to add a Gatling to the department's resources if he saw a chance.

"Did he tell you why?" he asked dryly.

"No need. The commission will recommend that if Chief Joseph and his Nez Percés don't leave the Wallowa they're to be driven out. The Indian Agent at Lapwai will ask 'em to leave and they won't. Then he'll ask General Howard for troops to do the job."

"And that means fighting?"

"Do you think Joseph will go without a fight?"

"I don't know. I never saw him. How many men has he?"

"Six, maybe seven hundred, if all the malcontents join him."

"That's not much."

"Too much unless General Howard reinforces the garrisons at Lapwai and Walla Walla. They've less than two hundred men between 'em."

"They still won't need us. There's plenty of troops at Fort Vancouver, and they can get upriver by steamer in a hurry."

John Shelby shook his head. "Four companies of infantry . . . maybe a hundred and twenty men? Too few and too slow. I think they'll send your troop, and that's why you got the Gatling."

Win Slade nodded and excused himself. The band leader was announcing the dance saved for him on Susanne's hop card. He found her with Cass Carter, who handed her over with a wink.

"I'll sit this one out with your mother, Susie, and see if I can't charm her into watching me instead of you."

They were standing by the door of the ladies' retiring room, and Cass nodded approbation at the appearance of the soldier guard.

"You look good, men. You can take a break, one at a time, and get yourselves something to eat. Mind that punch though."

The two soldiers beamed at him. When he had gone in search of Abigail Smith, Michael muttered to his cohort.

"I'll have first go. Won't be long."

There was no one in the buffet room except a white-jacketed soldier minding the table, and he cut Michael a thick slab from the joint of beef, offering it on a chunk of crusty bread. The meat was sadly underdone, to Michael's taste—like most soldiers he preferred it roasted dry and brown—but he chose it over the goose and venison on the table. He ate it carefully to avoid gravy spots on his white gloves, and washed it down with a cup of punch, which seemed far too mild to warrant Lieutenant Carter's warning. He had another, and as he finished it Brigid appeared at the door into the hallway.

Adelaide Suter had just told her and Angelina they

272

might visit the buffet. Brigid was not hungry but she wanted to see everything, and curiosity led her to the buffet room. Michael's reaction was characteristic. Before she could protest he swept her into his arms and they were circling to the sweet lilt of waltz music.

"Oh, Michael," she gasped, "you'll get us in trouble."

"Nah, nah! Not to worry. They're all dancin' in there."

He was good. He led firmly but he was light on his feet, and Brigid's worries were lost in pleasure. She had never thought to have a chance to dance this night.

But Michael was having trouble keeping his mind on his flying feet. Each time he completed a sweeping circle Brigid was propelled against him, and her bosom, offered up by the borrowed corset, clung momentarily to his chest. Even through his wool dress coat he could feel its warmth and gentle resilience.

"Ah, Bridey," he whispered, "ye're a lovely thing!"

"Whisht, now! Just dance and hush your tongue. Isn't the music grand?"

He whirled her around the table, her eyes closed in delight, until the soldier waiter cleared his throat noisily.

"Well, damn me!" boomed a hearty voice. "Just look what I've been missin', will you?"

It was General Quinn, seeking punch, but distracted by the red hair and alarmed green eyes peeking over Michael Brennan's arm.

"Ah, Brennan!" he laughed. "I might ha' known it."

"Beg pardon, sir. I didn't see the General come in."

"Hah! No need for pardon, man. Can't blame you watchin' that beauty instead of me."

"It's General Quinn," Michael hissed to his speechless partner. "Say somethin', for God's sake!"

"G-good evenin', yer honor," Brigid stammered, applying the only title she could think of at the moment.

"Sure an' I'm not much of a soldier, miss, but God knows I'm no judge. Private Brennan, will ye not do me the honor of introducin' me to your lady?"

Michael for once was having trouble with his tongue, and Brigid took matters into her own hands with a respectful curtsy to Quinn. She wanted no misunderstanding of this situation.

"I'm Brigid O'Donnel, sir. I work for the Carters, an' I'd ought to be in the ladies' retiring room, but Missus Suter said I could get a bite to eat, an' . . . well, the music is so grand, Michael an' me we just . . ."

She was out of breath and she watched Quinn as if he were about to eat her, but her ingenuous explanation had charmed him. Without a word, he lifted her from Michael's arms and waltzed her away to the music from the ballroom.

"Oh, sir . . ." Brigid protested helplessly. Michael disappeared silently. There was no help he could offer her now.

"Brigid O'Donnel," chuckled Quinn, "you'd not deny me a turn with a pretty girl like yourself, now would ye? If I don't tell a soul, who'll be the wiser?"

General James Quinn knew what he was doing, and he took pleasure in it. He thought army women were responsible for a deal of foolishness about rank and status, and dancing with Brigid made him feel delightfully wicked. Also they were Irish, the both of them, and he knew more about the poverty of Brigid's life than anybody on Belknap's Officers' Row. He was as courtly and charming with her as he had been with the post commander's wife, but in his pleasure he did not know how much trouble he made for her.

Lieutenant John Shelby, returning for a cup of punch perhaps beyond his need, watched this surprising scene for a long minute, then boldly asked for a dance with Brigid himself. General Quinn relinquished his partner without a thought other than that this pretty girl with her red hair and green eyes deserved a whirl in the arms of a younger man. Filling his cup at the bowl, he wandered blithely back into the ballroom.

Brigid's uniform—as intended by Mrs. Carter and Mrs. Brenner—indicated her status to Jack Shelby, but if General Quinn had danced with her he saw no reason why he should not. He knew he could not think of leading this surprising girl onto the dance floor, but that only made a stolen waltz in the buffet room more exciting.

Brigid gave the problem no thought at all. First Michael and then the general had danced with her, and Quinn had given her over to this big, handsome lieutenant without a question. He was not as good a dancer as either of them, but he held her close and kept his gray eyes on hers until she blushed with pleasure. She had all the rough and bawdy admiration from soldiers that she allowed, but this was different—exhilarating in its difference.

The music slowed and so, reluctantly, did Brigid's lieutenant. As the waltz ended he held her close and his lips brushed her forehead.

"I wish," he said, "I'd known you were here before."

The silence was broken by a hiss like that of an angry cat. Brigid prized herself out of Shelby's arms to see Mrs. Smith on Major Gregg's arm in the door.

"Oh, God above us!" she gasped.

Shelby stared openmouthed as Major Gregg drew the furious woman away.

"Don't worry," Shelby assured Brigid. "I'll handle this."

"Oh, I've got to go. I shouldn't be here."

"Are you sorry you danced with me?"

"No! I didn't mean that."

"Then don't worry. Listen . . . I want to see you again. When can I?"

"When can you what?" Brigid asked distractedly.

"See you. Talk to you. I don't even know your name. Please . . . when can I see you?"

She realized he was serious, and the idiocy of the thing overcame her. She giggled wildly.

"God preserve you, man . . . you're stark mad! But I thank you for the dance—it was lovely." On impulse, she stood on tiptoe to give him a quick, warm kiss,

275

then fled to the cloakroom. Michael scowled at her ferociously as she skipped past, but she ignored him.

Jack Shelby's notion that he could soothe Abigail Smith was a lost hope. She spread disaster as she departed the buffet room. Convincing Major Gregg that he had just witnessed a major crime, she descended upon the Carters, demanding that their maid be expelled at once.

"I don't understand," said Louise Carter. "What in the world has happened, Mrs. Smith?"

"Happened? That redheaded hussy is dancing with an officer in the buffet room. It's disgraceful and you must put a stop to it!"

The Carters peered into the hallway, wondering what to expect, and found Lieutenant Shelby at rigid attention before Major Gregg. They caught only his final words.

". . . return at once to your quarters, Mister. I will discuss this with the post commander, I assure you."

"Oh, my!" murmured Louise.

"What in the devil is going on?" demanded Cass.

"I don't know, but I'll find out," Louise assured him. "And you stay away from that major."

Shelby brushed past them, his face frozen, and—ignoring his wife's warning—Cass made for Gregg.

"Oh, damn!" muttered Louise, hastening after him. Before either officer had a chance to speak she had a hand on the arm of each of them.

"I'm famished," she announced sweetly. "Won't one of you gentlemen give me something to eat?"

Major Gregg was nearest the table, and he set about filling a plate for her. Lieutenant Shelby, on his way out, stopped at the door of the ladies' cloakroom.

"I'd like to speak to the young lady who just went in there," he told Michael who came to attention with a noisy clatter.

"Which young lady does the Lieutenant mean, sir?"

"The one who just went in, soldier! That's the one I want."

"Sir, there's two of 'em in there all the time, and others come an' go, sir."

"Oh, hell!" Shelby exploded, and he reached for the curtains. Michael took a formal step to his left, blocking the doorway.

"Sir, the lieutenant can't go in there. That's the ladies' retiring room."

"I know that, damn it! I want a word with the young lady who just went in there. You tell her, or I will."

"Beggin' the Lieutenant's pardon, sir, but he can't do that. May I suggest, sir, that the Lieutenant asks the next lady goin' in to tell her?"

Shelby's face flamed. Michael had outmaneuvered him completely. His last admonition had been delivered loudly enough to attract the attention of several couples, and with a muttered curse, Shelby gave up.

In the buffet, Major Gregg handed a laden plate to Louise Carter and hurried away. She handed it to Cass.

"You eat it. And don't you go near that man again."

In the cloakroom she bore down on Brigid. "What happened?" she demanded. "Why is Mrs. Smith so angry with you?"

"Oh, Missus Carter, I don't know! Missus Suter said I could go to the buffet, and . . ."

"Well, why didn't you tell Mrs. Smith you had permission to be there? What's this about you dancing with someone?"

"I didn't have a chance to tell her, ma'am! You see, while I was there a gentleman came in an' he just started dancin' with me an'— Oh, Missus Carter, I didn't mean to do anything wrong!"

Louise Carter's frown was forbidding, and Brigid looked appalled.

"All right, Brigid. It can't be all that serious, but that silly woman—" She broke off abruptly. "We'll straighten it out tomorrow, but I want you to go home now. I'll tell Brennan to walk you over."

"Oh, ma'am, there's no need for that! I'll go if you want, but you needn't send him."

"Yes, I want it so, Brigid. Now get your things on."

While Brigid pulled on her moccasins, Mrs. Carter whispered instructions to Michael.

"Yes, ma'am. I'll take her home and be right back, ma'am."

In the chill, waning moonlight he steered Brigid along the plank walk, his boot heels ringing in the silence. After a moment she sniffed, plaintively.

"What happened, Bridey?"

"Oh, Michael, I'm in terrible trouble!"

"And when were you not? What's that damned lieutenant got to do with it?"

"What lieutenant?"

"You know. He tried to go into the ladies' room after you."

"Oh, no!"

"Damn right, he did! What's he want of you?"

She stared at him, her eyes round and worried. "It wasn't my fault! I swear it wasn't."

"What, damn it? What happened?"

"Nothing! I don't even know who he is. Don't look at me like that! Damn it, you started it all!" She jerked her arm out of his grasp and began to cry. "Oh, sweet Saint Anne, what'll I do now? That Missus Smith is gonna get me for sure!"

Michael stopped and pulled her into his arms and she wept against his chest.

"Don't cry, Bridey. It'll be all right. Here." He tugged a handkerchief from his sleeve and mopped her face with it.

"It's like I told you, Brigid, you need a man. You're wantin' somebody to take care of you so's you won't be always gettin' into trouble."

"God knows," she sobbed, "I need help, but it's men that make me all my trouble. You . . ." She pushed him away. "You made me dance with you! You gave that old man the idea!"

"I'm not sorry I danced with you, Bridey, but I wish to God that general hadn't seen us. Did Missus Smith see you dancin' with him?"

278

"No!" she wailed. "He let that lieutenant have me, an' she came in an' saw us."

"Oh, damn! Whyn't you tell him no, you idiot?"

"No? Jesus, Mary, an' Joseph, what's the difference? If it's all right to dance with that old man, what's wrong with the lieutenant? Will you tell me that?"

"If you don't know, you'll not learn from me! Where's your brains, girl?"

"Gone! I've none left me, or I'd never have taken a job with these crazy people! This army is a madhouse run by the loonies, an' I wish I'd never heard of it!"

She pulled away from him and ran for the Carters' door, but he caught her before she could pound on it.

"Brigid, listen to me!"

"Get away!" she panted. "Get away from me or I'll yell for the sentry. I know that much about your damned army . . . If I yell he'll come runnin' an' I'll swear you laid hands on me. Leave me be, damn it!"

Mah Kim opened the door to peer at them in astonishment, and Brigid slipped past him before Michael could stop her. He shook his head and sighed, and after a moment Mah Kim closed the door softly.

9

After General Quinn's party there was a day of reckoning at Camp Belknap. Three of the five offenders against army custom were brought to the bar.

Major Gregg had explained at length to Major Suter why he ordered Lieutenant Shelby to leave the party, and he seemed to expect something to be done about it. With no great enthusiasm, Suter summoned Shelby to his office.

"I apologize, sir," said Shelby sincerely. "I went into the buffet and found General Quinn dancing with a very attractive young woman. On the spur of the moment I asked if I might have a dance. Of course I know now who she is, and I know it was improper of me."

Major Suter winced. "General Quinn was dancing with her?"

"Yes, sir."

"Well . . ." Suter scrubbed his chin reflectively with his knuckles. Young lieutenants were not necessarily excusable for copying the follies of generals, but this did make a difference. His wife had told him she gave the girl permission to leave the cloakroom, so Quinn was the real culprit. Obviously no one was going to take him to task for dancing with the Carters' maid. Damn General Quinn, he thought bitterly. And damn

280

Gregg, too. He was not going to disrupt his little garrison just to placate that obnoxious major.

"Very well, mister," he told Shelby. "I accept your apology, and that ends the matter as far as I am concerned. I suggest you be more careful in future, though."

Adelaide Suter had been instructed to deal with young Mrs. Randell, and she found an opportunity while the ladies were dismantling the buffet room and reclaiming their treasures. She took Arabella aside for a quiet talk.

"You're new to this life, my dear," she said mildly, "but you must know it is unwise to treat a senior officer in such fashion."

Arabella Randell was not evasive. "I am sorry, Mrs. Suter. Not," she added defiantly, "for what I said to that odious man, but if I've made any trouble for you."

"You've made no trouble for me, child, but that wretched major is on the staff in Washington and those people have the memories of elephants. Has it not occurred to you he might do your husband a great disservice? A bad word in Washington can hurt a young officer terribly."

"Oh, no! He wouldn't!"

"But, my dear, he might! You must learn that rank has its privileges. I know how unpleasant it is to be put out of your house by someone senior to you. God knows, it has happened to us often enough—but it is the custom. And it is very unwise to retaliate."

"But he can't! He mustn't hurt Jack just because of what I did. Can I not apologize to him? Would that help?"

"Absolutely not! It would just rub it in. The worst thing you can do is try to apologize to him. He is a very unpleasant man." She put her hand on the younger woman's and her eyes twinkled. "It was very foolish, my dear . . . but you did it very well. Now, just don't ever do it again."

Brigid's was the worst session. When Mrs. Carter returned with her basket of punch cups, she put them on the kitchen table with a grim face. Abigail Smith had explained in great detail her complaint against the Carters' maid.

"Brigid," she said, "I wish to speak to you. In the hall, if you please."

Brigid followed her apprehensively out of Mah Kim's hearing into the chilly hall.

"I want to know exactly what happened last night. Mrs. Smith says she found you dancing with Mr. Shelby. Is that correct?"

Brigid swallowed convulsively. "Ma'am, I did dance with the young man, but—"

"But I told you not to leave the cloakroom!"

"Oh, Missus Carter . . . I couldn't help it! Truly I couldn't. Missus Suter said I could go to the supper room, and there was no one there except the soldier, and then that nice man with the pretty uniform came in and—"

"What man?"

"The one with the big gold sash an' all the things on his coat."

"General Quinn?" Louise Carter looked astonished.

"Yes, ma'am . . . that's the one. He's Irish just like me. He didn't even ask me. He just started to dance with me." Brigid twisted her hands in her apron and watched her employer helplessly. "What could I do?" she asked plaintively. "I couldn't tell him to stop, could I?"

"For goodness' sake, why not?"

"Well . . . you said he's a general. You can't tell a general to stop, can you?"

Louise Carter had a terrible impulse to laugh, but she mastered it. "And Mr. Shelby? How did he get into this?"

"Ma'am, he just walked in whilst I an' the general were dancin', an' he made a little bow an' asked could he dance with me, an' the general let him do it." This came out in a breathless rush and Louise Carter looked puzzled.

"But, Brigid, why didn't you—"

282

"Oh, Missus Carter, I know it was wrong now. Michael told me when he walked me home. But I didn't know what to do. I just thought . . ."

"What did you think?"

Brigid dropped her eyes. "I thought if it was all right dancin' with the general t'would be no harm with the young man—Mr. Shelby."

"Oh, Brigid!"

"I'm so sorry! I swear I didn't mean to do wrong. I know I'm not supposed to dance with officers, but what could I do?" Her green eyes filled with tears and she sniffed loudly. "An' now . . ." she wailed, "that Missus Smith is goin' to make trouble for you too, isn't she?"

Louise Carter's eyes snapped. "I am not concerned about that. I can see it was not entirely your fault, but Brigid, you . . ." She stopped. She was trying to think of a suitable way to point out that Brigid had attracted unwanted attention to herself by what she wore to the party. But Brigid had worn the dress prescribed, and there was no way to be specific without being indelicate. Louise sighed and gave up.

"Well . . . this has been very unpleasant, but I do not think you meant any harm. I expect you have learned a lesson and will be more cautious another time."

"Y-yes, ma'am. I surely will." Instead of relief, this mild reprimand provoked a flood of tears, and Louise Carter was distressed by them.

"Come now, Brigid. We shall say no more about it. Dry your eyes and let us put this behind us."

Brigid nodded her head, scrubbing her eyes with her apron. "I'll not make that mistake again, ma'am," she murmured. "I swear I won't."

Mah Kim put a steaming pot of tea beside her mug on the kitchen table and made comforting noises. There was no doubt whose side he was on. Brigid gave him a wan smile and sniffed into her mug.

I don't care about that damned old Missus Smith, she thought defiantly. I don't see why it's any skin off her backsides if I have a dance at their party. I had fun dancing with that general. She brightened up at the thought. And with Mister Shelby, too. She gave Mah Kim a real smile, remembering how the big, good-looking lieutenant had stared at her and held her close. It had been more exciting dancing with him than with General Quinn or Michael. Michael! She put down her mug with a bang.

My God, she thought, what if somebody says something to that general about dancing with me and he tells I was dancing with Michael first? Oh, Mary, Mother, won't they skin us both alive!

There was only one small bright spot. She hadn't told on Michael, and if no one found out he started the whole thing by dancing with her, she would really have something to hold over his head now. She beamed at Mah Kim and poured herself more tea.

"Did you open a can of milk today?" she asked him smugly.

10

Lieutenant Shelby's prediction of the results of the meeting between Chief Joseph and the government commission was not just punchbowl talk. It was quite accurate, but by the time General Quinn and his escort departed Belknap all roads to the north were snow-blocked and official confirmation was delayed.

The Civil and Military Commission to Washington Territory and the Northwest was formed to negotiate with the so-called Non-Treaty Nez Percés, a group that refused to accept the terms of a treaty forced on their people in 1863 by the United States government. The Nez Percés had been assigned in 1855 a large reservation at the junction of Oregon, Washington, and Idaho, but discovery of gold within it in 1863 led to its drastic reduction in size. A majority of the Nez Percés moved onto the shrunken reservation in Idaho, but some clung to their ancestral homes nearby.

Since no gold appeared in these areas, the Indians were allowed to remain, but by 1876 a rising tide of white settlers coveted them for farming land. The lush valleys leading into the Snake River near its confluence with the Salmon were occupied by small bands of Nez Percés who had never relinquished them, and despite its weighty title, the commission seemed concerned only with these lands. Mr. Jerome, the chairman, made this clear when he met Chief Joseph and his adherents in November of 1876 in the church of the Christian Nez Percés on the Lapwai reservation.

"Thirteen years ago," said Jerome, "the Nez Percés sold all their lands except those set aside for them here. Why do you not accept that treaty?"

Chief Joseph explained patiently. The Indians who signed the treaty lived on the land reserved for them. They had no right to sell the lands of Nez Percés who lived elsewhere.

"Not so," said Mr. Jerome. "Among white people, the majority rules, and the rest must do as they decide. It is the same for Indians."

Joseph disagreed. Those Indians who adopted the white man's ways and his God might have to do as the white man ordered, but there were other Nez Percés who had their own ways and religion. The First Man, said Joseph, left no marks or lines on the earth to indicate which parts belonged to one people or another. He put the Nez Percés where He wanted them and they could not disobey Him.

Jerome dismissed this as pagan. Dreamers, he called the Nez Percé religious leaders—radicals who preached sedition against the white man's government. Their philosophy about a First Man who left no lines on the earth was meaningless. Nez Percé chiefs had sold their land, and lines had been drawn. Joseph and his people must live within them.

With that edict the commission withdrew, recommending to Washington that if the Non-Treaty Nez Percés would not peaceably abandon their homes and go upon the Lapwai reservation, they should be placed by force upon it.

Alarmed, the Indians left the church to discuss this order in a more comfortable place. Just as Camp Belknap was settling into snowbound isolation for Christmas, they gathered at a traditional and near sacred place of assembly—Tahpahlewam, or the Camas Meadows, by the Salmon just below its juncture with the Snake River. The principal leaders present

286

were Chiefs Joseph, White Bird, Looking Glass, and Too-hool-hool-sote; joined by a sub-chief of the Palouse Indian band named Hush-hush-cute, or Naked Head. Too-hool-hool-sote was a noted orator and first to address the gathering. He began—as was his custom—at the beginning.

"From before the time of my father's father and his father's father we have known that the white man would come here. The prophet Swopscha of the people of the Wana Pums foretold their coming. He said a white-skinned people would appear one day bringing strange customs and wonderful things. Some would be good for the Indian, but others would bring war and bloodshed and sickness. In the end, said the great prophet, the bones of the Nez Percés will strew the ground like driftwood along the shores of the great river."

There was a murmur of agreement. The chiefs and old men and as many of the young warriors as could crowd into the smoky lodge nodded recognition of this ancient prophecy.

"The white man came," continued Too-hool-hool-sote, "guided by an Indian woman they had stolen beyond the mountains toward the rising sun. They were greeted with kindness and respect because good things had been told about them by one of our own people, the woman Watkuese—She Who Returned from a Faraway Land."

Again his audience nodded and murmured. They knew that story by heart, but Too-hool-hool-sote was not deterred by agreement.

"Watkuese was stolen from a Nez Percé camp in the buffalo country by the Iskoikenic—the scheming Blackleg Indians—who sold her to a people living nearer the sunrise, who sold her to the white men. She lived with them many snows before she ran away and returned to her own people. She told that they had been good to her. They did not treat her as a slave, and when the first white men came here she told the grcat Chief Hohots Ilppilp, 'Do them no hurt. These are the people who were good to me.' "

He paused to scowl at the young men in the back of the lodge. "Never forget," he warned them, "that the Blackleg Indians are a bad people. When they are around you have to be careful of your horses and your women."

There were grins and nudges among the young warriors at this familiar advice, but the chiefs looked glum. They had not gathered to talk about horses and women. Too-hool-hool-sote noted their displeasure.

"The Nez Percés listened to the words of Watkuese, but the white men have not been good to us. The blood of our people is on their hands. They have stolen our cattle and our horses." He paused until there was total silence in the lodge.

"My brothers, we have kept the peace, but now the white men want to steal our homes, too. I am against this!"

There was an expectant rustle in the audience. Everyone was against this. What they wanted to know was how Too-hool-hool-sote would stop it. But he was too clever an orator to tell everything at once. He wanted to be called back again to explain his feelings, so he hunched his shoulders and stared at the chiefs before him.

"Who speaks now?" he demanded truculently.

A younger chief arose, Ippakness Wayhayken, whose name meant Looking Glass Around Neck, but who was called simply Looking Glass by the white men. His band, which numbered perhaps thirty fighting men, lived in a single village called Alpowai on the Clearwater River by the reservation.

"I too am against this, but what can we do?" He looked around the lodge. "We are only a few Indians. If we do not obey, the white general with one arm will bring soldiers to make us do what he wants."

There was a growl from the young men, and Looking Glass nodded. "You are thinking of the horse-soldiers in the fort on the reservation. They are no match

288

for Nez Percé fighters, but when they have been tricked and beaten there will be foot soldiers who come slowly but carry the long rifles. There will be guns on wheels—big ones and the little one that shoots faster than a man can count. I think we must talk with the one-arm general. Maybe he will listen when we talk as one warrior to another."

His words were greeted by a groan of disbelief, and Hush-hush-cute won permission to speak. He was only a sub-chief, and his little band lived far away on the Snake River in Washington Territory, but he had been a notable fighter and as an orator he was second only to Too-hool-hool-sote. He began with a sly dig at Looking Glass.

"Ippakness Wayhayken wants us to do what the white men say we must do. He and his people live close to the reservation. So close that if all the rest of us do what is ordered, maybe the white men will let him stay where he is."

It was a rude remark and everyone overlooked it, but there were a few grins. Hush-hush-cute then said he was opposed to giving up his home and very much opposed to moving onto Lapwai reservation. Larger bands would take all the good land and there would be none left for his few people. Maybe, he said, if we have a talk with the one-arm general he will let us move to the Umatilla reservation below Walla Walla on the other side of the Blue Mountains. It was not a new suggestion. It had many supporters because the Nez Percés and the Umatillas had intermarried for years and their ties were strong. Clearly there were many in the lodge who approved the idea, and Hush-hush-cute sat down, pleased with himself.

The council went on, and in their lodges the women waited. They learned at night what had happened, because their men came home. It was too cold and there was too much snow for the usual festivities accompanying a council; the men could not race their horses or make pageants of old battles and triumphs. There was so much snow that even the white men who had built trading stores along the river did not climb the bluffs to barter whiskey for buffalo robes. The chiefs would not let the young men go down to the stores, so it was a very sober council. It closed on a peaceful note, too. The fighting strength of all five bands was hardly two hundred warriors, and the war party among them was outweighed.

Chief Joseph, whose band was the largest, was for peace and more talk, and he was supported by Peopeo Kiskiok Hihih, whose name meant White Goose or Swan but who was known to the whites as White Bird. His was the second largest band, and when he supported Joseph the rest joined him. It was decided that in the spring, Ollicut, Joseph's handsome younger brother, would ask Mr. Monteith, the Nez Percé Indian Agent, to arrange a talk for them with General Howard. They would promise to move to one of the reservations—Lapwai or Umatilla—in exchange for the right to hunt and fish at will on their own lands.

This would be a satisfactory solution. They were rovers at heart, and no one would mind spending a part of the year with relatives on the reservation if they could visit their old haunts when they wanted to. Only Too-hool-hool-sote was glumly doubtful. As he had expected, he was called up once more to say what was in his heart.

"Who is it who lives above?" he asked gravely. "Is it First Man or second man? You are second man. I am second man. We are but children. He who lives above set me down where the rivers flow and the mountains stand. I must not make him angry by going somewhere else. You think you can trick the white men, my brothers, but I do not think you will. I have no willing mind to listen to anyone telling me I must move to a different place from that which was given me by First Man."

11

The soldiers' Christmas ball at Camp Belknap lacked the elegance of the officers' party for General Quinn, but it was the traditional high event of the year. Ingenuity and weeks of planning made up for scanty funds to support it.

Half the unused cavalry barracks was renovated for dancing and entertainment, and the messroom behind the barracks was readied for a late supper. Company funds were lavished on the soldiers' Christmas Day dinner, but poker and crap games following the November payday had been levied to buy a few refinements for the party supper. Against the weather, barracks and messroom were connected by a tunnel of cedar tips woven onto a pole frame, and the snow was shoveled out to make a path which was planked to keep guests out of the mud.

Decorations were much the same as those used by the officers, but with an addition that indicated the nature of the party. Private Keesmaier, whose skill at drawing maps earned him a permanent job on the adjutant's staff, produced cartoons for the walls. Lithographed portraits of President Grant and General Sherman took the place of honor over the fireplace, but other walls bore Keesmaier's neatly framed caricatures of all the sergeants of Camp Belknap. His wit was as

291

keen as his draftsmanship, and not a few sergeants needed a genial holiday mood to face their wicked likenesses. Satiric portraits of officers were inadvisable, but with an eye on his job in post headquarters, Keesmaier had drawn one of the post commander. It was a flattering sketch of Major Suter with a full beard, in a Major General's uniform, conspicuously dated "1886."

One end of the big barrackroom was screened off by a curtain made of army blankets pinned together and strung on a wire. This would provide a stage for tableaux and skits.

In deference to the younger guests, whose early attendance was traditional, the party began promptly at seven. A big Christmas tree, decorated with paper chains and strings of berries and popcorn, filled a corner of the room. Major Suter agonized about fire in the crowded room, so the candles were only lit for a brief time when everyone had arrived. Beneath the tree was a mound of gifts—one for every child on the post old enough to make his or her way unaided to the tree. Corporal Brody, the cavalry farrier, was big enough to serve as Santa Claus unaided, but in a padded red suit with cotton-wool trim and beard he was monumental. As soon as everyone on post except the guard had arrived, he emerged from behind the curtain with a chorus of "Ho-ho"s that set the children shouting in delight.

The gifts were small, but they represented a lot of work and forethought, and no one thought them insignificant. For each child there was an apple and an orange, brought all the way from California by rail and wagon, a little bag of hard candies, and a special surprise provided by Lieutenant Slade.

He had been in Salt Lake City for a few days the previous summer, and had discovered in a dry-goods emporium a quantity of ancient, shopworn birthday-party "crackers." After some hard bargaining, he bought the lot from his own pocket. They were little paper tubes with ruffled ends and a dangling ribbon which, when pulled, was supposed to produce a minute
292

pop inside the tube and then a tiny, pot-metal favor attached to its end.

Not one delivered the snap it was supposed to—age had defused them—but that made little difference to the children. Each came forward to receive his gifts when Brody called his name, and being old enough to go alone for your gift for the first time was a never-to-be-forgotten event.

The Carters were escorted to the party by Michael Brennan, stiff and impressive in his dress uniform. One of the traditions of this annual affair was that officers and their families received a "surprise" invitation delivered by a soldier to their homes. That he found the family in its best dress impatiently awaiting him was gravely ignored by the bearer of the invitation, who led his guests to the festive barracks.

Brigid walked with Michael, subdued and unusually deferential despite her excitement—and anticipation of the effect of the first appearance of her Wanamaker silk dress. There had been no question about her donning it for this occasion. Mrs. Carter nodded smiling approval of its splendor, and Amanda voiced consensus of Carter opinion in a hushed whisper.

"Oh, Brigid . . . you're bee-yoo-tiful!"

Her view was obviously shared by the garrison when Brigid emerged from the cloakroom at the party, candlelight shimmering on her red hair and in the ample folds of her skirt. She rustled back to Michael, who put a gilt edge on her triumph when he stared open-mouthed and then breathed softly, "Glory be to God, Bridey!"

When all the gifts had been distributed, there was a special tableau just for the children. The blanket curtain was drawn back to reveal Joseph looking fondly at Mary, who was peering into a cradle made of a ration box surrounded by trusses of straw. The Three Kings, their boots showing beneath too-short robes of burlap, marched in to present gifts with solemn speeches of admiration, and it was impressive despite Angie Couza's hissed prompting of Balthazar, who forgot his lines.

293

The choice of Angie to play the part of the Virgin Mother entertained the soldier audience mightily, but under the eyes of their sergeants they managed a respectful silence, until the curtain was drawn on this nostalgic scene to thunderous applause.

After this the children were packed off home in charge of older brothers and sisters, all except those who were too small to share in the festivities or be left at home. They were already settled in one of the small rooms formerly occupied by unmarried sergeants. Blankets and quilts had been spread from wall to wall there, with a dozen infants nested in them—some asleep and oblivious of noise, a few wide-awake and eying visitors with bright, curious eyes.

"Like a shoebox full of squirrels!" said Louise Carter, looking into this impromptu nursery.

The band—the same that had played for General Quinn—struck up a rousing tune and the senior non-commissioned officer, Ordnance Sergeant Timothy O'Hara, led out Mrs. Suter for the grand march. Major Suter partnered O'Hara's monumental wife, Rose, and with a fine eye for subtle distinctions in rank the remaining officers and sergeants paired off with each other's wives for the dance.

There followed a scramble among bachelors for the younger women of Belknap, and to Michael's visible distress he was outmaneuvered by Lieutenant MacKeever, who captured Brigid. Ben MacKeever was a popular officer though, and as he whirled his pretty girl along the rank of envious soldiers he winked triumphantly and won himself a grin of approbation.

After the grand march the officers and their ladies braved the chill of the passageway to the decorated messroom to admire the delicacies prepared for supper, which would be served later. Samples were pressed on them, and Cass Carter ate a large helping of potato salad despite his wife's stricken look.

"What's the matter, Weezie?" he whispered as they made their way back to the ballroom for their coats. "You know they like you to try everything."

Louise shivered. "Oh, Cass, it's not that. I just remembered that potato salad was George Custer's favorite dish. They always made it just for him in the Seventh."

"Good Lord, woman! What a thought! Come on, the Brenners have asked us for Christmas punch. If you're going to think about things like that, you need a drink."

They made their farewells with praise for the beaming hosts and departed with the other officers and their wives. Brigid was puzzled by this early departure until she watched the skits and tableaux that followed. Soldiers in comic approximations of costume parodied their sergeants and officers so wickedly their audience roared with laughter. These sly presentations alternated with songs and dancing as the party, freed of restraint, grew merrier.

She missed not a dance—indeed she needed help to keep her suitors in order because she granted every request happily and there were simply not enough dances to go around. Private Noonan escaped from the band to beg a dance with her, and even the disgraced Mario managed two turns around the hall with her before Michael intercepted them at a break in the music.

"You needn't have done that," she murmured. "He was minding his manners perfectly."

"I was afraid he'd get excited," Michael replied. "And God knows he couldn't stand another crack on the head with your skillet."

Brigid giggled, and clung tight as the band leader spurred on the dancers with a loud chant: "Oh, swing those girls, those pretty little girls . . . those girls you left behind you!" Michael whirled her off her feet in a breathless swing as the music crashed to an end.

"Let me rest a minute," she begged, panting. "I've no breath left in me."

Benches were provided along the walls for the weary—no woman in that room missed a dance for any other reason—and Michael led Brigid to a place beside Molly Magruder, wife of K Company's first sergeant. When she was seated he brought her a cup of punch—a heavy, handleless china mug that required both her hands to hold it. The punch was uninspired—lemon powder dissolved in water with sugar and nutmeg grated into it—but it was cool, and Brigid drank thirstily.

"Can I not bring you a cup, Missus Magruder?" he asked Molly.

"You can that, Brennan, but it wants some help. When you've drawn it, do me the goodness to step behind that curtain and ask Sergeant Magruder, for the love of God, to put a little in it for me."

Michael grinned and nodded. The senior sergeants, exercising their special status, had withdrawn behind the curtain to indulge themselves in something a little more serious than the punch. He took Brigid's mug from her, too.

"Maybe the First Sergeant will do the same for yours, Bridey."

Molly Magruder was probably between thirty-five and forty, but she looked ten years older. Hard work had worn away all but the traces of what must have once been a striking black-Irish beauty. Her hair, piled in a loosening coil, was sleek and lustrous though the black was liberally streaked with gray. Heavy brows over wide cheek bones accentuated a length of lean jaw. Her mouth was wide and thin-lipped, but when she smiled and her black eyes sparkled, the ghost of an impish charm showed itself. Her ancient dress hung slack on her lanky figure, giving her a scarecrow look, but her silent scrutiny was making Brigid nervous.

To her surprise, Molly nodded approvingly. "A Cork man is a limb of the devil, but by God they've an eye for a pretty girl. Are you fond of Michael Brennan, Brigid?"

"No more than any other," Brigid replied simply.

"Oh? He's more than a little fond of you, I'm thinking. Has he asked you to wed him yet?"

Brigid looked startled. "He's got no reason to think I'd have him, Missus Magruder."

"Not even when your time with the Carters is out?"

That startled Brigid even more, and she looked at the older woman in surprise. Molly chuckled.

"Sure and Sergeant Magruder has told me of your promise to the Lieutenant's good lady. I like that. You're a good girl, givin' an' keepin' your word as you have, but sure there's an end to it one day, is there not?"

"Oh, yes. But I tell you truly, Missus Magruder, when my time here is done I've a mind for something more than Michael Brennan or another like him."

"And what would that be?"

"I want to go back to a city . . . San Francisco, maybe. They say it's a grand town."

"All on your own, with no man to keep you safe?"

"Safe!" Brigid laughed. "God knows Michael Brennan's no lad to keep a girl safe."

"Oh, aye! I'll warrant that, till he's stood before the priest with you right and proper."

"I don't know," Brigid said. "There's precious little a soldier has to give a girl beside himself—and a cruel, hard life."

"Ah, it's hard enough, God knows," Molly sighed, "but there's worse."

"Oh?"

"Come on, girl! Ye're not that innocent . . . or did Missus Carter take you straight from your ma's care?"

"I've no family that I know of. I was raised by the good Sisters in Boston and I've made my way without a man this far. I'll look a bit more before I take me one."

"Well, you've the looks and spirit to go that way, but it's a rocky road, it is. And San Francisco's a wicked big town."

Brigid smiled placatingly. "Maybe I've not had the luck to meet a man as charmin' as your sergeant, Missus Magruder."

Molly's laugh was a joyous bark. "Charmin' is it? Saints above us, he'd not know the meanin' of the word. He's a good man, but I'd never call him charmin'.""

"How did you come to meet him, Missus Magruder, if I may ask?"

"Sure and you may. I've no shame for that story. I came to Tennessee at the end of the war with a wild Mick in a crazy regiment of drafted men from New York. The scrapin' of the barrel they were—so bad the army took their flag away and scattered 'em far and wide . . . leavin' Mary Keenan in Chattanooga with no Mick, no money, and no place to go."

"Couldn't you go back home?"

"Hah! My da would have whipped the hide from my back if I'd shown my face to him again. I was in trouble for sure, and that good man, Patrick Magruder, put out his hand to me." She chuckled softly. "To look at the little bantam you'd never think he had a tiger's heart, would you now?"

"He looks like he can take care of himself, surely," Brigid answered cautiously.

"Never you doubt it! I was bedivilled one night by a big, black-hearted sod of a horse-soldier and Pat Magruder laid him out like a corpse. Sergeant-major in a Connecticut regiment he was then. He took me with him to Batten Rooge, and when they mustered his regiment out he signed on in this one and I went with him."

She paused to eye the blanket curtain with a scowl. "What in the devil has become of your Brennan?"

"Shall I ask someone to fetch him?"

"Nah, nah! I've not finished my story yet." She was silent a moment; then she chuckled. "Cap'n Short was company commander then—Cap'n Luther Short. That was in sixty-six. He wanted Pat in his company bad, but he said I couldn't stay. That made Pat so mad he married me an' told Cap'n Short we was wed an' he could have both of us or none of us. Holy Mother, how that man Short could swear! He could make the leaves turn brown an' fall off a tree, an' he blistered my Pat

298

somethin' awful. But he had to have him, so he took us both an' we've been in K Company ever since."

Brigid thought of the dreary succession of God-forgotten little posts that must have meant, and shuddered. Molly Magruder did not notice.

"It's Pat Magruder's company now—and mine too. He's worked hard for his place and I've worked hard for him. One day he'll be Sergeant-major of this regiment, and then we'll have us a house all to ourselves, just like O'Hara and Couza."

She gave Brigid a fierce, proud look. "He's a good man, Pat Magruder. I was naught but a tramp when he took me, but never a word of that have I heard from his mouth since. Sure an' with him his company comes first, but that's no bad thing for me. I'm as proud of the company as he is."

Her intensity startled Brigid. It was the first time any of these women had said such things to her. They seemed a hard-eyed, workworn group of drudges with no thought beyond their washboards, their cramped room in a leaky barracks, and their endless, bickering gossip about each other. Brigid tried to find something to say, but Molly was not finished.

"It's a hard life, right enough. None will tell you different. You're wantin' somethin' better, you say, an' I hope you find it, but don't put us down, lass. You're thinking we do it just for bad rations and a roof with a hole in it?"

Brigid blushed, dismayed by the accuracy of that question. "Oh, Missus Magruder, I never . . ."

Molly nudged her to silence. "Whisht, now! Here's Michael Brennan back at last. Man," she told him in mock surprise, "I thought they'd done you in back there."

Michael's face was red, but he delivered two brimming cups without spilling a drop. "The First Sergeant's not a man to be hurried, Missus Magruder," he explained gravely.

"Dear God, and I know that well," she replied, tasting her punch. "Ah! That's more like it."

Brigid sipped hers cautiously and gasped. The insipid lemon drink had been laced with raw whiskey that gripped her throat and made her eyes water.

"God save us!" she croaked. "What did you put in it?"

Michael and Molly both laughed. "Come dance with me then," he urged. "That'll save you."

Brigid was silent, grateful for a waltz instead of the more demanding square dances favored by the soldiers, and Michael looked down at her, smiling.

"What did she say to make you so quiet, Bridey?"

"That all soldiers are devils an' you're the worst," she sniffed. "Whisht now, an' dance." But she made up for her sharp words by resting her flushed face against his chest for a moment, and he beamed triumphantly.

To her surprise, at the next break First Sergeant Magruder asked for a dance. Sergeants Couza and O'Hara had danced with her—stately excursions befitting their age and rank—and she expected more of the same, with perhaps some unpleasant questions if Molly had put him up to this. But the band launched into a riotous polka, and it quickly became clear that Pat Magruder had not come to ask questions. Around and around he whirled her as the music picked up speed, and Brigid, minding her flying feet, knew she was in the arms of a famous dancer. So did the others. By the time the music crashed to an end they were alone on the floor, the rest drawn back to give them room and cheer them on.

Magruder acknowledged his audience with a casual wave and made Brigid a jerky little bow before he led her, gasping for breath, back to Michael and Molly.

"I swear," he said gravely, "I never thought to see your like at the polka, Molly, but Miss O'Donnel's near the mark." With another jerky bow he handed her over to Michael. "T'was a pleasure, miss, and I thank you for a grand dance."

Brigid watched him lead his Molly toward the blanket curtain and then looked up at Michael.

"Does that mean I got a good grade?" she gasped.

He laughed and squeezed her hand, tugging her onto the floor. There were countless more dances, and Brigid lost all track of time in the excitement of pursuit by so many eager men. There were good dancers and terrible ones, but none were unmannerly. To be sure, they whispered fervent compliments in her ear, and some held her too close, but that was more often clumsiness than effrontery. She noticed a few soldiers who had found a bit too much of something more than punch, but if they grew noisy they disappeared between a pair of more sober comrades.

In deference to the season, there was naturally a clump of mistletoe on every chandelier, and a girl was likely to be kissed a couple of times in every circuit of the room. Brigid learned to manage this. A few men stole a kiss on her lips unexpectedly, but most were more circumspect. Maneuvering her obviously under a bunch of the magic berries, her partner would clear his throat, looking down at her to make sure she was aware of her vulnerability. It was easy then to lift her cheek and reward him for his kiss with a little gasp and demurely lowered eyes. They loved it, and Brigid shared their pleasure.

But eventually she noticed some of the older couples leaving and demanded of Michael what time it was. He looked stricken.

"You're never thinkin' of goin' home?"

"I doubt I can dance another step, Michael. Tell me what time it is, please."

Reluctantly he showed her his watch and she gasped. "Dear God, it's after four o'clock! Oh, I've got to go!"

"Why? We can rest a bit if you want."

"No! The children will be up at dawn, and I can't lie snoring in bed. Come on, Michael, please . . . take me home now."

The air outside was so cold it hurt to breathe, but he walked her slowly, and by the time they turned the corner by the adjutant's office, his arm was around her waist. Bundled in her great sheepskin coat, it was hard

301

to tell where her waist was, but he hugged her tight and slowed his pace even more.

"Bridey," he said, "I'd not like to think I need a bit of mistletoe to get a kiss from my girl."

She sniffed. "You surely found every bunch when you danced with Angie Couza."

"Angie helped put those things up. She knew where every blessed one was hung."

"Ah, poor Michael . . ." she giggled. "Chased by all the girls."

"Not all." He turned her to him and tipped up her face to kiss her lips long and warmly. She shut her eyes, and her response startled them both. "Merry Christmas, Bridey," he whispered.

"Oh, Michael! Thank you." He had wrapped his cape about her, holding her close against him, and in that moment she felt an alarming fondness for him. Slipping her arms around his waist under his coat, she sniffled happily.

"What's the matter?"

"Nothing. I'm just happy. It's the best Christmas I ever had . . . not like all those lonesome ones."

"You need a man, Bridey . . . a man to keep you safe an' see you're never lonesome again."

He rested his chin on her head and drew a deep breath. She was so little and so defenseless, it was hard to believe she had ever shrieked and shook her fist in rage at him.

"Brigid?"

"Yes?" Her voice was muffled against his chest.

"Brigid, will you marry me?"

She went stiff in his arms. "What did you say?"

"I said, will you marry me?"

"Oh, Michael . . ." She seemed to be laughing and crying at the same time. Her mittened fingers gripped his ears and pulled his head down to kiss him again.

"God love you, Michael Brennan," she whispered. "You're a devil, but you can be a sweet man when you've a mind to."

Their mingled breath made a moist cloud in the

shelter of his cape, but he could see the tears shining in
her eyes. Her hands pushed gently against his chest.

"Well, damn it, Bridey . . . will you have me?"

"Don't be rough now! Mind your tongue this night."

"I don't want a lecture! I asked would you have
me."

"I know you did, Michael. I'm tryin' to think what
to say."

"You mean you'll not, then?"

"Oh, Mike . . . I guess I'm tryin' to say I just don't
want to be a spike an' live on Suds Row in this lost
place. They're good women, those soldiers' wives, but I
don't want that. Can't you understand?"

He growled something unintelligible and she gave
him a little shake. "Don't be mad, please. God knows,
I'm proud you'd say those kind words to a girl like me,
but . . ." She shook her head. "It's just that I'll not be
a soldier's wife."

His hands pulled her roughly closer and his mouth
came down on hers, hard and hurting and hungry. She
gave him back his kiss for a brief moment then fought
free.

"Will you be a soldier's woman, then, Bridey
O'Donnel?" he demanded harshly.

She twisted away from him, laughing. "In the snow
an' all? God save us, was there ever a man such a fool
as to want to make love in this? They'd find us in the
mornin' frozen in a terrible indecent lump!"

"There's your house! The Carters are still at Brenners'—look at the lights!"

"With that crazy pagan Mah Kim waitin' for me an'
two innocent kids listenin' for reindeers on the roof?
God, Brennan, you are daft!"

"Ah, hell, Bridey!"

"Don't swear like that an' spoil a grand evenin' now.
Come on an' walk me home like a nice man."

"I'm not nice, damn it! I want you, Bridey . . . any
way you'll have me."

She tucked her hand in his arm and tugged him
along the walk, muttering darkly to himself, and in the

veranda of the Carters' house she gave him another long kiss.

"Don't sulk now," she told him. "I oughtn't, but so help me, I'm fond of you, Michael Brennan. Ask me again when you've got yourself out of this damned army and found a decent job that'll keep me in great style."

He swore explosively and grabbed for her, but she slipped the latch and was inside the door before he could catch her.

"Merry Christmas," she whispered as she shut the door.

12

Not long after the country went to the polls in November to elect a new President, the army grapevine began to report unusual troop movements in the East. Even rumors reached Camp Belknap late, however, and the garrison there heard nothing until after Christmas of 1876. By then even the Portland newspapers had noticed something odd.

Major Suter read one of these reports at officers' call, snorting with astonishment. The *Weekly Standard* noted that the navy had brought the *Wyoming* up the Potomac River to Washington, anchoring the vessel where her guns could cover bridges into the city from Virginia and Maryland.

". . . and a company of Marines has been stationed at the Chain Bridge!" concluded Suter. "For God's sake, you'd think Jubal Early and his rebels were loose in the Shenandoah again! Who are they afraid of?"

"Something to do with this damned election, I'd wager," said Captain Smith. "What do they say about that?"

Suter studied the paper. "Tilden claims a hundred and eighty-four electoral votes and Hayes is thought to have a hundred and sixty-five. Four states contested. If Tilden carries any one of 'em, we've got a Democrat for President."

"I know Oregon's in a mess. Who else?"

"Florida, Louisiana, and South Carolina. They all sent in two sets of electoral votes just like Oregon." Suter looked puzzled. "That means the Congress will decide who's to be President, doesn't it?"

Nobody knew. Belknap's officers included no authority on disputed presidential elections.

"Mathilde's people in Pennsylvania," said Doctor Brenner, "wrote that Congress has set up a commission to rule on the contested votes. They don't think that's legal."

"Hah!" snorted Carter. "Congress makes the laws, doesn't it?"

The confusion was not surprising. Most army officers below the rank of general avoided any involvement in politics and were consequently ill informed about them. They carried this practice so far as to refrain from voting even when their nomadic existence permitted it. Indeed, they had been scandalized when a few ill-governed army wives in Wyoming took advantage of that territory's women's suffrage law to vote.

Cass Carter brought the subject up at supper that night. "Thank God," he said, "Oregon's got no such fool law. I know you wouldn't vote, Weezie, but there's some here who would."

"I beg your pardon," Louise replied, "but I assure you I would vote if I were allowed to."

"What? The army's got no business in politics!"

"Politics is one thing and voting is quite another. I am not in the army, and just because you stick your head in the sand each election does not mean I would."

"But the President is commander-in-chief of the army! Suppose he turned out to be a man I'd voted against?"

"You would both survive handsomely. If women had the vote I doubt we'd be in this remarkable situation."

"What situation?"

"Why, it's quite clear to me. Because the presidential election is contested, the southerners will be able to bargain their support for what they want—and they'll get it. Mr. Grant obviously wants Mr. Hayes elected. If the southerners in Congress support Hayes, he will promptly approve their all-white legislatures. Furthermore, just as soon as Mr. Hayes is in the White House he will be obliged to withdraw the troops from Louisiana and South Carolina. The Negroes will be returned to slavery."

"Weezie," said Cass plaintively, "where in the world do you pick up this nonsense?"

"Not in the *Army and Navy Journal*," she replied tartly. "You really should read some other newspapers once in a while, Cass."

Louise Carter's prediction proved uncomfortably accurate. The Electoral Commission created by Congress was composed—after some juggling—of eight Republicans and seven Democrats, and by the middle of February it had declared Hayes the winner in Florida and Louisiana. Democrats screamed fraud and threatened violence, and General Sherman drilled troops in the streets of Washington. On February 23 the commission declared—by its usual vote of eight to seven—that Hayes was winner in Oregon too. Only South Carolina remained to be decided, and the Democrats in Congress—some of them, anyway—planned a filibuster in the House, which they controlled if the southern Democrats remained loyal.

The filibuster failed. On February 26 the House recognized Democratic governments in Louisiana and South Carolina, and the next day the Electoral Commission gave the latter state's votes to Hayes. At four o'clock on the morning of March 2, Thomas Ferry, President *pro tempore* of the Senate, announced to a weary Congress that Rutherford Hayes was the nineteenth President of the United States. At midnight on March 3, 1877, the forty-fourth Congress adjourned its last session—without passing a military appropriation bill for the new fiscal year.

That kind of news reached every post in the army in a hurry. Major Suter announced it at officers' call, and Cass Carter came home for his dinner raging. Since the

307

children shared the noon meal with their parents, Brigid helped Mah Kim set the table and then took a place herself between William and Amanda.

"What exactly does this mean?" Louise Carter asked her sputtering husband.

"It means that after June there isn't any money to run the army! I suppose we can buy rations on credit, but there won't be any pay. What in the name of God has got into that fool Congress?"

Louise looked smug and Cass glared at her. "All right! Tell me."

"They want to make certain that Mr. Hayes keeps his promise to withdraw all the troops from the South. They won't give him any money to pay the soldiers unless he does. I think it very clever of them."

"Clever! By God, I hope you still think so when I have to borrow money to feed us!"

"Now, Cass," she murmured, "an army officer's credit is always good, and I doubt Mr. Hayes will delay very long giving them what they want."

Brigid was curious but not alarmed. The threat of no money was serious, but if Mr. Hayes couldn't find a way to pay his army, she doubted the Brunings would let their daughter's family go hungry. Or without a maid, she hoped. But Lieutenant Carter got her sudden and undivided attention when he abandoned the Congress as a topic of conversation and grumbled that Lieutenant Shelby had returned to Belknap with some dire rumors.

"He came all the way from San Francisco just to bring rumors?"

"No, Weezie. He's been up at Walla Walla, scouting an extension of the telegraph line to Fort Lapwai."

"I should have thought he would have gone back to San Francisco by steamer. What in the world did he come here for?"

"Damned if I know. He's here, though, full of nonsense about a Nez Percé outbreak this spring."

"Did he bring orders about that?" Louise asked very softly.

"Not that I know of. Just talk. If I were Suter, I'd tell him to keep his mouth shut. All this talk about fighting is going to get people excited."

Brigid was thinking of a hasty kiss she had given John Shelby in the buffet room at General Quinn's party and his insistence on seeing her again. Was it possible he had made the long, hard detour via Camp Belknap to see her? It seemed unlikely, but it was an exciting idea.

"Why," demanded Louise Carter, "must there be trouble with the Nez Percés? Doctor Brenner says they are the most intelligent and civilized Indians in the country."

"I suspect they are, but they're still Indians, and we haven't been very intelligent in our dealings with them."

"What have we done?"

"First we promised them some land they wanted, and then we found out we wanted it. Now we've told them they've got to get off it."

"How does that involve us?"

"Now, Louise! The Interior Department has told the Indian Agent at Lapwai reservation to get the Nez Percés out of the Wallowa Valley and onto the reservation. Mr. Montieth will tell them to move and they probably won't. Then he'll write a note to General Howard and ask him to make them go."

"Does General Howard have to do what Mr. Montieth wants?"

"Of course. That was all settled in Washington months ago. The Indian Commissioner probably asked the Secretary of War if the army would help, and Mr. Cameron said it would. General Sherman has told Howard that if the Indian Agent needs help, he's to give it— 'in the interests of peace.'"

"But Mr. Cameron is no longer Secretary of War."

"Doesn't matter. Hayes threw Cameron out and put in McCrary, but if McCrary didn't like the idea he would have said so by now. No, Shelby's right about that, I expect. The Nez Percés have been told to leave the Wallowa Valley by April, and if they don't, we'll have to push them."

"And Mr. Shelby says they will fight?"

"He does. Just like all young shavetail lieutenants, he's itching for a fight."

"Old first lieutenants know better, of course," said Louise bitterly. Cass grinned at her.

"We all get tired of mending barracks and doing fours-right on the parade ground. Fighting is what we're hired for, Weezie."

She stood up abruptly. "Ah! Well, I hope the Congress will decide to pay you for it. I shouldn't want you doing it for nothing."

With that retort she marched out of the dining room, the children and Brigid staring at her in astonishment. Carter chuckled.

"I shouldn't tease her like that. I'll just go and apologize, and she'll be all right."

The kitchen cleared, Brigid decided to visit the post trader's store. Prudence Morton had promised to save her the next hundred-pound flour sack to be emptied, and that was a prize not to be missed. From a sack that big she could make herself a new nightgown without having to stitch several pieces together. Her route was circuitous, for the snow was too deep to go directly, and she had to follow the few paths that had been shoveled out and kept clear.

The bag, Prudence reported, was not quite empty. Business was slow. "Tell you what," she said. "If Dad doesn't sell it soon, I'll pour what's left in another bag and then you can have it. I promise." She leaned across the counter to whisper eagerly, "Did you hear what happened at Couza's? You know Angie's sister Maria, don't you?"

Prudence always had the freshest and most scandalous stories of the goings-on in the sergeants' quarters, and the two girls gossiped happily, heads together, until a soldier joined them at the counter and put his hand over Brigid's. It was Michael Brennan.

310

"Where did you spring from?" Brigid demanded, tugging to free her hand.

"You were so busy telling dirty stories you didn't see me come in?"

"Oh, Michael!" Prudence giggled, "they were not dirty stories! Shame on you for listening."

He held Brigid's hand beneath the counter and she stopped pulling. Every encounter with Michael was still a fencing match, but since Christmas she had been more lenient about small liberties like this. Prudence detected the surrender and shook a warning finger at her.

"Don't trust him, Brigid. He's bad!"

"Prudence," growled Michael with a fierce scowl, "why don't you go count cans or something?"

Brigid laughed and he looked at her hopefully. "You going back to Carter's now?"

She nodded. "Unless you want to buy about ten pounds of flour."

"What would I do with that?"

"I don't know. I want the sack, and she can't give it to me till it's empty."

"I can get you a piece of canvas. Would that do?"

Both girls burst into laughter, and he scowled again.

"What's the matter with that? What d'you want it for?"

"None of your business," Brigid told him, still laughing, but she put her arm through his and pulled him toward the door. "Come on, now. If you won't buy the flour you can walk me home."

That took his mind off the canvas, and he pulled open the door for her. She stopped abruptly at the threshold. Lieutenant Shelby was stamping snow from his boots on the stoop, and when he saw Brigid his face lit up happily.

"Miss O'Donnel! I've been looking for you." He pulled off his shapeless beaver cap and made her a formal bow. Brigid's eyes sparkled. Maybe, she thought, he did come all this way just to see me. At least he's found out my name. He was even handsomer than she remembered, despite the shaggy buffalo coat and floppy hat worn by officers and soldiers alike in these cold regions.

"You're just leaving?" asked Shelby.

"Yes, sir."

"Mayn't I walk you home then?"

"Well—ah—Private Brennan was going with me, but . . ." She left that dangling, and Shelby took his cue.

"Ah! I guess I'll have to rank Brennan out of that privilege." He grinned at Michael, and Brigid struggled with laughter at the look on the latter's face. Shelby took Brigid's arm and escorted her carefully down the single step to the trader's porch.

"You know," he told her gravely, "you must not call me 'sir.' Have you forgotten we had a dance together not so long ago?"

"Oh, no! But I'd as lief not talk about it."

"Did you get in trouble?"

"Enough," she said plaintively.

"All right . . . I'll make it up to you. You'll have to show me which way to Carter's. I don't recognize this place with all the snow."

They had more of an audience than Michael Brennan by this time. Prudence had joined him on the stoop, and several people had gathered at the step. Noting these interested spectators, Brigid blushed—and discovered a familiar figure she had been seeking.

"Squis-Squis!" Pulling away from Shelby, she approached the Indian girl, holding out her hand. "Where've you been? I've been looking everywhere for you. You haven't taken the things I left for the baby, and—"

She broke off, shocked at the girl's face. If possible, Squis-Squis looked worse than she had when Brigid first saw her. Her face was not so thin, but her eyes were puffy, and the alert, hungry look had been replaced by one of sullen indifference.

"Where's the baby?" Brigid demanded, making rocking motions with her arms to explain the question.

Michael Brennan left the stoop and touched her arm. "The baby's dead, Bridey. I thought you knew."

"No! My God, when did it happen? Why didn't you tell me?"

She shook off his hand and moved toward Squis-Squis, who backed away, her moccasins squeaking in the snow.

"Ah, you poor thing! I'm that sorry for you." Brigid followed the Indian girl, who continued to back away, her face cold and sullen. Michael tugged at Brigid's coat.

"Leave her be, Bridey. She won't—"

"Watch it!" said someone by the porch. "Here's her man."

Petoe's intentions were obvious. Ignoring the whites, he walked toward Squis-Squis. When he was in reach of her he lifted a threatening hand and growled something in their own tongue. She shrank from him.

"He's going to hit her!" shrilled Brigid indignantly. "Stop him!"

Shelby was nearest, and he stepped between Petoe and the girl. "That's enough!" he said. "Leave her alone."

Petoe simply walked around the young officer and reached for Squis-Squis, who dodged, hissing some imprecation at him. To Brigid's astonishment the girl skipped away to take refuge behind Michael, peeking over his shoulder at her angry husband, or owner, or whatever he was. Petoe followed her and Michael squared off, facing him.

"Look out, Mike! He's got a knife."

Michael's reaction was quick and practical. He jerked off his fur cap with the dangling earflaps, and buried a fist in it to make a clumsy but effective guard against a blade. Lieutenant Shelby threw open his coat to show his officer's uniform, and stepped again between Petoe and his target.

"Stand out of the way, Lieutenant!" growled Michael, moving cautiously to keep the Indian in front of him. "He'll cut you."

"He's not going to cut anybody," said Shelby, leveling a finger at Petoe's angry face. "I told you to stop. If you pull that knife I'll put you in the guardhouse. Do you understand what I say?"

Either Petoe understood or he decided Squis-Squis was not worth his trouble. He spun on his heel and walked away.

"Oh!" gasped Brigid, "Jesus, Mary, and Joseph!" Her openmouthed admiration of Shelby was too much for Michael. He clapped his hat on and disentangled himself from Squis-Squis.

"Scat! Get away with you now!" He reinforced his command with a brisk slap on her narrow bottom, and she dodged away.

Shelby tied his coat and recaptured Brigid's hand, which was not difficult. She stared at him big-eyed and breathless.

"Shall we go?" he asked, smiling. Clinging a little more tightly than necessary to his arm, she nodded.

He walked her back to the Carters' as slowly as possible, and by the time they arrived Brigid was glowing. John Shelby, she decided, was not like any other officer she knew. He treated her as if she were a lady, not a maid, and the admiration in his eyes was exciting.

"Now . . . when are we to have another dance together?" he asked when they reached the Carters' front veranda. Brigid was sufficiently at ease by then to give him an impish smile.

"You're not to talk about that, remember?"

Louise Carter must have caught sight of this surprising scene from a window, for she opened the front door with a disapproving glint in her eye.

"Good afternoon, Mr. Shelby."

Brigid jerked her hand from his. "Oh, Missus Carter . . . you remember the Indian girl and her baby that time in the kitchen?"

"Why, of course, Brigid, but what—"

Brigid gave her no time to finish her question. "The baby died and the girl was at the store an' that Indian

314

she belongs to came after her. He was goin' to hit her an' he had a knife an' Mister Shelby stopped him."

She had run out of breath and Louise Carter stared at John Shelby in surprise.

"Good heavens! I trust you called the guard?"

"No, ma'am. There was no need. He stopped when I told him to. I thought it best to walk Miss O'Donnel home, though."

"Why, that's very thoughtful of you. Lieutenant Carter has returned to the company, but won't you come in and have a cup of tea? You must be frozen."

"I'd like that, ma'am, very much, but perhaps I'd better wait a bit."

"Oh, come in, Mr. Shelby! We're too far back in the woods to be formal. Come!"

As soon as the door had closed on them, Louise Carter put things deftly back in order. "Brigid," she said crisply, "please ask Mah Kim to bring tea to the parlor." She gave John Shelby a warm smile. "Come in. I've a hundred questions to ask you about San Francisco. Do you know I've never been there?"

In the kitchen Brigid hustled Mah Kim into a clean white jacket and dispatched him with the silver tea service and a dozen of Mrs. Carter's hoarded sweet biscuits. She would rather have taken them herself, but that seemed unwise. Mrs. Carter had specified Mah Kim and she could think of no reasonable excuse for replacing him. Damn, she swore softly to herself. I'd like to talk to him some more. He's fun. That was such an odd thing to think of an officer that she giggled in surprise at herself.

While she fumed in the kitchen, John Shelby disarmed his hostess. He drank one cup of tea, ate one biscuit and rose promptly at the end of fifteen minutes of easy small talk. He did not know it, of course, but he had earned Louise Carter's highest order of merit. Young and a bit dashing, she later reported to her husband, but he obviously comes from a good family.

"I'm sorry you missed Cass," she told him in the

315

hall. "Could you not return when he is here? I'm sure he would like to see you."

"Thank you, ma'am, but I fear it's not possible. I'm off early tomorrow morning. Please give Lieutenant Carter my respects, and I thank you very much for the tea."

"Not at all. It was my pleasure. And thank you for looking after Brigid for us. Are you going directly back to San Francisco?"

"As directly as I can, ma'am. They say the stage roads are clear, so I should have no trouble reaching the railroad."

"I hope you have no difficulty. Since you're going straight to San Francisco, may I ask a favor of you?"

"Of course, anything. What can I do?"

"Would you take a letter to Mrs. Faison for me? Her husband is Captain Faison, and he is stationed on Angel Island. I believe that is quite near Division Headquarters, is it not?"

"It is indeed. The launch goes to the island every day, and I'll see she has it by the first boat after I arrive."

"That's most kind of you. I shall write it tonight and send it to you the first thing tomorrow morning. When you see her, please give her and Captain Faison my best regards."

Next morning's breakfast found the Carter house without bread. It was bake day for the post, and by midmorning the orderly or Mah Kim would pick up three days' supply from the post bakery behind the hospital, but breakfast without toast would bring a lecture on poor management from Lieutenant Carter. Brigid bundled into coat and moccasins and ran for the bakery to get enough for breakfast.

The two civilian bakers employed by the commissary had been at work since midnight, and the wonderful odor of fresh-baked bread surrounded the little stone house. The heat of the ovens had softened the snow

316

piled on its roof until yard-long icicles hung from its eaves in a glittering frieze. Half a dozen other early-comers were gathered about the door, stamping to warm their feet.

Brigid joined the line, thrust her mittened hands deep into her sleeves, and tucked her chin into the collar of her sheepskin. What a day to run out of bread, she grumbled. If I'd only thought, I could have borrowed a loaf from Angie yesterday. The man in front of her stooped to peer into the hood of her coat.

"Mornin', missy. You in there sommers?"

"Hello, Mr. Hanst. I wish I weren't." It was the burly quartermaster woodcutter who had told her where to hide supplies for Squis-Squis. "Did you hear what happened yesterday?" she asked him.

Peter Hanst defaced the snow with a big splash of tobacco juice, leaving amber beads of the stuff congealing in his beard.

"Yup. Pity 'bout that gal."

"Why, nothing happened to her. Mr. Shelby ran that crazy Indian away. Michael said the baby died, though."

"Y'ain't heard 'bout the gal, then?"

"What do you mean?"

"Guard found her in th' road behind th' infantry cookhouse 'bout midnight. Froze stiffer'n ary board. Somebody done beat her till she couldn't crawl off."

"That Indian! Did they catch him?"

"Naw. He's gone. Couldn't find hide nor hair of him."

"I hope they catch him and kill him! Hanging's too good for that sod."

"Maybe." Hanst spat accurately into his previous target in the snow.

"What do you mean, 'maybe'?" she exploded. "He did it! He tried to yesterday at the store."

Hanst sighed. "Y'ought never git messed up with them Injun sluts, missy. If'n Pee-toe whupped her to death, he had good reason."

"I don't believe it! She was a good girl."

317

"No better'n th' rest of 'em. Ever since her baby died, she's been hangin' 'round th' barricks fadiddlin' whusky an' eats outa th' sojers."

"Doing what?"

"Now, missy, ain't no way to say it plainer that ain't gonna make you mad."

"Oh!" Brigid considered that for a moment and it made her angrier. "Well, it's his fault then. Why didn't he feed her?"

"I reckon he hadn't a helluva lot t'eat hisself, an' he shore didn't have no whuskey to give her."

"So? Is that reason to beat her up and leave her to freeze to death?"

Hanst looked frustrated. "Ain't no way to tell what reason he had—if he done it. He was smart enuf to clear outa here 'fore anybuddy could ask him. Anyhow, it ain't no-way certain he done killed his woman. One o' them sojers could jest as likely got hisself drunk last night an' knocked that hoor silly 'thout meanin' t' kill her. Wouldn' be the first time it happened."

That explicit alternative shocked Brigid into silence, which lasted, to Peter Hanst's relief, until he had his bread and departed, avoiding her angry look.

Because of the deep snow, the garrison stood reveille in barracks these days—a brief formation—but Lieutenant Carter was late returning for his breakfast because all the officers were summoned to Major Suter's office immediately afterward.

When he did return, his account of the night's happenings was less graphic than Peter Hanst's, but since Suter had ordered questioning of all the soldiers, it was clear that Hanst was not the only one who suspected someone other than Petoe might be responsible for the sordid killing.

Brigid set about her morning chores troubled by some hard thinking. The more she thought, the worse she felt.

Michael had brought the girl and her baby into the Carter kitchen and helped feed them. That was reason enough for Squis-Squis to run to him for help when Pe-

318

toe threatened her. But there could be other reasons too. Hanst said Squis-Squis had been sleeping with the soldiers. Which soldiers?

Brigid put down a lamp and stared at it. She knew a lot about Michael Brennan. Maybe more than anyone at Camp Belknap. Michael wouldn't beat a woman and leave her to die in the snow, not even if he were drunk. And she had never seen him drunk.

But take her to bed? Ah, now, that was something else. Quite possible. She picked up the lamp chimney, stuffed her rag into it, and twisted to get the soot out.

If she asked him, he'd just raise his brows and grin and say, "What's a man to do? I asked you to marry me, didn't I? You wouldn't have me on either side of your blanket." This imagined retort so infuriated her that she didn't hear Mrs. Carter calling until the second time.

"Yes, ma'am?"

"Where is Schroeter, Brigid?"

"At the barracks, ma'am. They're holding a meeting or something."

"Oh . . . that's right." Brigid's explanation hardly described what must be happening at the barracks now. "Where is Mah Kim?"

"Bakery, ma'am. This is Saturday."

"I thought you went for bread early this morning."

"I only got one loaf for breakfast, Missus Carter. He went to get the rest of this week's ration."

"Oh. Damn it all!"

Only extreme irritation could provoke that sort of language from Louise Carter, and Brigid looked astonished.

"Do you want something, Missus Carter?"

"I must get this letter to Mr. Shelby before he leaves, and it is very late already. I shall have to ask you to bring it, Brigid."

"Yes, ma'am," Brigid replied, promptly forgetting her suspicions of Michael. "Where do I take it?"

"To the bachelor officers' quarters, of course. Just give it to the orderly and tell him it's for Mister Shelby.

319

Tell him—Oh! The orderly won't be there either." She considered a moment, tapping the letter irritably against her knuckles. "It can't be helped. You can't go upstairs, of course, so just put it on the hall table and call out, 'Letter for Mr. Shelby.' Then come straight back."

The planked walk past the Brenners' house to the zoo, as the garrison fondly called the big log structure housing its unmarried officers, had been kept clear of snow, so it was hardly a minute's walk for Brigid. The wind had dropped, and it was not as cold as when she had made her early-morning trip to the bakery. The sun was dazzling on the snow; warm enough to set the icicles dripping in the screen of junipers between the Brenners' and the bachelor quarters.

Brigid pushed open the front door and advanced cautiously into the wide, gloomy cavern of the hallway. In the absence of the orderly, the fire in the stove was low—so low she could see her breath on the chilly air. Skipping along the walk, she had cherished the thought that Jack Shelby just might happen to be in the hall when she entered. The idea of just the two of them all alone together was dangerously exciting. She was disappointed.

Putting the letter in the middle of the table where it could not be missed, she called in a small voice, "Letter for Mr. Shelby!"

There was no response. Not a sound. Perhaps he had already gone. A pair of saddlebags and a scuffed leather valise piled by the door belied that, and she tried again, a bit louder. She was peering doubtfully up the staircase when an amused voice behind her made her jump in alarm.

"I wish we had a mail-carrier like you in Frisco."

Jack Shelby was standing in the kitchen door in his shirtsleeves, toweling his face vigorously. Obviously he had just finished his morning shave.

"Oooh! You scared me," Brigid gasped. Her heart thumped in alarm, but his broad smile and admiring look dispelled that. Gray eyes he's got, she thought, and bonny bright ones too. A strapping great handsome bucko he is, and you, Brigid, had better get yourself out of here.

She ignored her own advice, fascinated by those level gray eyes. "I . . . I brought your letter from Missus Carter. The orderly was away, and so is Mah Kim."

"I'm in luck, aren't I?"

"It's right there," she pointed to the table.

"I see it."

"Well . . ." Brigid drew a shallow breath. "I'd best . . ."

"Take off that coat? You're right. It's cold enough in here, but you'll freeze when you go out if you don't."

"Oh, I can't stay. Missus Carter wants me straight back. She's . . . uh . . . waiting for me."

Instead of going, she managed to back herself against the big table, and now Jack Shelby was barring the way. She had to tip her head back to look up into his smiling face.

"There's not a soul in the house," he assured her. "Now, can I ask when I'm to have another dance?"

"Oh, go on!" she managed. "You're teasing me."

"Never that, Brigid!" He twitched out the knots in the thongs lacing her sheepskin coat. "I can't dance with you in that thing."

"Dance with me! What are you talking about?"

"I can't wait for a proper ball . . . this will have to do."

She grabbed the coat before it slid from her shoulders, but it was open from throat to floor, and his hands were clasping her slim waist. He began to hum tunelessly, and swept her in a series of circles across the waxed plank floor.

"Mr. Shelby! Somebody will come . . . stop, please!"

"Nobody's coming. I'll stop if you don't like it, though."

After his shave he had splashed his face with bay rum. Its penetrating odor tickled her nostrils and set her head spinning as if she had taken a sip of toddy. I do like it, she thought. Oh, my, I do. She savored the rough touch of his wool shirt against her face and let him spin her mindlessly around the hall. The brassy clamor of a distant bugle brought them to a halt.

"Damn!" Jack Shelby swore. "Fatigue call. That means they've finished."

"Oh! I must go! The orderly will come now."

His hands slipped up under her arms, pulled her in and lifted her a little, his wrists nudging the swell of her breasts.

"Brigid?"

"Mmmh?"

"Look at me, Brigid."

She did, and he kissed her, and she let him do it. More than that. She returned his kiss.

"That wasn't a real dance," Shelby whispered. "It doesn't count. I think Mrs. Carter will come to San Francisco to see her friend soon. Be sure you come with her, and I'll take you dancing at the Occidental."

"What's that?"

"It's a grand hotel, and they dance every night there. Would you like that?"

"Oh, yes!"

"It's a bargain." He kissed her again, and helped her retie her coat. Her fingers were trembling so, she could never have managed that unaided.

"Don't forget!"

"Oooh . . . Mr. Shelby! I won't." She fled, her face flaming.

13

The following day was Sunday, welcomed by the garrison because deep snow forbade the usual inspection and full-dress parade out of doors.

Belknap had neither chaplain nor chapel, but for those who found Sunday uncomfortable without some semblance of a religious service there was an informal gathering at midmorning in the big courtroom in the bachelor officers' quarters.

The officers and a few soldiers took turns reading a selection from the Bible and leading the assembly in the Lord's Prayer, nearest to common ground for all. When Major Suter presided, he assumed his book of Episcopalian Church Services was acceptable to all, and read from it in accord with the season. This being the fourth Sunday in Lent, he selected a morning lesson from Micah that proved uncomfortably apt in view of the trouble brewing in the north.

"Hear ye now what the Lord saith," he intoned. "Arise, contend thou before the mountains and let the hills hear thy voice . . ."

In conclusion there would be a hymn or two, led by Abigail Smith or Sergeant Benoni's wife, Maria. Maria had never had an hour's music instruction in her life, but her sweet, happy voice was a relief from the severity with which Mrs. Smith attacked a hymn.

323

Michael had never attended one of these gatherings, but on this bitterly cold Sunday he found reason to make a beginning. He wanted words with Brigid O'Donnel, and a chance encounter, stretched to include walking her home, would allay Mrs. Carter's suspicions. His visits to the Carter house had become more frequent since Christmas, and he had noted a questioning look in the lady's eyes of late.

To insure a welcome, he wheedled out of the company cook two empty flour sacks—hundred-pounders. He still did not know what Brigid wanted them for. He had tried to get that out of Prudence Morton, but she would not tell.

Despite repeated shaking, the bags exuded a fine dust of flour, so he wrapped them in newspaper and stuffed them in the pocket of his coat. He was settling his cap to go when Private Ryan appeared at the foot of his bunk with a sly smirk on his face.

"You goin' to Carter's, Mike?"

"I'm going to church. Why?"

"You're goin' to *church?*" The astonishment in Ryan's voice was unfeigned. Michael gave him a sour look. He had no affection for Ryan, who had wormed his way into a permanent job dog-robbing at the bachelor officers' quarters and used it to evade all company duties. Not all orderlies were worthless, but Ryan, in his opinion, was proof of the average soldier's conviction that worthless men sooner or later became orderlies.

"That's what I said, isn't it?"

"All right," Ryan answered hastily, "no need to take on. Ye'll be stoppin' at Carter's after then?"

Michael glared at him impatiently. "What the hell's that to you, Ryan?"

With a look of studied innocence, Ryan dropped a pair of small, fur-lined mittens on Michael's bunk. "I was only thinkin' ye could give these to Brigid. If ye're not stoppin' there, I c'd take 'em meself."

Michael studied the mittens in silence. They were unmistakably Brigid's, but Ryan's smirk puzzled him.

Since his encounter with Corporal Wortman, few men in the company—least of all Ryan—made fun of Michael Brennan, and none courted his wrath with remarks about Brigid. His fruitless pursuit of that pretty redhead was common knowledge, but so was his reaction to any joking about her. He could not fathom what the sly man was up to.

"Where'd you find these?" No man in his right mind could mistake the tone of that question, and Ryan's response was studiously cautious.

"Lootenant Shelby give 'em to me before he went off with the mail-rider yesterday."

"Oh? And told you to give them back to Miss O'Donnel?"

"Sure, Mike. How'd I know whose they are?"

Michael drew a deep breath, and Ryan shifted to put the bunk between them. But he misjudged his man. Michael could see where this was leading. Straightfaced, Ryan would dole out scraps of information, relishing the questions that extracted them. He would not have that pleasure, Michael decided grimly. He picked up the mittens and put them in his pocket.

"Right. I'll see she gets 'em."

Hearing not a word, he sat through the brief service, eyes fixed on the shining coil of hair beneath Brigid's chip hat two benches in front of him. His rage at Shelby and Ryan was almost comforting in its intensity but when he tried to imagine how the lieutenant had come by Brigid's mittens it nearly choked him.

Standing in the back of the room as it emptied, he glared ferociously at Brigid until he caught her eye. Her reaction was anything but helpful. She put her nose in the air and sailed past him without a word, even though William and Amanda hung back to greet him.

"Good morning, Brennan," Mrs. Carter said in a surprised voice. "I'm glad to see you here."

That was all. Not even a suggestion that he stop for a cup of coffee in the kitchen. Seething almost audibly, Michael trailed the Carter family down the walk to

325

their quarters, made his way through the snow to the back entrance, and waited impatiently until he heard someone moving about inside. Brigid opened the door to his knock, but not enough to let him enter.

"What do you want?"

"And good morning to you too, Miss O'Donnel! I brought you something. You want me to leave it on the stoop?"

Grudgingly, she let him in, watching in silence as he put the package of flour sacks on the table. Since she made no move to open it, Michael did so. Then he pulled the mittens from his pocket and dropped them on top. They raised a little puff of flour.

Brigid picked them up and put them behind her back. "Thank you. I'll not be needing the bags."

"All right. Pity I can't bring you what you need most—a little sense!"

"I've enough not to stand here and listen to your bad mouth, Brennan!" She jerked open the door. "Get out, now!"

His big hand lifted hers from the latch and he shouldered the door shut.

"Not until I've had my say."

"Say it to the stove then. I'll not listen to you!"

She tried to go, but her hand was trapped and he held her fast. For a second he thought she would kick him and burst into yells of rage, but she mastered it, crimson with the effort.

"For the love of God and all his holy angels, Bridey . . . what are you doin', foolin' around with that lieutenant?"

Her answer was almost incoherent but she got it out, her imprisoned hand jerking with every word.

"Missus Carter asked Mr. Shelby to take a letter with him. There was no one here but me, an' . . . I brought it to that . . . that place where he was stayin'. I must have dropped the damned mittens when I put it on the table. In the hall!" The last three words were shouted. Michael's expression was unchanged, and she jerked furiously to get away from him. "I don't know how you got your hands on them, but you've no right to talk to me like that!"

"I got 'em from that maggot Ryan—him that's dog-robber for that place." His voice dropped to a growl. "He says Mr. Shelby gave 'em to him an' told him to bring 'em back to you."

"Oooh! He's a dirty liar, damn his eyes!" She wrested her hand free and rubbed her wrist sulkily. "Damn you too, Michael! You hurt me!"

"That Georgia stud'll hurt you worse! God save us, Bridey, don't you know you can't have any truck with an officer?"

"I will if I want to! I'm not in your damned army!"

"Ah, Bridey . . . He only wants one thing from you. Soon's he's got it he'll laugh in your face!"

"That's funny . . . comin' from you!"

"Now, damn it, I asked you to marry me, didn't I?"

"Yes, when you couldn't find any other way to get around me!"

"That's pretty mean, Bridey. I asked you fair an' square."

His hurt was genuine, and she looked defensive for the first time. "Well, it's not your place to be talkin' to me like that."

"It's the God's truth! Somebody's got to tell you." That stung her, and she fought back.

"You pick your company, Michael Brennan, an' I'll pick mine."

"What the hell does that mean?"

"You think I didn't see that Indian girl run to you when her man went for her? I know what's been goin' on in the barracks with her. How was she, Brennan? A little smelly, I don't doubt, but that didn't bother you, did it?"

Michael's eyes narrowed angrily. "Are you sayin' I killed that girl?"

"No . . . I'm not. But last night wasn't the first time she was down there."

"Bridey," he said grimly, "I may be hard up, but I'll never be that bad I got to lay an Injun on the meat-

327

block in the cookhouse. Who in God's name filled your head with that crap?"

"That's no worse than what you said about me an' Mr. Shelby!"

"Ah, for God's sake! I could lay every squaw from here to Idaho an' nobody'd give a tinker's damn save Doc Brenner. You jump in the straw with that smart-ass lieutenant, an' there'll be hell to pay an' no change!"

"Ooooh! Don't you dare say that to me!"

The pitch of this discussion had risen to reach beyond the kitchen, and Cass Carter put down his paper and frowned.

"What in the world is going on out there? Who is that with Brigid?"

"I think," replied Louise, "it's Private Brennan."

"Well, damn it all, he can't come to my quarters and yell at her like that. I'll put a stop to this!"

"Now, Cass," his wife murmured. "It sounds to me as though Brigid is doing her share of shouting. I shouldn't interfere if I were you."

"Why, Weezie, that's not like you! We can't have that going on."

"Just give it a moment more. I suspect she will put him out shortly, and that's good."

Cass looked baffled, and she smiled at him sweetly. "Brennan has been visiting us rather often since Christmas, or hadn't you noticed?"

"Well . . . yes, I suppose so. I haven't been counting."

"He has. And I must confess I have been troubled about it. He's a good-looking rascal, and I would prefer to see a little less of him around Brigid."

"Then why don't I tell him so?"

"Because, my dear, it will be more effective if Brigid does that." There came faintly to their ears the thud of the kitchen door, and Louise Carter smiled again.

"There! He's gone, and from the sound of that conversation I doubt that he will be back soon."

Book Three

1

May of 1877 brought spring and fresh rumors of the war to Camp Belknap. The road to Canyon City was open, and every mail-rider brought a packet of newspapers. The Portland and Lewiston journals reported developments breathlessly.

General Howard met the recalcitrants among the Cayuse and Umatilla Indians—the Columbia River Renegades, he called them—and frightened them into sullen obedience. Then he went to Fort Lapwai to meet Chief Joseph and the other Non-Treaty Nez Percés. Too-hool-hool-sote was their spokesman. His truculence was dangerous, but he was their best orator.

The Indians made their transparent bid for freedom in exchange for a promise to settle on a reservation. It was too late. Daily contact between Nez Percés and white settlers bred daily trouble in the valleys of the Wallowa and Grand Ronde Rivers. General Howard would have no warrior talk. They must go onto the Lapwai reservation—not the Umatilla—and there would be no roaming anywhere without a written pass from the agent. Furthermore, they had just thirty days to reach Lapwai.

It was a cruelly illogical deadline. The rivers overflowed with the spring run-off. Bringing women, children, horses, and cattle across them now would be

331

murderous. The Indians balked and the newspapers shouted war. At Camp Belknap, trader Morton looked up, baffled from his copy of the Lewiston *Teller* at Dr. Brenner who had come to purchase tobacco.

"What they got to fight about, Doc? It says right here they can have all the land they want on the reservation."

Brenner sighed. "I guess they'd rather have their own land, Mr. Morton."

Dispatches from Department Headquarters were as ominous as the newspapers. Two troops of cavalry were ordered to the Wallowa Valley, another to Lewiston. Two companies of infantry from Vancouver moved to Walla Walla and two more encamped at Wallula, prepared to move north or south at need.

The talks at Lapwai stretched into a third day, and Too-hool-hool-sote conceded bitterly that the Nez Percés would move as required, but they could not do this in thirty suns. General Howard was adamant, and the old orator turned again to his Dreamer faith with its First Man and his unmarked earth. Howard was an evangelist as well as a soldier—his own people called him the Praying General—and this appeal to a pagan religion angered him. He leveled a finger at Too-hool-hool-sote.

"Do you intend coming on the reservation peaceably, or shall I put you there with my soldiers?"

Said the chief, "You have brought a rifle to a peace council. You do not want to talk. If you mean we have but thirty suns to gather all our people and our flocks, my answer is no. We will have to fight."

Whereupon General Howard arrested the Nez Percé spokesman and locked him in the Fort Lapwai guardhouse. It was an unheard-of thing to do at a council.

But it had the desired effect. Chief Joseph and the others bowed their heads and accepted the "protection papers" granting them thirty days to settle on the reservation. All except Hush-hush-cute. Because his band lived so far away, he was granted thirty-five days, but he would not accept the paper.

"I do not want it," he said caustically. "I might get it dirty."

General Howard returned to Portland and telegraphed success to General McDowell in San Francisco: ". . . . .Non-Treaty Nez Percés constrained compliance with order of government. Thirty days allowed to gather scattered people and stock. Location on reservation selected and agreed upon. . . ."

By the second week of June, Portland papers reported that the Nez Percés were moving peacefully toward the reservation and all danger was past. The whole of the Northwest breathed a sigh of relief. When General Howard's "Columbia River Renegades" were told that the Nez Percés had submitted, they too chose peace.

At Camp Belknap the garrison relaxed and enjoyed good weather. Almost every day the temperature reached seventy degrees, and Sweetwater Canyon burst into a riot of color. The Carter children chafed under their mother's rule that they could not leave sight of the post, and begged Brigid to intercede for them. Brigid suggested a picnic.

They would go, she explained to Mrs. Carter, with the wood detail. Corporal Wills would take them in his wagon up a pretty little valley branching north from the canyon above the post, and they would return with Wills and his soldiers in the afternoon.

The quartermaster hired civilians to keep Belknap in firewood, and three of them were working at the head of the valley, where they had built a lean-to for shelter at night. Every few days soldiers came from the post with a wagon to haul away the wood they had cut and stacked.

"All right," conceded Louise Carter, "it sounds safe enough. But not today, I hope. Today is the thirteenth."

Brigid smiled. Mrs. Carter had never before been superstitious. "Oh, no, ma'am. It's day after tomorrow he's going."

Louise Carter's concern about the thirteenth of June would haunt her later. General Howard's month of grace for the Non-Treaty Nez Percés expired on the fifteenth, and by the night of the twelfth they were across the Salmon on the Camas Meadows, a stone's throw from the reservation. One day's march would bring an end to the crisis, but they never made that crucial final march. An event beyond foreseeing by General Howard or any other white man intervened.

Among Chief Joseph's young men in the camp at Tahpahlewam was a warrior named Wahlitits, whose father had been murdered by a white man in 1874. Tipyahlanah Siskan, a sub-chief called Eagle Robe by the whites, had objected to infringement on his land by a settler named Larry Ott. When Ott began plowing a field Eagle Robe considered his own, the Indian threw stones at the white man and flapped his blanket at the plow horse. Ott stopped plowing and shot Eagle Robe, who died a few days later, sending a last message to his young son.

"I know my days are short upon this earth . . . tell my son, Wahlitits, for my sake and for the sake of his brothers and sisters, to hold his temper. . . . When I am dead, tell him all I have said, and lastly of all, not to wage war on the whites."

Wahlitits took no revenge for his father's killing. His restraint might have brought him no trouble had he not grown up to be a remarkably strong and handsome young man with a quick eye for pretty girls. On the eleventh of June he persuaded one of them to join him in his lodge. Her mother found her there next morning and whipped her out, upbraiding Wahlitits for his behavior.

"You were no man when your father was murdered by the whites," she snapped at him. "Why don't you go after *them* instead of my girl?"

Wahlitits ignored her, but that night on the Camas Meadows there was a Kissing Dance and while Wahlitits was courting the girls a young man tapped him on the shoulder. He was a relative of the seduced maiden.

"So," he said, "here you are again at your old tricks.

334

You are very stylish with the girls, but we know you are a coward."

Wahlitits considered that remark and looked at his accuser. "Do you mean what you say?" he asked.

"I do. You are a coward. There is your father's grave. He was murdered by a white man and you don't have the courage to kill the man who did it. He is living just across the river right now and you do nothing."

Addressed thus in the presence of many people, especially the Nez Percé maidens, Wahlitits was abashed.

"All right," he said softly, "you will be sorry for what you have spoken."

He remained the rest of the night in his lodge, but at daybreak on June 13 he recruited two friends, and they rode down to the bank of the Salmon River where the whites lived. They could not find Ott, but about twelve miles above Slate Creek they found Richard Devine, an old man who lived alone. They killed him. Next morning they went to the John Day ranch, where a white man named Harry Elfers lived. Elfers was hated by the Indians because he set his dogs on them when they crossed his fields so they killed him, too. There were two other white men at Elfers's house, and they were both killed. Mrs. Elfers and her children were not molested, but Wahlitits and his friends took weapons, ammunition, and all the horses they could find. Riding south, they encountered a storekeeper named Charlie Cone, whom the Indians liked because he always traded fairly. Cone recognized the horses and asked if they had bought them.

"No," said Wahlitits. "We killed him and took his horses. We don't kill you because you are a friend. You get all your friends and go to Slate Creek settlement quick. Get in a house and stay there. You stay inside and you won't be hurt. You run around and somebody will kill you."

The Nez Percé War had begun. But by no means could word of this beginning have reached Camp Belknap by the fifteenth of June, when Corporal Wills took Brigid, William, Amanda, and three soldiers in his wagon to get a load of wood. At the head of the valley where the woodcutters were working he found a great quantity of logs stacked by the road. More than a wagonload. He sent the full wagon to the post with orders to return for another.

The road ended at the stacked wood, but a trail led into the forest where the thunk of axes and crash of falling trees marked the woodcutters' presence. Brigid left her basket with a warning to the soldiers to stay out of it, and walked up the trail with the children to watch the cutting. The woodcutters, rough, whiskered men, greeted them happily. They made much of Amanda, but it was Brigid who brightened their day. After a while two of them returned to their work, leaving the third to whet his axe and talk to Brigid. She sat on a felled tree, luxuriating in the sunlight striking through the newly leafed forest. It was warm and quiet and peaceful until suddenly the woodcutter dropped his stone.

"Oh, shit!" he said softly.

"Watch your tongue, man!" exploded Brigid, but the expression on his face snapped her head around to see what had alarmed him.

Four Indians were standing in the trail. Their hair was braided and tied with scraps of cloth beneath floppy black hats. Each wore a blanket around his shoulders, buckskin leggings or nondescript trousers showing beneath. Each cradled a rifle in his arms.

One of them took off his hat. He was a young man and he had a narrow stripe of red paint across his forehead. It ran back over his head in the part of his black hair.

"Hal-lo," he said pleasantly and advanced to the seated woodcutter. His companions followed. Two were as young as he; the third was an old man with the wrinkled, leathery face of a mummy.

Shifting his rifle, the first Indian reached down to take the axe from the woodcutter. Holding it by the blade, he tested its edge with his thumb.

"Good!" he grunted approvingly.

336

"Glad you like it, friend," said the white man, holding out his hand for the axe. Without sound or warning the Indian swung the axe handle in a short, violent arc against the woodcutter's head. He slumped over with a groan, and Brigid clutched the children to her, horrified.

She could hear the busy axes of the other two, but the woods screened them from view. Whether they heard the blow or simply came back to get their companion was not clear, but both of them suddenly appeared in the trail a little way down the slope and stared in surprise. One of them was carrying his axe and a rifle.

He dropped the axe, but before he could raise the rifle one of the young Indians shot him. The remaining woodcutter spread his hands to show he was unarmed.

The first man, felled by his own axe, groaned and stirred. The Indian who had struck him leaned over to examine him. After a moment he put the muzzle of his rifle against the white man's chest and pulled the trigger. The shot was muffled, and when the Indian lifted his weapon a curl of smoke rose from the scorched shirt.

A chorus of inquiring yells came from the soldiers, and two of the young Indians faded into the forest, prowling alertly toward the sound. The third watched Brigid narrowly. With a child under each arm, she was frozen in terror like a rabbit hearing the hawk's dive. The Indian gestured with his chin down the trail and gave her a questioning look.

"S-soldiers," she managed, in a whisper.

"Aha!" he said, and called a low-voiced warning to his friends in their own language. There was no reply. The third woodcutter remained standing in the trail where he had entered it.

The Indian put the muzzle of his rifle against Brigid's ribs and pushed. She wanted to cry out, but her tongue was locked in her mouth. He raised it until it caught under her breast, and she could feel the front

337

sight digging into her flesh. Watching her reaction, the Indian grinned.

The old man said something in a scornful voice. A second comment brought an angry hiss from the young Indian. He jerked the gun muzzle painfully upward and walked away into the forest.

The old Indian remained. After a moment he came forward, and Amanda whimpered when he put out a clawlike hand to touch her hair. He stroked it and his wrinkled face changed minutely. Not his expression, because there was none. Just a small rearrangement of his features.

"Go," he pointed down the trail. "Don' run."

They stared at him in disbelief, and he repeated the order.

"Don' run. Walk slow. Injun say stop . . . you stop. Go now."

The children stared at her questioningly and Brigid decided nothing could be worse than just standing there waiting to be killed.

"Come," she said. "Do what he says."

William first, then Brigid, clutching Amanda's hand, they stepped over the bodies of the two dead woodcutters and came to the third, who had not moved.

Brigid thought he was paralyzed with fear. They would simply have to walk around him and leave him there. But his eyes were alert and questioning.

"Turn around," she told him quietly. "Turn around and walk in front of us."

With no sound but the occasional clatter of a pebble dislodged by their feet, they went down the trail.

The swift murder of the two men made everything so unreal that their descent was just another part of the nightmare. It could not be considered an escape. At every careful step Brigid expected to meet the blazing rifles of the three young Indians. To her horror she saw one of them standing among the trees, but he did nothing. He just watched them file past. No one dared look at him, and they continued to pick their way downhill with exaggerated caution.

A bend took them out of his sight and they came to the woodcutters' shanty. The sole survivor of its occupants stepped out of the trail and reached into the lean-to for his rifle and cartridge belt.

"Oh, don't!" whispered Brigid urgently. "They'll kill us."

"Maybe . . . maybe not."

"What are you going to do?"

He was stuffing cartridges into his Winchester as quietly as he could, dropping several in his haste. He stooped to pick them up.

"You an' the young'uns keep goin'. Soon's you're in the open, run like hell fer them woodpiles. Don't stop fer nuthin'. If them soljers got the brains God give a chickadee, they'll be in there waitin' fer ye."

"But what about you?"

"I aim t' git me one o' them bastids. Couple maybe, if they's young an' crazy enuf. Git on, now."

There were six stacks of cordwood at the bottom of the slope that led from the forest to the end of the wagon road—three on each side of the track, ready to be loaded onto the wagon. Corporal Wills had seen that they would make a passable fort. He had not run up the trail to find out what the shots meant, but with his two remaining men had thrown down enough of the four-foot logs to block the openings between the stacks to a height of several feet.

When he saw Brigid and the children come out of the forest, he vaulted this barricade and trotted toward them, his Springfield at the ready. The other two soldiers were closing the lower end of their makeshift fort. As he met Brigid midway of the slope, there was a shot and a yell on the ridge above. The Indians had encountered the remaining woodcutter.

"You've got to help him!" Brigid panted.

"Nothin' I can do for him, Red. *Run, now*—you kids run!"

Brigid took a child in each hand and ran. A soldier met them at the woodpile and tossed the two children in like bundles. Brigid scrambled in unaided, and he never even glanced at her ankles when she hiked up her skirt to climb the log barricade. His eyes were fixed on Wills, who was walking backward down the trail, watching the edge of the forest.

The woodcutter was still in action, for there was an occasional shot and a few Indian yelps high on the ridge. Wills climbed into the little fort and surveyed it grimly.

Each stack of wood was four feet high and eight feet long, with a gap of about a foot between stacks. If a man stayed out of the gaps and below the level of loose logs closing the ends of the double row, nothing could hit him. It was better than being caught in the open, but they might be there a long time. Gathering canteens, the corporal sent one of his men scrambling down to the creek to fill them.

"How—how will they know we're in trouble?" gasped Brigid.

"I doubt they can hear the shootin' that far, but Ferris will when he comes back with the wagon. He'll get help. Wish we had somethin' more to hold water. What's in the basket?"

"There's a jar of lemonade."

"Good. We'll have a party. Watch out, now."

There was no climactic battle to tell what had happened to the third woodcutter. Either one of the sporadic shots got him or he had abandoned the field. The arrival of the Indians at the edge of the clearing was announced by a bullet slamming into the logs with a solid thump.

"All right, Red—get flat on the ground an' keep them kids down." Wills nudged one of the soldiers crouched behind him. "Gause, you take the bottom end an' I'll take this one. Dickey, you gotta watch both sides."

There was another shot from the trees, marked this time by a drift of smoke, and Wills slammed a response at it with his rifle. It took the Indians a long time to encircle the little fort. One of them worked his way through the woods until he could cover the lower end, where he and Gause exchanged cautious shots at long intervals. Another, up where the trail disappeared among the trees, was more troublesome. He could shoot into the fort until Wills and Dickey piled up enough logs at that end to block him. A third produced an almost fatal surprise. Unseen, he crawled under the shelter of the creek bank to within twenty yards of the lower row of stacks. He announced his arrival with a slug that came in through the gap and cracked into the logs above Dickey, who was crouched on the opposite side.

Dickey screamed and rolled into the center of the enclosure, clutching his head. He rolled over Amanda, who shrieked until Brigid hauled her free of the groaning soldier. Wills pulled Dickey's hands from his face to look at his wound.

"Christ, man! You're all right . . . that's just a splinter." A sliver of wood blown from the logs by the Indian bullet had laid open Dickey's forehead. It was not serious, but it bled profusely, blinding and terrifying him.

"I'm blind . . . I'm blind! Oh, God, I can't see!"

"Get off yer ass an' get that Injun or he'll kill you next time. Get up, man!"

"I can't! I can't see."

There were two Indians shooting at the upper end of the fort now, and Wills had no more time for Dickey.

"How many of 'em are they, for God's sake?" he demanded of Brigid.

"We saw four."

Wills nodded. "That's how many is shootin' at us. Hope they don't draw any more."

Brigid wondered if the old man was shooting at them too. He must be, unless there was one she hadn't seen. At that moment the Indian in the creek got another bullet through the undefended gap, and this one narrowly missed Wills. He swore obscenely, but Brigid, deafened and terrified by the noise, hardly heard him. She was flat on her stomach, an arm over each child, trying to soothe Amanda's gasping sobs.

"God damn you, Dickey!" growled Wills, kicking the hapless man. "Get up an' fight, will you?"

But Dickey only cowered against the logs, clutching his face. He looked awful with blood staining his hands and dripping from his chin.

"I can't cover two sides of this damn place," swore Wills. "Can you shoot a gun, Red?"

Brigid stared at him big-eyed. "I never did before. I don't know how."

"Just stick the damn thing out an' shoot it. Anything to worry that bastard."

"I'll try. Billy, hold your sister tight an' don't either of you move, you hear?"

Clumsily, she worked the muzzle of Dickey's rifle into the gap in the logs and jerked at the trigger. Nothing happened, and Wills looked over his shoulder.

"You gotta cock it, Red. Pull the hammer back."

That took both hands for Brigid, and she managed it with a struggle. She was convinced the Indian would kill her if she got in front of the gap, but she was determined to try. Teeth clenched and eyes squeezed shut, she pushed the heavy Long Tom out and jerked the trigger again. The hammer fell with an empty click, and she opened her eyes cautiously.

Precisely at that moment the Indian in the creek slammed a shot into the ground at the outer end of her loophole. The bullet droned over her head, flinging a burst of dirt and wood chips in her face.

"Brigid!" wailed Amanda, and Wills thought she had been hit, but she was only flattened against the logs, scooping dirt from her mouth and sobbing in terror and frustration.

"It's broken!" she choked. "The damn thing is broken. It won't shoot."

Wills retrieved the rifle and flung open the breech block.

"You got to load it, dummy! There's an empty cartridge in it."

"That's not my fault!" sobbed Brigid.

"No, that son-of-a-bitch left it there!" He kicked

Dickey, who had managed to tear a sleeve off his shirt and wrap it around his head, covering his eyes and his ripped forehead. The soldier crawled blindly out of reach of Wills's boot.

"Look . . . you push this thing here an' lift the block. Get the empty hull out an' stick in another one. Slam the block down, cock it an' shoot it. You can do that, can't you?"

Apprehensively, Brigid watched him load the rifle. He gave it to her and she worked it into the loophole a third time, gripping it in a loose approximation of the way Wills held his own weapon. The result, when she jerked the trigger, was spectacularly successful.

Since she had kept her eyes shut, she had no idea where the shot was directed, but the slot between the log piles channeled it in the general direction of her target. The heavy .45 caliber slug hit a rock halfway to the creek, producing a lethal shower of rock chips and a lump of lead ricocheting into the willows with an awesome howl. The Indian was in no danger, but Brigid damned well had his attention.

At her end of the loophole the results were almost as spectacular. The loosely held butt of the heavy rifle slammed into her shoulder with the force of a kicking mule, driving her backward across the chip-strewn wagon track. Her thumb, gripping the throat of the stock, collided brutally with her upper lip, and in moments she did not have to feel it to measure the damage. She could look down and see it swelling.

Oh, you bastard. You black-hearted bastard. She cursed the rifle and the Indian indiscriminately. She began the intricate task of reloading with her back against the logs, and she felt one of them surge against her as the Indian put a bullet into its outer end.

Suddenly she was no longer terrified. All right, she muttered. God mend my hands and I'll have your red ass in hell this day. Her conviction that the Indian would kill her was supplanted by a grim desire to kill him first.

She reloaded the Springfield, and this time she kept

343

her eyes open. The Indian had to raise his head and shoulders above the bank to shoot at her, and the next time he did it she was waiting for him. Her second shot was closer. It stripped branches from the willows a dozen feet above him and it ruined his aim completely. Things at her end had not improved, however.

"*Ow* . . . Jesus, Mary, an' Joseph!" she wailed in anguish.

"You hit?" yelled Wills.

"No! This devil's-limb of a gun is killin' me!"

The corporal looked at her dirty, swollen face, green eyes blazing, and burst into laughter.

"Hold it tighter, Red. Pull it back against you hard, an' it won't kick so bad."

"An' how do I make the ugly bitch go where I want it?"

Wills rolled over to explain. "Put that thing on what you want to hit . . ." He indicated the foresight. "An' then line it up right in this notch." He put his finger on the V-shaped notch on the leaf sight in front of the block.

Brigid never sent the Devil his promised red meat, but the Indian never got another shot into her loophole either. She scared him so badly he took to popping up for quick wild shots without aiming. William puffed and hauled until he got the cartridge belt off the whimpering Dickey, and all through the long, hot morning he handed cartridges to Brigid as she tore up earth and mowed down willows along the creek. The sun turned the interior of the little fort into a bake-oven, stinking of wood chips and burned black powder.

When Corporal Wills nudged her wide-spread leg with a canteen, she sucked warm water from it eagerly and spilled a little into her hand to wipe her aching, sunburned face.

"Don't waste it," he warned. "May have to last us a spell. You all right?"

"I'm fine. But I'd give my place at God's golden chair if he'd just help me kill that red bastard."

"You'll get him. Don't get careless. Jesus! If I had

me a couple more like you, Red, we'd go after him."
He jerked a thumb at Dickey, huddled against the logs.
"Look at that worthless scum!"

Help came in midafternoon, announced by shouts
and a burst of fire on the ridge above the log piles. The
cavalry troop had arrived, led by Captain Smith and
Cass Carter, whose own company was far behind,
dog-trotting up the road behind Ben MacKeever.

Dismounted troopers scrambled through the brush
cloaking the sides of the valley and swept the lone Indian sniping at Gause before them. The rest of the
troop burst into the glade mounted, riding past the fort
in a thunder of hooves and barking revolvers. There
were no Indians in sight, but the troopers worked on
the principle that with all that lead flying none would
shoot back.

Carter vaulted off his horse into the log enclosure,
sweeping William and Amanda into his arms with a
shout of joy. Their happy reunion jammed the little
pen so full that Brigid was shoved against the logs.

A hand closed on her arm and she shouted in alarm.
Michael Brennan, red-faced and sweating, grinned at
her.

"Are you all right?" he demanded, peering at her
face. "What the hell happened to you?"

Covering her fat lip with her hand, Brigid squeaked
at him indignantly. "Nothing! Why'd it take you so
long to get here?"

Wills chuckled. "Don't make her mad. Close as you
are, she can drop you."

"What do you mean? What's she been doin', for
God's sake?"

Lost in the roar of cavalry firing, the shot from the
creek went unheard but the bullet cracked by Michael's
head so close he sprawled backward with a jerk.

"Get down, you big clown!" screamed Brigid. "That
Indian's still in the creek!"

The troopers had overlooked Brigid's enemy, and he
was still trying to kill someone. Lieutenant Carter flat-

tened his children on the floor of the pen and jerked out his revolver.

"You stay with the kids, Lieutenant—we'll get him," Michael shouted. "Get down, Bridey, an' hand me that rifle. What's the matter with him?" he indicated Dickey.

"Damned little," grated Wills. "He's just hidin'."

Dickey flailed the air with his hands and hunched away. "I'm blind! Leave me be!"

"Well, gimme his belt. I got to have some cartridges."

"There aren't any," shrilled William, wriggling free of his father's arm to hold up Dickey's empty belt triumphantly.

"Goddam, Red!" exclaimed Wills. "You shot 'em all?"

"She did?"

Brennan, pocketing a handful of cartridges given him by Gause, stopped to stare at Brigid. He understood now what had happened to her face. His arm about her shoulder caught her kneeling, off-balance, and he gave her a crushing hug.

"Good on you, Bridey!"

She pushed him away furiously. "Lemme go, you fool. You'll get us all killed."

"All right, Brennan . . . you ready?" demanded Lieutenant Carter. Michael nodded, and the officer rose to a crouch, emptying his revolver into the willows in a series of aimed, spaced shots. Wills elbowed Brigid aside to join the fusillade, firing as fast as he could reload. Michael scrambled over the logs at the lower end of the pen and flung himself toward the creek.

The Indian clung to his shelter, pinned down by the rapid fire from the log pile. Brigid tried to follow Michael's progress through the loophole, but it was impossible. Hunched against the logs, she hugged Amanda with one arm and sucked a scraped knuckle worriedly. God defend him, she prayed silently, even if he is a great fool.

The willows swayed and crashed where Brennan

346

dove into the creek and the Indian broke from cover. Michael's rifle roared, and Wills raised a bellow of triumph.

"You got him! He's down!"

Everyone stood up to see. Brennan, wading knee-deep in the creek, stopped to take careful aim. His rifle crashed again and he waded out of sight behind the willows. After a little he climbed onto the bank above the fort and walked back, his trousers streaming water.

"You get him?" demanded Carter. Michael nodded.

"What kind of Indian is he?"

"Don't know, sir. I pulled him out on the bank. Maybe the scouts can tell." He looked at Wills. "You got any more hid out around here?"

The corporal shook his head. "I'd think not. There was only four of 'em."

"Nobody hurt except him?" Carter indicated Dickey.

"No, sir. An' he's not hurt as bad as he's makin' out."

"They killed two woodcutters," said Brigid, "an' there was another one up there. Maybe they killed him too."

"How'd you know that?" demanded Michael.

Brigid looked apprehensive and Lieutenant Carter put an arm around her shoulders. "Not now. You can tell us when we get home. That way you'll only have to tell it once."

Lieutenant Slade and a dozen troopers crowded around the log fort, their stamping, blowing horses adding to the confusion. The cavalrymen stared at Brigid with rapt attention.

"Somebody's got to go through those woods before we leave," said Carter, "but I'd like to start back now. Louise will come looking for us if I don't get these kids home quick."

"You go on," Slade told him. "Go with the captain, and I'll keep some men to check the woods. We didn't bring any scouts, so we'll have to haul Brennan's Indian back to find out what he is. We got another one on the ridge to put with him."

"Is he an old man?" asked Brigid softly, and they all looked at her in surprise.

"I haven't seen him, miss," replied Slade. He turned to his troopers. "Anybody know?" One of them nodded and held up a strange looking carbine.

"Young buck, Lootenant. Took this off him."

Carter looked at the weapon. "Remington seven-shot bolt action. Takes our cartridges, too."

"Reckon you could get us some of those, Lootenant?"

There was a chuckle at the trooper's question. Indians with repeating rifles were a sore spot for the army and its single-shot Springfields.

Winfield Slade was still curious about Brigid's question. "Why did you ask that, miss?"

"I . . . I just wanted to know."

"I know," announced William. "He was a good old man. He liked Amanda's hair."

"Saints above us!" muttered Michael, staring at Brigid in amazement. "What all have you been into this day?"

"That's enough," Carter interrupted. "I said later. Now let's get going."

He took Amanda in front of him on his saddle. William wrapped Dickey's empty canvas belt around his small waist and buckled it proudly before climbing up behind a trooper. It was visible evidence of his part in the fight, and he would not be parted from it. Its owner had less attention than William. Dickey's appearance was dramatic—his shirt sleeve glued to his face by dried blood—but Wills had been explicit about the nature of his wound.

One of the cavalrymen offered his horse to Brigid, but before he could reach her, Michael Brennan had lifted and settled her sidesaddle on the animal. She retaliated by chatting happily with her mount's owner and ignoring Michael, who led the horse.

Half a mile from the scene of the fight they encountered Cass Carter's company, raising the dust of the wagon track in a fast-moving column. At sight of his

348

company commander with Amanda in his arms, Ben MacKeever voiced a comment that would be overworked that afternoon.

"Thank God," he said simply.

The infantrymen set the returning pace, and it was late afternoon before they crossed Sweetwater Creek by the post bakery. Every woman on the post and the few remaining men were gathered to meet them. K Company opened ranks to let Louise Carter run to her husband, who lowered Amanda gently into her arms.

Louise Carter's face over her daughter's head was terrible. She was close to explosion with anxiety, and when she saw Brigid her overstrained nerves let go.

"What did you do?" she demanded in a harsh, strained voice. "How could you?"

Brigid stared at her, appalled. She was unprepared for this savage reproach, and William defended her.

"That's no fair, Mama!" he shrilled from behind his trooper. "Brigid got us away from the Injuns. They caught us an' they killed two of the men just like that . . ." He tried to snap his fingers and failed. "But she talked to the old man, and then she just turned around an' made us all go in front, an' we walked away like there weren't any Injuns there."

He spread his hands, fingers curled as if trapping something between them, and lowered his voice dramatically.

"They had us! They were gonna kill us. But Brigid wasn't scared. She just walked away from 'em an' they didn't do a thing."

His audience listened enthralled, and William plowed on. Pulling off his cartridge belt, he held it high.

"See? One of the soldiers was hurt, an' Brigid took his gun, an' she an' me, we shot every bullet in this whole belt! I bet we killed ten Injuns, didn't we, Brigid?"

Louise Carter looked from her son to his father in openmouthed astonishment, and Cass Carter chuckled.

"At least ten. There were hardly any left for us

when we got there. Brennan got one and Win Slade's men got the other."

"That's a fact, Missus Carter," put in Corporal Wills. "Beggin' your pardon, ma'am, but Red here is one helluva good soldier."

"Oh!" gasped Louise. "Oh, Brigid, forgive me! I was so frightened." She held out her hand to Brigid, who slid down from her horse, and Louise Carter put a finger to her cheek. "Whatever happened to your poor face?"

There was laughter among the soldiers. Every one of them knew that badge of first experience with the clumsy, hard-kicking Springfield rifle.

"Oh, my poor baby!" Louise Carter hugged Amanda, tears bright in her eyes. "Come, let's go home."

She looked at the soldiers watching her.

"Thank you," she said softly. "Thank you all."

At the sideboard in the dining room, Cass Carter poured himself a generous glass of Mr. Bruning's Pennsylvania bourbon, and a smaller one for Brigid. She tried it gamely. By that time Major Suter had arrived, and the Brenners crowded into the room as well.

William was the spokesman. From time to time, when his account of the epic defense of the log fort got out of hand, Cass Carter looked at Brigid, who nodded in corroboration or smiled painfully at an outrageous claim. When the story had been told and retold, Suter turned a serious face to Carter.

"What's your feeling, Cass? A few wandering renegades, or something more?"

"I don't know, Major. We don't even know who they are. Slade will bring in the two we killed, and maybe the Indian scouts can tell us."

Brigid's lip had subsided a little by next morning, but when Louise Carter saw the big purple bruise on her shoulder she was horrified.

"Good Lord, child! Does it hurt?"

"Yes, ma'am, but it'll be all right. Corporal Wills says it happens to everybody the first time."

Major Suter sent a courier to the telegraph station at Baker City with a report for Department Headquarters, but it would be days before there was a response to that. Meanwhile, Camp Belknap increased its guard and waited.

That night Michael Brennan and Corporal Wills knocked on the kitchen door, and William's shout of delight brought the elder Carters on the run. Michael had set a brand-new forage cap with brass crossed rifles at its peak on Brigid's flaming hair.

"Sharpshooter O'Donnel," he said solemnly, "you are now a member of Company K, Twenty-first Infantry. Stand tall, soldier!"

"What about me?" crowed William. "I helped her with the cartridges."

Wills produced another cap from behind his back, and the ceremony was repeated noisily. Someone had cut a ring for Amanda from an empty cartridge and filed it smooth. Two of her small fingers would not fill a .45 caliber ring, but her mother smiled and promised she would keep it safe until it could be worn.

"We could use a couple more like these in the company, Lieutenant," Wills said of the two recruits in their new caps. "They put the fear o' God in that Injun that hid in the crick."

"What about the other woodcutter?" asked Brigid softly. "The one that . . ."

Michael shook his head. "They found all three of 'em. He didn't run away."

"God rest his brave heart," murmured Brigid.

Louise Carter broke the silence with a surprising gesture. She put her arms around Brigid and kissed her cheek.

"God bless you too, Brigid. You were brave as any man there."

Embarrassed by her own display of emotion, she blew her nose and asked Mah Kim if there was coffee for the visitors. He set out cups and a fresh pie with a

351

sly glance at Brennan. William demanded coffee too, and in recognition of his stature as an authentic hero he had a cup, though there was more milk than coffee in it. Michael showed him how to break down the back of his stiff new forage cap so it did not look so new, and explained the art of polishing the brass crossed rifles.

"You do it right," he assured William, "an' before you know it they'll look just like mine."

He displayed his own cap, with the insignia almost smooth with a mirror shine, the lines depicting the locks and barrels all rubbed away by hard polishing.

The more memorable events of the fight talked over once again, Mrs. Carter started her children for bed and the two soldiers rose to take their leave. Brigid let them out the back door and Wills moved away, but Michael drew her onto the stoop.

"Now what?" she demanded suspiciously.

"I just wanted to say something I couldn't say in there." He smiled at her fondly. "You're one hell of a girl, Red."

"Well . . . now you've said it. And don't call me Red!"

He laughed. "With Wills tellin' everybody the tale of your great fight with the Indian, you'll never shed that name, Bridey." He gave her shoulder an affectionate squeeze and she winced.

"You'll have it after that Long Tom shoulder is gone, I'll wager. How's your lip?"

Incautiously she raised her face to show him, and he kissed her before she knew what he was about.

"Oh, get on with you!" She pushed him away. "Don't be tryin' your tricks on me."

She flounced back into the kitchen, slamming the door behind her, and Mrs. Carter, mixing condensed milk and hot water for Amanda, looked up in surprise.

"What the matter?"

"Nothing, ma'am. I didn't mean to shut it so hard."

But her face was bright red, and Louise Carter gave her a puzzled look.

2

Major Suter's reaction to the incident at the woodpile did not end with a report to Department. He tripled the Belknap guard—two men on every post and a full detail on call in the guardhouse—and he dispatched patrols—infantry probing the mountains, and cavalry on the southern plateau. They encountered nothing but a courier riding hard from Baker City. Within an hour of his arrival, a bugler on the veranda of the adjutant's office sounded officers' call with a strident urgency.

"It's started," Suter told his assembled officers, "and it's bad. The Nez Percés hit the settlers around Mount Idaho, and General Howard sent two troops from Fort Lapwai. The Indians whipped the hell out of them. Thirty men killed, according to this report."

He shuffled the messages in his hand. "We have orders. Howard thinks the Indians in the Weiser Valley may go north to join the Nez Percés. Our cavalry is to get across the Snake River into Idaho as fast as possible, to guard the Weiser River crossings. Mr. Slade will take the troop, and Captain Smith will command here in my absence. I'm going to Fort Boise to get it ready for the troops coming from California."

That explained the look on Captain Smith's face. Everyone knew he was unfit for field duty, but to be left behind while his own troop rode out was a blow that earned him sympathy.

"Troops from California!" exclaimed Surgeon Brenner. "Is it that bad?"

"Bad enough for Howard to order up damned near every man in this department and ask General McDowell for more."

"What about my company?" Carter asked.

"You're not forgotten. You're to send six men with the Gatling gun to Fort Klamath. Captain Jackson's troop leaves there for Roseburg and the railroad as soon as they join him. Howard wants them at Lapwai." He fixed Cass with a warning finger. "Jackson's under orders to leave Klamath by next Monday. You'll want good men, all mounted, and a double team for the gun."

Carter stared at him in astonishment. "Klamath's two hundred and sixty miles from here, Major! We're to get that gun there in five days?"

"We'll all leave at daybreak tomorrow. Send your detachment to Linkville at the bottom of Klamath Lake. I doubt that Jackson can get through the mountains to Roseburg this early in the year, so he'll go south to Linkville. If they miss him there, they've got till the first of July to catch him. There'll be a train at Roseburg for Jackson on the first, and I want your men and the gun on it. Understood?"

"Yes, sir. And the rest of the company?"

"Stays here. Howard wants someone watching the Paiutes."

"They won't make trouble!" Carter protested.

"We don't know who killed those woodcutters, Cass, and because we haven't found any Indians doesn't mean there aren't any more around."

He rapped on his desk to still the whispering.

"I expect to leave here at seven o'clock in the morning, and we've got a lot to do. Cass, pick your men and put a good noncom in charge. They'll take only rations enough to get them to the railroad. Don't bother with ammunition for the gun. They can get that at Vancouver or Lewiston—Howard's setting up a depot there. Slade, you'll take thirty days' rations and ammunition, and that means wagons, but remember . . . Carter has the pick of the mules. Have you any questions, gentlemen?"

His answer was the shuffling of boots as they edged toward the door.

"All right. Let's get ready."

The officers erupted from the headquarters to find their sergeants waiting, and Cass took Magruder with him to the quartermaster stable. The gun team and mounts for his men would determine if they won their race for the coastal railroad, and he meant to choose them himself. The barracks exploded into activity. Within minutes cavalry troopers streamed across the parade to the stables, stumbling under their loads of equipment. Nightfall put no end to their work, lanterns flaring in the barracks, stables and storehouses, and it was midnight before Cass Carter returned to his quarters. William and Amanda were long abed, but his wife and Brigid awaited him with anxious faces.

"The cavalry's going," he told Louise, "not us. We're only sending six men." Her eyes closed for a moment in a silent prayer of thanks.

"How long will it last?" she asked him.

"Lord, Weezie, who knows? Could be over before they get there, or it could go on for months. Is there any coffee?" Brigid jumped to fetch him a cup.

"Get where? Where are they going?"

Cass grinned. "Slade's taking the cavalry north of Boise to watch a river. Our men will go with the Fort Klamath troop to Lapwai. That's where the fighting is."

"Mister Slade? What about Gid Smith?"

"He'll stay here in command. Suter's going to Fort Boise."

"Who are you sending? Ben MacKeever?"

"Oh, no. Corporal Wortman with Katz, Chandler, Kieran, Cobb . . . and Brennan."

"Oh, my!" Louise glanced at Brigid.

"Can't help it," Cass said, finishing his coffee. "If

this gets worse the rest of us will go, and I can't spare my sergeants. Wortman's all right, but he's never seen any fighting. Brennan has."

"But I thought he and Brennan . . ."

"No matter. Brennan's a good soldier—better in a fight than in garrison. He'll take care of Wortman. If he had the stripes, I'd give him the command."

Despite Major Suter's angry impatience, it was eight o'clock before his troops were ready to move. The difficulty was the civilian teamsters on the cavalry wagons. For combat duty they drew eighty-five dollars a month in coin—not depreciated greenbacks like the soldiers—but even that was not enough to hurry them.

The cavalry trumpeter put the column in motion with a series of bugle calls: "mount," "twos right," and "forward." As it passed the guardhouse, Lieutenant Carter's four-man fife and drum corps saluted it with a march.

"Oh, Dear, What Can the Matter Be?" was hardly comforting, but it was appropriate. As Lieutenant Slade turned at the headquarters to lead his troop off the post, Carter's musicians changed their tune, and a sigh rustled through the women watching their men depart.

At parade or a dance it was a merry tune, but at a time like this it broke your heart. Angie Couza began to sob—a lament for the whole column, perhaps, for it was hard to tell which individual held Angie's warm heart at any time. Brigid's throat closed painfully. The ancient plaintive words of that song left no Irish girl unmoved:

> . . . I'll not fall prey to all their wiles—
>   Their charms shall not ensnare me,
> For my heart turns back to Erin's isle,
>   And the girl I left behind me.

"There goes your man," Mrs. Magruder whispered in her ear. "Have ye not even a wave for him?"

The cavalry was through the gate now, the infantry

gun-crew following. Wortman led, behind him the Gatling was drawn by two mules in tandem, and Michael brought up the rear on a big, somnolent mule. He passed so close to Brigid she could have put out her hand and touched him, but her impulse was slow. He caught the movement from the corner of his eye and looked back. For a long moment his eyes held hers. Then he grinned and winked. She tried to push her way out of the knot of women, but Molly Magruder gripped her arm.

"Ye'll not go runnin' after him, now. Leave that foolishness to Couza."

"Let me go!" Brigid protested. Molly shook her head.

"Don't be teasin' him, girl. You don't even want him."

Brigid jerked her arm free and started for the house, colliding blindly with Louise Carter.

"Oh, dear!" murmured Louise. "Don't cry, Brigid! Please, don't cry!"

3

After the army's initial defeat at White Bird Canyon, General Howard turned out the Department of the Columbia. By telegram he directed his adjutant general in Portland to "Order to Lewiston every available man in the Department. . . . I wish these movements perfected in the shortest possible time."

One of the units swept up by this order was Captain James Jackson's B Troop of the First Cavalry at Fort Klamath. Jackson marched through the Cascade Mountains and up the Oregon coastal road to Roseburg. The Belknap infantrymen were waiting for him there with their Gatling gun, and after he loaded his men and horses on the cars for Portland, Jackson never stopped long again. He meant to join Howard's war in the north.

Transferring to steamboat at Portland, he moved up the Columbia and Snake Rivers to Lewiston, where he picked up a pack train of a hundred and twenty mules, loaded with ammunition and supplies for Howard. From Lewiston he pushed southeast in pursuit of his General, and the closer he came the more harrowing were the reports of the local citizens.

The Nez Percé withdrawal from their victory at White Bird Canyon had been far from a rout. Catching one of Howard's scouting detachments beyond help, they wiped it out, killing Second Lieutenant Rains, ten troopers of the First Cavalry, and the civilian scout Rains was trying to find. Seventeen civilian volunteers were surrounded near Norton's Ranch on the road from Lapwai to Grangeville, and stood off the Indians for an hour until troops came to their help. This engagement had provoked bitter charges in the Lewiston *Teller* that the First Cavalry had been slow and cowardly in relieving the besieged civilians.

Jackson reached Grangeville, in Idaho Territory, a day's march behind Howard, to find the little town humming with news of a terrible battle fifteen miles away on the Clearwater River. It had been going on all afternoon, said the citizens, and Howard was in serious trouble. The entire Nez Percé nation—treaty and nontreaty alike—had swarmed down on Howard's four hundred and fifty men.

One of General McDowell's aides from San Francisco, Captain Birney Keeler, sent for a firsthand look at the war, had joined Jackson at Lewiston. The two captains agreed that they should push on as fast as possible, and by midmorning of the twelfth, marching down the east side of the Clearwater, they could hear the steady crackle of rifle fire and the occasional boom of a howitzer.

Their road snaked across a rolling prairie just outside a succession of gullies running to the bluffs bordering the river. These were shallow washes where the road crossed them, but they were deep and wide, with a thick lining of brush, where they drained into Clearwater Canyon. In the intervals between gullies, nearly flat tableland extended from the road west to the brink of the bluffs, and General Howard's force had inexplicably wedged itself into one of these intervals.

The only cover or concealment in the compartment seemed to be tall grass, in which Howard's position was marked by clouds of powder smoke. Michael Brennan, astride the lead mule of a pair hitched in tandem to the Gatling gun, could see more than Wortman, who had dismounted to jog ahead of the gun on foot.

"What are they shooting at?" yelled Wortman, "I don't see any Indians."

The answer was painfully apparent to Michael. He guessed Howard had tried to seize the bluff and failed, finding himself boxed in on the plateau by Indians lining the bluff and tree-choked gullies on three sides of him. It was as if the General had got himself onto a pool table with Indians in the pockets on all but one side.

Jackson wanted to charge into the fray, but he dared not leave the pack train unguarded. If he detached enough men for that, the remainder would be too small to count. He solved the problem by dismounting his troopers in a screen around the pack train and driving the whole unwieldy mass into Howard's perimeter. The Indians responded at once. Warriors popped up from the wooded gully on the south side of the compartment and banged away furiously at the approaching column. Several pack mules went down, but miraculously, none of the men were hit.

General Howard sent help. Out of the smoke came a small body of troops in open order, firing steadily. Filing by their right flank, they inserted themselves between Jackson and the Indians in the gully, and as Michael flogged his mule past them he saw that they were artillerymen, fighting as steadily and effectively as any infantry.

Troop B and its horde of braying, bucking mules swept onto the plateau, which proved not as flat as it seemed from the road. There were humps and folds in the ground beneath the grass, and in one of these they found General Howard's pack train and a makeshift field hospital.

Howard had sent Captain Miller and his artillerymen to help Jackson, but when Miller found himself near the beginning of the southern gully with a crowd of excited Nez Percés standing up to shoot at him, he exceeded his orders. He wheeled his gunners by their right flank, and with a whoop they charged the gulley, firing as they went. They were equipped with the infantry's trowel bayonets, glittering wickedly in the hot sun as they crashed into the brush, and the Indians scrambled to get out of their reach.

The unexpected charge had help from the perimeter. A stubby little mountain howitzer bounced out behind a trotting team, the crew running alongside. Two hundred yards from the gulley they dropped trail, and in minutes they were banging away over the heads of Miller's men, plowing the gulley with shell. All over the field, men stood up to wave their hats and cheer the ridiculous little gun and its crew.

But Miller's rush left a number of Indians behind, who saw a vulnerable prize in the howitzer. A dozen mounted braves broke cover, whooping and riding hard for the gun, with more behind them advancing on foot. The crew switched to canister and blew the horsemen away, but not the Indians crawling through the grass to reach them.

The artillery lieutenant who had brought out the howitzer went for help. Appearing like a jack-in-the-box at the edge of the hollow where Jackson's pack-train was sheltered, he found the Gatling gun.

"Bring it out!" he yelled at Corporal Wortman. "Get it up there and cover my gun."

Getting the Gatling team out of the milling pack mules was hard, though, and the lieutenant displayed an impressive talent for swearing. Once out of the hollow, the untrained mules balked flatly. No power on earth was going to take them into that whistling, crackling hell on the flat.

"Unhook 'em and run it up by hand!" shrieked the lieutenant. "Where's the ammunition?"

Wortman pointed at two lead mules with ammunition packs, heads down and fighting frantically to get back to the mass of animals.

"Blindfold the bastards and drive 'em out! Come on, men . . . let's get this gun moving!"

He flung himself, with Wortman, Brenner, and the rest of the crew, against the wheels of the Gatling, and they heaved it over the broken ground to within a

361

hundred yards of the howitzer, which was firing as fast as men could load it, the crew wrestling shells from the packs of a dead mule beside it.

"Right here!" panted the officer. "Open up an' keep 'em off my gun." He was gone, running for the howitzer, and Michael loaded the Gatling while Wortman spun the crank. For a wonder, it did not jam, and its breathless, cracking roar was a welcome sound.

"Ammunition!" bawled Michael. "Bring some more —quick!"

A blindfolded pack mule, fighting like a demon, was hauled as close as possible, but he would not stay. Stripping the packs onto the ground, they let him go, bucking and braying, into the smoke. Knocked sprawling by the animal's lunges, Michael followed him with a curse. "I hope the son-of-a-bitch runs over an Indian," he swore bitterly.

The artillerymen in the gully were advancing in fine style, but the Indians left behind were behaving like no Indians Michael had ever seen. Swept by howitzer and Gatling fire, they kept coming in short rushes covered by rifle fire from their prone comrades. The howitzer crew stood fast until the Indians were within seventy yards, before they broke and left their bronze antique undefended.

A dusty, sweating cavalry captain cantered up to the Gatling and surveyed the scene coolly. His horse was as calm as he.

"Run it back, Corporal," he told Wortman quietly. "Get yourself some room, before they're on top of you. If they try to move that howitzer, fire at it."

"No!"

The artillery lieutenant was back, wild-eyed and gasping. "You can't leave my gun out there! Keep 'em off it till I get some men."

"They can't hurt that goddamn yacht-club cannon, mister," the cavalry officer told him, "and the Gatling's no good this close. Get it out of here, Corporal!"

More than willingly, two of the crew snatched up the trail and two more grabbed the wheels, running the gun back faster than it had come. Indian bullets kicked up grass and dirt at their heels to inspire them.

But the lieutenant was a real artilleryman, and he would not abandon his howitzer. He went back to it by himself, and for some unknown reason Wortman went after him.

Michael watched in amazement. Wortman had never shown any heroic tendencies before. Running after a crazy lieutenant into a crowd of fighting-mad Indians struck him as such monumental lunacy, he was never able to understand why—after a moment—he went scrambling and stumbling after Wortman and the officer.

Reaching the howitzer, Michael flung himself behind the dead mule and peered over its neck. Wortman was sprawled by the gun, handing something to the lieutenant, who was on his back under it. It must have been a shell, for the officer got to his knees and calmly jammed the thing into the muzzle of the howitzer.

Bullets snapped and howled around the little gun, and one of them slammed into the mule, driving a rasping grunt from the animal. For a moment Michael thought it was still alive, but the mule's head was inches from his own, and the protruding tongue clenched between thick yellow teeth belied that.

"The rammer!" shouted the lieutenant. "Give me the rammer!"

He was prone again, one hand stretched behind him, and Wortman was looking around helplessly. Michael sighed. The rammer was leaning on the mule, far out of Wortman's reach. Inching forward, Michael grabbed the thing and began an agonizing approach to the howitzer, his chin furrowing the dirt. From that position he could see no Indians, but he had no desire to. Bullets cracked over his head like boards slapped together, and one ricocheted off the iron rim of a gunwheel with a throbbing howl that drove him flatter yet. He pushed out the rammer staff until Wortman could reach and hand it to the lieutenant.

363

"Good!" said the officer. "Now get a friction tube."

"What's he want?" Wortman yelled at Michael.

"It's what you shoot the goddamn thing with, I think. Must be in the pack."

Together, flat on the ground, they rummaged through the ammunition chest until Wortman held up a compartmented wooden box holding slim gray tin tubes.

"This it?"

Brennan nodded, and Wortman extracted a tube by the wire ring at its end.

"Leave it alone!" yelled Michael. "It'll go off if you pull it!"

"What'll I do with it?"

"There's a hole on top of the gun at this end. When that damn fool gets it loaded, you stick it in the hole right up to the ring an' hook a lanyard to it. Get out of the way of the gun and jerk the lanyard."

"That's easy enough," said Wortman, getting to his knees and peering at the breech of the howitzer.

"Get down, man!" yelled Michael, "You want to get your ass shot off?"

Neither Wortman nor the lieutenant paid any attention. The officer knelt at the muzzle of the gun, driving home the canister round he had loaded, and Wortman inserted the friction tube in the vent, which he had finally found.

"Not yet," said the lieutenant calmly. "Got to prick the cartridge first."

Michael shut his eyes. He supposed it might help if these two lunatics got the gun to fire, but he doubted they would live to do so. Deep in the grass as he was, he could hear the high-pitched shrieks of the Indians drawing nearer, and with them the lieutenant's cool instructions to Wortman.

"Now you can put it in. Push down hard so it goes in the powder bag."

It was unreal. Two supposedly sane men fiddle-dicking with that toy cannon while God knows how many Indians were seriously trying to kill them.

"Where's the lanyard?"

"I don't see one."

"Should be a spare in the fuze pouch."

"Lieutenant, I don't know what a fuze pouch looks like."

"There it is . . . right there. Hand it to me."

Michael opened one eye. Wortman raised up to hand the officer a greasy cord with a wooden handle on one end and a snap-hook on the other. As the lieutenant took it, Wortman sprawled backward behind the gun with a coughing grunt.

Michael heard the bullet hit him. He crawled forward, twisted a hand into Wortman's shirt collar, and dragged him back to the scant shelter of the dead mule.

The slug had gone in just above Wortman's breastbone, and he was breathing with a deep, snoring gurgle. I got to get him out of here, Michael thought, appalled at the wound. Quick, too, or he's got no more chance than a whore's prayer.

"Grab hold of my belt," he told Wortman, straddling the prone man, "I'm goin' to drag you out of this."

"Nugh!" said Wortman wetly. His usually ruddy face was ashen, and his groping hand caught Michael's collar.

"The belt, damn it—not there!"

"You . . ." choked Wortman, tugging feebly.

Michael bent his head to hear what he was trying to say.

". . . got . . . your . . . stripes back . . . you son-of-a-bitch . . ."

Having loaded his howitzer almost single-handed under heavy fire, the lieutenant now decided to shift its trail. It was not pointed exactly where he wanted it. The earlier rapid firing had seated the trail firmly in the ground, and he had to stand up and kick it to get it free. When he had, and the gun was laid just where he wanted it, he dropped on one knee outside the wheel and jerked the lanyard.

The roar of the little howitzer was deafening, but that was the least of its impact on Michael. The crew had removed the locking rope from the wheels as soon as the gun was seated, and with its trail shifted, it leaped backward when it was fired.

The lunette at the end of the trail smashed into Michael's shin, and he screamed. Since he was sprawled flat, belly down and hugging the ground as tightly as possible, there was no give.

"You hit?" asked the lieutenant.

"The gun! Pull it off me . . . get me loose!"

Heaving up the trail, the officer pulled Michael's leg from beneath it and the Irishman bellowed in pain.

"It's broken! The goddamn thing broke my leg!"

"Hell!" said the lieutenant. Obviously he had meant to keep on firing the gun, but now he had to do something about Brennan.

"I'll get you to cover," he said disgustedly.

"You better look at Wortman, first . . . he's hit bad."

"When did that happen?"

The officer crawled to Wortman and crouched over him.

"He's dead."

Michael rolled over to look. Wortman's face was proof. Like the mule's, it reflected death that struck suddenly but not fast enough.

"You sure your leg's broken?" asked the lieutenant. "We got to slow those Indians down before we can get out of here." He handled Michael's leg again, and Michael swore explosively.

"Don't pull it, Lieutenant! Goddamn it, it's broken!"

"I guess it is. All right, I'll put one more round into 'em and then we'll go."

Michael groaned in pain and fury. The lieutenant was his only chance of getting back to the perimeter before there were Indians all over him, and the damned fool was going to play grab-ass with his cannon again.

The officer worked just as carefully as before, loading the howitzer as deliberately as if he were on a practice range. He jerked the lanyard and Michael heard the canister slashing into the brush of the gully, and rejoiced at the dismayed howls that greeted the storm of leaden slugs. There was a perceptible slackening of the Indian fire, and relief flooded him. Now they could go.

But first the officer gathered up all the remaining friction tubes and threw them as far from the gun as he could. Michael watched him in sweating wonder.

"All right. Can you hop on your good leg?"

"You bet, Lieutenant! Let's get outa here!"

The officer paused long enough to pat Wortman's shoulder affectionately. "Brave man. I'll come back for him."

He will, too, thought Michael. He wondered if the lieutenant was a genuine hero or just plain crazy. The officer pulled him up and they went off at a shuffling trot, arms around each other's shoulders, Michael's broken leg swinging painfully as he hopped along.

Miller's artillerymen had broken the heart of the Indian attack. They swept the southern gully clean, and the rest of Howard's men rose to join them, driving the Indians from the bluff and the northern gully too. Michael could hear the shouts of triumph as the lieutenant handed him over to a medical orderly at the field hospital. The officer did not stay. He went off at a trot, and Michael knew where he was going.

"What's the matter with him?" asked the orderly. "Where's he going?"

"Not crazy," grunted Michael. "He's been there a long time. You got any water?"

"We've sent for some. We can get at the spring now. Where you hit?"

Before Michael could answer, a tired, blood-spattered surgeon appeared. He listened to Michael's mumbled explanations, then cut the laces of his brogan, pulled it off, and slit the trousers and wool longjohns beneath them.

367

"No blood." he said, prodding the big blue lump on Michael's shin. "What did this?"

"Ow! Jesus, Mary, and Joseph, Doc! Don't poke it! A goddamn howitzer ran over me."

"You're a hell of an artilleryman. Can't you get out of the way of your own gun?"

"Not my gun! I'm a doughboy, an' I hope to God I never see a gun again as long as I live. Ow! Easy, Doc ... please!"

"It's broken," chuckled the surgeon, "but it's not bad. Bone didn't come through."

He pulled splints and bandage from a medical pack and grinned at Michael.

"This is going to hurt like hell when I set it because I'm not about to waste any chloroform on a big ugly Mick like you. We'll just see how tough a doughboy you are. You can swear . . . or you can take a lap on the beads. Just don't thrash around, now."

Dusk closed over the groaning hollow, but the day's heat lingered and the wounded begged for water. The medical orderlies hauled it uncomplainingly from the distant spring in canvas buckets, and Michael dozed fitfully until it was his turn. When they woke him and gave him a cup he gulped it thirstily.

"Easy," warned the medic, "there's plenty now. Couple of people want to talk to you."

The artillery lieutenant was squatting by a nearby fire talking in low tones to a tall civilian. When Michael finished his water, he pointed at a knapsack beside him.

"That belonged to your friend. Thought you'd want it. I want his name and outfit, because I'm going to see that he's mentioned for bravery in this fight."

"Did he get buried?" Michael asked irritably, and the civilian chuckled. Michael squinted to see who had laughed.

"I was only laughing at the way you said it, soldier. No disrespect. First things first, eh?"

"This is Mr. Sutherland," said the artillery lieutenant. "He's a newspaper correspondent. Your friend was brought in, and he'll be buried tomorrow with the others."

"How many others?"

"Twelve that we've found. Maybe more—got dark before we had a good look. What was your friend's name?"

"Wortman, sir. Corporal Henry Wortman, Company K, Twenty-first Infantry."

"K Company? Oh, you came with the Gatling, didn't you? Where from?"

"Yes, sir. From Camp Belknap. We came with Cap'n Jackson's troop from Klamath."

"Ah, yes. Just in time for the finish, weren't you?"

Just in time to get run over by your damned cannon and get Henry Wortman killed, thought Michael sourly. He said nothing, though. He thought the lieutenant was a little crazy and he wanted no truck with newspaper writers. No good came of their fancy accounts of a fight. But the civilian was squatting beside him, holding out a cigar.

"Smoke, soldier?"

No use letting prejudice get between me and a good smoke, Michael decided, accepting the stogie. Mr. Sutherland brought a glowing branch from the fire to light it.

"I can't get much out of the lieutenant here," he said. "Can you tell me what happened with that howitzer?"

Michael pulled on his cigar until it glowed, and nodded his thanks. "Not much. I an' Corporal Wortman an' the lieutenant went out there after the crew ran off, an' shot that damned thing at the Indians for a while."

He eyed the lieutenant and remembered the swollen, tallow-colored tongue of the dead mule.

"The lieutenant an' Wortman did most of it. After Wortman was hit an' I was hurt, the lieutenant loaded an' fired it by himself."

369

Sutherland was scribbling, leaning to the fire to see his notebook. "You didn't tell me that part, Lieutenant."

The young officer grinned, and winked at Michael. "You might not have believed me, Tom. Had to get somebody else to tell you that. I couldn't do all that without help. This soldier and his friend did as much as I did."

Well, thought Michael. That's handsome of him. And he's not the fool I thought he was. He drew deep on the cigar. It was fresh and good. Sutherland stopped writing and looked at him.

"And your name . . . ?"

Michael studied him cautiously, and the correspondent smiled.

"You and Wortman and the lieutenant did a mighty brave thing with that gun. I just want to make sure General Howard and a lot of other people know about it. That's all."

Michael nodded. "Brennan, sir. Private Michael Brennan, K Company of the Twenty-first."

"You from Camp Belknap, too?"

"Yes, sir."

"Thank you, Brennan. I promise it won't do any harm."

The lieutenant and the correspondent moved away, and Michael rolled over to relight his cigar at the fire. He saw Wortman's knapsack, and after a while he went through its contents. The only thing of immediate value was a can of sardines, but the key was gone and he had lost his pocket knife.

The medical orderly came back with a mug of coffee and a handful of hardtack crackers. He opened the tin for Michael, generously refusing a sardine in return. Michael wolfed them all, soaking his crackers in the oil and enjoying them greatly.

If that civvie correspondent does what he says, he thought, I might get my stripes back. With Wortman dead, there was a chance. He flipped the empty sardine tin into the darkness and lay on his back to watch the stars.

"I'd as lief had 'em off somebody else, Henry," he said softly, "but I thank you. And for the sardines, too."

4

With the departure of the cavalry, Camp Belknap's effective strength consisted of the twenty-nine infantrymen remaining in Cass Carter's company. Their difficulty was compounded by Captain Smith's insistence that a regular routine be maintained. He might be unfit for campaigning, but he would not command a slack post.

There were no more reports from Department, but Colquohon in the infantry company had a letter from his friend, Private Kieran, who had gone with the Gatling gun. Wortman's detachment had reached Roseburg in time to take the cars north with Captain Jackson's troop, and they had found Fort Vancouver all but deserted. The four companies of the Twenty-first Infantry stationed there had all gone to join General Howard. The letter was dated July 4, and closed with the remark that "tomorrow we leave for the front."

On the seventeenth, the mail-rider was back with nothing official, but he reported rumors in Canyon City of another terrible battle somewhere near Mount Idaho.

"Sounds like they're still talking about the first fight," Cass told Louise. "Perry's disaster. That was near Mount Idaho."

She looked puzzled, and he scowled. "It was a

disaster. Perry took his troop and Trimble's into a trap. The Indians hit them and I think they broke."

"What does that mean?"

"Broke and ran. Perry had over a hundred men. He lost thirty-four killed and two wounded. That means he was whipped and he abandoned his wounded on the field. The Indians must have killed everyone they found. That's the only way you have casualties like that."

"My God . . . how horrible!"

She found him that night sorting his field equipment on the floor in the hallway. "What are you doing?" she demanded in a whisper.

"Just getting ready."

"But Major Suter said you have to stay here to guard this post!"

"That's right. But if there has been another fight . . . as bad as the first . . . they'll want us." He looked at her and got to his feet quickly.

"Now, Weezie . . ." he began, but she pulled away from him.

"Have you heard something you haven't told me?"

"I've never done that to you."

"But you know, don't you?"

"I don't know anything. I've just got a hunch."

She stared at him, the tears spilling down her cheeks, and when he held out his arms she came to him.

"I don't want you to go!"

"I haven't gone yet. Come on . . . it's late. Let's go to bed."

A courier from Baker City arrived next morning while they were at breakfast, and before they had finished an orderly brought a summons from Captain Smith.

"I'll finish packing for you," Louise said.

"But I don't know what he wants," Cass objected.

"You've got a damned good idea. And so have I. Go on now, and let me know as soon as you can."

When Carter, Brenner, and MacKeever had gathered, Smith read them his news.

"Howard met the Indians on the eleventh and twelfth. He calls it the battle of the south fork of the Clearwater River."

"Casualties?"

"Thirteen killed and twenty-seven wounded."

"Ah! He whipped them, then."

"I'd say so."

"Any from my company? If they left Vancouver the fifth, they could have been there."

Smith studied the long telegram. "Yes. Wortman killed. Brennan wounded. I don't see any more. Doesn't say if Brennan's serious."

"Damnation!" growled MacKeever. "What happens now, sir?"

"Howard says the Nez Percés have started for Montana on the Lolo Trail. The Second Infantry is on the way from Louisiana, but he won't wait for them. As soon as Major Sandford brings up the California troops from Boise, he's going after the Indians."

"Sandford? What happened to Major Suter?"

"Doesn't say. Perhaps he'll stay at Fort Boise to meet the Second Infantry. They could come in that way."

"But what about us?" MacKeever persisted.

Smith suddenly looked old and very tired. "They're stripping us. My troop goes north with Sandford, and you're to replace them on the Weiser. Doctor, they want you at Fort Boise. God knows what for."

"What about Belknap?" Carter asked. "They can't leave it with no garrison at all."

"Troop A, First Cavalry, is ordered here from Camp Bidwell in California."

"But that'll take days! Do we wait until they get here?"

"No. You go at once."

"What will you do in the meantime?"

"Hang on. Fort up and hang on, that's all. You'd better get your people ready, Cass. We've still got two

374

wagons, and I suppose you'd better take 'em . . . if you can find enough mules." He managed a smile. "Good thing you're going, Doctor."

"Why, for God's sake?" Brenner demanded.

"The mules will need you."

Cass returned to his quarters within the hour, but there was no need to explain what had happened. The activity in the infantry barracks made it obvious. He found Louise and the children kneeling on his bedroll while Brigid tugged at the straps.

"What in the world is in it?" he asked wonderingly.

"I put in what you'll need," Louise replied brusquely. "When do you go?"

"By noon, I expect. Doesn't take long to get twenty men ready."

"Do you know where?"

"Yes, damn it! To watch the Weiser River so Win Slade can take the cavalry north to join General Howard."

Louise managed to keep the elation from her eyes. "That sounds rather dull," she said quietly. "You must eat before you go. Brigid, will you tell Mah Kim we require dinner by eleven, please." She turned back to Cass. "Was there another battle?"

"Yes. A big one, apparently. We whipped them but it must have been touch-and-go for a while." Brigid returned from the kitchen and he gave her an unhappy look. "Uh . . . our detachment was in the fight." The way he said it fixed both women instantly.

"What—?" Louise began, but Brigid's harsh whisper interrupted her.

"Michael's dead?"

"No! Wortman was killed. Brennan's been wounded. I'm sorry, Brigid, but that's all we know. It could be bad or it could be only a scratch."

It was Amanda, proper little Philadelphia lady, who was first to voice the lament that Irish Brigid was stifling with her hands at her lips.

"Oooh . . . poor Michael!" she wailed.

Brigid reached her first. On her knees, she hugged the little girl and rocked her to and fro.

"Don't, Amanda! He's all right . . . I know he is!"

"How do you know? Papa said he's hurt!"

"He'll be back . . . you'll see!" Her own eyes were brimming dangerously. "Nobody could stop that big Mick from coming home. Please don't, Amanda . . . You'll make us all cry, baby!"

At noon the remainder of K Company marched away, Cass Carter at the head of the tiny column and MacKeever at the rear. Dr. Brenner rode the seat of the first of the two baggage wagons, and there were neither fifes nor drums to play them off to war. He had found all the musicians fit to shoulder a Springfield and march. The nine men he had declared unfit would remain with the few troopers left behind by the cavalry to guard Camp Belknap until a relief garrison appeared. They did not gather with the women to bid farewell to K Company. Their status was not a popular one.

5

Captain Smith organized the remainder of his post with grim efficiency. The next morning he gathered all the women and children at the bachelor officers' quarters and laid down the rules. The big log building was the most defensible house of the post, and it would be their fort. Every family was assigned a space in it, and required to bring bedding and food to be stored there. The windows on the ground floor were blocked up by burlap bags filled with earth, and loopholes were punched through the chinks between the logs on both floors. There was not a trumpeter left, but the quartermaster blacksmith made an iron triangle to be hung in the porch of the adjutant's office.

"When you hear that struck by the guard," Captain Smith told them, "no matter where you are or what you are doing, come here at once, as fast as you can."

Spare rifles and all the ammunition left in the magazine were moved into the big downstairs hall of the building, and barrels of water were put in all the rooms.

"Some of you"—he smiled at Brigid—"already know how to use a rifle. Sergeant O'Hara will give instruction to any others who care to learn. I suggest you attend his classes."

His preparations were impressive, and they kept everyone busy for quite a while but nothing happened, and feminine interest in Sergeant O'Hara's rifle practice waned quickly. Louise Carter, abetted by William and Brigid, attended the first three sessions and then dropped out.

"I can load the wretched thing, and if anyone gets close enough to me, I suppose I could shoot him with it. It's noisy and it hurts, though, and I see no purpose in practicing further to be miserable."

The twenty-one soldiers left behind were organized into a detachment under the command of Ordnance Sergeant O'Hara. Sergeant Couza had never been anything except a commissary sergeant, and was considered unqualified to lead a combat force. He was assigned the job of supervising the makeshift fort into which the bachelor officers' quarters had been converted, but Mrs. Smith supervised him so closely that the establishment quickly became known as "Fort Abigail."

Sergeant O'Hara's defense force soon showed its true worth. O'Hara was sixty years old, and unable to dominate his unruly command, which was accurately described by the more experienced ladies of the garrison.

"Coffee coolers is too good a name fer them sorry boogers," Molly Magruder announced. "Shammin' sick or lame to git outta goin' to the war. They wouldn't fight if ye locked 'em in the sink with an Injun."

Smith divided them into three details—one on guard, one in reserve in case of emergency, and one to patrol outside the post. The latter was the first to get into serious trouble. Seven men under Acting Corporal Davis of the cavalry troop were dispatched on a swing around Camp Belknap to look for signs of Indians. Instead of a swing, Davis's patrol marched east to Glenn's Store, a settlement of about twenty-five people on the main stage road from Boise to Baker City. They were gone for two days before a civilian rode over to ask Captain Smith what his soldiers were doing in the saloon behind the stage station. Didn't he need them at Camp Belknap?

378

Outraged, Gideon Smith mounted one of the few remaining quartermaster mules and rode the ninety miles to Glenn's Store himself. He rounded up five of the miscreants and drove them back, but the trip put him to bed for a week. The other two did not reappear for days, and when they did they brought enough whiskey to circumvent Smith's new orders.

Henceforth, he decreed from his bed, the patrol will not go more than ten miles from the post in any direction. Obediently, Sergeant O'Hara led his heroes up Sweetwater Canyon a few miles, but instead of returning that night, they camped out and the whiskey appeared. What happened then was never clear. O'Hara and one man got back to Belknap next day with a confused story of an attack by Indians on the patrol's camp. The triangle on the adjutant's veranda was beaten, and every soul in Camp Belknap fled to the bachelor officers' quarters.

For an entire day, the remaining soldiers and the women peered grimly from their loopholes waiting for attack. There was none. One by one, O'Hara's stalwarts drifted in—each with a different story. The last two showed up three days later with a Paiute Indian woman they claimed to have captured from their attackers, but their story was damaged by the attitude of the woman, which was hardly that of a captive.

"God hold us in his hand," commented Dinah Wool, "if we're beholden to that lot to save us from the murderin' Injuns!" Dinah's husband was a sergeant in Cass Carter's absent company.

On the twentieth of July the mail rider brought a copy of the Portland *Standard* that displaced the antics of the defense force as a topic of conversation. It contained a lengthy account of the battle of the Clearwater by a correspondent named Sutherland who was with General Howard's force. Most interesting was a full column by Sutherland on the heroics of an artillery lieutenant named Otis on the second day of the battle.

According to Sutherland, Lieutenant Otis and two brave soldiers had made their way to a howitzer, aban-

379

doned by its crew in the face of an Indian charge, and served the gun until one of the soldiers was killed and the other wounded. The dead man was Corporal Wortman and the wounded soldier was Private Brennan, whom the officer had carried on his back out of danger. Interviewed later by Sutherland, the lieutenant said the bravery of the two soldiers had saved the day—they had enabled a battalion of General Howard's force to turn back the Indians and sweep them from the field.

"I found the wounded soldier, Private Brennan, in the field hospital after the battle," Sutherland wrote, "and asked him for his account of the action. 'It was the lieutenant's fight,' he told me. 'After Wortman was killed and I was hit, he fired the gun till there was no more ammunition. Then he fixed it so the Indians couldn't use it, and he carried me off with the bullets flyin' that thick you could stick out your hat and catch a pound of 'em.' As modest as he was brave, this big Irish soldier, giving all the credit to his dead corporal and the young lieutenant. I doubt the heroism of these three good soldiers will earn them the praise it deserves from their countrymen safe in the East, but it is to be hoped the Army will recognize their mighty deeds."

"Glory be to God!" said Molly Magruder when the post trader read this thrilling story to an enthralled group of women in his store. "I've no doubt he played the man, but Michael Brennan never talked like that at all, at all. Does it tell how bad was his wound, Mr. Morton?"

"No." Sy Morton studied the paper and shook his head. "That's funny. It never says anything about that at all. It says the wounded had a hard journey to Grangeville, and from there they'll be taken to Fort Lapwai. This time of year the steamers get within three miles of there. Anybody bad hurt'll be in Portland in a week."

"If he gets to Portland, they'll never get him beyond," muttered Mrs. Magruder with a wicked look at Brigid. "They say the town is full of handsome women."

Sunday, July 22, began on a depressing note and ended in a shambles. When the women of the garrison gathered at Fort Abigail for the quasi-religious service that morning, Captain Smith chilled their hearts by reading the grimmer portions of the Order for the Burial of the Dead, for Corporal Wortman.

"Man that is born of a woman," he intoned solemnly, "hath but a short time to live, and is full of misery. He cometh up and is cut down, like a flower; he fleeth as it were a shadow, and never continueth in one stay. In the midst of life we are in death: of whom may we seek for succor but of thee, Oh Lord. . . ."

Brigid, raised by the Sisters in the conviction that good Catholics who attended other people's church services put their souls in danger, was badly shaken. As long as these affairs seemed more social than religious, she had quelled her conscience. But Captain Smith's prayers for the soul of Corporal Wortman, killed in action short days after he grinned at her as he rode out the post gate, were too painful to be ignored. When she was back in her room she spent some time on her knees by her bed, soliciting forgiveness for her sins, comfort for Henry Wortman, and a safe return for Michael Brennan.

With a garrison of twenty-one, Captain Smith had finally given up formal guard mount, but that afternoon there was not even a man-for-man exchange on post. Old Sergeant O'Hara reported to the post commander with tears in his eyes that the evening relief was unable to mount guard at all. Somehow they had smuggled a demijohn of pop-skull liquor into the guardhouse, and only three of the seven were conscious. Those three were so sick it was doubtful they would ever go on guard again.

There was no use swearing at poor old O'Hara. He frankly admitted he could not control the collection of skulkers left in his charge. In despair Smith wrote a plea to Major Suter for a lieutenant, or at least a good young sergeant, to whip some semblance of discipline into the dregs that had been left to guard Belknap. He would return the man as soon as the cavalry troop from Camp Bidwell arrived, but unless he had some help, he feared for the safety of the post. The full measure of his despair was the fact that he sent this plea to Fort Boise by a quartermaster civilian farrier, not trusting any of his enlisted men to take it.

6

Two weeks passed with no response to his request for assistance and Captain Smith began to think there would be none. He guessed Major Suter had his hands so full at Fort Boise he could spare no one, but on August 4 help arrived unannounced in the form of Second Lieutenant John Shelby.

The young officer's distaste for the job was obvious. Well on his way to the scene of action in the north, he had been diverted by Major Suter from the California troops passing through Boise. When Shelby described the unit from which he had been stolen, Captain Smith's respect for Suter's achievement rose.

General McDowell was obviously stripping California to help Howard. Of the five troops of cavalry in that department, four had gone to the field force and the fifth was under orders to Belknap. Of six artillery companies, three had gone north as infantry with three of the seven real infantry companies plus two more from Arizona. As a final measure, McDowell had mounted yet another artillery company on worn-out horses and shipped it out as cavalry, and it was this makeshift troop to which Shelby had attached himself as a means of getting to the war.

With the demand for fighting troops so insistent that California coast artillery was being converted to infantry and cavalry, Major Suter's achievement in diverting a healthy young lieutenant to Camp Belknap—even temporarily—deserved admiration.

"I know how you feel, mister," Smith told the lieutenant. "It won't be long. The Bidwell troop ought to be here by the middle of the month, and then you can go. I doubt that you or anybody could get this guard detachment into the field, but I expect this post to be properly guarded and that's your job."

Shelby acknowledged it glumly and handed over a pouch of mail. Belknap's cavalry troop had left a quantity of it in Boise when it departed for the fighting, and while Shelby was there, Cass Carter's miniature infantry company had passed through, leaving more. The infantry was bound for Middle Valley, a mining district a hundred miles northeast of Boise.

"What in the world for?" demanded Smith.

"Major Suter said the Weiser Indians have been quiet so far, but the miners in the upper end of the valley are afraid the Nez Percés will circle back and stir them up. K Company was sent to see that that doesn't happen."

"All twenty of 'em, eh?" Smith commented wryly. "That ought to be a great comfort to the citizens of Middle Valley." He glanced through the official messages Shelby had brought, and grunted at one of them.

"I see Carter's had a report on the Clearwater fight. Here's a warrant to promote Private Brennan to corporal—if he gets back here. Well . . . you'll have the bachelors' quarters to yourself, mister. You can take an orderly from the detachment if you find one you trust. I want you to put a heavy hand on that bunch. Old Sergeant O'Hara can manage the housekeeping, but don't expect any more from him. The old man's as crippled as I am, damn it!"

From the veranda of the adjutant's office, John Shelby surveyed Camp Belknap and swore silently. It had taken weeks to persuade the division signal officer he could be spared from the telegraph lines, and finding a place in the makeshift cavalry troop had been a stroke of luck. It was no prize, but it was a way to get to the fighting, and when Major Suter ordered him out of it to go and hold old Gideon Smith's hand he had protested bitterly—so bitterly he very nearly got himself in trouble.

Damn Camp Belknap, he muttered. Damn Suter and this poor old excuse for a post commander. There was only one bright spot in the whole gloomy mess—Brigid. He looked at the packet of letters in his hand—letters from Lieutenant Carter to his wife which he had not handed over to Captain Smith. He meant to deliver these personally to the Carters' house.

Ordnance Sergeant O'Hara was shuffling his feet at the foot of the steps. With his sparse gray whiskers, he looked like an elderly, apprehensive mouse.

"Has the Lootenant got any orders fer the detachment, sor?"

"How many men on guard, Sergeant?"

"Siven, sor. Pullin' double tours—four hours on post."

"Turn the rest of them out for retreat—every manjack of them—and I'll inspect them."

"Beggin' the Lootenant's pardon, sor . . . we got no bugler to blow retreat, an' Cap'n Smith said jist send a man to take down the flag without no formation."

"Sergeant O'Hara," Shelby said grimly, "you don't need a bugler. You just whisper into that guardhouse that I want them all on the parade ground at five-thirty sharp. You got that?"

"Yiss, sor!"

When he knocked on the Carters' door, Brigid opened it and stared at him in astonishment.

"Good afternoon, Miss O'Donnel. It's a pleasure to see you again. Is Mrs. Carter home?"

"Why—ah—yes," Brigid managed, coloring prettily. "I'll call her, Mr. Shelby. Won't you come inside?"

She was bursting to know what brought him back to Belknap this time, but the children, curious as mice, were at her heels already, and she had no opportunity to ask. They hardly knew Lieutenant Shelby, but William was not deterred by that.

"Have you seen my dad?"

John Shelby's handsome face lit with an engaging grin. Squatting Indian-fashion beside his saddlebag on the veranda floor, he began to unbuckle it with deliberate slowness.

"I sure have, and he sent something for both of you. I think I put it in here."

Amanda's eyes glowed. "Oh! What is it?"

"Amanda!" Brigid warned her. "Mind your manners."

When the bag was finally open, out came the treasures—for Amanda a pasteboard box whose faded label announced it contained a complete set of French dolls, one little boy and two little girls with numerous changes of costume for each. For William there was a sturdy case-knife, wood-handled with brass bolsters. The gifts were greeted with shouts of delight.

"Children? Brigid? Who is there?" Louise Carter called from the back of the house.

"Mama! Mama, look what Papa sent me—just look!" Amanda departed in a rush, scattering sheets of uncut costumes for her family of pasteboard dolls, and William followed, brandishing his knife. Brigid trapped him as he passed her.

"Don't you run with that knife open! Close it up, now!"

Shelby watched smiling until they were gone; then he drew something else from the saddlebag. Unwrapping a length of none-too-clean flannel, he handed Brigid a small glass bottle. She read the label in wonder.

"Murray and Lanman's Famous Florida Water!" She sniffed it cautiously. "Perfume! For me . . . from Mr. Carter?"

"No, indeed. From Mr. Shelby."

"Oh, my! Oh, my goodness! Mister Shelby, I—" Whatever she had to say was lost in the return of the children and their mother.

"Mister Shelby! You've seen Cass? The children said you brought these from him."

"I have indeed, Mrs. Carter. I saw him at Fort Boise last week."

Louise Carter's eyes found the letters by the bag on the floor, and she tried not to stare at them hungrily.

"You've just come from Fort Boise? You must be dead tired! Are you . . . that is . . . Shall you stay here for a while, or . . . ?"

Shelby gathered up the letters and handed them to her, smiling.

"Oh, thank you! Thank you for bringing them . . . but you must have something. Tea? Coffee? No! Not after that ride . . . a toddy?"

"Mrs. Carter, I couldn't keep you from those letters. Let me come back tomorrow, after you've read them, and I'll tell you everything I know. I'll be here until the relief garrision gets in."

"John Shelby, you're a kind man!" she thanked him, blushing. "If you are free for supper tomorrow, come and tell me everything."

"I'd be honored, ma'am."

"Splendid! We shall expect you." She was already edging toward her room, clutching the letters to her breast.

Brigid brought her perfume from behind her where she had concealed it, and sniffed the bottle rapturously. "Oh, Mr. Shelby, how can I thank you? You'd oughtn't to have gone to that trouble for me."

"Brigid, it was no trouble at all. I wish it were grander, but Boise City doesn't have much to offer."

"Grander! Oh, my! I never had *any* before. I don't know what to say."

"You've said it very prettily. I'm glad you like it. I hope I shall see you tomorrow at supper."

Closing the door behind him, Brigid cautiously loosened the stopper of her bottle of perfume and inhaled the fragrance. Good Saint Joseph and sweet Saint Anne, she exclaimed to herself, imagine him bringing this all that way just for me. Through the front window she caught a glimpse of his broad shoulders disappearing up the walk past the Brenners' house, and she shivered with excitement.

Supper next evening fueled her excitement. Because Lieutenant Shelby could tell them about their father, the children were included at table, and that meant Brigid could be there too. She longed to wear her best dress, but that was out of the question so she donned for the occasion one of the lightweight cretonne gowns Mrs. Carter had bought her at Wanamaker's. Because of the generally chilly weather at Belknap she had seldom worn it, and it made a suitable impression with the addition of a broad green ribbon in her red hair.

"Why, Brigid, how nice you look!" Mrs. Carter remarked as she checked the table before Lieutenant Shelby's arrival, Mah Kim watching suspiciously from the kitchen. He had set the table carefully, and now there were two women circling it, looking for something wrong.

He misjudged Brigid's intentions. She was only trying to keep enough distance between herself and Louise Carter to prevent her employer from detecting the first application of the precious Florida Water. In the process, she overlooked Amanda, who wrinkled her nose and commented that something smelled awful good. Brigid made a hasty retreat to the kitchen.

Supper was happy and prolonged. John Shelby ate enormously, praised everything, and congratulated Mah Kim effusively on his apple pie. Between courses, he told of seeing Lieutenant Carter and his company as it marched through Boise for its new station far up the Weiser Valley.

"They look pretty ragged now," he chuckled, "but tough. I wouldn't want to pick a fight with them. You should see your dad," he told the children. "He's riding the biggest mule in Idaho and he calls it 'Wagner.' "

"What an odd name!" exclaimed Louise Carter. "Did he get it from someone named Wagner?"

"No, ma'am. He said every time that mule brays at

388

the dawn he expects a troop of Valkyries to ride over the hill."

"Good heavens! Imagine Cass remembering that opera. I thought he slept through it. But tell me, Mister Shelby, is there likely to be fighting at this place where he's gone?"

"I don't think so, ma'am. I understand General Howard has changed his plans about going north over the Mullan Road. He will follow the Nez Percés directly, wherever they go, and they'll not turn back with him pushing them."

"What about you? Will you be able to catch up with General Howard after you leave here?"

"I mean to, ma'am. Just as soon as the new garrison arrives. I'll catch up somehow."

After supper he had only a moment with Brigid alone. She put the children to bed and hurried back to find him making his thanks to Mrs. Carter in the hallway.

"Have you everything you need, Mr. Shelby?" Louise Carter asked him. "You must have found Fort Abig—the zoo, I mean" she corrected herself with a giggle "in pretty desolate condition."

"There is one thing," he replied. "Have you a small mirror I could borrow? I broke my shaving mirror, and I can't find one anywhere in the whole place."

"Why certainly. We must have one somewhere." She went to search, and as soon as she was gone, Shelby took Brigid's hand. She pulled it away and put it behind her, out of temptation's way, but she gave him a warm smile. He studied her admiringly. The cretonne dress was determinedly modest, but the light material clung to her small curves delightfully. Leaning closer, he sniffed appreciatively.

"You're wearing your perfume. Do you like it?"

"Oh, yes! Thank you for giving it to me."

Before he could say more, Mrs. Carter returned with a small, oval mirror. "It's a bit feminine, Mr. Shelby," she said doubtfully, "but it will be better than nothing."

"It certainly is, and I'll take good care of it. Thank you and good night, ma'am, Miss O'Donncl. It was a grand supper."

Next day the old regime returned with a vengeance for the guard detachment. There was morning inspection in ranks—unsatisfactory—followed by close-order drill and fatigue duty, during which the post was scoured for trash and the plank walks swept free of a month's encrustation of mud. At retreat there was full-dress parade for the lowering of the flag, and their new young West Pointer required no drum or bugle to help him form his troops.

"Oh," sighed Angelina, "he's so handsome! Richard —you stop that or I'll tell your dad!"

To disguise her interest in Mr. Shelby, Angie had turned out the two Brenner boys to watch the parade. They lacked her interest in the formation and were wrestling happily.

Molly Magruder made a rude noise. "All of you are the same! A new man on post and you get the twitches. Just look at the redhead, would you?"

Brigid had adopted Angie's transparent tactic to watch Shelby, deploying William and Amanda as her screen. But she had outdone Sergeant Couza's daughter in one respect. She had tied her red hair in a bright green scarf that fluttered in the breeze like a signal flag as her sparkling eyes followed Shelby marching around his formation and barking orders. When he rounded the little line of soldiers and started back for the flagpole, he could hardly miss her breathless interest. Angie sniffed disgustedly.

"Oh, aye!" muttered Molly. "If Michael Brennan gets back he'll find that one's mind on higher things than an Irish buck-private."

7

Two days later Molly's prophecy was put to the test when a small train of four wagons pulled into the post with supplies from Canyon City. A squeal of delight from Prudence Morton greeted Michael Brennan, seated beside the lead driver with his right leg propped ostentatiously on the dashboard.

"Oh, Michael! Thank God you're back safe and sound!"

"I'm safe enough, darlin', but not all that sound." He climbed down gingerly and Prudence looked worried.

"Nah, nah, Prue . . . it's nothin', truly." He gave her a big grin. "It's all healed up, an' I only favor it to wheedle a kiss from pretty girls. You got one for me?"

"Oh, you . . . !" She lifted her lips, blushing furiously.

Dinah Wool, chortling, picked up the cane he had left against the wagon wheel and poked him in the back with it. "If ye're goin' to kiss every woman on the post, Michael, my boy, ye'll be needin' this!"

"Dinah, darlin' . . ." He turned to fend off the cane and bussed her soundly. By that time half a dozen more women and a horde of children had gathered around him, shouting welcome.

"Come on, now!" Michael ordered brusquely. "Can't

391

have all this pushin' an' shovin'. You girls line up so's I don't miss anybody." That futile command brought him a gale of laughter and they crowded closer, the children tugging at his coat and the women giggling as he tried to kiss each one. Molly Magruder threatened him with a clenched fist, but he gave her a smack on her lean cheek.

"Ah, you devil . . ." Her eyes were suspiciously wet. "I never thought I'd see the day I'd be glad to lay eyes on you, Michael Brennan!"

"Now, Missus Molly, you knew damned well I'd be back. I'm near as hard to kill as that man of yours, I am." He searched through the group of women, scowling. "I'm thinking there's a few missing, ain't there?"

"We hardly knew you was comin', Michael," Prudence told him, clinging to his arm, "but I declare . . ." she added sourly, "the word spreads fast."

She was referring to Angelina, running down the plank walk, skirts lifted high to free her flying feet.

"Michael! Oh, Michael!"

"Prop him up, girls!" Dinah Wool warned. "He's goin' to feel this one."

She was right. Angie flung herself into Michael's arms with a shout of joy and he staggered under the impact.

"God save us, Angie! You'll finish what the Injuns couldn't. Be easy with him, girl. He's hurt."

"You'd never know it to look at him," muttered Prudence. Michael put Angie aside, gasping, and peered at the empty walk along Officers' Row.

"Where're you going?" Angie demanded with a pout.

"I vowed I wouldn't miss a one, luv . . . even if I've got to hunt 'em down. I'll be back for seconds in a little."

He hobbled off, leaning heavily on his cane, and the women groaned derisively.

Halfway to the Carters', William met him and their reunion was manfully joyful. "Michael!" demanded the boy eagerly. "Where were you wounded? Will you show me? Will you?"

"T'was naught but a trifle, Will," Michael answered. Then he stopped to consider William's eager face. Sooner or later the nature of his injury would be known, and it might be wise to have William on his side when that happened. He put an arm around the boy's shoulder and dropped his voice to a whisper.

"I'll tell you true, Will, there's nothing wrong with me. Oh, I put on a little . . . just for the girls, you know. Whisht, now, an' I'll tell you the truth of it . . . if you promise not to let on to anybody."

"Oh, no! I'd never do that, Michael!"

So, in return for his promise, young William was first to know all about Michael Brennan's unglamorous wound at the battle of the Clearwater.

At the Carters', William flung open the door, shouting: "Mama! Mama! Look who's here!"

That cry brought the women of the Carter household running. Amanda was first, and she flung herself into Michael's arms with a shout.

"Brennan . . . Michael Brennan!" Louise Carter gripped his shoulders and shook him gently. "Oh, I'm glad to see you back! Are you all right?"

"Sure, ma'am, I'm fine, I am." He set Amanda aside gently and stood up, smiling. "What's the word from the Lieutenant? All well, I hope?"

"Oh, yes! Mr. Shelby saw him in Boise City and he's all right. They've had no fighting there."

"Mr. Shelby's back?"

"Yes, he's to command the guard until they send someone to take care of the post. Oh, my . . ." She studied him, shaking her head, "You're thinner. Have you been in hospital all this time?"

"Until a week ago, ma'am, but I'm right as rain now."

"We're proud of you, Brennan. We read the story about you in the newspaper—about you and Corporal Wortman. But come in! Come in the kitchen and let us find something for you to eat. Brigid—" She broke off suddenly, puzzled by these two. They stood apart staring at each other, and Michael Brennan's lean face was serious.

"Hallo, Brigid," he said softly.

Her hands twisted in her apron, Brigid took a deep breath. "Oh, Michael . . . I'm that glad you're safe! Did they hurt you bad?"

"Lord, no! I'm all right, Bridey. I . . ." He shot a sidelong glance at Mrs. Carter and grinned broadly. "I'm glad to be back, though."

"Come!" said Louise Carter. "Come and tell us all about it."

In the kitchen he put his arm around Mah Kim's narrow shoulders and gave him an affectionate shake. "John, you crazy pagan! Have you got some pie for me?"

Mah Kim hissed explosively and hurried to put coffee and a wedge of pie on the table. "Missus Carter . . ." Michael said with his mouth full, "would you believe I dreamed about this pie?"

Amanda on his knee and William at his shoulder, he told them about the battle of the Clearwater—a sanitary version for the sake of the children—full of smoke and noise and grand doings, with none of the painful truth.

"Truly, 'twas none of the fighting I feared, but those doctors after," he said. "Nine days it took us to get from the battlefield to the hospital at Fort Lapwai, and every blessed day those ghouls prowlin' about lookin' for some bit of a poor soldier to cut away. Ahhh! That was the bad part!"

That was as near as he got to the brutal truth of the fight, and Louise Carter's white face forbade him more.

"Have you seen Captain Smith yet?" she asked him.

"Why, no, ma'am . . . I've just got here, and I . . . well, I wanted to ask about the Lieutenant."

"I suppose I shouldn't tell you before you've seen him, but I can't help it. You're to be promoted, Brennan. I've a letter from the Lieutenant that says you're to be corporal for your bravery in the battle."

Michael shook his head seriously. "I'm proud to hear it, ma'am. But I wish to God I didn't have the stripes from Henry Wortman. He was a brave man, he was."

He sighed and pushed back his empty plate. "Speakin' of the Captain . . . I'd better get myself down and report to him." He grinned at William. "I'd not want to make him angry, and him just waitin' to give me my stripes again."

At the door he paused until the Carters had gone, then looked down at Brigid's flushed face. "I swear," he told her, "I was kissed by every female in the post before I could get here. Have you none for me then, Bridey?"

"I'll wager you did!" she snapped. "And any you missed are waitin' for you outside, no doubt." She gave him an unsatisfactory peck that made him scowl ferociously.

"I thought you were glad to see me back. By God, and that's small proof!"

"I am glad . . . but that's no reason to stand here in front of God and everybody huggin' and kissin' you, Michael Brennan!"

Mr. Shelby, he said grimly to himself as he limped back toward the adjutant's office. So that jumped-up Rebel bastard is back in the woodpile again. She won't have a soldier, but she likes that damned lieutenant sniffin' around her.

Captain Smith rose from his desk and came around to shake Michael's hand.

"You've done us proud, Brennan," he said gruffly. "I'll wager no other detachment took the casualties we did. I was damned sorry to hear about Wortman, and I'm glad to get you back." He noted the cane and asked about the wound and Michael explained what had happened.

The officer chuckled. "Don't put it down, man. It goes in the books as 'wounded in action,' and that's what counts. I had one of those once when I was a lieutenant. Walked back through a village after a fight and some little squirt shot me with an arrow—right in the butt. By God, I couldn't sit down for a week, and I was damned if I'd explain what happened." He winked broadly at Michael. "Keep the cane a while and fool the girls, eh?"

"I'll not be needing it, Captain. I'm for duty if there's a job for me."

"Nonsense! We can use you, that's certain, but I'll have you down as 'sick in quarters' for a week at least. Give you a chance to get these sewed on." He handed Michael the warrant for promotion to corporal.

"That's well-deserved, Brennan. If Lieutenant Carter hadn't sent it, I'd have raised hell with him. Congratulations!"

"Thank you, sir."

"That's all right. Now you take it easy for a week, and then I want you to help Mr. Shelby knock some heads together. There isn't another noncom on the post can handle that pack of rascals left to guard it. Report to him in a week—unless that leg gives you trouble. We've got no doctor here now, so don't take any chances with it."

Michael viewed the prospect of soldiering for Lieutenant Shelby with acute distaste. On the veranda, he folded the promotion order carefully and put it in his pocket. That wasn't so easy come by, he thought, and if that young buck makes me trouble, the stripes will come off first. Might be, he decided, a smart thing to favor this leg until the new garrison arrives and Mr. John Shelby takes himself off to the wars. With any luck, that fool will get himself killed and I'll talk some sense into that daft redhead at Carter's.

For a week he loafed, luxuriating in the attention of the women of Suds Row. They fed him and made much of him, listening—half-believing—to his stories of the Clearwater and his bold deeds there. The only flaw was Brigid. She avoided him, amiable enough when he sought her out, but only as long as he kept his distance.

Angie Couza seized the chance to monopolize

Michael until Mrs. Brenner, exasperated, sent word she would put a chair in her veranda for him if he would only bring Angie when he came. His good fortune held, for on the day his leave was up, Troop A of the First Cavalry clattered across the plank bridge into the post to take over. They had come a hundred and eighty miles across country from Camp Bidwell, at the intersection of the Oregon, California, and Nevada boundaries, and their horses were badly jaded. That was of small consequence to the women of Camp Belknap, who welcomed the dusty, sunburned troopers. The scandalous behavior of the guard detachment had not been comforting.

John Shelby's joy at the arrival of Troop A was unbounded. Now he could get on to the war, and he would make damned certain he did not go via Fort Boise. Major Suter would have no second chance to block his path.

The new troop had only one officer, and Gideon Smith was sorely tempted to renege on his promise to Shelby that he could go as soon as it arrived. He would sleep better if there were two lieutenants to share his responsibility, but he lacked the toughness to hold Shelby longer. The young man had done a remarkable job with the guard detachment in his brief stay. They no longer shambled about the post like loafers, and they saluted the post commander even if they were on the other side of the parade ground from him. When Shelby demanded permission to go, Smith granted it reluctantly.

"You don't intend to leave now, do you, mister? Hell, it's three o'clock in the afternoon!"

"First light tomorrow, sir."

"That's better. Which way are you going?"

"I will take the stage at Canyon City, sir—I'll leave my horse there with the mail-carrier—then to Walla Walla and hope the steamers are still running upriver to Lewiston."

"Well . . ." The elderly captain suddenly looked

wistful. "Good luck, mister. I wish to God I were ten years younger."

I'm glad you're not, thought Shelby as he headed for the post trader's store. I wouldn't be here if you were. I've lost a lot of time, but it wasn't all bad. He thought he might find Mah Kim at the restaurant, and he was right. Sy Morton hoped the new troop would bring it business, and the entire Chinese family that managed the establishment was cleaning and making ready. Naturally, Mah Kim had found some excuse to join this effort.

Beckoning him aside, Shelby gave him a folded note and a twenty-five-cent piece. Mah Kim pocketed the coin and studied the face of the note with polite interest.

"I want you to take that now," Shelby told him. Mah Kim nodded and put the note in his pocket. It dawned on Shelby the man couldn't read and hadn't the least idea what he was to do with it.

"It's for Miss O'Donnel," he explained impatiently. "I want you to take it to her." Mah Kim nodded again, energetically, his face blank.

"Brigid, damn it!" Shelby exploded. "Take it to Brigid!"

"Ah, Missy Bridge! Yes, sah!"

Brigid received it with surprise. She did not know the handwriting, and could not fathom who would send her a note by Mah Kim. The scrawled initials enlightened her.

It was certainly brief and to the point. "I must speak with you for a moment. Will you meet me behind the Carters' house at tattoo?"

She studied the message with mounting excitement. It was the first such she had ever received. What in the world had got into John Shelby? Better you should ask what's got into you, Brigid O'Donnel, she told herself. He's a grand handsome lad all right, but he's a lieutenant, and if anyone saw him whispering to Carter's Brigid in the dark there would be hell to pay.

She tried to consider the facts soberly. She had

heard of officers who prowled after sergeants' daughters and servant girls. If Mr. Shelby were interested in her, he could hardly have anything but a quick tumble in the hay on his mind. But he had danced with her at General Quinn's ball and brought her perfume all the way from Boise City. She giggled to herself. If that's what he's after, it's surely been on his mind for quite a while. She folded the note and tucked it between her breasts, humming to herself. I think I'll just find out what Mr. Shelby is up to, she decided. It'll be good and dark by tattoo anyway.

Mah Kim watched this performance with a knowing grin, and she shook her fist at him in mock anger.

"Don't you smirk at me like that, you nosy pagan! And don't you dare tell anybody about this, you understand?"

Even August nights could be chilly in the Blue Mountains foothills, and Brigid shivered, tugging her shawl closer about her. The shiver was not entirely the work of the night chill. John Shelby's hand in the small of her back, urging her off the Carters' stoop, played its part. The moon was full and she needed no help to find her way along the path behind the Brenners' house, but she did not protest until they passed through the row of cedars marking the end of the line of family quarters. Before her loomed the bachelor officers' building, its logs silvered by the moonlight.

"This is far enough," she whispered. "What did you want to tell me?"

"We can't talk here. The guard'll be along any minute."

"That's time enough. What is it?"

"Please, Brigid . . . I've got to talk to you. You saw the troop from Bidwell come in this afternoon."

"And what's that to do with it?"

"I'm leaving tomorrow," he said softly, "for the front."

"Oooh!" It was more a long, indrawn breath than a reply. "Do you have to?"

"Of course. I want to. And I won't have a chance to talk to you in the morning."

"Oh, Lord, that's daft! Why do you want to go?"

"Come inside a minute and I'll try to tell you. Please?"

She knew she shouldn't, but she went, shivering with excitement. Inside the big log building it was so dark she didn't know what he was about until his arms were around her and it was too late. She gave up a kiss with token resistance, and was alarmed at her own response.

"God save us, but it's black in here! Do make a light, please."

She heard him searching the mantel for a lamp, and the squeak of glass as he found it and lifted the chimney. Then his match popped and flared, driving the darkness from around him.

"No one here but us," he assured her, "and the windows are blocked up tight."

"It's cold," she protested.

"I left a fire in my stove upstairs. I can get it going in a minute."

"Oh, no! I can't go up there!"

He gave her an exasperated look. "It would take an hour to get a fire going in this." He indicated the big hall fireplace.

"We don't need a fire. I can't stay that long anyway. What did you want to tell me?"

"This is no place to talk. What's the matter?"

She was looking apprehensively about her. She dared not go to his room, but the great, empty hall made her nervous.

"Someone will come!"

He slid the heavy bar through its hasps, locking the door.

"There. Back one's already barred. If anybody comes, he'll have to knock, and you can go out that way before I let him in. It is cold down here . . . let's go up."

"Oh, Mr. Shelby, I mustn't. I shouldn't be here at all."

He tipped up her worried face and smiled at her reassuringly. "Brigid, are you afraid of me?"

"Dear Lord, I am that!" She squirmed protestingly as he gathered her into his arms again. "Please, Mr. Shelby! . . . Let me go!"

"Not until you stop calling me 'mister.' "

"And what should I call you, then?" she demanded in astonishment.

"Jack. That's my name."

Her exclamation ended in a giggle. "You're an officer—I can't call you that!"

"Yes, you can. Come on, now—say it!" He kissed her until she conceded, gasping.

"All right . . . Jack! Now stop, please!"

Pushing him away, she tucked up her disordered hair and sought to distract him. "You said you wanted to talk. Why do you want to go to that awful war? You could just stay here till it's over, couldn't you?"

"Would you like that?"

"Don't be daft! I'd like you not to go and get your crazy self killed or hurt. Whatever makes you want to do such a thing?"

"If I didn't want to go, I wouldn't be in the army," he answered simply.

"Ah, come on! Lots of the soldiers didn't want to go."

"I'm not a soldier, Brigid. I'm a lieutenant. And I'll be one for twenty years if I don't get to that war and do something about it."

"God save us! You want to go kill Indians just to get yourself promoted?"

"That's about the only way now. But there's more. It's my job, and how else will I find out if I can do it?"

"Suppose you got hurt? I'd think your girl would rather have a whole lieutenant than a crippled captain . . . or whatever they'd make you."

"I don't have a girl, Brigid."

401

That was nonsense, and she let it pass. "They might even kill you! They killed Corporal Wortman."

"Somebody has to pay the piper for the dance," he said quietly. "It could be me."

She stared at him, appallèd. Another man might say that to wheedle a girl into his bed, but John Shelby meant it. It was not just blarney to get him a girl. Illogically, she remembered Michael Brennan's reaction to the same possibility. One night on Magruder's porch someone had asked if he never worried about being killed. "Nah," he said. "I'd make damn sure it was that red booger's woman did the keenin' and moanin' . . . none of mine." Shelby's serious acceptance of the possibility of death unnerved her. With Irish female illogic, she was suddenly and hearbrokenly sorry for him. She caught his head in her hands and pulled it down.

"Nah, nah, Jack," she whispered, "never say that!"

She was moved and a little frightened. Maybe he was one of those who could see his own death. There were people who could, she believed. But to go looking for it with that knowledge? Oh, God, how awful! She mourned for him, and that was poor armor against his wanting her.

"Brigid?" he murmured, his lips in her hair. Clinging to his hand, she let him lead her up the stairs.

He lit the lamp, stoked the stove, and had her in his arms again before she could puzzle out what crazy impulse had brought her to his room. If the ability to disentangle a woman from her clothes was any measure, Jack Shelby was no innocent. In minutes Brigid's back prickled with the cold as her breasts flamed in his hands. She flattened them against his chest, protesting.

"I'm freezing! Put out the light, please."

He understood that bit of illogic too and blew out the lamp obediently, but her body was all the more exciting as he bared it in the shaft of moonlight slanting through the window. His hands were gentle and maddening, and she scrambled into the bed to escape them for a moment. It was a poor defense. Within minutes

402

she understood that Jack Shelby might be a little fey, but he knew what to do with a girl. Compared to George Schultz, he was an artist.

Brigid disappointed him in only one respect. A certain amount of gasping was inescapable, but she was still afraid someone might hear them. She made love as silently as possible, and he was perturbed.

"What's wrong?" he demanded.

"Great God, man . . . get on with you! What do you want?"

"You don't say anything!"

"I've not got the breath in me for that! Come on!"

Afterward, she teased him gently about it and he chuckled. "Where I come from, a girl lets a man know how she feels. But . . ." He kissed her gently. "I swear I never felt like this before. Oh, God, Brigid—you're so lovely!"

"Where do you come from, then?"

"Savannah. Do you know where that is?"

"How could I? I was raised in an orphans' home and the good Sisters spent more time teaching us not to do things like this than about wicked places with a name like Savannah."

"Why's it wicked?"

"It must be! Look at you, tumblin' the Carters' nursemaid like this. God's great fool that I am! Dear Lord, if Missus Carter knew, she'd put me out with a curse!"

The thought sent her groping in the dark for her clothes, and Jack Shelby clutched at her hastily.

"What's the matter? What are you doing?"

"I'm going home! You said you wanted to tell me something, and look at me! Shame on you, Mr. Shelby!"

"Brigid . . . stop it! Be still a minute!" He had to pin her, wriggling, to the bed and kiss her into submission.

"Brigid . . . if I get back . . ."

There it was again. She put her hand over his mouth hard. "Jack, for God's sake, don't say that any more!"

403

Burrowing under his chin with her head, she spilled hot tears on his chest and he rocked her soothingly, not understanding what had frightened her.

"Brigid?"

"Yes?"

"What I wanted to tell you . . . ask you . . . Would you marry me?"

It took a moment for that to penetrate her anguish for him. When it did, she sat bolt upright and peered at his face, half-revealed in the moonlight.

"What are you talking about?"

"Would you?"

"Jack Shelby, you're as mad as a March rabbit! How could you marry me?"

"Why shouldn't I?"

"Because, you idiot, lieutenants can't marry nursemaids!"

"They can if they want to."

"Dear God . . . you are touched!"

"Not at all. You're a beautiful woman, Brigid, and I love you. You've no reason to be ashamed of what you are."

"I'm not ashamed! But, man, do you think there's an Officers' Row in the whole army would have the likes of me? Come on! You're raving." She struggled exasperatedly to escape him, and he kept her only by unfair tactics.

"Ow . . . ouch!" she squealed, gripping his hands. "Let go . . . you hurt!"

"Not until you shut up and listen to me. I'm serious. I've loved you from the first time I saw you, Brigid, and I want to marry you."

"Now . . ." she soothed. "You're just excited."

"I am, sure, but I mean it. Don't you know that?"

"Ah, Jack . . . maybe you do, but that's crazy. If I was daft enough to listen to you, we'd be in hell for the rest of our lives."

"That's a terrible thing to say!"

"It's true! We couldn't stay in bed all the time. You'd ruin yourself and I'd be comical. I don't under-

404

stand your army, but I know it's got no place for me. I'll not live on Suds Row with the soldiers' women an' I can't ever be an officer's wife. It's mean of you to ask me."

She had a hard and painful truth there, and he had to admit it. "What if I got out?" he asked after a moment.

"Out of the army? What would you do then?"

"I don't know. We'd go home and I'd find something."

Brigid sighed. "And your family? It isn't only the army that doesn't like Irish nursemaids."

"There's only my mother. My dad was killed in the war . . . fighting against the army I'm in now. She'd never say anything."

"She'd be thinkin' it, though . . . an' so would her friends. Sure an' there's some too decent to say it to your face, but there's more would have naught to do with me—or you—if you married me."

"We don't have to go home," he said slowly. "We could go somewhere that nobody knows anything about us."

Brigid stared at him in wonder. She didn't think he was teasing her. This was more than just bed talk. He meant it.

"When?" she demanded cautiously. "When would you do this?"

"As soon as I get back from this war."

She shivered. At least he hadn't said, "If I get back."

"Are you angry, Brigid?"

"Ah, no!" She bent to kiss him. "No girl's angry when a man asks her to marry. I'm that proud you did, Jack."

It was a lovely dream, and she savored it for a moment. Married to Jack Shelby . . . in San Francisco, maybe. No. The army was there, and his friends would see them. Someplace else? There wouldn't be a place for them. She wrapped her arms about her naked breasts and shivered again.

405

"You didn't answer me. Will you?"

"I'll tell you when you get back," she evaded, with a sick feeling in her stomach. It was hard to say that with any assurance. The feeling had settled upon her that he would not come back.

She dressed, shivering with cold, for the stove had gone dead entirely. "Oh, Lord," she mourned, "what time is it? If Missus Carter catches me slippin' in, I'm done for."

"I'll walk you back . . . and we'll tell her."

"No! Not yet! If she's up, I'll say I was at Mortons'. Prue will swear it was so."

The lamp on the downstairs mantel was thickly sooted. He had left it burning too high. Brigid felt her way down the stairs and their creaking made her nervous. At the door she slid back the bar and flung a worried look at the guttering lamp. It would silhouette her plainly when she went out.

"I'll move it," he told her. He put it on the bottom step and returned quickly.

"God hold you in his hand, Jack Shelby," she whispered to him.

"You won't go away? You'll wait till I come back?"

"I'll be here. For God's sake be careful of yourself."

He pulled her into his arms and held her tight. The water barrel by the door had been long unchanged, its surface thick with dust. Something skittered across it, leaving a tasselled wake, and Brigid jumped. Only a Jesus-bug, she saw, but it startled her. She let him kiss her, but she wanted to go now. He begged again to see her to the house, but she shook her head, slipping out of his arms and through the door.

He means it, she told herself wildly. He really wants to marry me. Oh, God! Could we make it work?

Then, as she ducked under the cedars, the cold absolute certainty that he would never live to marry her or any other girl returned and froze her heart. She was suddenly and desperately afraid. How do I know that? Dear God, she panted, I don't want to know things like that!

406

She covered the remaining distance to the house with flying feet and flung herself into the kitchen, shaking with relief. It was warm and dark and silent and there was no one to ask where she had been . . . or what it was she knew.

Oh, God, she prayed, silently, make it easy for him, will You not?

8

Next morning, the bugler of the new cavalry troop brought the entire garrison out of bed with a start. Reveille was to be expected, but he followed it with officers' call on a brassy, urgent note that roused everyone.

There was only one officer with the Bidwell troop, and he had bedded himself down in the empty set of quarters between the Suters' and Carters' houses. Every family in Officers' Row heard his boots clattering on the planks as he ran for the adjutant's office.

"Stop!" Louise Carter fixed young William with a steady finger. "You shall have your breakfast before you leave this house. If it's bad news, it will be here shortly."

It was bad enough. The dusty, exhausted civilian in Captain Smith's office had ridden ninety miles in less than twelve hours. He came from a tiny settlement called Stonehouse, clustered about the bridge where the Bosie–Walla Walla stage road crossed the Malheur River.

"Southbound stage fer Boise come in on a dead run 'bout dusk yestiddy. Driver tol' us he run inter a bunch o' Injuns jest below Glenn's Store not two hours before. Said they was a funny ol' geezer leadin' 'em could talk Amurrican. They wuz all carryin' weepons an' they stopped the stage in th' road. Ol' Injun asked how to git to Chief Winnemucca's farm, an' where wuz the sojers."

"Was anyone hurt?" Captain Smith broke in.

"Naw. Didn't lay a finger on no one, but they sure skeered hell outa ever'body. Driver told 'em to follow th' Malheur to th' north fork an' then ride up it nigh to Castle Rock an' they'd find old Winnemucca's place. Seems they was a queer mix. One o' the passengers said they wuz Bannocks and Sheepeaters an' maybe some Paiutes in the bunch. Th' ol' feller tol' the driver they come from the reservation up by Pendleton—them You-ma-tilly Injuns done drove 'em out. They wuz lookin' fer Winnemucca and his Paiutes, an' they said if anybuddy tol' th' sojers 'bout 'em bein' here, they'd kill him fer certain."

"Did they bother anybody at your town?"

"Kee-*rist*, Cap'n! Even an Injun'd have trouble findin' Stonehouse. Ain't nuthin' but the stage station and maybe four-five shacks. But them Injuns is headed this way an' somebuddy's got ter ketch 'em up. We knowed there's no sojers left at Boise, an' that's why I come here. You got to go git them boogers, Cap'n! They run onter them settlers in the Malheur Valley an' they'll like as not kill 'em. Stage driver he said they wuz purely mean lookin'."

Captain Smith looked questioningly at Lieutenant Max Weisendorf commanding the cavalry troop from Camp Bidwell, and the lieutenant shook his head.

"We'll go if you say so. But I've got to have a good guide and my horses are worn out. Sir, we've come a hell of a long way in the past week. We'd do better dismounted."

The civilian made a derisive noise. "Them Injuns ain't a-gonna wait fer you to walk 'em down, Lootenant!"

Smith tugged at his sideburns in a nervous gesture, and Lieutenant Shelby cleared his throat. He had arrived moments behind Weisendorf.

"We've got twenty men who can ride, and mules to

mount them. If Lieutenant Weisendorf will give me ten more of his best horses, I'll round up those Indians, sir. They don't sound like they're looking for a fight anyway."

The civilian from Stonehouse snorted derisively. "You ketch them Injuns, Lootenant, an' you mought have t'eat them words."

Shelby gave him a cold look. "You want to help me find them? I suppose you know this country, don't you?"

"You bet yer ass I do, but I ain't scoutin' fer no army less'n I git paid fer it. Them fellers with Gin'l Howard, they's drawin' eighty dollars coin ever' month to find Injuns fer him."

Gideon Smith's jaw set angrily. "If those Indians get at the Paiutes, you and all your friends might have to fight, Mr. Houser . . . without being paid for it."

Houser looked pained. "That's whut I'm here fer, Cap'n—to git you to go after them renegades. You got sojers, an' they git paid regular fer chasin' Injuns."

"I mean to do just that, mister!" Smith's voice startled them all. "But I need a guide. I'll hire you, but the pay is two dollars and fifty cents a day, and not in coin. You'll get a voucher, and you'll get your pay just like the rest of us—in greenbacks when the paymaster gets here."

The civilian considered the proposition silently. "Ain't much of a deal," he muttered after a moment. "But I'll do it. You're likely not to find 'em less'n I do."

"Good. What's your full name?"

"Houser . . . Tom Houser."

Smith wrote it down. "All right, Mr. Houser, you're signed on as a scout. Shelby, see that he gets some breakfast and a mule."

"Don't want no mule. I got a horse."

"You rode him all night, didn't you? Get him a mule, Shelby." He turned to Weisendorf. "Can you mount ten men to go with Mr. Shelby?"

Weisendorf's face was a study in frustrated rage.

410

"Sir, I told you I can go after those Indians! My horses are beat—that's all. There's nothing wrong with my troopers."

"No one said there is, mister!" Smith's voice retained its unwonted edge. "I haven't been a cavalryman for forty years without knowing what a long march does to horses. Yours are worn out, and I need your men here." He leaned forward and pointed a finger at the two lieutenants.

"Now you two listen to me! If the Paiutes join the Nez Percés we've got a general war on our hands. This post has to be protected, and the cavalry troop can do that without horses. If the Indians attack the settlements east of here, I've got to send troops to stop them. That's your job, Weisendorf, and your horses need every day of rest they can get before you have to go. On the other hand, there's a slim chance a small force can surprise those Indians from up north before they get to the Paiutes, and that's Shelby's job—with whatever men I can spare him."

Both lieutenants considered this surprising outbreak for a moment and then looked at each other. Old Gideon Smith had suddenly and forcefully put a new light on their situation. Weisendorf was first to speak.

"I didn't think of that, Captain. I apologize. I'll have ten good men and the best horses I've got ready whenever you want them." He turned to Shelby. "D'you want a good sergeant with them?"

O'Hara, who had taken Houser to the kitchen for breakfast, was back, and spoke up before Shelby could answer.

"Sor, Corp'ril Brennan has turned out the guard detachment, an' they're saddlin' up now."

"Who the hell told him to do that?" Shelby exploded.

O'Hara's mouse-whiskers twitched. Leading the civilian to the cookhouse, he had encountered Brennan kicking soldiers out of their bunks. "I smell a fight, Pop," Brennan had said. "Tell the cook to get us some

411

bacon and coffee, quick." There was no use telling this angry lieutenant that.

"I did, sor," the old sergeant said. "I reckoned the Lootenant would be wantin' 'em, an' Brennan's as good a noncom as any, sor." He stared defiantly at Shelby, and Lieutenant Weisendorf smothered a chuckle. Captain Smith had obviously surprised everyone by taking command of his own post, and now this antique wisp of an ordnance sergeant was standing up to Shelby. Smith backed the sergeant.

"That's all right, O'Hara—well done! Brennan's a good man. Mister Shelby . . . ?" He turned to Shelby, who nodded.

"I know Brennan, sir. If he's fit, I'll take him."

"Good. You understand what I want you to do?"

"Why, bring those Indians back, sir. Is there anything else?"

Smith sighed. "Quite a bit, mister." He emphasized his orders with a jabbing finger. "First . . . If Houser can find them and you can surprise them before they get to Winnemucca, bring them here. Second . . . If they've already joined the Paiutes, you are not to try to cut them out. You will stay the hell away from those Indians and find out what's happening, and let me know as fast as you can. Your job, Mr. Shelby"—he spoke slowly and very distinctly—"is to stop a war— not start one. Do you understand?"

John Shelby nodded. On the veranda, Weisendorf gave vent to a soft, admiring whistle. "He may be crippled, but there's nothing wrong with his head. I had him all wrong." He grinned companionably at Shelby. "I'm not so sure I want your job, after the way he spelled it out. You don't want a good sergeant?"

"No, thanks. Seems I've already got one." They stared at the circus on the parade ground. Mules and infantrymen were circling each other noisily in a confused tangle, just beginning to show a semblance of order. The motivating force was Corporal Brennan, moving among them with an authority that seemed to impress even the mules.

"What th' hell is all this, Mike?" demanded a sulking infantryman. "We're post guard—not no goddamn pack o' Garryowens!"

Brennan stopped to examine him gravely. "Weaver . . . what are these?" He touched the new stripes on his blouse.

"Aw, come off it, Mike! That candy-ass Lootenant ain't—"

Michael gathered the slack front of the soldier's jacket in his big hand and lifted. "Weaver," he said softly, "that lieutenant can't give you nuthin' but pack-drill fer bein' the slob you are, but I ain't no lieutenant. I'm Corporal Brennan to you, an' if you don't shut yer mouth and move yer ass into ranks, I'm gonna stomp a mud-puddle in it an' walk it dry!" He pushed his face within an inch of Weaver's. "From now on, soldier . . . when I itch, you scratch. You got that?"

By the time John Shelby had returned with his pistol belt and saddlebags, Brennan had the Belknap detachment, mules and all, ranged in a decent column of fours. Weisendorf's ten troopers were at the rear and there seemed no doubt in anyone's mind about who was ramrodding this mixed force. The near lead infantryman was holding the reins of a big, hammer-headed roan mule, and when Shelby rode onto the parade ground, Michael gathered this beast and led him out to meet the officer.

"Detachment's formed and ready, sir," he reported, saluting. "Full belt an' twenty rounds in the saddle bags. Three days' rations on each man, an' enough oats for the mules if we feed light."

"How's your leg, Corporal? Can you keep up?"

"I'll be the last one you lose, sir," Michael answered, and there was more to that response than the words said. Shelby nodded.

"Good." Then he grinned, suddenly and surprisingly. "I'm glad to have you, Brennan. Let's go. Take the rear of the column, and I want no stragglers."

"Mount . . . ho!" Shelby sang out, and with some unmilitary scrambling the infantrymen gained their saddles. The army had no scabbard for the long infantry Springfield, and with their rifles slung across their backs the doughboys looked like raffish cossacks. Shelby led his column between the infantry barracks and the adjutant's office, past the quiet women gathered there. The detachment marched out in silence, broken only as the end of the column slouched past.

"Watch yer ass, Michael," Molly Magruder said.

"Which way?" Shelby asked his civilian guide when they were clear of the post. Houser pointed east at the meandering line of bluffs.

"Jest follow them till we hit the river, an' keep goin' to the north fork. Stage driver told them Injuns they'd find Paiutes up there a ways. Might git there first if you kin move these fellers fast enough."

That was the problem—getting enough speed out of the mule-mounted infantry without ramming them into an ambush. Shelby studied the bluffs for a moment. If he hugged them close, his left was protected, so he sent four of Weisendorf's troopers to the right as flank guards. To insure speed, he would set the pace himself. With Houser, four troopers and the Bannock Indian scout assigned him by Captain Smith, he formed an advance guard. Houser eyed the Indian scornfully.

"You can talk to these people?" Shelby snapped.

Houser grinned and dropped his hand to the butt of the Winchester scabbarded under his left leg. The lieutenant shook his head.

"My orders are to bring them in, and that's what I mean to do. I need somebody who can talk to them."

"Jeezus, Lootenant! You think they gonna lissen to you?"

Shelby ignored him. "Brennan, you're in charge of the column. Stay far enough back so you can deploy if we run into trouble, but you've got to stay close enough that you can see me—all the time."

"We'll keep up, Lieutenant."

414

"All right. See to it. If you need me, send a man up."

Giving Shelby and his party a six-hundred-yard start, Michael set a course as close to the bluffs as possible without following all their erratic indentations, and his straight line across the dusty flats permitted fair speed. The mules were fit, and they could keep up a racking trot for lengthy periods, though that gait soon reduced the infantrymen to misery. It was past ten o'clock that night before they bivouacked among the springs feeding the middle fork of the Malheur, but they had covered forty miles since leaving Belknap.

At dawn next day they picked up the old wagon road across the open plateau and followed it fast until they struck the river again, lower down its course. More cautiously, they continued to the juncture of the south and middle forks forming the Malheur proper and down that until their shadows reached a dozen feet before them in the late afternoon. Brennan had dropped back to swear at the end of his column when he heard a shout from the lead soldier. A wooded spur of mountains reached into the flat ahead and the trooper pointed to it.

"Man come outa there, an' him an' the Lootenant is talkin'. See 'em?"

"Yeah. He wants us to stop, he'll tell us. Keep movin'."

When they rode into the trees they saw a swift, shallow stream boiling down the rocky slope to join the Malheur. Shelby, Houser, the Bannock scout, and a stranger squatted on a sandbar where the latter scratched lines with a twig.

"Loosen your girths and walk those mules a while before you let 'em water," Brennan warned the men.

"Ain't we gonna unsaddle?"

"When I tell you to. Get off yer ass, Ritchey, an' walk that mule."

The conference on the sandbar seemed heated. The stranger was urging something on Shelby, who was shaking his head.

415

"How far have we come today?" he demanded when Brennan joined them.

"Thirty, maybe thirty-five miles, sir."

"That's what I thought." Shelby turned back to the civilian squatting between him and Houser. "We'll unsaddle and take a break till midnight."

"Goddamn it, Lootenant, they'll git away!"

Michael nudged Houser and jerked a thumb at the stranger. The guide flipped a pebble in the water.

"North fork. Them Injuns ain't got here yet. Done stopped a ways downriver. This here is Ned Meagher from th' Teneysville militia comp'ny. They followed them Injuns to where they turned inter th' mountains, an' Cap'n Russo done sent him to fetch us."

Apparently this was the first time anyone had mentioned Russo by rank, and Shelby scowled. "A company? How many men?"

"Eighteen," said Meagher.

"State militia? Sworn in?"

"Naw! Warn't no time fer that. What difference? Y'all come to help us, how come you don't git on with it?"

"Captain" Russo's force sounded more like a posse than militia to Michael, but he held his tongue and watched Shelby.

"How many Indians?" the Lieutenant demanded.

"Maybe thirty. Not more'n a dozen bucks an' a couple half-growed young'uns. Rest is women an' kids."

"They know Russo is following them?"

Meagher looked pained. "You ever follow a Injun 'thout him knowin' it, Lootenant? I reckon they jest stopped to see what Cap'n Russo is up to. Soon's they count how many men he's got, they'll move again."

"Where'd they stop, Ned?" Houser put in.

" 'Bout half a mile up a little crick midway from here to where the river comes outa the mountains agin."

Shelby looked at Houser, and the guide explained. "River cuts through a canyon fer the next twenty mile east. Mountains on both sides. Ain't no way to come

416

on that crick he's talkin' 'bout lessen you follow th' river."

"Can't they go north into the mountains?"

"Ain't likely. If they mean to git to the Paiute reservation, they'll come to this fork. It's bad, but it ain't near as bad as climbin' up through them mountains."

"Sounds to me like we've got 'em in a box," Shelby said. "What if they start this way? What will this Russo do?"

"Well, hell, Lootenant! He ain't no damn fool. He cain't stop them Injuns with what he's got. He'll git outa their way an' follow 'em, I reckon."

"All right. If they don't move until daylight we'll be there to help him. If they come upriver tonight, we've got 'em between us."

"Why wait on the bastids? Let's go git 'em!"

"If I try to push these mules fifty miles in a day they'll quit on us, that's why."

Michael nodded. "They need a break." To his surprise, Houser agreed.

"He's right, Ned. We got them Injuns 'tween a rock an' a hard place. Cap'n knows what to do. They start this way an' he'll hightail somebody up here t'tell us."

They picketed the mules with a feed of grain in their nosebags, posted guards, and built a few small fires under the stream bank to brew coffee and fry bacon. Shelby walked the guard posts with Brennan and asked about reliefs.

"I'll change 'em every hour, sir. That way they won't go to sleep on post and everybody will get some rest."

When they returned to the streambed, Houser shared his coffee with them and Shelby questioned him about the trail downriver.

"Some good an' some bad, Lootenant. They's an old trail, an' it ain't too rough where it ain't washed out." He shook his head. "Some places you jest gotta git in the water and slosh through it."

"We'll make a lot of noise."

"No more'n that damn river. They won't know you're comin' lessen they got a buck out watchin' fer

417

you." He scowled at Meagher. "Neither will Cap'n Russo, come to think of it. I'd purely hate to walk inter that bunch sudden-like. Soon's you're done with yer cawfee an' fat-back, Ned, how's 'bout you slippin' back down there an' tell 'em we're comin'?"

Meagher grunted. "You're bound t'git my ass in a sling, ain't you, Tom Houser?" But when he finished his coffee, he stood up and tucked his rifle under his arm.

"Y'all bring my horse. I kin make better time without him. Fer Chrissakes, don't drag ass gittin' down there, now."

Midnight was cold and dew-wet under the trees when Brennan moved from man to man, shaking them awake with a whispered caution against noise. The night was clear, but it was pitch-dark in the grove and the mules had to be saddled by feel. Brennan worked his way along the line of fretful animals and swearing men, muttering instructions.

"We'll lead out from here. Grab the tail of the mule in front of you and hang on. If you fall, catch up quick."

"What if he kicks?"

"Kick him back, but don't let go."

Once out of the trees there was enough starlight to see the dim bulk of the mule ahead, but when the canyon closed in it was as dark as a pocket, and man after man went down with a splash and a curse. The column floundered grimly downstream.

Once in a while they came upon a stretch of gravel or even a meadow bordering the river, and the pace improved, but it was slow, painful work and it was taking too long. Lieutenant Shelby swore bitterly but there was no way to go faster. By nature a cautious beast, a mule could be led down the stream in the dark, but he would not be hurried. When rocks slipped and turned under his hooves, he stopped, tested, and chose another route. That kind of independence did not make for speed.

After what seemed hours of this agonizing crawl,

there were streaks of dawn in the eastern sky whenever the looping turns of the canyon offered a glimpse of it. Surprised mule deer crashed away from the banks of the stream in terror, and each time they did the column froze in place.

"It's only a friggin' deer!" Michael swore bitterly, shoving at a man crouched in the icy water. "Get on with you now!"

"How the hell I'm gonna know it's a deer? Could be a goddamn Injun, couldn't it?"

"The Injun," Brennan panted, "will shoot you in yer great, clumsy ass, man. The deer won't. Now, move, damn it!"

The column came to a confused stop, each man blundering into the one ahead, and Brennan thrashed his way forward, hauling his mule after him. There was light enough to see Meagher and a stout, bearded man, standing in the water talking to Shelby.

"They're breakin' camp right now!" rumbled the bearded civilian. "Come on . . . let's go!"

"Where are your people, Russo?"

"Right at the mouth of the creek, but I've only got eleven. Some went back to Stonehouse last night to get help. We thought you'd quit on us."

"Where are the Indians?"

"About five hundred yards up the creek, in a deep hollow. They aren't goin' to stay there all day! I tell you they're packin' up to go right now. If you'll move, you can catch 'em before they get out!"

"I'll just take a look." Shelby handed his reins to Houser and waded toward the bank. The bearded man caught his arm.

"You don't need to look! Get these goddamn soldiers out of this river and ride for that hollow. You can see it as soon as you're on the bank. You fiddle-dick around here till they see you, and they'll scatter like rabbits. You'll never find 'em again!"

Shelby wavered and Houser thrust the reins of his horse back into his hands.

419

"He's right, Lootenant! You wanta git 'em afore they see you, you gotta go now."

"All right! Let's get up there. Move 'em out, Brennan!"

There was no reasonable way to carry out that order, but Michael grinned at the young officer. He might not know what he was doing, but he had no doubts about it. He was damned if he was going to wade all the way back to the end of the column, though.

"Out!" he bellowed at the half dozen men in sight, standing knee-deep in the swift water. "Pass the word! Get out, mount up, and follow the Lieutenant!"

He lunged for the bank himself, kicking up a shower of spray that glittered in the first rays of the sun. The mule balked, then scrambled after him, and above the splashing he heard the order being shouted upstream.

Out of the water, he found himself in a thicket of vines, broke through them, and clawed his way into his saddle. Kicking the mule hard, he burst into a parklike meadow rising gently to forested slopes a quarter-mile distant. The hollow described by Russo was obvious, not four hundred yards up the slope. Smoke from the Indians' fires threaded up from it, feathering in the dawn breeze.

Halfway to the hollow an Indian woman in bright-colored skirts stared at him openmouthed. Perhaps she had started for the river for water or maybe only to relieve herself in privacy. She gave a shrill, penetrating cry, hiked up her voluminous garment, and went up the slope faster than he had ever seen a woman move in his life.

Shelby, his revolver held high, galloped up the slope with Houser close behind him. Right and left, men broke from the brush along the riverbank and pounded after him, yelling.

Houser flushed a small boy, stark naked, from a clump of grass too small to hide anything, and the child darted toward Brennan, caught sight of him, and reversed his course with the agility of a rabbit. Zigzagging downhill, the youngster threaded his way through

420

the shouting soldiers and disappeared into the brush with a flash of small bare buttocks as he dived for safety.

The Indian camp in the bottom of the hollow was revealed in segments as Michael whipped his mule to the edge. A dozen hasty tepees had been pitched in the basin gouged out by ancient wanderings of the creek, the tips of their lodge poles level with the rim. It was ten or twelve feet deep, the raw, shale-studded earth of its sides almost perpendicular. A good hiding place, Michael thought, but a death trap to be caught in.

There seemed more than thirty Indians in the bottom of the pit—ponies, children, dogs, men and women, all in frantic motion, but as man after man appeared at the rim, rifles ready, this was stilled. The Indians stared up and the soldiers watched them—as if everyone waited for a signal calling the next movement in this strange confrontation.

Michael's tense body relaxed a little. This was no war party. Hostile Indians would never have trapped themselves in this deadly pit, and these were shabby Indians—no war paint; lean, sore-backed ponies; too many children and dogs and too much cheap, white man's camp gear. He saw few weapons—a Winchester or two, but more antique muskets and a few shotguns.

Directly beneath him something winked in the sun, just striking into the hollow, and he leaned forward to see what it was. A young woman scowled up at him. The memory of Sappa Creek and another black-haired girl—dead on her back in the sand—crowded in on him. This one was very much alive, gripping an old, warped lance with the homemade blade and straggling tuft of feathers pointed at him. The sun caught a movement of the blade, and his mule backed nervously.

Several of Russo's men had come up the slope on foot, puffing from their run. One of them paused long enough to catch his breath, then took aim with his rifle at an Indian below. For a frozen moment everyone

421

watched; then a trooper beside Brennan put his carbine to his shoulder.

"Hold it, soldier!" Michael shouted. Simultaneously Lieutenant Shelby leveled his revolver at the civilian.

"You!" he said harshly. "Put that rifle down!"

The man stared at him in astonishment. "What in hell we waitin' fer?" he demanded.

"Put it down, I said!"

"Well, Jeezus! We jest gonna look at 'em?"

"There'll be no firing unless they start it. Russo . . . did you hear me?"

Shelby did not look for Russo. He kept his eyes and his revolver on the man with the half-lowered rifle, and Michael noted that approvingly. Wouldn't it be a kick in the tail, he thought, if I wind up liking Brigid's damned lieutenant. He backed his mule and circled to his right until he was behind the angry civilian. The man looked back into the muzzle of the long Springfield.

"You heard the Lieutenant," Michael told him gently. "Put it down, now."

Shelby and Russo argued hotly and the lieutenant won. Russo grudgingly repeated Shelby's order about not firing. The Bannock Indian scout was summoned, and with a deal of unintelligible debate singled out an old man whom he identified as the leader of this band. Shelby struggled to communicate through the Bannock with this ludicrous figure.

His skinny body wrapped in a blanket, bare feet protruding beneath it, the old Indian refused to talk at all until his badge of office—a dilapidated black hat with a single upright feather—was brought him by the women.

Where had they come from? The Umatilla reservation on the northern border of Oregon. Whether because the Umatillas did not like them or because they objected to Umatillas was not clear. What did they want? They wanted old Winnemucca, chief of the Paiutes. They liked Paiutes. Were there any Nez Percés among them? Silence. Several times repeated, this question finally resulted in an old woman being thrust forward to glare at Shelby, her toothless gums bared defiantly.

"He's lyin', Lootenant! Every one of 'em's a Nez Percé," snorted Russo.

Young Joseph's rebellious Nez Percés had established a reputation that hardly matched these sad-looking Indians, and Shelby brushed aside the charge. Abandoning his attempt to establish what kind of Indians he had caught, he tried to tell them what he wanted of them.

"Tell him they can't go to the Paiutes," he instructed the Bannock.

In response, the old Indian delivered a lengthy oration, translated briefly into: "He don' like."

"I can't help that. I will take them to the army post."

More talk.

"He don' like."

"If he doesn't come with me, these people will shoot him!" A wave at Russo's surly "militiamen."

More debate between the Bannock and the old man squinting up from the bottom of the pit.

"Why they shoot? He is friend."

Young Shelby was reaching the limit of his patience. He was shouting now, though every word had to be transmitted by the Bannock not three feet from him. The difficulty of communicating through an interpreter was lacerating his nerves.

A ten-word sentence in English became a minute's oration in the hands of the illiterate Bannock. The old man in the pit would respond at even greater length, and after a moment's consideration the Bannock would shrug and say, "He don' like." This lunatic exchange was building dangerous tension.

"Tell him put down the rifles . . . Come out one at a time . . . We are going to the army post!"

Mules shifted and stamped nervously, and their riders scowled—at Shelby and the Indians. "Goddamn!" muttered one of Russo's civilians. "No need to shoot 'em . . . gonna talk 'em to death!"

Before the old Indian had finished his response to Shelby's last order, the Bannock shook his head. "He say no."

"Damn it! That's an order!" the lieutenant exploded. He jerked his fist in the startled Bannock's face. "He's got to do what I say! Tell him put down those rifles and come out of there or—"

He broke off, stuttering in frustration. Or what? What could he do?

An Indian solved the problem. He worked the lever of his Winchester with a metallic clang.

Every man on the rim of the hollow understood he was jacking a cartridge into the chamber of the repeater. At a distance of twelve feet, two of the four men who shot at him hit him.

An animal roar burst from the crowded Indians— panic and fury mingled. The entire circle of soldiers and civilians opened fire in a shattering blast of sound. There was more than screaming in response. Those few Indians with weapons fought back.

A blast of birdshot enveloped Michael and his mule, searing his hands and driving the animal into a paroxysm of braying leaps. Some of the Indians had more effective weapons. Michael saw a soldier throw away his rifle and fling himself out of his saddle. Before he was clear, his mule's head dropped between his forelegs and the animal somersaulted over the edge of the pit, snatching his screaming rider with him. The Indians fought to get out of the way as man and animal cartwheeled into them.

It was a good deal like shooting fish in a barrel, and little more effective. The mounted infantrymen were terrible marksmen and their mules were entirely out of control. Nevertheless, it was difficult not to hit something in the struggling mass of Indians. The children were the most appalling. They screamed, and Michael had never heard an Indian of any age scream.

Resistance by the Indians ceased almost at once under this unequal and murderous fire. Those who had weapons threw them down or held them over their heads in sign of surrender. They never had a chance, and they were trying to quit, but the excited men above continued to shoot despite Lieutenant Shelby's hoarse bellows to "Cease firing!"

Michael heard his order, and knew it would never check this madness. He drove forward, striking up rifles and pushing men back from the edge of the hollow.

"Cease firing, goddamn it! Cut it out—stop!" He added his voice to Shelby's, and men stopped shooting to stare at him in astonishment. The firing slowed, checked as much by the choking clouds of black-powder smoke as by Brennan's and Shelby's furious shouts.

But Michael's course, hemmed between the circle of men and the edge of the pit, was a perilous one. A bucking horse slammed into him, shunted him too close, and he felt his mule's hooves break through the overhanging lip.

A horse would have killed himself and his rider, dumping both over the edge in a wild struggle to regain his footing. Not a mule. When the ground gave beneath him, Michael's animal wrenched himself around to confront the fall, sat on his haunches and tobogganed down the steep slope, braking his descent with short, jabbing thrusts of his forelegs.

Without interference, Michael and the mule would probably have reached bottom upright and undamaged, but as soon as he pitched over the edge he knew he was in trouble.

Directly beneath him was the Indian girl with the lance. She should have been scrambling out of the way, but instead she set the butt of her lance in the ground and carefully adjusted the blade to impale Michael. Frowning in concentration, she stepped out of the path of the nine hundred pounds of man and mule sliding down on her, leaning far forward to keep the lance in place.

There was no possibility of shooting her and no way

to change the trajectory of the mule. Michael struck at the lance blade as it touched his belly.

All he achieved was to drive the point down so it slipped between his leg and the slick leather of the McClellan saddle. Slicing through the flesh of his inner thigh, the blade followed the curve of the saddle up through his buttock until it stuck fast in the cantle. The resistance seated the butt of the lance, pinning Michael to his saddle until the shaft splintered and broke.

Skipping aside, the girl clapped her hands delightedly, her squeal of triumph audible through Michael's anguished bellow. The mule regained his feet and shied violently from the yelling Indians, Michael standing in his stirrups to jerk at the stub of lance. It was fixed in the saddle, not in him, but it had done its work. Blood soaked his trousers and spattered on his hands.

Jesus, Mary, and Joseph, he groaned—the bitch has done me in. Rolling off the mule, oblivious of the Indians, he groped in his bloodsoaked crotch to find out what damage she had done. An old woman belabored his shoulders with a stick until someone drove her away.

"Corp! Brennan . . . where you hit?" A soldier tried to pull him up and Michael looked at him blankly. "God almighty, man! You're bleedin' like a stuck pig!"

Michael groped for the man's coat, lurched toward him. The world turned soft and white and silent. He sat down hard with a groan, bent forward, and went limp.

"Brennan? Oh, Jeez! Somebody gimme a hand! Gotta stop him bleedin'."

Of the four days following, Michael Brennan knew little. There was not even a medical corpsman with the column, and the remedies applied by his comrades were as damaging as the loss of blood. They could stop it temporarily with compresses soaked in icy water, but when he was moved it began again. Miraculously, he survived the wound and the treatment.

John Shelby doubtless saved his life. It was obvious if they tried to carry him either up or down the

426

Malheur River the trip would kill him. Houser insisted it was the only way out, but Shelby ignored him. He sent a rider downriver to Stonehouse with instructions to bring a doctor if he could find one, and a wagon without fail. He would take his captives, his soldiers, and his wounded straight south through the mountains to the edge of the great plateau where the wagon and doctor should meet him.

He stayed on the nameless little creek just long enough to let the Indians bury their dead. Then, with Brennan and one other soldier in litters, he led his awkward command across the Malheur and up the pine-clad slopes between it and the plateau.

9

Brennan gave little trouble. He was rarely conscious. The other man had caught a blast of buckshot in his legs, stomach and chest, fortunately not at close range. Most of them were located and extracted with a knife point, but several were unaccounted for, and the idea of these somewhere inside him made the soldier afraid and querulous.

By good fortune, beyond the crest of the low mountain range Shelby's column found a winding valley with a tolerable slope. Indian captives showed the soldiers how to make travois for the wounded men, and with drag ropes to slow the descent, these proved better than the hand-carried litters. The wagon was waiting on the flat, but no surgeon.

"Ain't no doc nearer'n Malheur City, Lootenant," said Houser, who had brought the wagon, "an' you wouldn't let that devil drench a mule. He ain't been sober since the war."

Shelby swore, but there was nothing he could do. Russo and his "militia" had gone directly home down the Malheur River—only Houser had stayed on to draw his pay voucher from Captain Smith. This left Shelby with only a few more soldiers than Indians, and he was afraid if he took too much time the Paiutes might come looking for their intercepted visitors. With misgivings, he assigned six of Weisendorf's cavalrymen to escort the wagon.

"I'm going to take these Indians on as fast as I can. You follow me." Brennan's ashen face was frightening, and the lieutenant frowned. "He needs help quick, but a rough trip will kill him. Take it slow, but keep moving. I'll send help as soon as I can."

It was a hellish trip. It took six days even though the troopers moved night and day, stopping frequently, however. Brennan was feverish and could not swallow coffee—the only hot drink they had. The other man rejected it too—insisting he had a buckshot in his stomach, though the vigor of his complaints belied that. On the fifth day, a dozen more cavalry troopers appeared.

"Lieutenant got in yesterday," the sergeant in charge of them said. "We started as soon as we could. Any trouble?"

"No Injuns, if that's what you mean. Got a right sick doughboy, though. He's stopped bleedin' but I reckon that's because he ain't got any left. Why didn't you bring the doctor?"

The sergeant looked at Brennan and swore feelingly.

"There isn't one. Post surgeon's gone to the war, and there's nobody at that hospital but a steward. Come on. Let's get moving."

The Indians who survived the brief, unequal exchange of fire on the creek bank gave no trouble on the march back to Camp Belknap. Their wounded traveled in travois and kept up with the column. A rider from Lieutenant Shelby alerted the post, and Captain Smith met the captives with every trooper in Weisendorf's command, mounted with carbines across their saddles, ready for action.

The show of force was unneeded. It only frightened the Indians. Their old leader, who had somehow escaped death in the slaughter pit on the creek, shouted for the Bannock interpreter. The Indians milled nervously on the parade ground, surrounded by a ring of soldiers, while Smith, Shelby, and Weisendorf tried to get out of the Bannock what the old man wanted.

He wanted to know what would happen to him and his people.

Tell him, said Smith, that they will be kept under guard until they can be sent back where they came from.

This produced a tumult among the Indians when it was translated, and the troopers shifted watchfully in their saddles.

The old man said his people did not want to go back. The River Indians would kill them all. He did not want to be killed at Camp Belknap either, and if the soldiers kept on standing in a circle around them, they would start killing Indians again. His women began to wail and some of them were singing—a wild, desperate sound.

Captain Smith said they had to stop singing.

The old man shrugged.

When you know you are going to die, you sing . . . was the gist of his reply.—If you take us back to the Umatillas, they will kill us. If you keep us here, the soldiers will kill us. It was a time for singing certain songs.

"Well, what in hell does he expect us to do?" Smith demanded.

"Sir, I understand they're friends of the Paiutes," Shelby answered. "The old man told me they want to go live with their friends. The Bannock says they're looking for some Paiutes who live by Castle Rock, about forty miles from here."

"Can't have that!" snapped Smith. "They'll make trouble."

The two lieutenants looked at the shabby, wailing Indians, and then at each other. Captain Smith had reverted to normal. The old man was determined to get these Indians off his post and back to their reservation no matter how difficult it might be. The wailing of the Indian women grew louder, and Weisendorf looked at

430

the women and children of the garrison, watching from the edge of the parade ground.

"Sir . . . Captain Smith," he said softly, "this could blow up on us any minute. May I suggest, sir, the first thing to do is move this bunch outside the post before it does."

"Where, mister?"

"What about that meadow just above the bakery?" Shelby asked. "They can camp there, and maybe they'll settle down a little."

It was only slightly less difficult than negotiating with the old Indian in the funny hat, but Smith eventually agreed. He rode off to examine the meadow, and the two lieutenants got down to business.

The old Indian consented. But no guard, he insisted. As long as the soldiers were there with their rifles ready, his people knew they were going to be killed. Why a guard? The Indians wouldn't run away. The old man gestured at the soldiers. They are afraid of us? Send for Chief Winnemucca of the Paiutes, he said. He is a friend of the white men. He will tell the old white man with the whiskers what to do.

Weisendorf looked gloomy. Smith would never agree to no guard. But Shelby had an idea.

"We'll post a guard where they can't see them . . . in the bakery and the hospital and the storehouses. Tell him we'll send for his friend at Castle Rock. Stop telling him they've got to go back to that damned reservation, and give them some food. I didn't have any to give them. I'll bet they simmer down and make no trouble at all."

"That makes more sense," said Weisendorf, "than I've heard all day. They've been disarmed, haven't they?"

"Sure. Haven't been searched for knives, but this isn't the time for that."

"Agreed. Let's do it."

So the Indians were edged off the parade ground through a gauntlet of troopers to the meadow beside Sweetwater Creek, above the bakery. They put up a few tepees, and Weisendorf sent rations from his own troop kitchen. The singing stopped.

Lieutenant Shelby packed his gear again and wrote another note to Brigid. But he couldn't find Mah Kim, and he did not want to risk another messenger. He couldn't find Brigid either, because she was careful not to be found.

Early the next morning he joined the mail-rider departing for Canyon City, and the two of them waited at the adjutant's office for the mail to be brought out. While they waited, the wailing began again in the Indian camp.

"What's up?" Shelby demanded of Weisendorf, who had walked onto the porch, red-faced and swearing to himself.

"The old fool sent the Bannock to tell them they're going to be taken back to the reservation under guard. I couldn't stop him."

"Hell!" exclaimed Shelby, kicking his horse away from the stoop.

"Where are you going?"

"To talk to that old man. He's got more sense than Smith."

He rode off at a trot. Passing the bakery, he warned the nervous guards crouching behind it not to show themselves. Then he rode into the Indian camp and dismounted.

The guards stayed out of sight as he had told them, but there were four civilian teamsters standing in the road by the bakery in plain sight. Two wagons loaded with bacon and dried goods—peas, beans, coffee—had been unloaded the day before at the commissary storehouse, and the drivers wanted to look at the captured Indians.

The soldier guards, whom Shelby told not to follow him or show themselves, apparently did not even watch him very closely. The teamsters had the only credible account of what happened after Shelby reached the Indians, and they were not in agreement on all of it.

The agreed items were: Shelby got off his horse and

432

a little Indian boy held it. The old man put on his hat and came to talk to Shelby. The women stopped wailing to listen, and the few remaining Indian men gathered about Shelby and their old leader. Two of them seemed to have an altercation of some sort. Then one of them stepped forward, put a pistol to the back of Shelby's head, and pulled the trigger.

The muffled shot turned out Camp Belknap. The Indians milled around, apparently trying to gather their belongings to flee. The guards burst out of the bakery and the outhouse behind the hospital, and several of them fired their rifles in the air.

Weisendorf's bugler at the adjutant's office blew boots and saddles, and in minutes the meadow was swarming with armed troopers.

The Indians had no chance to run away. They were rounded up, driven into the quartermaster corral, and searched thoroughly for more weapons. No women were brought from the post for this, and the Indian women and girls were searched by soldiers. They were too frightened to protest. That was all. The Indian who had shot Shelby was easily identified and taken to the guardhouse. The lieutenant's body was put across his horse, which was led to the hospital.

There was obviously nothing to be done for him, but that was the only place to take him.

10

Six days after the Indian girl caught Michael Brennan on her lance, the cavalrymen lifted him carefully from their wagon to a bed in the Camp Belknap hospital. The soldier who said he had a buckshot in his stomach had been such a nuisance that they handled him less gently. The elderly hospital steward left in charge by Doctor Brenner peered at the wad of blood-caked undershirt packed between Brennan's legs, and clucked deprecatingly.

"Turn him over on his belly," he directed.

After another examination, he repeated the clucking noise and rubbed his hands on his white jacket.

"My God!" he said softly.

"Are you goin' to sew him up . . . or somethin'?" demanded one of the troopers.

"I don't know how. Besides, if I mess with him he'll start bleedin' again."

"For Chrissake, man! It took six days to get him here . . . you got to do somethin'! Why don't you—"

"Did he eat anything?"

"Crackers an' coffee an' fatback? What d'you think?"

"I'll give him an enema."

"Mary, Mother of God! . . ."

One of the soldiers nudged him. "There's a lady here, Corp."

Flipping the blanket over Brennan's appalling backside, the corporal turned to face Mrs. Carter, Brigid close behind her. They both looked bad, but when they saw Michael's still face they looked worse. Louise Carter caught her breath in a gasp.

"Is he hurt badly?"

"Yes, ma'am," said Moser, the hospital steward.

"Well, what are you doing about it?" Mrs. Carter burst out.

Moser spread his hands helplessly. Mrs. Carter looked as if she had been crying for a week, and he hadn't thought Brennan was that important to her. Brigid spared him an attempt to answer the question. She peered at Michael, put both hands over her mouth, and gulped noisily.

"Don't start that again, Brigid!" Louise Carter snapped. She glared at Moser. "Do you know what to do?"

"Oh, yes, ma'am! I'm goin' to do it right now."

"He can mix physic an' pop boils, but I wouldn't let him set my cat's leg, Missus Carter." Molly Magruder pushed through the cavalrymen, elbowing them aside to look at Michael.

"Oh, my! He does look bad." She put an arm around Louise Carter's shoulders and steered her to the door. "I'll take care of him, missus. You'd oughtn't to be here. You men get outta here, too. Scat, now!"

"Can I help, Missus Magruder?" Brigid asked in a muffled voice.

"Sure you can. Moser! Come back here."

Removing the blanket, she studied Michael's filthy, blood-stained bottom critically, and Brigid gulped again.

"I'll not need you if you can't stand the sight of him," Molly warned. She pulled at the dreadful undershirt and Michael groaned.

"Well . . . the big *omadhaun*'s alive anyway. That's something. Moser, fetch us a pan of hot water."

Gently, skilfully, she soaked the filthy cloth free of Michael's wound. Brigid shut her eyes and swallowed hard.

"Just hold up his leg," said Molly disgustedly. "You can do that, can't you?"

From time to time Michael groaned under this torment, but Molly persisted. When she had the wound clean, she demanded gauze from Moser and packed it into Michael's crotch.

"Is that all?" Brigid asked.

"I don't know any more about it than old Mousey here," replied Molly. "I dassen't do any more. We'll keep it clean an' try to find a doc." She replaced the blanket gently. "An' hope the booger lives till we do."

"That's unlikely," said Michael in a weak voice, "with a pack of witches mishandlin' my privates like that."

"God preserve us!" exclaimed Molly delightedly. "You'd come back from the dead for that, wouldn't you, Brennan?"

"You know more about that than me, Molly. What's left down there?"

She chuckled. "Damn close thing, boy! An inch the other way an' you'd make soprano in the choir." She patted him on the bottom.

"Just tell me one thing, will you, Michael?"

"What?"

"How'd you get all those feathers in your ass?"

Brigid's giggle ended in a sob, and Michael looked at her in surprise.

"I'm all right, Bridey . . . don't cry. You heard what Molly said."

"I doubt she's weepin' for you, lad," said Molly. "Come on, Brigid. Stop now."

"Who's she cryin' for, then?"

Molly gathered bloody bandages and dropped them in a bucket by the bed. "John Shelby, I suppose."

"Shelby!" Michael groaned and propped himself on his elbows. "What are you sayin'? Nothin' happened to Shelby!"

"He's dead," Brigid sobbed.

Michael glared at Molly. "How can he be dead? What's she talkin' about?"

"He's dead all right," Molly replied harshly. "He went in that Indian camp yesterday, and one of 'em shot him. They ought to burn that red son-of-a-bitch alive! It was the same one that beat his woman an' left her to freeze in the road last March."

Sunday morning Michael awoke without pain but something worse—a numb stiffness in his midriff. He pushed himself up in alarm to look at his wound, and the pain returned. Moser heard him gasping and brought a cup of coffee. Michael tried it and gagged.

"Gah! That's awful. Lemme have some water."

He gulped half a cup thirstily and immediately felt queasy. Moser shrugged helplessly.

"You want a biscuit?"

Michael shook his head. He lay still, staring at the whitewashed wall, trying to sort out the sounds of the awakening post, until the door creaked and Brigid put her head in cautiously.

"Can I come in?"

"Sure. Come on."

"I brought you an orange." She perched on the rail of the stripped cot next to Michael's and peeled the fruit. He studied her serious face, amused by the concentration she gave this task. She must have come straight from the Carters' kitchen in her old sweater and corduroy skirt, an ankle-length apron tied about her waist and her hair in braids falling over her shoulders.

"Here." She held out a segment. "It's kind of dry, but Missus Magruder said it's what you need."

"Oh, Lord, that's good! I could eat a dozen of 'em."

She frowned. "I'll see if Mr. Morton can get some more. I snitched this one from the Carters."

"You'll get in trouble again," he grinned, reaching for her hand.

She looked worried, but it was not about the orange.

"You're hot, Michael. Have you taken a fever?"

"I'm all right. Tell me about Shelby."

"I don't know much. I heard the Indians yelling. They were camped up the creek a little way, and I couldn't see. I ran onto the veranda and I saw Mr. Shelby ride up there and after a little we heard a shot and some soldiers came and said the Indians were trying to run away." She stopped, and Michael saw she was crying.

"And then?"

"They came back after a while with Mister Shelby on a horse."

"He was alive?"

"Oh, God . . . no! He was lying across the horse with his . . . his head hanging down . . . all bloody." She put her face in her hands and sobbed. "I saw him . . ." she whimpered. "Oh, Jesus, Mary, and Joseph, it was awful!"

Michael patted her knee, and after a while she sniffed and mopped her eyes with her apron.

"I'm a useless thing, aren't I?" she asked. "Blubbering like a fool when I came to cheer you up. You didn't like him, did you?"

"Jack Shelby? No, and he didn't give a damn for me either, but he was a good man. I'll say that for him."

"Even if he left you behind . . . after you were hurt?"

"He had to do that. He did everything he could for me—and for that one." He jerked a thumb at the soldier with the unlocated buckshot, who was awake and staring at them curiously. Michael shook his fist at the man. "Turn over, damn it! Don't just lay there lookin' at her."

"I want some breakfast," said the soldier mournfully.

Brigid started up, but Michael restrained her.

"Then go an' get it, why don't you?"

Groaning, the soldier wrapped his blanket about him

438

and crawled out of bed. He shuffled away, hunched over painfully.

"He's hurt!" Brigid protested. "You oughtn't to talk to him like that."

"He can't be hurt bad if he wants breakfast. Let him go." He turned back to Brigid, scowling. "Weren't there any guards on those Indians? Didn't anybody go with Shelby?"

"Oh, Michael . . . I don't know! I told you I couldn't see."

"Did they kill the Indian who did it?"

"That Petey—or whatever his name is? No. The soldiers put him in the guardhouse."

"That was dumb! Now somebody's got to hang him."

"I hope so! I hope I can watch."

"You were that fond of Jack Shelby, then?"

Brigid dropped her eyes. "That damned Indian's got it coming, hasn't he? He killed Shelby and I suppose he killed that Indian girl last winter, too."

"Well . . . I'm glad you've decided it wasn't me, but you didn't answer my question."

She was not angry, just sad. "Jack Shelby was a good man. Just like you said. Yes . . . I was fond of him. He was good to me."

There was a long moment's silence, and then she stood up. "I've got to go. They haven't had breakfast yet." She frowned at Michael's flushed face. "I wish Dr. Brenner were here."

"Don't worry about me, Bridey. I'll be all right. Thank you for the orange."

"I'll find you some more of them."

"You'll come back, then? You aren't mad because I asked you that about Shelby?"

"No," she gave him the ghost of a smile. "I'm not mad. I'll be back."

He felt hot and dizzy and he dozed fitfully, awakening from one of these feverish naps to find old Sergeant O'Hara sitting beside him.

439

"Hullo, Sergeant," he rasped. "I'm glad to see you. Maybe you can tell me what the hell's goin' on here."

"A bad thing, lad; that's what's been goin' on. How d'ye feel?"

"I hurt like hell, Sergeant."

"Well, an' that's not surprisin'. They tell me you got quite a hole in you. Has Moser had a look at you this mornin'?"

"He was here with a mug of coffee made out of rat droppin's an' worse, but I haven't seen him since."

"He didn't change your bandages?"

"I wouldn't let him if he wanted to. That nipplehead doesn't know whether to wind his ass or scratch his watch."

O'Hara chuckled. "I guess you're all right, then. Your mouth's as bad as ever."

"Tell me how the lieutenant got killed."

The old man scowled. "That was a bad business, lad. I don't know the ins an' outs of it, an' I doubt anybody ever will, now. Them Injuns was jumpy as a long-tailed cat in a room full o' rockers, but Mr. Shelby, he got 'em here without no trouble. He brought 'em through the post after that troop of horse soldiers was lined up on the parade ground, an' they made camp up the crick a little way. He was real careful with 'em—didn't want no guard around the camp to make 'em skittish."

"No guard at all?"

"Couple men in the bakery to watch they didn't slip off, but that was all." O'Hara tapped his nose with his forefinger. "I'm thinkin' the Lootenant told 'em if they'd be quiet an' sit tight he'd help 'em get what they wanted."

"What was that?"

"To go stay with old Chief Winnemucca an' his Paiutes. Hell, there's not above twenty of 'em left. I don't see how they could make trouble no matter where they went. Anyhow, whatever Mister Shelby told 'em, it did the trick. They made no trouble at all until

440

yesterday mornin' when Cap'n Smith told 'em they'd have to go back where they came from."

"Why'd he do that, for God's sake?"

O'Hara looked pained. "Thirty years I been tryin' to figure out why officers do fool things like that. I'm damned if I know, but he sent that Bannock scout to tell 'em an' they started raisin' hell."

"So then he sent Shelby?"

"No—that's one fool thing he didn't do. I was in the headquarters with him, an' I know that for a fact. Mr. Shelby was all packed up to go to the war, an' I s'pose he just took it in his head to go up there alone an' try to settle his Injuns down before he left."

"Alone? The guard didn't go with him?"

"He told 'em to stay in the bakery so the Injuns couldn't see 'em while he talked to the old man—that old fart who says he's chief. The guard saw Mr. Shelby get off his horse, an' then one of those Injuns put a pistol to his head an' blew his brains out—or whatever he had in place of 'em."

"Jesus! Missus Magruder and Brigid said it was the same Injun used to work for the quartermaster here—that bastard who beat up his woman an' left her to freeze to death. Where'd he come from?"

"It was him all right. Petoe, his name is. We didn't know that till after we took him to the guardhouse. I guess when he ran off from here he joined up with this bunch. They say he was with 'em on some reservation up north where the other Injuns didn't want 'em."

"Funny the Lieutenant didn't know him right off. He broke up a fight between him an' his woman the afternoon before the guard found her in the road."

"I remember that. I guess Mr. Shelby never took a close look at him."

"Any idea where he got the gun?"

O'Hara shrugged. "Wouldn't be hard to hide a pistol. The boys tell me Mr. Shelby never did shake 'em down good enough to make sure nobody had a gun hid."

"Ah, hell! If only I'd been there. That's crazy, not

441

searchin' those bastards! What's Cap'n Smith goin' to do now?"

"Well . . . just what he always does, I guess," O'Hara said disgustedly. "Wait for somebody to tell him what to do. Mr. Weisendorf told him he ought to give that Injun a drumhead court-martial an' hang him before noon tomorrow, but the Cap'n wouldn't do it. He sent a courier to the telegraph station yesterday, an' I'm thinkin' we'll just sit here playin' grab-ass till Department gives him some orders."

"You mean those Indians are still camped up there on the creek with nobody watchin' 'em?"

"Ah, no, lad! We clapped those boogers in the quartermaster corral with two squads outside—loaded an' ready. An' this time we searched every mother's son of 'em right down to the hide—women and kids included. They didn't like that, either."

O'Hara got up from the bunk rail, rubbing his lean backsides and grimacing. "I got to be goin', or Rosie will be takin' on. Our girl, Grace, is home for a while. She's the one married a corporal in the artillery at Fort Canby." He winked at Michael. "Poor sod got turned out for a doughboy an' went to Montana with Gen'ral Howard. Is there aught I can get for you?"

Michael shook his head. "No, I thank you, Sergeant. It's a sad tale you've told me, but I'm glad to have the straight of it."

"Oh . . ." O'Hara paused. "There's a feller wants to talk to you. I almost forgot about him. Says he writes for the newspapers. You feel up to seein' him?"

"What's he want to talk about?"

"The fight, I s'pose. He's been pesterin' everybody about it."

"When'd he get here?"

"He was here before Mr. Shelby got back. Said he was lookin' for somebody could tell him about that fight up north where Wortman got killed, but I guess he's onto this one now."

"Sure, I'll talk to him. I can tell him anything he wants to know."

"I doubt that," O'Hara said sourly. "Never seen a feller so full of questions. Matter of fact . . ." he added reflectively,, "I never seen anybody got up like this feller before."

"What d'you mean, Sergeant?"

"You'll see. He'll be right outside, I'm thinkin'. You take it easy now, Brennan. Molly says we got to find a sawbones for you, but I'm damned if I know where."

"Ah, those women fret too much, Sergeant. Don't you start."

O'Hara departed, and within minutes the door opened to admit a man of about Michael's age, slim, wiry, clean-shaven, and, as the sergeant had said, very strangely garbed. Michael eyed him curiously.

His jacket of faded canvas reached almost to his knees, open in front to reveal a knitted sweater or vest that was almost as long. Beneath these were cord knickers and buckled canvas gaiters, the inside of the legs of the knickers reinforced by canvas, authentically saddlestained. It was a unique outfit, but practical and well-worn.

Michael found the jacket particularly intriguing. The unbuttoned flaps of the breast and side pockets displayed a row of cartridge loops sewn onto each pocket. These were empty, but verdigris stains at each loop indicated they had been filled with brass cartridges once.

"Corporal Brennan?" The man held out a hand. "I'm Charles Ritter, special correspondent for the San Francisco *Chronicle*."

Michael took the outstretched hand, still studying the unusual jacket. "Sure an' I'm pleased to meet you, Mr. Ritter. Sergeant O'Hara said you're wantin' to know about the battle of the Clearwater. I was there."

"Yes, the sergeant told me that, but—" He broke off and looked down at his jacket. "Something wrong?"

"You a hunter, Mr. Ritter?"

"No. Why do you ask?"

"That jacket. I thought you newspaper fellers weren't supposed to carry a gun."

"Ah!" Ritter grinned. "Well . . . last year I was

443

working for a London paper in the Balkans. Got so bad at the end it was fight or get caught by the Turks. I didn't want that."

"Where's that—the what-did-you-call-it?"

"Balkans? In Europe. The Servians revolted against the Turks, and got whipped as usual."

Michael caught one familiar word—"Servians"—and nodded. He remembered that Tomchik, the giant Philadelphian, was a Servian.

"I knew a Bohunk once," he said. "I'm surprised anybody could whip an army of 'em. What did you want to know about the Clearwater?"

Ritter seated himself on the adjacent cot, pulling out a notebook. "I'd like to get to that later. Right now I'm trying to find out about this fight on the Malheur River, where you captured the Indians."

"Didn't you talk to Mr. Shelby?"

"No. I meant to, but I was too late." He shrugged. "That was a sad thing that happened. Your troopers spoke highly of the lieutenant. They said you were second in command. Can you tell me about it?"

"Sure." Michael settled himself as comfortably as he could, quite willing to answer Ritter's questions. He reckoned he owed his stripes to the last newspaper correspondent he had talked to.

"It wasn't right on the river, you know."

"Yes, but I can't find anyone who knows the name of the creek where you caught up with the Indians. Do you?"

"Lord, no! I doubt it's got a name."

"How did you come upon their camp?"

"There was some civilians from Teneysville followed 'em from the stage road. We joined up with them and they showed us the camp, and we surrounded it just at dawn."

"The Indians fired on you?"

"Oh, no. Mr. Shelby talked to 'em. There was a lot of talk. He told 'em they had to come with us, but they didn't want to. He was tryin' to get 'em to put down

444

their guns and surrender, and the civilians wanted to start shootin', and—"

"Ah! Wait a minute . . . " Ritter scribbled furiously in his notebook. "These civilians—they were under your lieutenant's command?"

"They didn't think so, but he straightened that out. They had a man called himself a captain . . . Said they were militia, but they'd not been sworn in. Mr. Shelby was in command, all right."

"So he called on the Indians to surrender. Then what happened?"

"One of 'em jacked a cartridge into his gun. That tore it."

"He shot at you?"

"Didn't have a chance."

"Who killed him? The soldiers or the civilians?"

"Jeez! That'd be hard to say. Soon's he worked that gun, all hell broke loose."

"The Indians fought back?"

"They sure did!" Michael held out his hands to show a pattern of red and blue spots on their backs. "I got those right off."

Ritter studied the spots curiously. "Birdshot?"

"Right. I was lucky. The other man hurt took a load of buckshot in his belly."

"The Indians had only shotguns?"

"Hell, no! They had rifles too."

"And there were only two soldiers wounded?"

"Far as I know. Only two of us in hospital, anyway. Anybody else got hit, it wasn't bad enough to count. I don't know how the Indians made out."

"I do," said Ritter, thumbing his book. "There were thirty-three Indians in that pit," he read. "Nine men, thirteen women, and eleven children. Two men, five women, and four children killed; three men, four women, and two children wounded, and one child missing. There are twenty-one Indians in the corral out there now . . . nine of them wounded."

Michael gaped at him in astonishment. "How in hell did you figure all that out?"

"Talked to the Indians. They told me."

"You can talk to 'em?"

"The old man speaks pretty good English."

"By God, he wouldn't when Mr. Shelby was tryin' to get him out of that hole!"

"Maybe he didn't think it was good enough for the spot he was in. Did it ever occur to you, Corporal," Ritter asked gravely, "that those Indians were trying to surrender when you opened fire on them?"

"Great God, man! Whatever gave you that notion?"

"Why did the troops start shooting?"

"I told you! One of those bastards loaded his gun!"

"A Winchester, was it?"

"Hell, I don't know! Could have been a Henry. Had a lever anyway, an' the son-of-a-bitch worked it."

"Wouldn't he have to do the same thing to unload it?"

Michael gave him a long, disgusted look. "Mister, are you tryin' to say you think that Indian was unloading his gun?"

"It's possible, isn't it?"

"Well . . . hell! I s'pose so. No other way to unload that kind of gun. But, God almighty . . . what a fool thing to do! If he was that crazy, it's a mercy somebody killed him!"

"And the women and children too?"

"Now just a damn minute, mister! Nobody meant to kill any squaws or kids either! What the hell you think's gonna happen when they're all mixed up like that—the squaws shootin' too, like as not!"

"I wouldn't be surprised if they were," said the correspondent quietly. "What choice did they have? They tell me you were wounded by a woman. Is that right?"

"It damned sure is! That fiddlin' bitch . . ." Michael's indictment of the Indian girl went unfinished. He was damned if he would explain to this snotty civilian how he had been wounded. Before he could think of another way to finish, the door opened to admit Molly Magruder, carrying a basket with a napkin

446

spread over it. She looked at Michael's flushed and furious face and put the basket down abruptly.

"That's enough now, I'm thinkin'," she said softly. Ritter got to his feet.

"We weren't quite finished, ma'am. Perhaps—"

"No. That's enough for the while. Come along now." She nudged Ritter toward the door. "You oughtn't to get him riled up like that, mister. He's hurt right bad."

"Oh? He said he'd been hit with birdshot."

Molly swore under her breath. "You think that big Mick is laid out like he is with nothin' more than birdshot in him?"

"He was wounded twice?"

"That's right, an' I wish to God we could find a doctor for him. He needs that more'n he needs you right now." She shut the door on Ritter, turning back to Michael at once.

"Damn it, Molly—" he began, and she shushed him angrily.

"Damn it yourself, Michael Brennan! You talk too much." She sniffed curiously. "Mah Kim sent you somethin' good to eat, but . . . " She sniffed again. "First I'm goin' to have a look at those bandages. You don't smell too good to me."

11

Molly Magruder's nose had not deceived her. "Jesus, Mary, and Joseph!" she muttered when she uncovered the wound. There was no doubt it was festering. The lips of the ugly gash were inflamed and swollen, a red stain spreading from it into his groin and down his leg.

"What's amiss?" Michael grunted.

"I don't know. Quit thrashin' around, will you."

Moser was small help. He sniffed and shook his head. "Proud flesh. That's a bad one."

"I can see that!" Molly exploded. "What's to do for it, man?"

"I don't know. I'm no doctor. Let's try a hot pack and see if that'll draw the crud out."

They packed Michael's crotch with bandages soaked in hot water, and he groaned and squirmed, but his fever was up and his eyes glazed. Molly offered food, but he wanted only water, and after a little he dozed off, breathing harshly. The hot compress drew a quantity of vile-smelling drainage, but the wound looked no better for it. Brigid returned after supper and stared at him aghast.

"Oh, Missus Magruder . . . he's real bad, isn't he?"

"He is that, an' likely to get worse, I'm thinkin'."

"Will he die?"

"Oh, hell, Bridey, I don't know! He might if we

448

don't get somebody who knows what to do for him. Have you seen Peter Hanst around today?"

"No. What can he do?"

"He can hump his idle butt to Canyon City an' get us a doctor, if that fool captain won't send for one." She eyed Brigid grimly. "Can you change these bandages and look after him for a bit?"

"I . . . guess so. Where are you going?"

"To find Hanst, girl! Where else?"

"All right. What do I do?"

"When that pack gets cold take it out and put on a hot one. There's clean linen here, an' the kettle's on the stove. Not too hot, mind. Don't scald the poor sod."

Brigid put off this task as long as she dared, then set her teeth and plucked out the cold compress. Michael's nakedness was tolerable, but the ugly, evil-smelling wound appalled her. Shuddering, she stuck to her task until she had replaced the old compress with a fresh, warm one. His indifference to this was alarming. It was impossible not to hurt him, but he only groaned and tossed. Brigid put her hand on his face and gasped. My God, she thought, he's burning up.

With considerable difficulty, she got him onto his back and bathed his face and chest with cool water. He mumbled and sucked at the soaked cloth, but when she tried to give him a cup of water it spilled from his mouth and he brushed it away clumsily. She wished Molly would come back, but it was a long time before the sergeant's wife returned.

"How is he?" Molly demanded.

"He's quieter, but my God, he's hot. I've kept a cold rag on his head but it doesn't help much. Did you find Hanst?"

"Wasn't easy, but I did. He'll go tomorrow."

"Oh, thank the Lord! How long will it take?"

"He could make it back in three, maybe four days—if he can find a sawbones."

But Wednesday passed and Thursday as well with no sign of Hanst. The weather turned fiercely hot, the

449

thermometer reaching ninety-five by noon some days, and Michael's hospital room smelled like a charnel house.

"He may die," grumbled Dinah Wool, "but I'm thinkin' we'll have to finish him with a stick, he's that tough. Phew! How can a man smell like that an' not die?"

Michael survived. Probably because the women nursed him so determinedly. Molly and Brigid took turns with the others—Dinah, Sabine Busch, Maria Benoni—watching over him day and night. Sophy Krause of the cavalry troop joined them in their vigil; even Rose O'Hara and Anna Couza took a turn. Mrs. Brenner produced from her absent husband's private stores a jar of phenol crystals, from which, by experiment, the ladies manufactured a nonlethal solution of carbolic acid with which to cleanse the suppurating wound in Michael's thigh and buttock.

"Du lieber Gott!" murmured Sabine Busch, sniffing the mixture cautiously. "You will cook him alive, yet!"

Applied to Michael, the solution foamed in a way that seemed to justify her concern, but the wound did look better for the treatment—not so angry and swollen. On Friday, five days after his departure, Peter Hanst reappeared. He came alone, and Molly Magruder swore at him luridly.

"You old goat! You spent my money in some saloon an' you found no doctor?"

"You gave him money?" Rose O'Hara exclaimed. "What did you expect, then?"

"I gave it him to eat—not drink, damn it!"

"I didn't drink it, woman," rumbled Hanst. "I been waitin' fer the sawbones to git back frum Portland."

"What's he doing in Portland?"

"He went t' git married."

"Oh, hell, he'll never get back! Did you leave word for him to come?"

"I went to Baker City t'try to find another one. They got one, but he won't come."

"Then you haven't done a damn bit of good, have you?"

The woodcutter's whiskered face wrinkled in a sly grin. "Could be. I seen the feller at th' telegraft office. Asked him t' find out where at is the nearest army sawbones."

"So?"

"Doc Brenner's comin' back."

That got their attention. Everyone spoke at once.

"When?"

"You old fool! Why'nt you say so first off?"

"Dear Lord . . . somebody run tell Missus Brenner!"

Angie Couza, who had brought a pan of fresh biscuits, ran to find the doctor's wife, and Molly shushed the chattering women.

"When will he be here, Peter?"

"He wuz up at Kamiah, lookin' after some o' Ginnul Howard's folks. The man said he'd be startin' south first day o' September."

"That's tomorrow! How long will it take him?"

"Week maybe. Could be sooner. Told him t'git word to th' Doc he's needed."

"If you weren't so damned hairy, I'd kiss your ugly mug," Molly told him.

Hanst sighed. "Long's I ain't gonna git kissed, you reckon I c'ld git somethin' t' eat?"

"Here!" Molly gave him Angie's biscuits. "There's coffee on the stove. Can't get these things into Brennan anyhow."

"He do look right peaked. Whut's he livin' on?"

"Soup, and that's got to be spooned into him."

So the weary vigil continued, but with more hope now. Michael looked as bad as he smelled, but he was holding his own. The fever was intermittent as the infection in his wound waxed and waned, and now and again one of the women sitting by his bed found his hollow eyes on her, clear and alert for a little while.

"Dinah, love?" he whispered late one night to Cor-

poral Wool's wife. "What are you doin' here? Where's
Ed?"

"Oh, Michael . . . he's still at the war. How do you
feel?"

"Like I been stomped an' hung out to dry. How long
have I been here now?"

"It's goin' on ten days, Michael."

He struggled to raise himself and look at his wound,
but he was too weak. Dinah pushed him gently down.

"No use lookin' at it, lad. It's doin' a little better."

His nose wrinkled and he shook his head wearily.
"Not if it's me makin' that fearsome smell. God above
us, girl, how do you stand it?"

But the fever was upon him again before dawn, and
when Brigid came with Molly to relieve Dinah Wool,
they exchanged a frightened look.

"Oh, God! Will Dr. Brenner never come?" Brigid
whimpered. "Molly, I don't think he's goin' to make
it."

"I don't know about Doc Brenner, but this one
will," Molly said grimly. "We'll get him through somehow." She changed Michael's bandages, gagging at the
odor. "Got to get that proud flesh out of there . . .
that's what's doin' this to him."

Michael was flushed and panting, muttering to himself and twisting weakly on the bed. "Get me that jar
of stuff Missus Brenner brought, Bridey. I'm goin' to
make it strong enough to burn that filth off him."

The carbolic solution she mixed was strong enough
to wrench a hoarse groan from Michael as she dabbed
it on his wound, but after a little he fell into a fitful
sleep, still mumbling unintelligibly.

Thursday, the sixth of September, brought a courier
from Baker City with a packet of telegrams for Captain
Smith, but no word of the doctor.

"He wasn't there when I left, ma'am," the soldier
told Mrs. Brenner, "but that was two days ago. My
horse went lame on me."

Two of Gideon Smith's telegrams were clear enough. Department wanted the Indians locked in the quartermaster corral sent north to the Umatilla reservation at once, escorted by as many of Lieutenant Weisendorf's cavalrymen as necessary. The Nez Percés had been engaged at Camas Meadows and driven from Idaho into Wyoming. No further trouble was expected in Oregon. The second order settled the matter of Petoe. He was to be turned over to the civil authorities in Canyon City, where it was expected he would be tried for the murder of Lieutenant Shelby.

Weisendorf shrugged. "I doubt it makes much difference who tries him, Captain. The civilians will hang him quicker than we could."

"What do you mean by that, sir?" Smith bristled.

"You would have to get at least three more officers here before you could hold a General Court, and when it found him guilty Washington would have to review the case before you could hang him. Good riddance, I'd say, sir."

"Well . . . you've got a point there, mister. Now tell me what in the devil you make of this one." Smith handed over a third message, and Weisendorf studied it curiously. After a moment he blinked and shook his head.

"Relayed from Washington through Division and Department . . . in four days! Who sent it?"

"Looks like the Adjutant General's office. What in hell are they talking about?"

" 'Require immediate, full report, details of engagement on Hanging Woman's Fork,' " Weisendorf read aloud wonderingly. "Isn't there more? Must be another page somewhere."

"There isn't. That's all of it. I never heard of any such place! D'you suppose the damned thing's been sent here by mistake?"

"It's certainly addressed to you, sir . . . 'Commanding Officer, Camp Belknap.' Can they be talking about Shelby's fight? That was on the Malheur River."

"That's the only engagement we've had around here,

but where in the world did they get that name for it? Besides, I sent Department a full report on that two weeks ago."

An explanation of this curt demand for information arrived the following day with Dr. Brenner, who rode into Belknap just before dusk, though the revelation was delayed by the excitement generated by his appearance.

"Thanks be to God an' all His holy angels—you're here!" panted Molly Magruder, who had run the length of the walk in front of Officers' Row to meet the doctor.

"Well, Mrs. Magruder, it's nice to be welcome," Brenner said, smiling. "Who's having a baby?"

"Nobody. It's Brennan, sir . . . he's real bad."

"Again? What happened to him this time?"

Molly explained as the doctor turned over his horse to a trooper and walked toward his quarters. "All right . . . all right, Mrs. Magruder. I'll have a look at him shortly." He chuckled at her expression. "You will allow me to have a word first with Mrs. Brenner, will you not?"

It was a long word, and Brigid and Molly waited impatiently until the doctor had his supper—Mathilde would not hear of his leaving until he had. Michael was sitting in bed, spooning up soup noisily, when Brenner arrived at the hospital.

"Brennan," demanded Dr. Brenner, scowling, "why in the devil can't you get yourself decently shot when you get in a fight? Last time you got run over by a howitzer, and now Mrs. Brenner tells me some Indian stuck a spear in you."

"It's the God's truth, Doctor," Michael told him, grinning. "A big old dirty one to boot."

"I can tell that," Brenner said, wrinkling his nose. "Well, I'll just have a look at you. Ladies, will you excuse us, please?"

454

"His backside's no stranger to us, Doctor. We been coddlin' it for the last two weeks."

"I don't doubt it. What have you done with Moser?" The expression on Molly Magruder's face made him laugh again. "All right, I know. Nevertheless, I'd be pleased if you two would step outside for a bit. Here . . ." he tucked a folded newspaper under Molly's arm. "Your hero's got his name in the news again. Read it while I'm having a look at him."

They went into the steward's office under the big hanging lamp, and Molly spread the paper on the table. It was a six-day-old copy of the Portland *Weekly Herald*.

"I don't see anything," Brigid said, puzzled. Molly put her finger on a smudged column with bold black headlines.

"That'll be it."

" 'Massacre on Hanging Woman's Fork'? Whatever . . . ?"

"Whisht now, girl, an' let me read."

It was a long article, two and a half columns of small print. They read it together, Molly Magruder's scowl growing blacker with each line.

MASSACRE ON HANGING
WOMAN'S FORK

LITTLE BAND OF INDIANS TRAPPED—ALL BUT EXTERMINATED BY U.S. ARMY—TWENTY INDIANS KILLED OR WOUNDED—FIFTEEN OF THEM WOMEN AND CHILDREN—ARMY OFFICER SHOT BY CRAZED CAPTIVE—SECOND MASSACRE ON SAME SPOT IN FOUR YEARS

Vengeful soldiers and citizens surround fleeing Indians and gun them down—soldiers run amok on haunted stream— young Indian maddened by soldier brutality turns on captors—kills army lieutenant who commanded the troops

Baker City, Oregon, August 29, 1877. From Special Correspondent Charles Ritter to San Francisco *Chronicle*.

Frustrated in its pursuit of the Nez Percé Indians far to the north, the U.S. Army on August 20th took savage revenge on a small band of thirty-three Indians surrounded beside an aptly named stream in southeastern Oregon. It was not the first time the banks of this tributary of the Malheur River have been stained by Indian blood.

This correspondent has spoken with survivors of the most recent atrocity, who insist they were only trying to evade their blue-coated pursuers, and is assured of the veracity of the Indian account. An old man named Kot-kot-hy-nih, leader of the unfortunate Indians, told me their story himself in the corral at Camp Belknap, Oregon, where the army has penned up the few survivors of the massacre.

"We were nine men, thirteen women, and eleven children," said Kot-kot-hy-nih. "When the soldiers stopped shooting, eleven were dead and nine were wounded. Only five were men. A little boy ran away into the forest and we do not know what has happened to him." After the killing—it cannot be called a battle—Kot-kot-hy-nih and the pitiful remnant of his people, including the wounded, were marched by the soldiers for four days to Camp Belknap where they are now imprisoned under close guard.

Their crime was flight from the Umatilla Reservation in the north, where they were persecuted by ancient enemies among the Columbia River Indians who live there. They sought sanctuary with their friends, the Paiute Indians, who live on the headwaters of the Malheur River in Grant County, Oregon. Only a few miles from this haven, they were seen by white settlers who instantly formed a "militia company" and pursued them, sending to nearby Camp Belknap for help from the soldiers stationed there.

The Regulars came quickly and eagerly. Citizens and soldiers soon found the frightened Indians hiding under the banks of Hanging Woman's Fork. There was a brief parley between Kot-kot-hy-nih and lieutenant John Shelby, who commanded the troops, but according to Corporal Michael Brennan, Shelby's second-in-command, negotiation failed and shooting began without further attempt to obtain a peaceful surrender. The inequality of this affair is revealed by the army casualties—two soldiers slightly wounded by pellets from the shotguns which seem to have been the principal armament of Kot-kot-hy-nih's few warriors.

When the exhausted remnant of the band reached the army post, they tried to explain what they were seeking, but next day came the stern order of Captain Gideon Smith, commandant of Camp Belknap: "Back to the Umatilla Reservation under soldier guard!"

The Indian men accepted this cruel fate stoically, but their women set up a wail of despair, and it was then that the army suffered its only real casualty.

Lieutenant John Shelby, who had led the army pursuit and capture of the band, rode alone among the captives—his exact intentions unknown to anyone. He was seen to dismount and engage in words with the old leader of the Indians, but while they spoke, a young warrior named Pe-toe, maddened by the wrongs he had suffered and the cries of the helpless women, did a terrible and hopeless thing. Drawing from beneath his blanket a pistol, he shot and instantly killed Lieutenant Shelby.

The angry soldiers drove the Indians at once into a corral and locked them there under heavy, armed guard. All the captives, even the women and children, were given a searching examination for more hidden weapons. The young brave who killed their officer was loaded with chains and flung into the camp guardhouse to await trial for murder, the outcome of which is almost certain if his case is dealt with by a military court.

History has repeated itself with cruel exactitude on Hanging Woman's Fork. In June of 1873, when the army crushed the Modocs of California, a little

457

band of those redoubtable Indians escaped the final trap and fled into Oregon. The Modocs had assassinated General Edward Canby while he negotiated for their surrender in their fortress among the California lava beds, and there was to be no mercy for them. Their leader, Captain Jack, did not escape. With three of his lieutenants he was hanged, and the severed heads of all four, pickled in alcohol, were sent to the army's Medical Museum in Washington, D.C.

The few who escaped capture fled, and the pursuit, said General Jefferson C. Davis, who replaced Canby, "partook more of a chase after wild beasts than war." Some fugitives reached the forested haven of the Malheur Mountains, more than two hundred miles distant, and, thinking they had eluded pursuit, encamped upon the banks of Hanging Woman's Fork. There they were surprised by the soldiers who fell upon them and killed all but a few.

The army must not be proud of that earlier success, for no record of the action is to be found except in the memory of Indian survivors—if any remain—and one white man in Oregon. He was once a scout for the army, and he told this correspondent the story of the first massacre beside this haunted stream.

Doubtless the army has reported a brisk victory there over recalcitrant allies of the Nez Percés. That is a logical story, though persons familiar with the sad plight of our noble Indians may read between the lines. Such perceptive readers will find confirmation of their suspicions in the facts here reported by this correspondent.

Molly required longer to finish than Brigid, who was rereading some of the more lurid patches with a horrified expression by the time the sergeant's wife reached the end and made a disgusted, spitting noise.

"That miserable son-of-a-bitch!" she hissed.

"Who?"

"Who else but *him!*" Molly put a blunt finger on Ritter's name at the head of the first column. "That sneakin' louse with his fancy jacket with all them bullet-loops on it. Damn his eyes! If Major Suter'd been here, he'd have kicked his ass off the post before he cooked up this devil's stew."

"Is it true?" Brigid whispered, big-eyed. Molly stared at her disgustedly.

"I've no doubt bits an' pieces of it are . . . but the bastard has put an ugly face on it, now. For God's sake, don't look like that, girl! You know these men better than this feller does. You know Brennan well enough. D'you think he gunned down a pack of women an' kids in cold blood like this clown says?"

Brigid bit her knuckle and said nothing.

"What's the matter with you, Bridey, for God's sake?" Molly demanded.

"Haven't you heard him?"

"Heard who? What're you talkin' about?"

"Michael. You've been in there with him when he was out of his head. He said it over an' over . . . 'I didn't mean to kill her. I didn't know she was a woman.' I heard him say it, but I didn't know what he meant."

"Oh, for God's sake! He was burnin' up with fever, sayin' anything that came into his head. Maybe it was somethin' that happened . . . " She broke off, scowling.

"Petoe's woman . . . Squis-Squis?" Brigid's question was almost inaudible.

"No! I'd not believe it! That bastard shot Mr. Shelby in the back, didn't he? You think he wouldn't beat his woman to death?"

The door opened and Dr. Brenner came in before Brigid could reply. He nodded at Molly approvingly.

"Looks like you took a hot iron to him, Mrs. Magruder. What was it?"

"Some stuff Missus Brenner gave us, Doctor. It was in a jar, an' she told us to mix it with water."

"Ah! Phenol. You must have made it mighty

459

strong." He patted her shoulder. "It's all right. He'll have a hell of a scar, but I think you've burnt the infection out of him. I've just trimmed him up a bit, and I think he'll be all right now." He glanced at Brigid. "What's the matter?"

Molly repeated her spitting noise. "She's gaggin' on that . . . that crap there."

"The newspaper? Ah, they all do that. Makes the papers back east copy their stuff. I wonder where he got that name? I never heard of a creek with a name like that. Probably just made it up. I wouldn't let it bother you, ladies." He smiled at them kindly. "I gather you two have been sitting up with Brennan every night?"

"Most everybody took a turn, Doctor. We didn't know what we ought to do, but we didn't want to just leave him be."

"You've done just right. I'm sorry I wasn't here, but I doubt there was a lot more I could have done for him. He doesn't need you now. I'll have a word with Moser and he'll call me if I'm needed. You two go along and get yourselves some sleep."

12

"Well, damn it . . . he got it from somebody! He didn't just make it up!"

The commanding officer of Camp Belknap was determined to discover where Charles Ritter had found his name for the creek on which Shelby had caught the Indians. He had worked himself into one of his rare spells of authority, and the men gathered in his office eyed him cautiously. There were two officers, Dr. Brenner and Lieutenant Weisendorf, and three sergeants: O'Hara, Couza, and Weisendorf's troop first sergeant.

"We've asked every soldier he talked to," said Brenner quietly. "Brennan never heard the name before. What about the civilians on post? Trader Morton or the woodcutters or that scout you hired to go with Shelby?"

"Houser? He was gone five minutes after I paid him. I don't think Ritter got to him, but I never thought of Morton."

Sy Morton swore innocence, but he identified the culprit. "Hanst," he said. "That writer feller bought old Pete enough beer to pickle him. Why don't you ask Hanst?"

"Sure I talked to him," the woodcutter said. "I seen

what he wrote. Damned good, too. I was scout for Gen'l Crook when he was in these parts."

"Peter," Doctor Brenner said grimly, "you can't read a line. What do you mean, you saw what he wrote?"

"Miss Prue, she read it to me. I was a scout. That's a fact."

"Nobody said you weren't. Did you tell him that damned creek is called Hanging Woman's Fork?"

"Why, shore, Doc. That's its name."

Gideon Smith sighed painfully. "Will you tell me why—how in hell it got it? Nobody else around here ever heard of it."

Hanst looked disgusted. "Beggin' your pardon, Cap'n, but you army fellers jest don't pay no heed to what's happened hereabouts. Had you asked any of us old timers, we c'd of told you. That writer feller, he asked."

"So he did. Will you tell me now?"

"Shore. Glad to. After the sojers whupped them Injuns down in Californy, a few of 'em got away—that was three, four years back. The cav'ry chased a bunch up this way and caught 'em on that same crick. Killed damn near all of 'em, they did."

"Soldiers from this post?" Smith asked.

"Naw. They come frum down in Nevada somewheres. They come in here after the fight, an' I learned the story frum the scout that was with 'em."

"What story, man?"

"About the fight, Cap'n. They snuck up on them Injuns jest like Mr. Shelby, an' they got most all of 'em. They brung in maybe three or four—all of 'em wimmen, as I remember."

"But the name? Hanging Woman's Fork. That's what you told Ritter, isn't it?"

"Now, Cap'n," Hanst said patiently, "that come later. I ain't got there yet."

Captain Smith shut his eyes and prayed for patience. "All right, Mr. Hanst, tell me about the name."

"Used to be a feller called Phineas, hunted an' trapped up in them mountains north o' th' river. Seems like an Injun gal got away frum th' sojers an' Phineas he found her. Took her up, he did, an' she stayed with him nigh on a year. Some kinda Californy Injun she was, but a man like Phineas, he warn't partiklar. I seen 'em couple times, an' Phineas he tol' me she was a mite queer in th' head but all right under a blanket."

Hanst gave the captain a knowing wink, and Smith closed his eyes again.

"Anyhow, th' sojers buried them Injuns they kilt, but they din't do too good a job of it. Nobody ever buries a dead Injun right good, I reckon. Some of them no-good Paiutes dug 'em up an' scalped 'em, an' I guess Phineas's gal found out about it. She took on somethin' bad. Tol' him her dad wuz one of 'em killed on that crick, an' she wanted to go see if he'd been dug up. You don't happen to have a seegar or some tobaccy, do you, Cap'n? I'm plumb out, I am."

Lieutenant Weisendorf handed over a sack of flake tobacco and a folder of papers, and everyone waited while Peter Hanst rolled himself a bulbous cigarette and lit it.

"I thank you, mister. I ain't too good at rollin' 'em, but it's better'n nuthin'. Where was I?"

"Phineas's Indian girl." Dr. Brenner reminded him.

"Yeah. She kept after Phineas till he had t' take her back where the sojers had killed her folks. Warn't nuthin' but bones left, but she figgered some o' them wuz her dad. Said she jest had t' git him inter th' ground right or he'd never be quiet. Phineas tol' me she carried on 'bout that till he got skeered. Figgered if he din't help her git them bones buried, she'd never be no good fer nuthin'. Him an' her, they buried everythin' they c'd find, an' then he went off meat-huntin' an' left her in camp. She wuz singin' an' carryin' on, Phineas said, an' he wuz glad t'git out of that fer a spell."

The ill-made cigarette sputtered and went out, and Hanst made a disgusted face. Sergeant Couza produced a cigar for him, and again there was a pause while the woodcutter lit the cheroot and puffed on it happily.

"Ol' Phineas, he was gone quite a spell, but he got

him a deer an' come back to camp, lookin' fer his gal t'
skin it out an' cook him some steaks. First thing he
seen was one o' his dogs by th' crick with its throat
cut. Same thing with both his horses. His tent was
burnt an' his things was strewed all over, an' his gal
was settin' there, keenin' an' wailin' like them Injun females do. He cut hisself a stick an' made to whup some
sense inter her, but she had his shotgun an' when he
started fer her she let it off right at him."

Hanst stopped to relight the cigar, and after a moment Lieutenant Weisendorf broke the silence.

"She killed him?"

"Aw, hell no! How'd I know the story if she done
that? She missed him clean, an' he wuz gonna frail her
butt, but he thought about it some an' figgered warn't
no use in that. She was plain crazy. Phineas reckoned
he'd never be sure she wouldn't cut his throat some
night, so he took and hung her frum a big ol' tree
right by that crick. She'd done ruint near six hundred
dollars worth o' gear an' horses, an' Phineas, he was
right put out with her."

There was a long silence after Hanst stopped. Captain Smith shook his head. "That's the first time I ever
heard that. When did they start calling the creek by
this name?"

"Injuns did soon's they found that gal hangin' frum
the tree. Phineas, he jest left her there. You ask any of
them Paiutes over to ol' Chief Winnemucca's place an'
they'll tell you that's its name."

"And you told Ritter this story?"

"Shore did. He asked me whut is th' name of that
crick, an' I tol' him. Ain't nuthin' wrong with that, is
there? I'da told you, had you asked me."

Spurred by the curt demand from Washington, Captain
Smith submitted a second report of Shelby's engagement with the Indians, longer but no different in the
essentials. Shelby's death, he repeated, precluded an
officer's firsthand report of the affair, but all details had

464

been confirmed by Shelby's second-in-command, Corporal Brennan.

Brennan, he added, had been badly wounded by an Indian woman. He deserved commendation for his part in the action. A Medal of Honor was not warranted, but he suggested a Certificate of Merit—a recommendation doomed to fail. In the thirty years it had been in existence, the certificate had rarely been awarded, perhaps because it carried with it a special compensation of two dollars a month extra pay.

Michael was flattered to learn this, but not hopeful. Since Sappa Creek he had been dubious of army decorations, particularly for actions derided by the press. Charles Ritter's lurid account of the Massacre on Hanging Woman's Fork had been widely copied by Eastern journals.

More tangible reward arrived in a letter from Brigadier General Quinn of the Connecticut Militia, which he read on the stoop of the hospital, enjoying the sun and the attention of Angie Couza and Sergeant O'Hara's daughter Maureen.

"I have seen the newspaper accounts," wrote Quinn, "and Captain Smith's reports. His recommendation for a Certificate of Merit is foolish. Your gallantry deserves more than Smith can manage . . ."

Michael skipped over this welcome praise, seeking what he expected from a practical man like Quinn. He grunted with satisfaction when he found it.

" . . . so I have taken the liberty of putting in motion a few wheels on my own account. My friends in San Francisco assure me you will shortly receive orders transferring you to a job on the Division staff requiring a sergeant's stripes. This is all I can manage at the moment, but in a month or two I will communicate with you concerning a job here in the East I have in mind for you if you are agreeable. . . ."

Angie gave him a solicitous look. "Bad news in your letter?"

"Not at all, at all. A kind word from that great man,

General Quinn, that's all." He beamed at her. "By the bye, ladies, have either of you seen Brigid about?"

The angry snap in Angie's eyes urged caution on him, and he added, "I've not seen her these three days past, and I must be givin' her my thanks for all her kindness when I was so low with my wound."

Maureen made an unpleasant sound. "I doubt your thanks will sweeten her temper."

"She's angry, then?"

"She's been readin' those damned newspapers," Angie snorted. "She says you an' the rest of the boys are no better than murderers."

"Does she now?"

But it was clear that no message borne by this pair would be of use, so Michael bided his time until Molly Magruder looked in on him a little later.

"Sure an' I'll tell her you're wantin' to speak with her, Michael, but I doubt it's worth it. You'd not believe the things that girl has been sayin'."

Molly must have been persuasive, though, for after supper Brigid appeared. She put a napkin-covered pan on the table and eyed him coldly as he peeked beneath the cloth.

"God be praised! A whole apple pie. Bless your kind heart, Bridey!"

"Mah Kim sent it."

The chill in her voice warned him, and he proceeded cautiously. "I'm in your debt for more than pie, Bridey. Dr. Brenner says had it not been for you an' Molly I'd likely not be here to eat it."

"I'd have done as much for any man hurt like you were."

"Now, those are cold words!"

She gave him a sour look. "I've naught else for you, Michael Brennan. I suppose your job is killin' people, but I don't like it an' I don't like you for doin' it."

He shrugged. "As you say . . . it's my job. Like it or not, I'm bound to do it."

"Innocent women an' kids, too?"

"Innocent! Jesus, woman . . . you've good reason to

know what that slut did to me with her dirty great spear!"

"Good on her! Trapped in a hole with soldiers all around, shootin' at her with their guns. I'm glad she got a bit of her own!"

"Ah, Bridey," he sighed, "you're takin' those newspapers for whole cloth, I fear."

"I've no need for them," she bristled, fists clenched on her hips. "More nights than I want to count I sat here listenin' to you rave—the fear of God on you, I'm thinkin'."

"What did I say?" he demanded, astonished.

" 'I didn't know it was a woman', you said. 'I didn't mean to kill her.' Over an' over you said it, till I was like to go out of my wits."

He whistled softly. "Did I, now? God, I was off my head, wasn't I?"

"And sayin' the truth for once, I don't doubt! Which one was it troubled you, Brennan? One of those in that hole?—Or was it you that beat up that poor girl an' left her to die last winter?"

He groaned. "You know I didn't do that thing, Bridey! I may have killed a woman once—"

"I knew it!" she shouted triumphantly. "You were that near to dyin', you told the truth for once, didn't you? I knew it—"

"Shut up a minute, will you not?" he exploded. "I killed no woman nor child in that hole! I never killed that girl last winter either. Once, a long time ago, I may have done so, but that was in another fight an' I'm not sure at all."

"That's an excuse?" she yelled. "I'll have none of it, Brennan! It's a dirty business you do, an' don't tell me you don't like it! I think," she hissed venomously, "you'd as lief kill a woman as anybody, an' I'll have naught to do with that kind of man. I'd be afeared to walk out with the likes of you."

She marched to the door and jerked it open, pausing for a final explosion.

"You can rest easy, Brennan! They've taken that

poor dumb Indian that killed Mister Shelby off to jail in Canyon City. They'll hang him before he can get at you for killin' his women."

The hospital rocked as she shut the door, and after a moment Moser put his head in and looked about curiously.

"What was that?" he asked.

"The wind blew it shut," Michael told him. "Bring a knife an' some coffee, an' I'll give you a piece of apple pie like you haven't had since you came to this damn place."

13

By the last week of September, Michael was up and limping about Camp Belknap, visiting every house that offered a meal and feminine company except the Carters'. He had no welcome there, though Mah Kim smuggled an occasional pie to the hospital. Dr. Brenner ordered long walks, and on some of these William and Amanda kept him company, but not Brigid. She avoided him, and when they met by chance she sailed by without even a nod, to the undisguised delight of Angie and Prudence. Both offered to soothe any loss Michael felt.

The news from the war was scant, though there were ugly rumors of bad behavior by two troops of the First Cavalry. At Camas Meadows Chief Joseph's braves had turned, one dawn, on their pursuers, driving off most of General Howard's pack mules. Two troops of the First and one of the Second Cavalry had gone in pursuit, following too far and too fast. The Nez Percés turned again, and in the confusion an order was given the cavalry to withdraw. It was obeyed so promptly by the First that Captain Norwood's troop of the Second was cut off and surrounded by Indians. General Howard got them out with infantry and a howitzer, but there were hard words said about B and I troops of the First. They had chased the Nez Percés all the way

469

from Oregon to the Wyoming border, only to falter when they finally made contact.

On the morning of September 28, Michael was having a cup of coffee on Sergeant Benoni's back porch when the hospital orderly pounded on the front door.

"Corporal Brennan!" he shouted. "Is Brennan in there?"

"He is," Mrs. Benoni told him. "What's wanted?"

"Dr. Brenner wants him at his quarters. Right now."

Michael excused himself and was met at the doctor's door by Angie, who looked harried.

"Where've you been? Doctor's waiting for you in the front room, and he's got company."

The company was a serious young man in a dark suit with a white shirt and cravat—unusual civilian attire at Belknap.

"Brennan, this is Mr. Shaw," said the doctor. "He's an attorney from Canyon City. Shaw, I think this is the man you're looking for." He indicated a chair and Michael eased himself into it.

"Mr. Shaw," continued the doctor, "is one of the lawyers defending Petoe. You know he's being tried for killing Lieutenant Shelby, don't you?"

"Yes, sir. I heard that."

"Well, Shaw has asked me for help I can't give. I think you can . . . if you want to."

"Help defend that Indian, sir?"

"That's up to you. I want you to hear him out, though."

He nodded to the civilian, who rearranged some papers on the floor at his feet and looked at Michael.

"My partner and I were hired by the Council on Indian Rights in Baltimore, Corporal. Petoe's being tried by the federal district court in Canyon City, and it's been in session since last Tuesday. I guess you know how most folks feel about this case."

"Yes, sir. I feel the same way."

"You want to see that Indian hanged, is that it?"

Michael shrugged. "I didn't think they could do any-

470

thing else with him. He shot the lieutenant in the back, didn't he?"

"That's right. He admits it."

Michael looked at Dr. Brenner, but got no help from him. "I guess I don't understand, mister," he told Shaw. "If he admits it, what can you do for him?"

"Well, so far we've only heard the district attorney, and he's preaching to the choir. He calls it murder and most everybody seems to agree with him."

Michael didn't want to tell the young man he was wasting his time because that seemed so obvious. He shrugged.

"So do I."

The lawyer smiled. "Next week is our turn. We're going to prove it wasn't."

Again Brennan looked at the doctor. This couldn't be a joke, he decided, because the doctor was taking it seriously. That worried him. He had a soldier's ingrained distrust of lawyers, so he watched Shaw warily and said nothing.

"First," continued Shaw, "we're going to make sure they can't hang him. Then . . . "

Michael leaned forward to stare at the lawyer in disbelief, and Dr. Brenner laughed.

"Wait. Listen to him."

"Do you know the difference between murder and manslaughter, Corporal?" asked Shaw.

The answer was watchful silence.

"It's like this." The lawyer held up a thumb. "You kill a man with malice and deliberation—that's murder. If you're convicted you hang." He folded the thumb and held up his forefinger. "But . . . if you kill him without premeditation under great mental stress, that's manslaughter. You'll probably do time, but you won't hang."

It was obvious that this lesson in law was going to get no vocal response from Brennan and Dr. Brenner intervened.

"Mental stress. How're you going to prove it?"

Shaw counted on his fingers again. "Witnesses. In-

471

dian Agent at Umatilla reservation—Columbia River Indians threatened to kill the old man and all his band, so they ran away. Shelby's Bannock interpreter—when Shelby caught them he told them they had to go back. They objected, and he killed eleven of them—"

"That happened four days before Petoe killed Shelby!" Michael objected.

Shaw continued. "Bannock interpreter—morning after the Indians got to Belknap he told them again they had to go back to Umatilla . . . on orders by the post commander. Teamster from Canyon City was here that morning and saw it all . . . saw what happened when the Indians got that order." He grinned again. "He calls it 'one hell of a hoo-raw.' We'll call it great mental stress, and between us we'll make our point."

"All right," said Brenner. "How about premeditation?"

"Easy. Petoe couldn't plan to kill Shelby. He didn't have a gun."

"What'd he kill him with?" demanded Michael truculently.

"Jerked a pistol away from another Indian. Teamster saw him do it, and the Indian who had the gun will swear to it. Petoe didn't plan anything. He just went crazy."

Dr. Brenner looked at Michael and chuckled. "You believe that, Brennan?"

"Well, sir, that's not the way I heard it, but I wasn't there. I don't see it makes any difference whose gun he used, and there's something else Mr. Shaw hasn't talked about."

"What's that?" demanded Shaw.

"Lieutenant Shelby ran that Indian off the post last spring. I'd say Petoe hated his guts a long time before he killed him."

The lawyer nodded. "It's possible. The doctor just told me about that. The district attorney brought it up, but he thinks Petoe got in a fight with a soldier—you, I gather. He doesn't know Shelby was here then."

472

"What if somebody told him?" asked Brennan.

Shaw gave him a long look. "Who's going to do that, Corporal?"

"I guess you want me in that court for something, mister. What if they ask me?"

The lawyer shrugged. "Tell 'em. That won't stop us. This is just the beginning, Corporal. We mean to get that Indian off scot-free."

That was too much for Brennan. He snorted disgustedly. "You going to tell me how, mister?"

Shaw nodded. "I am, because we need your help to do it." He leaned over to study one of the papers on the floor, and after a moment he asked quietly, "Have you ever killed an Indian, Corporal?"

Michael's jaw dropped. "I . . . yes, I guess so. Wait a minute! You mean, did I ever just walk up to one and shoot him?"

"No. The doctor says you've seen a lot of fighting, in the war and after that, too. It wasn't all hand-to-hand, I suppose. Didn't you ever draw a bead on a man who hadn't seen you and knock him over?"

Michael considered that slowly. "It's possible," he conceded.

"Would you call it murder . . . or manslaughter?"

"Christ on the tree, mister! I wouldn't call it either. What d'you mean by that?"

"Just what I said. You killed the man. What do you call it?"

"Damn it to hell! I was in a fight. If he'd seen me first he'd have killed me."

"I know that. But you killed him. Now what do we call it?"

Michael shook an angry finger at the lawyer. "I'm a soldier, mister, not a goddamn bandit! If I kill a man in a war, it's not murder or manslaughter or any other fancy name, so long's he's carryin' a gun an' ready to use it on me."

"So . . ." said Shaw softly. "If you were tried by a court for killing a man like that . . . how would you defend yourself?"

473

There was a long silence. Shaw and the doctor watched Brennan's face curiously. After a while the doctor nodded and stood up.

"I think we could use some coffee. I'll just see if Angie won't make us some."

Angelina brought the coffee, eager to know what was going on in the front room, but they took her tray and shut the door and she could hear nothing through it.

Shaw seemed to be waiting for something, and Dr. Brenner broke the silence. "Will you help him, Brennan?"

"Do what, Doctor?"

"When the shooting started on that creek, did you think you were in a war?"

Michael stared at him in astonishment. "You got another name for it, sir?"

Brenner grinned. *"Das ist das Wesentliche!* That's all he wants. Will you stand up in court and say that?"

"I'll say it anywhere. It's a fact."

"Good. You go to Canyon City with Shaw, and when he asks you did you think you were in a war, you tell him. That's all."

"What good will that do?"

"If they believe you," said Shaw, "they might turn that Indian loose. Does that make a difference?"

"I'd as soon see the son-of-a-bitch hung, mister, but if my sayin' we were in a war gets him off, that's his good luck. I don't give a damn."

"All right," said the doctor, "you'll go. I'd better have a word with our post commander first. Don't worry, Shaw. He'll see the light. I'll just ask Mathilde to set a place for you two at dinner, and you can start north as soon as you've eaten."

14

Saturday, October 6, was beef-issue day at Camp Belknap. The contractor had driven in a bunch of scrawny steers, which were killed and butchered at once. A representative from each kitchen on the post joined the line waiting at the commissary storehouse to draw rations of fresh meat.

Troop kitchens put their share in two-wheeled handcarts which—by post commander's order—had to return to the company cookhouses along the road fronting the stables instead of directly across the parade ground. They left an unsightly trail of blood spots when loaded.

Enlisted wives with laundress status drew their rations free of charge like the soldiers. Civilian employees paid cash, and beef drawn by an officer's orderly or cook was charged to his account at eight and a half cents a pound. All soldiers and their families were convinced that the best cuts of meat were reserved for officers, though it was doubtful there were any choice cuts of the tough, stringy meat available this time of year. There was no pasturage near the post to recover the animals from their long drive to get there.

"I don't see," grumbled Maria Benoni, "how a damn cow can live when it's all gristle like this." She prodded a chunk of dark, muscular meat disgustedly. "I wish the Major was here. He'd not let 'em issue this crap."

"Can't be long, ladies," said the commissary butcher cheerfully. "Them Injuns got by the cav'ry on the Yellowstone, an' they're headed straight for Canada. Troops can't follow 'em across th' line, an' I'll wager they're back home afore snowfall."

"Michael's back," Prudence whispered to Angie. "I saw him come in just as I left the store."

"Did you talk to him? What's he been doin' in Canyon City all week?"

"Didn't have a chance. He went straight to the hospital—lookin' for Doc Brenner, I s'pose. Maybe you can find out at supper tonight."

Michael had delayed only long enough to unharness the doctor's horse and give him a quick rubdown before seeking out Brenner, who greeted him with a questioning look.

"They turned him loose, sir. Mister Shaw got him off."

"Good! Tell me."

Michael sat down and stretched his legs with a groan. "He fooled 'em. For the first three days they thought all he was tryin' to do was get Petoe off the murder charge. He might have done it, too. I swear, if Shaw had quit on Wednesday, he'd have got that Indian off with a jail sentence."

"How?"

"It was right funny. That government lawyer took the better part of a week provin' Petoe shot Mister Shelby and makin' a case that he's a mean, no-good Indian who had been plannin' to murder Shelby ever since the fight on the creek. Shaw said there was no question Petoe killed Shelby, but the Indians he lived with ought to know best what kind of man he is. Then he called 'em up to say what they thought."

Michael chuckled.

"You know how serious they are. Shaw'd ask 'em a question and they'd think it over. Is Petoe a mean Indian? They'd nod, and after a while they'd say, he's

476

mean. Is he a no-good Indian? Yep. He's no good. Did he plan to kill Mr. Shelby? They'd look surprised and shake their heads. That Petoe, they said, he couldn't figure out how to kill a fieldmouse, much less a man. Hasn't got sense enough to come in out of the rain. Then the government lawyer would go at 'em. Did Petoe kill the lieutenant? Sure. Why'd he do it? No idea. Nobody knows what a damn fool like Petoe is goin' to do. He's a crazy Indian. Then they'd tell some fool thing he did while he was livin' with 'em, and pretty soon they had the whole courtroom laughin'. That's all that government man could get out of 'em—Petoe's a crazy Indian. He finally gave up, and everybody thought it was all over."

Michael shook his head wonderingly.

"Shaw had me fooled, too. I thought he was goin' to quit, but he was playin' a smart game. I guess he wanted to make sure he'd got the rope off of his Indian's neck before he made 'em turn him loose."

"What happened then?"

"Thursday morning Judge Heber asked Shaw if he had anything more to say, and Shaw let him have it. He used a lot of fancy words, but all he said was that Petoe and the Indians were in a war with the soldiers and you can't try a man in the civilian court for killin' his enemy in a war. That woke 'em up. Judge Heber looked like he'd swallowed his tobacco, and the government lawyer started hollerin' that you can't have a war unless somebody declares one. He wanted to see that in writing, but Shaw said the Indians can't write and the government doesn't declare war on Indians—it just sends the army out to get 'em. They argued for a while, and Judge Heber asked Shaw how could he prove there was a war. Shaw said if the Indians and the soldiers thought there was one it didn't take a piece of paper to prove it, and he started callin' up Indians to tell what they thought about that."

Brenner held up his hand. "Coffee?" he asked. Michael nodded and the doctor opened the door to shout for the orderly. When the pot had been brought and their mugs filled, he settled into his chair and grinned at Michael.

"Go on."

"All the Indians said that when Shelby caught 'em at the creek he started a war. The government lawyer wanted to know what their chief thought, so Shaw called him up—the old man with the black hat. He wouldn't take it off. He's got no teeth, and the interpreter had a hell of a time makin' out what he said. But he made his point. He said the war didn't start on that creek. It started when the first white man showed up out here and began stealin' from the Indians, and it's been goin' on ever since. He said somethin' else that got translated as 'the only good white man is a dead one,' and that started everybody laughin' again. Shaw asked if they wanted more Indians, but the judge said no, that's enough. The government lawyer got his turn, and he said maybe the Indians thought there was a war, but what about the army? Mr. Shelby was commander, but he was dead, so how could Shaw prove what the soldiers thought."

"And then Shaw called you up?"

"Yes, sir. He asked was I at the fight and was I wounded there and was I Mister Shelby's second-in-command. I said yes, and the government lawyer wanted to know what was Captain Russo doin'. Shaw had an answer to that. He had a paper to prove the state never called up Russo and his people, so they were nothin' but a posse and none of 'em had any rank. Then Shaw asked me did I think I was in a war, and I told him yes and so did every man with me. He quit then, and Judge Heber let the government lawyer have a go."

"What did he say?"

"That we were peace officers. Just because we were soldiers didn't make it a war, and what did I think about that?"

Michael drained his coffee and put the mug down with a clang.

"That candy-ass civilian! I told him. When I enlisted

in the army nobody said I was a peace officer. The army tells me to go and fight Indians, I don't think I'm some kind of policeman. I'm a soldier, and I thought I was in a war, and when one of those Indians hit me with a load of birdshot I damn well knew it. He kept askin' me and I kept on tellin' him. After a while Judge Heber asked me, and I told him, too. I guess then they believed me."

"Was that the end of it?"

"Oh, no! The government lawyer said if there ever had been a war, it ended when the shootin' stopped on the creek. Petoe killed the lieutenant after the war was over. Shaw fixed that one, too. He called up a white teamster from Canyon City who was here when Mr. Shelby was killed. That teamster wasn't happy about it, but Shaw got it out of him. The Indians hadn't been disarmed . . . they weren't locked up . . . there wasn't even a guard on 'em that anybody could see. Not till after Shelby was killed. Shaw said the war wasn't over till that happened, and did they want some Indians to tell about it?"

"What did the judge say?"

Michael grinned. "He looked like a cat that got into the turpentine. He said he didn't want to hear any more out of anybody. Shaw and the government lawyer both tried to talk, and Judge Heber just told 'em to sit down and shut up."

"He threw the case out of court then?"

"No, sir! He put the evil eye on that government lawyer and said he wasn't about to have this damned case back in court again. Then he lit into the jury. He told 'em there wasn't but one thing he'd hear from them. This Indian, he said, has got to be acquitted. What he did was an act of war. He said it real slow and real plain, and they heard him. They didn't even go out and think it over. They talked to each other for a minute and then the head man got up and said, 'Your Honor, we find Petoe not guilty.' Didn't even say what he was not guilty of, but everybody knew. That was the end of it."

"So! And how do you feel about it?"

"I don't give a damn for that Indian, but what Mr. Shaw said about there bein' a war is right. I wouldn't have stood up for him unless I believed that."

"How about when the word gets around? A lot of people won't understand what you did."

Michael got to his feet. "Corporal and below, I can handle them."

Brenner nodded. "Good. What about your leg? Is it still bothering you?"

"I can handle that too, but how long am I goin' to have this limp, Doctor?"

"Maybe the rest of your life. Depends on what got sliced in there and how it mends and what you do with yourself. Do you know there's orders for you in the adjutant's office?"

"San Francisco?"

"You knew they were coming, then?"

"I had an idea."

"Well, I won't ask how you got that. Congratulations. Sounds like a damned fine job. Sergeant's stripes come with it?"

"I think so, sir—unless somebody stops that. But I want you to know, Doctor, I didn't finagle that job."

Brenner chuckled. "Hell, man, I wouldn't blame you if you did. I'd say you've got a good friend somewhere . . . back east, maybe?"

Brennan shrugged. "From what you say, I'll be needin' more than one."

"Yep. I hope not, but just in case . . . I've got something for you that will help."

The surgeon pushed a paper across the table. It was a printed form, the blanks completed in pen and ink in a small, crabbed hand. Michael read it carefully and looked puzzled.

"You're goin' to have me discharged, sir?"

"Not if you don't want to."

"That's a medical discharge, isn't it?"

"Not at all. That's a certificate of temporary disability. It's my professional opinion that you may be all

480

right in a few months—or you may never get over that wound. You can tear it up or you can keep it. Call it an insurance policy if you like."

"What would I do with it, sir?"

"Brennan, I don't think that limp will bother you unless you go back to humping a pack and a rifle thirty miles a day. It certainly won't bother a staff sergeant at Division Headquarters. If you like your new job, you can forget about this paper. If you don't like it . . . for one reason or another . . . you give this to the Division medical officer and ask to go before a disability board. When the board meets, it will probably require my endorsement on this certificate, and I'll give it to 'em. I'll tell 'em I thought that leg might go bad on you, and I'm not surprised it has. Now do you understand?"

Michael studied the paper and then the doctor. After a moment he grinned.

"I used to have a sergeant in Kansas always said he was happy as a man with his discharge in his pocket." He folded the certificate and put it away in his coat. "Always wondered how that would feel."

"Well, now you know. What did you do with my horse?"

"In the corral, sir. I'll take a currycomb and brush to him now, and tomorrow I'll wash down the buggy." He thought a moment. "Doctor, I'd just like to—"

Brenner held up a warning hand. "Don't thank me, Corporal. That's nothing but a certificate of a surgeon's opinion, and don't you get to thinking it's anything else. Now get out of here and let me go to work."

15

On the ninth of October, Lieutenant Weisendorf's troop bugler sounded a routine reveille, wiped the mouthpiece of his bugle on his sleeve, and headed for the cookhouse to get himself a cup of coffee. The orderly ran onto the adjutant's porch and yelled at him excitedly. Standing in the road, the trumpeter put his instrument to his lips and burst into an unorthodox fanfare that roused the post in surprise.

"Rally Round the Flag, Boys," he blared, then exhausted his repertoire of extracurricular music with a joyous rendition of "Forty Miles a Day on Beans and Hay in the Regular Army, Oh!" After that he simply blew all the daily bugle calls—plus fire call, pay call, stables, and the charge—in bewildering succession.

"It's over!" yelled the orderly, pounding on the porch railing with the office coffeepot. "Rover . . . rover . . . the war is *over!*"

"What the hell's the matter with you, soldier?" roared Sergeant O'Hara, rounding the corner of the building at a trot.

"It's over, Sarge! Chief Joseph surrendered! The Injuns have quit!" He waved a buff telegram form in the air. "Just got here!"

Captain Smith hurried up the plank walk from his quarters in carpet slippers, his cape over his long flannel nightshirt. Some of the women who had begun to gather about the adjutant's office tittered in amusement.

"What's all this?" he demanded.

The orderly pointed to an exhausted horse at the hitching rail.

"Rider just in from Baker City, sir. Telegram from Montana. Gen'ral Miles caught them Injuns forty mile from the Canada line an' the whole lot surrendered."

That was glad news, but there was no answer to the women's first question—when will the troops come home? Not until two days later did a courier from Fort Boise bring a partial answer.

"The cavalry in General Howard's column turned back on the twenty-seventh of September," Smith told the officers and sergeants assembled in his office. "They're marching to the railroad in Utah. They'll take the cars there and get off at Winnemucca."

"What about the infantry?"

"Ordered back to Fort Boise."

"But when will they be here?"

"Doesn't say. Just says they'll leave the Weiser Valley and march to Fort Boise. Dr. Brenner is ordered to meet them there. They want a surgeon."

"Have they been in a fight?"

Smith looked serious. "No mention of a fight. I've heard of no trouble in the Weiser Valley."

Brenner gave him a wry look. As usual, Captain Smith was making a mystery of it.

"They've probably got a few sick, that's all. I'll start today and send word back as soon as I find out."

The gathering broke up, talking loudly, and the women fell upon them outside the headquarters. The cavalry wives crowed with joy and sympathized with their glum infantry companions.

"Doc Brenner will find out," Sergeant O'Hara told them. "He's goin' to meet the comp'ny at Fort Boise, an' he'll send a rider back as soon as he gets there."

Brenner stopped for a while at the Carter house, then went on to his own to pack up his equipment.

Moments later, Brigid opened the kitchen door and shouted for the children.

"William . . . Amanda!" There was no answer, and she glared at Mah Kim. "Where'd they go?"

"I dunno, Missy Bridge. What you want?"

"Their mother wants them. Which way did they go?"

He shrugged and looked blank.

"Don't plague me, Mah Kim! Missus Carter's goin' away and she wants to talk to them."

"How she go 'way? You said you go San Francisco pretty quick. You can't both go 'way!"

That was a sore subject with Brigid, and her face flamed. "I know, damn it! But she's got a chance to go see Mr. Carter in Boise, an' I've got to stay till she gets back."

"Hot damn!" said Mah Kim. "That's good."

Brigid's promised year with the Carters had stretched to sixteen months, but she had never given up her dream of a city job. She had badgered trader Morton until finally, not a week past, he had found her a place in San Francisco. Brigid was torn. She said she had to wait until Lieutenant Carter came home from the war, but Mrs. Carter refused. If Brigid had found a job, she should take it or she might lose the chance. In the end, with guilty tears, Brigid had accepted her release. Now she was stalled by Louise Carter's sudden decision to go to Boise, and Mah Kim's delight was no comfort. She whirled on him furiously.

"You know where they are, you sneaky pagan! Tell me!"

"They just take lil' walk, Missy Bridge."

"By the creek? You know they're not supposed to do that unless somebody goes with them!"

Mah Kim's guilty silence was eloquent, and Brigid exploded.

"Brennan? Damn it, I told you I'd skin you alive if you let him in here again! Which way'd they go?"

"I dunno. Don't say."

Brigid shook her fist at him and flounced out the door, swearing.

Michael, William, and Amanda were sitting on the big rock that sloped into the stream behind the bakery. The water was too cold for fishing, but the children were tired of walking, so Michael had rigged a pole with cord, hook, and bobber. As Brigid's angry shouts drew nearer, he hunched his shoulders.

"I think she wants you kids."

William ignored the warning. "Lookit the bobber, Michael! Look! You got a bite!"

"Nah, nah. When you got a bite, Will, it goes right under."

"So!" Brigid's exclamation behind them was angry.

No one looked at her. They all watched the bobber expectantly.

"William! Amanda! What d'you think you're doing?"

"Fishing."

"Oh, aye! One idiot waitin' for another! Didn't you hear me calling you?"

"Sit down, Bridey," Michael said softly, "an' ease your temper a bit."

"You shut up! You kids get up here this minute—your mother's goin' to Boise an' she wants to see you."

"Papa!" shouted William. "She's goin' to see Papa! Can we go too?" He scrambled to the bank and set off running for the house.

Michael swung Amanda off the rock and she followed her brother, squealing delightedly.

"When's she going?" Michael asked.

"Right now. With Dr. Brenner."

"And you? I heard you were going to quit and go to San Francisco."

"I was," snapped Brigid. "Mr. Morton got me a job there, but Missus Carter's goin' to see the Lieutenant, an' she can't take the kids. Somebody's got to stay an' look after them."

"There's plenty would do that, but I hope they don't."

"What's that mean?"

He got to his feet awkwardly and joined her on the bank.

"I'm glad you've got to stay," he told her, grinning. "I don't want you trippin' off to the city."

"What's it to you?" she shot back. "It's none of your business where I go!"

She marched off down the path to the house, and Michael limped after her, admiring the angry switch of her hips. She threw him a furious look over her shoulder.

"And where do you think you're goin'?"

"To help Missus Carter."

"You're not needed, thank you. Mah Kim an' I can see to her."

"Mah Kim makes good pie an' you make trouble, Bridey. You need a good head for real work."

"Oh . . . you go to the devil!" She hurried on, angrily aware that he was enjoying the view.

Dr. Brenner's buggy stood before the house, a soldier at the horse's head and another lounging in his saddle nearby. Louise Carter was comforting a sobbing Amanda.

"I won't be long, baby . . . I promise. Maybe Papa can come back with me."

Mah Kim dragged a fat carpetbag onto the porch from the house, and Michael took it from him and lifted it into the back of the buggy.

"Oh, Corporal Brennan!" exclaimed Mrs. Carter at sight of him. "I'm so glad—ah—" She glanced at Brigid's flushed face and faltered.

"Not to worry, ma'am," Michael assured her. "You needn't be thinkin' about us here. If Brigid an' Mah Kim need any help, I'll take care."

Brigid's face turned redder. "We'll be needin' no help, ma'am."

"Oh, Brigid, I'm so sorry to do this to you . . ." Louise Carter gave her a pleading look. "But I shouldn't dare go unless I knew you were here to care for the children. I promise I shan't be away for long."

"Sure, ma'am," Brigid murmured, "you mustn't worry yourself about it. I don't mind stayin' a bit longer."

Dr. Brenner appeared with Mathilde and his two boys, kissed them all, and handed Louise Carter into the buggy.

"Mathilde," said Louise, "I feel so guilty about this."

"Quatsch!" sniffed Mrs. Brenner. "I have had him for a whole month. I can spare him if he takes you to see your Cassius." She patted her husband's knee. *"Auf Wiedersehen,* Josef. *Gute Reise."*

The doctor smiled at her. "Let's go," he told the troopers, and clucked at the horse.

Since Michael had told no one but Doctor Brenner of his part in Petoe's trial, the Belknap garrison knew only that the Indian had been acquitted—news that was greeted with indignation. With the report of the Nez Percé surrender and the end of the war, no one paid much attention to the trial until the mail-rider from Canyon City brought a strange story. Petoe had been acquitted, he said, because a soldier told the court some crazy story that got him off.

He was accused of being crazy himself, but he insisted it was true and that the soldier had come from Camp Belknap. Those who knew Brennan had gone to Canyon City put two and two together and began to speculate. There was a good deal of talk, but not in Brennan's presence. He did not seem inclined to speak of it, and no one wanted to press him.

The dedicated poker players of the post were not concerned though, and Moser, searching for Michael, found him in the farrier's shop with his usual cronies. Since the paymaster had last visited Belknap in June, just before the army stopped being paid, poker like everything else was "jaw-bone" as the soldiers said. With no money available, winnings were penciled on the wall of the shop to be paid if payday ever came again.

"That girl at Doc's house wants you," Moser told Michael.

"Oh, hell!"

Brennan got up from the blanket on the floor cautiously. His leg still hurt, but it had not stiffened, and Dr. Brenner said that was a good sign. Since the doctor had departed for Fort Boise the day before with Mrs. Carter, he supposed Mrs. Brenner wanted something.

"I'll be back," he told the farrier.

"If that Couza gal sent for *me*," muttered one of the players, "I'd not be back in a hurry. Deal, will you?"

Michael found Angie, face and fingers smudged, glaring at the Brenners' kitchen stove. "It smokes, an' I can't make it do right. Please help me fix it."

Michael sighed. The Brenners owned the most complicated kitchen range on the post. Cast-iron swirls and curlicues decorated its body, and a pair of fat iron cherubs climbed a grapevine supporting the overhead warming ovens. There were drying racks, water coils in the firebox—which had both front and side doors— two copper water tanks, and numberless knobs, levers, draft controls, and even a foot pedal to open the oven door.

"Good God!" he muttered.

He could find nothing broken, so he attacked the controls, but this produced only smoke. That summoned Mrs. Brenner.

"I don't know what ails it, ma'am," said Michael, wiping soot from his face. Mrs. Brenner looked surprised. She rearranged the controls, pulling, pushing, and adjusting levers in their ratchets. The stove stopped smoking and began to hum softly.

"Nothing is wrong with my stove, Corporal Brennan, except that someone has pushed what ought to be pulled." She gave Angie a cross look and returned to the front of the house. Angie giggled and hid her face in her hands.

"Now what was it you really want of me, Angie Couza?" Michael asked.

"Let's go to Mr. Morton's. You know who's there?"

488

"No, Angie. Who?"

"That newspaper feller. The one that wrote the story about Mr. Shelby catchin' the Indians an' put you in it."

"Is he now? What's he want this time?"

Angie shrugged. "There's two of 'em. They came to see Bender and Downey—those two in the new cavalry troop that got hurt in the big fight last August."

"Ah! The Battle of the Big Hole. Small wonder Ritter's back . . . he smells blood."

"What do you mean?"

"Bender says they killed more squaws an' kids there than we did with Shelby."

Michael had listened to Bender and Downey. They were a pair of military oddities with a curious story:

Assigned as recruits to the Second Cavalry at Fort Ellis in Montana, they had been shanghaied en route by Colonel John Gibbon when he took his understrength Seventh Infantry in pursuit of the Nez Percés. Gibbon caught up with the Indians at the Big Hole Basin in Montana, launched a surprise dawn attack, and inflicted heavy casualties on his quarry—more than eighty killed, Bender said, though he estimated half of these were women and children. Gibbon's force was too small to follow up the success, and the Nez Percés struck back, surrounding him. By the time General Howard's column drove off the Indians, Gibbon had lost almost seventy men of his total force of a hundred and eighty soldiers and civilian volunteers.

Both wounded, Bender and Downey had been left at Saint Joseph's Hospital in Deer Lodge, Montana. Somehow they had made their way south to the railroad in Utah, where a harried quartermaster put them on the cars for San Francisco. Neither of them protested. The adjutant general of the Division of the Pacific saw no way of returning them to Montana, so he assigned them to Lieutenant Weisendorf's troop of the First Cavalry, which brought them to Camp Belknap.

Downey might have sense enough to keep his mouth shut, Michael thought, but Bender would tell anyone

489

his lurid stories for a quart of beer. Ritter would have a field day with that one.

"Can we go?" urged Angie. "Everybody's there . . . even Brigid," she added wickedly.

"Brigid?" Michael scowled. "What about the Carter kids?"

"Mah Kim's at the house. He told me Brigid is there."

Michael considered that for a moment. "All right," he said. "Come on."

There was quite a crowd at the trader's store. Soldiers spilled out of the enlisted men's billiard room to cluster about two civilians standing at the counter, and at the far end of the room half a dozen women had gathered, ostensibly discussing with Prudence Morton the merits of some newly arrived dress goods. Michael left Angie with the women and joined the soldiers.

Conversation ceased when he arrived. Charles Ritter, still wearing his odd shooting jacket, lounged against the counter with an older civilian. Both of them looked at Michael curiously.

"Afternoon, Corporal Brennan," said Morton. "A beer for you?"

Michael nodded, and thumbed the porcelain stopper in its wire stirrup off the bottle Morton set before him. The older civilian held out his hand, beaming.

"Corporal Brennan, I hoped I'd see you. I'm Ben Hart, editor of the Canyon City *Herald*."

"Pleased to meet you, Mr. Hart," Michael replied.

Ritter nodded coolly.

"I guess I owe you an apology, Brennan," he said.

Michael put down his beer and watched the correspondent warily.

"When I said none of the soldiers were seriously wounded in that fight on the creek, I didn't know you'd been hit twice. All you mentioned was some birdshot. I should have got it right before I sent it to be published."

"That's all right," Michael told him. "I don't mind." His complaint with Ritter's story was not over the extent of his own wounds. Before he could say anything more, Ben Hart clapped him on the shoulder.

"Have another beer, Corporal—my treat. I got to tell you, I think what you did for that Indian was just great!"

The silence in the room this time was absolute. Even the women stopped whispering and watched expectantly.

"Damned near every man in Canyon City was set to hang that poor kid. They'd have done it, too, if you hadn't stood up for him like you did. I tell you, Corporal, that took guts, and I admire you for it."

"Well, I be goddamned! It's true, then," muttered one of the soldiers. Another said something obscene, and Morton looked at him angrily.

"Watch your mouth! There's ladies here."

Michael identified the offender. It was Private Weaver, who had never forgotten nor forgiven what Michael had said to him the day Lieutenant Shelby's detachment formed on the parade ground to go after the Indians.

"Tell us, mister," said Weaver unpleasantly, "just how Corporal Brennan got that pore Injun off."

If Hart noticed the disgust in Weaver's voice, he paid it no heed. He was only too eager to repeat the story.

"It was beautiful! Nobody thought that Indian had a chance. He couldn't even get a lawyer to defend him until that Baltimore outfit got those two men from Pendleton to take the case. They sure turned it around."

"What Baltimore outfit?" asked Sergeant Couza.

"The Council on Indian Rights," replied Ritter dryly. "They take a big interest in what happens to Indians."

"Well, sir," Hart continued, "those two young lawyers were good. They took about four days makin' a case that the Indian wasn't guilty of murder at all . . . only manslaughter. A lot of us think they did it. If they'd quit when they got that done, I'll bet Judge Heber would have told the jury they couldn't convict him of murder. He'd likely have got off with a jail sentence. But they didn't quit. That young Shaw said if he could prove the Indians and the soldiers were at war, the court couldn't even try that Indian."

"That's a load of crap!" exploded Weaver. "He shot that lieutenant in the back, didn't he? There wasn't any war goin' on when he did that!"

"Ah!" chortled Hart. "But Mister Shaw proved there was. He proved there was a war from the time the first shot was fired on the creek until the last shot was fired right here at Belknap."

"Jesus Christ! I don't—"

Morton slapped his hand on the counter and everyone looked at him. He pointed a finger at Weaver.

"I told you, soldier, to watch your mouth. One more like that an' I'll put you out."

Weaver grumbled, but he had no response. Sy Morton kept order in his store with a fourteen-inch iron cavalry picket pin—an awesome weapon nearly an inch thick with a knob on one end and a sharp point on the other. Only a fool disagreed with the trader when he armed himself with that.

Old Sergeant O'Hara, standing beside Couza, cleared his throat gently.

"Shut up, Weaver. Go on, Mr. Hart. How'd he prove there was a war?"

"Easy. He had more Indians than they wanted to hear tellin' 'em they thought they were in a war. Some of 'em said they'd been at war since the first settler showed up in these parts. All he had to do was get the army to say it was in a war, and that was it. Corporal Brennan did that. And did it damned well, too. After he got through, there was nothin' left but some shoutin' by that government lawyer."

"Well . . ." said O'Hara, "I guess there was a war when Mr. Shelby rounded up those Indians, but I'd say it ended when he brought 'em back here. How'd he get around that?"

Hart counted on his fingers, just as young Shaw had done. "The Indians had never been searched and fully disarmed . . . They were not confined . . . And they were not under guard—as far as they knew. All that happened after Mr. Shelby was killed, and that was the last shot of the war. You can't hang a man for killing an enemy in a war. Soon as Corporal Brennan spoke his piece for the army, Judge Heber knew they hadn't ought to have even tried that Indian. He told the jury to find him not guilty of anything . . . And that's what they did."

There was an instant rumble of confused response. Most of the soldiers had never questioned that there was a war, and when it ended was a technicality. What puzzled everyone was why Brennan had gotten himself involved in the matter. Hart sensed that. He put his arm around Michael's shoulder and beamed at his audience.

"You men ought to be proud of Corporal Brennan," he said. "That Indian was bein' railroaded right onto the gallows until he stood up for him."

It was not a convincing reason to be proud of Brennan. There was another outburst of talking with a few audible expressions of disgust. Michael disengaged himself from the editor's arm and beckoned to Sy Morton for another beer.

"Let me buy you one, Brennan," said Ritter. "I'd like to buy a beer for the smartest soldier in Oregon."

The onlookers fell silent once more, watching with interest. Michael was about to open the bottle Morton had just given him, but he put it down and looked at Ritter.

"Before I take that beer, mister, tell me why I'm so smart, will you?"

Ritter laughed harshly. "I don't want to disappoint my friend, Ben Hart, but I think you had a little more in mind than just saving that Indian."

"And what was that?"

"I'd guess those two smart young lawyers told you what the Baltimore Council planned to do if the good citizens of Canyon City put that Indian on the gallows."

He waited until every eye in the room was on him. "If the Indian was guilty of murder, then so was every soldier who stood around that hole on the creek bank and shot himself a squaw or two. You can't have a war that only works one way. If the Indian was hanged, the Council was going to bring charges of murder against your post commander and Lieutenant Shelby. Of course, Shelby being dead, they couldn't try him, so they would have tried his second-in-command—Corporal Brennan, the great friend and benefactor of the Indians."

The silence was absolute until Sergeant O'Hara began to laugh. He sounded more like a guinea hen than ever. He wheezed and chortled and pounded Couza on the back until the commissary sergeant began to laugh too. The two of them leaned on the counter and guffawed. The laughter spread. Hart's praise of Brennan made them suspicious, but Ritter's accusation delighted them.

"Take his beer, Michael," gasped O'Hara. "I'll buy you a dozen more, I will. You're pretty damned smart at that."

Ritter's face was white with anger. He rang a coin on the counter and jerked his thumb at Michael's beer.

"Now wait a minute . . ." said Michael. "If you hate payin' for it that much, I'll just drink Sergeant O'Hara's beer."

"I'll pay," rasped the correspondent, "but I won't drink with you. A war, you said? What kind of a war is it when you gun down women and children like you did?"

Michael shrugged. "You told me when I was in the hospital you'd just come from a war in the old country. How do they do it? Send in a white flag and say, 'Get your women an' kids out of the way, we're goin' to fight a while now'?"

"That's what a civilized army does!"

That was too close to what the man from the Baltimore Council had said for Michael to accept quietly. His eyes blazed.

"Well, why don't you educated folks teach these Indians your rules, then?"

"What good would that do?" barked Ritter. He pointed at Bender. "You all do it! He'll tell you how Gibbon and the Seventh Infantry hit the Nez Percé camp at dawn on the Big Hole without a warning of any kind. How they killed women and children . . . killed them in their beds! What kind of war is that?"

"I'll tell you, mister," Michael blazed. "It's the kind that started on Whitebird Creek last June, when the Nez Percés locked a woman an' her baby in a cabin an' burnt it to the ground. Don't tell me you don't know what your Saint Joseph an' his bucks did to Jack Manuel's wife an' kid?"

"They released the white women they captured in the Yellowstone Park!"

"So what! Howard was pushin' him hard then. What about Missus Chamberlain over by Idaho City? What rules were they usin' when they raped her an' cut her little girl's tongue out because she cried, watchin' the fun?"

Sy Morton was shaking his head, indicating the group of wide-eyed women at the other end of the counter, but Michael ignored him.

"You an' your rules! You make me sick to my stomach, mister. You said it . . . you can't have a war that only works one way. We fight this war the only way we know how, an' I guess we'll keep on doin' it as long as the Indians make the rules."

"That's right," put in Bender excitedly. "Those Injun women were shootin' at me at the Big Hole! What was I s'posed to do? They had a yellow-haired white girl they stole in the Bitterroot Valley, an' when she got away from 'em they gunned her down rather'n let her get back to her own folks. I saw that."

Michael drew a deep breath and mastered his anger. "Mr. Ritter, instead of worryin' about the rules, why don't you take a look at your army? If there was enough of it, we'd keep these damned Indians quiet till you an' the Baltimore Council could talk sense into

495

'em. That war should have ended right there at the Big Hole, but the Seventh Infantry only had a hundred an' fifty men . . . officers an' soldiers together. What good is a damned regiment with a hundred an' fifty men in it? And not a man-jack with a penny of pay since the Congress stopped the money! Here . . ." He pushed his bottle of beer at the correspondent. "Take a drink before you burn somethin' out." He grinned at the startled civilian. "You're right, Mr. Ritter. It's a hell of a way to fight a war. I take as much shame for it as you, but it'll take more'n you an' me to change it. Drink your beer an' let's call it quits, eh?"

Ritter studied the big corporal for a moment. Then, surprisingly, he smiled. "All right, Brennan. I'll drink with you on that."

The tension drained out of the crowd with an audible sigh, and somebody said plaintively, "After all that preachin', Mr. Morton, maybe these newspaper fellers'll help us get some back pay. Can I have a beer, jaw-bone?"

Ritter lifted his bottle to Michael. "No hard feelings about that story I put you in?"

"Hell, no, man! It made somebody so mad they're likely to make me a sergeant. I thank you for the help."

The women had moved to the door, whispering busily among themselves, and Michael dutifully gathered up Angie. Brigid had disappeared.

been confirmed by Shelby's second-in-command, Corporal Brennan.

16

It was growing dark outside when Michael and Angie left the trader's store. He had not spoken to Brigid all afternoon, and Angie was triumphant. She clung to his arm all the way to Brenner's, whispering excitedly, and at the doctor's back door she stood on tiptoe, head back and eyes shut expectantly. Nothing happened.

"Michael?"

The Carters' kitchen door had opened momentarily, casting a glow of lamplight across the porch.

"Michael!" Angie tugged at his coat.

"Huh? What, Angie?"

"Oh, you go to the devil!" she hissed. As she stormed inside, there was a soft giggle from the Carters' back porch.

"Bridey?"

"You better run. I bet she's gone for the broom."

He sat on the top step of the Carters' porch and peered at Brigid in the gathering darkness. She leaned against the door, her sheepskin coat thrown over her shoulders.

"That was mean of you. Why didn't you kiss her?"

He shrugged. "Are you really goin' away, Bridey?"

"I am. My year's done, and more. Missus Carter said I could go when she gets back from Fort Boise."

"To San Francisco?"

"Yes. I told you, Mr. Morton got me a job there. In the store where he buys his things."

"That's no more than you had in New York . . . less, maybe. I thought you wanted something better."

"I'll find it. Have to start somewhere."

"What's the name of the store?"

"Why d'you want to know?"

"I'll be lookin' in on you. I'm goin' to San Francisco too."

"What?"

"I'm goin' to San Francisco," he repeated.

"You've got a furlough?"

"No. I'm to have a job at Division Headquarters in the Presidio."

She looked suspicious. "You're jokin' me! How'd you get that?"

"I'll tell you if you'll come sit down. You're givin' me a crick in the neck, talkin' like this."

Curiosity overcame her caution, and she perched on the opposite end of the step, wrapping her coat about her.

"Aren't you in trouble for what that man put in the newspaper? I thought Captain Smith was mad at you."

"Not at all. General Quinn fixed it for me. He said the captain put me in for a medal or somethin', but that'll come to naught, so he got me a job on the staff in San Francisco and maybe a promotion too."

"Does Quinn know about that Indian, Petoe? What you did for him at the trial?"

"I doubt that'd make a difference. Quinn's got a good head on him." He gave her a grin. "He's lookin' after me, all right."

Brigid sniffed. "Don't be givin' yourself airs. He's Irish an' he's just takin' care of his own." He was silent for a long moment.

"Michael?"

"Yes?"

"When you went to Canyon City an' got that Indian off . . . was it because you were sorry for him . . . or was it what that Mr. Ritter said this afternoon?"

498

"What do you think?"

"I don't know. I didn't understand all that stuff Ritter said. Could they truly put you in court an' maybe hang you for killin' those Indians?"

Michael chuckled. "I hope not. They'd not have an army long if they start that."

"Not even for killin' women?"

"Bridey," he said solemnly, "I haven't killed a woman for a whole week."

"Damn it, Michael, don't make fun of me! I want to know."

"You're still thinkin' of what I said when I was off my head in the hospital?"

She nodded.

"A long time ago in Kansas, Bridey, I was in a bad fight with some Indians, an' I may have killed a squaw. I don't know. . . ."

The moon was up, silvering the floor of the canyon and driving luminous shafts through the mist rising from the stream. Brigid listened intently while he told her the story of the fight at Sappa Creek.

"Then you don't really know it was you that killed her?" she asked when he had finished.

"No, I don't. But I can't lay the spirit of that girl. Why does she devil me if I didn't?"

"Maybe . . . just because you're still sorry for her."

"I am that, God knows, but I wish she'd leave me be."

"Then were you sorry for Petoe, or just scared of what would happen if you didn't get him off?"

"What's got into you?" he exploded irritably. "I thought you didn't care what happens to me."

She was startled by his anger, but she would not give up.

"I . . . I just want to know, that's all. I don't understand."

She was braced for another outburst, but he was silent.

After a moment he said softly, "I doubt you'll ever understand, Bridey."

He stared morosely at the mist curling off the stream, and then he continued softly.

"I'm no freak. I don't like killing. I never meant to kill a woman in my life, but maybe I did. I guess I've killed a man, but it was in a fight an' he was tryin' to kill me. I never thought about it much till that lawyer got hold of me." He shifted uncomfortably on the step. "No . . . I'm not sorry for that damned Petoe. I hated Shelby's guts, but he was my lieutenant. And, no, I'm not scared of any Baltimore society siccin' the law on me. But damn it all"—he drove his fist into his open hand with a smack that made Brigid jump—"they can't say I'm just a tramp tryin' to play cops an' robbers!" He turned a baffled, angry face to her. "If this isn't a war . . . an' I'm not a soldier . . . what in hell am I an' what am I doin' here?"

Brigid had no answer for him. The complexity of his problem baffled her too, but not as much as his voicing it. In the year and a half she had known Michael Brennan, he had never voiced any doubt of himself. Now he was asking something of her beyond the obvious that he had always wanted. She stared at him in amazement.

"Well?"

She still had no answer, but her heart ached for him. She slid across the step and put her arm in his.

"I don't know, Michael. I wish you *weren't* a soldier."

"Hah! I'll bet you never said that to your lovin' lieutenant!"

"Hush!" She put her fingers on his lips. "I never loved him, but don't you talk about him."

"You went to bed with him, didn't you?"

Brigid studied his scowling face warily. He was just fishing. He had no way to know.

"That's none of your business, Michael Brennan," she told him gently. "You said that Indian girl haunts you. Well, John Shelby haunts me. He was a dead man before he went after those Indians."

"How in the devil did you know that?" he demanded in surprise.

She shivered. "I don't know. I don't want to know. I hope to God and all the blessed saints I never see that in a man's face again. An' him so young an' laughin' and good lookin' . . . just beggin' me for a little lovin'."

"Jesus, Bridey!" whispered Michael in awe. "You've never got the second sight! Can you look in a man's face an' tell what will happen to him?"

"No! Not before John Shelby, an' please, God . . . never again! It near frightened the wits out of me. Will you leave it be, now? I don't want to talk about it."

His anger forgotten, he found her hand and held it tight. "I'm sorry for you, Bridey. That's a fearsome thing. Come here—you're all cold."

"No!" She jerked her hand away—roughly—because she wanted him to hold her close and warm her.

"Tell me what you'll do in San Francisco. What kind of place did General Quinn get you?"

"I don't know. It doesn't matter. He says he's goin' to find me a job back east if I want it."

"Truly? But he's not in the army . . . not really. Mr. Carter calls him a holiday soldier. How can you work for him?"

Michael shrugged casually. "Maybe I'll quit the army—if his job's good enough."

"You'd desert? Run away?" Her question was awe-stricken.

He felt the paper in his coat pocket. "No need of that. Dr. Brenner gave me a certificate. If I give it to the doctors in San Francisco an' say my leg's gone all stiff, they have to believe me because the Doc wrote it all out. How it got hurt an' how bad it was, an' if it gets worse I should have a discharge an' maybe a pension to boot."

"Oh, Michael! I don't believe you. Let me see."

He showed the paper, but held it beyond her reach. "You can't read it out here. Let's go inside and I'll let you see it."

501

Surprisingly, she jumped to her feet and pulled open the door. "Shh!" she warned. "Don't wake the kids."

She could not see his grin in the dark. He was remembering Norah Brannigan in Lieutenant Coursey's vine-covered porch on Governors Island.

On tiptoe, she turned up the kitchen lamp and held out her hand. "Let me see that thing."

He gave it to her and watched her hungrily as she read it. She had thrown off her coat and she was wearing the soft black wool dress Mrs. Carter had bought her, with a big white collar. The collar was starched and its points, resting on her high, round breasts, rose and fell with her excited breathing.

"That'll get you out of the army?" she asked incredulously. "I can't make head nor tail of it."

"Doc says it will. I don't understand all those words either, but if he says so, I believe him."

Lips pursed, she read it again, frowning.

"Angie says Dr. Brenner made you talk to the Indian's lawyer. After that you went to Canyon City an' did what they wanted of you. Did they give you this for doin' it?"

He laughed and put the certificate away. "Bridey, you've got a crooked mind. You think they had to pay me off? Doc Brenner didn't make me go. I went because I wanted to, an' if what I said helped that Indian, that's just his good luck. I didn't say it for him. This"—he tapped his pocket—"is not payment for anything."

"You're sure?"

"I am that. Doc says he's just doin' what he's supposed to do for any soldier hurt like I was. But . . ." He looked thoughtful. "He knows there's some will be down on me for helpin' that Indian get off. Most folks wanted him dead an' didn't care how." He caught a strand of her hair and tugged gently. "I remember a redhead sayin' she wanted to watch him hang."

She made a face at him and tucked her hair back in place. "What's that got to do with it?"

"Maybe the doc has given me a way out if some-
502

body on Division staff hands me a hard time about it. I don't think they will. You heard Couza an' O'Hara this afternoon. The more that fool Ritter shoots off his mouth, the less trouble I'll have—in the army, anyway."

"Would you use it? Will you get out?"

"I might. If General Quinn has a grand place for me back east, I'd be tempted."

She twisted a button on his coat and murmured something, but he couldn't hear her.

"What did you say?"

"I said . . . is that the only thing?"

"Ah, no. . . . I can think of others."

"What?"

He had to bend to hear her soft question. He pulled her to him and smiled at her serious face.

"Brigid O'Donnel, do you remember me askin' you to marry me?"

She giggled, hiding her face against his chest. "Just before you wanted to roll me in the snow?"

"I don't need snow for that. I told you before, I want you any way you'll have me. Will you marry me, Bridey?"

"Oh, Michael . . . "

She was trying to think, and it was hard with his hands cupping her waist. He had turned to her for help outside, and that was the first time he had ever asked for help. She loved him for that. She loved him for other things, too. All that fighting and swearing at him wasn't the way she really felt. He hadn't promised he'd quit the army, but he'd hinted. If he was wondering why he was a soldier, she could make him see that he ought to quit. She felt warm and worried and excited all at once.

His fingers worked up her back busily, found the ribbon binding her hair, and pulled it free. When she lifted her face to his, it tumbled down in a great, glowing scarf over her shoulders. He parted it and kissed her until she gasped.

"Let me breathe!" she begged. "Do you mean it?"

"That I want to marry you?"

"I know that. I'm talkin' about the other."

"Ah, Bridey! You know I'm a weak man. I could never turn from temptation."

It wasn't much. Hardly a promise. But she hadn't the breath to argue now. "Don't!" she gasped, grabbing his hands. She was too late. His fingers had not idled while he kissed her. Her dress was unbuttoned to the waist, and it slid easily from her shoulders. She had not worn the corset since General Quinn's party, but he already knew that. Her chemise went with the dress.

It was too late for anything now. She flattened her breasts against him, pinning his hands with them, and kissed him passionately.

"Saints above us!" he muttered. "You haven't done that since Philadelphia. I thought you'd forgotten how."

"You devil!" she panted, her green eyes sparkling. "Come here an' I'll show you."

When he released her she clung to him, eyes shut and face flaming. His big hands roved over her hips and she felt the dress slipping again. She bolted against him.

"My God! You'll have me naked, Michael!" She flung a despairing look over her shoulder. "I'll bet Angie's watchin'!"

"Do her good, poor thing!"

She wrestled helplessly with him, giggling and using her elbows wickedly, but it was no match. Breaking free at last, she snatched up the tangle of clothing about her ankles.

"Come on!" she whispered. "You want the whole post watchin' us?"

He pursued her noisily, and she hissed for quiet. It was pitch-dark and cold in her room.

"D-don't light that lamp!" she warned.

"It never crossed my mind," he assured her, pulling off his coat.

"Oh, damn it!"

"What's amiss?"

"My garters! You've got 'em in a hard knot, an' I can't get 'em off!"

He could just make her out, sitting on the bed tugging at her stockings. Jerking the quilt from beneath her, he tumbled her in and followed, pulling the quilt over them. It stayed somehow, despite the struggle beneath it.

"Will you forget the damn garters?" he laughed. "They'll not be in the way."

"Let me go! Get off me, you big *omadhaun!*"

"Never! Stop fighting, now!"

He trapped her flying fists and pinned her helpless in the soft featherbed, kissing her until she moaned and squirmed against him.

"Oh, Michael . . . " she whispered. "Come to me, lover."

17

A loud rap jolted Brigid from sound sleep. Dawn light seeped through the drawn window curtains, and she pushed her hair from her eyes to stare at the door in alarm. Michael's trousers flung over the foot of the bed caught her attention and snapped her wide-awake.

"Oh, my God!" she moaned, jerking the quilt over his head and scrambling for the trousers. It was hopeless. His clothes were all over the floor. What if the children came in now?

A more imperative rap spurred her to frantic action, and Michael erupted from beneath the quilt with a questioning rumble.

"Shh! Someone's at the door!"

There was a nerve-racking squeal, as of metal on glass, and he reached to pull back the window curtain a cautious bit. He grunted in amusement.

"You got another bluecoat, Bridey. He's jealous."

Pulling the curtain open wide he revealed a large, irritable blue jay on the window sill, turning his head from side to side to peer through the glass.

"Ooh!" she gasped in relief. "That damned bird!"

"What's he want?"

"His breakfast, I guess. The kids have been feeding him. Lord, he scared the heart out of me."

She flapped a sock and stuck out her tongue at the

jay, who flew off with a startled squawk. Michael laughed and hooked an arm around her slim waist.

"Stop it, now!" she protested. "They'll be up an' lookin' for me. Let me go! You're like that damn bird—always after more."

"Nobody's up," he soothed her. "It's hardly daylight. Come here."

She defended herself halfheartedly for a moment.

"Please, Michael . . . don't! You'll rip it. Let me take it off."

"It's only a flour sack. I'll buy you a real one when we get to Frisco. When did you put it on?"

"I got cold," she murmured, measuring her warm length against him happily. "Pull the quilt over us . . . so they don't hear anything."

There was a slice of sunlight across the bed when she woke again, and she tumbled out of bed feeling guilty and happy at the same time.

"Now what?" groaned Michael.

"The kids'll think I'm dead. I've got to fix their breakfast."

"Where's Mah Kim?"

Her eyes sparkled. "I told him he needn't come early."

"Oh? When did you tell him that?"

"None of your business. Turn over now, an' don't watch me while I wash."

She gasped at the icy water but splashed gamely through a hasty bath, standing in the big ironstone basin and shivering mightily. In skirt and blouse, she sat on the bed, dragging a brush through her tangled hair.

"Button me up, quick. An' don't you dare come strollin' out of here into the kitchen."

"But I want some breakfast!"

"Then slip down the hall an' knock on the front door like you've just come. Aren't you supposed to be at the barracks?"

He groaned dramatically. "I'm just a poor wounded soldier, Bridey. I'm in the hospital."

507

Brigid rolled her eyes. "God's presence be about us! Wounded, are you? Then old mousey Moser'll be lookin' for you."

"Nah. He'll think I'm in Brenner's . . . or up at Morton's. Just hand me my trousers, will you, love?"

He got the trousers and a splash of icy water on his bare chest, dipped from the pitcher as she slipped out with a wicked grin.

The children's faces fell when they clattered into the kitchen and found Brigid shaking up the stove.

"Where's Mah Kim?" asked William sadly.

Brigid only made one breakfast—oatmeal. She had been raised on it by the Sisters and she thought it was good enough for everyone.

"He's late. Did you wash?"

Their murmured assurance was lost in a hearty banging at the front door. Michael's voice boomed in the hall.

"Anybody up?"

"We're in the kitchen," Amanda shouted and looked at Brigid hopefully. "Michael will want breakfast, too. You can't make him eat oatmeal."

"Good mornin', kids . . . and good mornin' to you, Brigid O'Donnel," Michael hailed them cheerfully.

Ah, the wicked man, Brigid thought, suppressing a giggle. You've gone and done it now, O'Donnel. But he was so big and handsome and ruddy-faced, she felt a glow of pride. He'd even shaved himself in the cold water, with Lieutenant Carter's spare razor, she supposed.

"What's for breakfast, Amanda?"

"You won't like it."

"What?"

"Oatmeal! Ugh!"

"Amanda!" Brigid shook a spoon at her threateningly.

"Well," said Michael. "Nothing wrong with a little porridge for starters."

"Starters! You're out of your head, Michael Brennan, if you think I've naught to do but make you some

508

kind of feast. Oatmeal there is, an' that's what you'll have."

"Ah, come on, Bridey. Look at these poor hungry kids. You dish up the porridge an' I'll just do us a bit to follow with."

To the children's delight, he mixed batter in minutes, and before they finished their oatmeal there was a growing stack of pancakes in the warming oven atop the stove.

He put a plate of these on the table and sat down, rubbing his hands.

"Is there butter?" he asked Brigid, and she sniffed.

"You've got fancy taste! Not even canned butter left. Brown sugar or molasses, that's all there is."

That proved quite satisfactory, and very shortly there was a demand for more pancakes. Michael started to rise, but Brigid pushed him back with a pinch, just to show him she was not to be taken for granted.

"Sit now. I'll do some more," she told him sweetly. There was a knock at the kitchen door, and Angie put her sleek black head in curiously.

"Oh, it smells good. Can I come in?"

"You are in," said Brigid tartly. "D'you want some pancakes?"

"No, thanks. We've had breakfast." She winked at Michael, who had the grace to look abashed.

"Missus Brenner wants to know if you've heard from Missus Carter."

"Of course not," snapped Brigid. "I'd have told you if I had."

Angie stood behind Michael, her hand resting on his shoulder, and Brigid eyed her grimly.

"Sit down, Angie, an' have a cup of coffee, will you not?"

"All right. Oh, you've got condensed milk!" She seated herself beside Michael and spooned the sweetened milk lavishly into the mug Brigid put before her.

"Don't the Brenners let you have any?"

509

"Not this kind. Missus Brenner says it gives you the flux, and she won't have it in the house."

Her clientele filled to bursting, Brigid returned to the table and her own coffee, frowning at Angie's fingers stroking the sleeve of Michael's dark blue blouse. Angie pinched the cloth between her fingers and rubbed it admiringly.

"That's nice. Bet I know where you got it."

Michael looked annoyed, but Angie chattered on. "I saw it when I went to get Dad's new vest from Hirschberger."

"Who," asked Brigid, "is Hirschberger?"

"He's the cavalry tailor. The one they left behind because he's got the neuralgy an' can't get cold or wet. He made a cape for Mr. Slade, an' there was lot's left over. He made this for you, didn't he, Michael? That's real officers' stuff—soft and nice. I like it. Did he just finish it?"

Michael stood up, scraping his chair noisily. "Well, I guess I better let Moser know where I am, or he'll be nosin' around lookin' for me. That was a grand breakfast, and I thank you, Brigid."

"I gotta go too," chirped Angie. "Missus Brenner will be worryin'."

"You shouldn't have stayed so long, then," Brigid told her. The fire in her green eyes promised trouble for someone, and Michael edged toward the hall door.

"Left my cap in there," he explained. "Good day, ladies."

Brigid fixed him with a glare. "I'll just have a word with you before you go, Brennan. Good day to you, Angie. I'll tell you soon as I hear from the Carters."

Angie lingered, her eyes on Michael, but Brigid pushed her out. Amanda had gone with a pancake for her blue jay, and Brigid prodded William.

"Don't let her go near that creek an' don't you get so far away you can't hear me call, you understand?"

"You sound just like Mama," William muttered gloomily. He pulled on his jacket and followed his sister out of doors.

"You do sound testy," Michael said. "What's the matter?"

"Shut that door." He closed it, and turned to find himself impaled on a stiff and angry finger.

"Now tell me," Brigid demanded, "why you'd have the tailor go an' make you a brand new army coat out of officers' stuff when you're goin' to get out of the army. You can't mean to wear that thing when you're a civvie, can you?"

Michael looked thoughtful. "That's a prudent thought, Bridey." He nodded. "You're goin' to make a thrifty wife, I'm thinkin'."

"Don't blarney me! Why?"

"Well . . . it'll go better with those doctors if I look sharp."

"I don't believe you. Come on—out with it!"

"That's a fact, Bridey, an' . . . well, just suppose they don't give me a discharge right away. You know how the army is. They fool around an' write letters to Washington an' all. I might have to wait a little bit, an' I couldn't get a coat this good at twice the price in San Francisco."

Brigid's face flamed. She was so angry she could only stutter.

"Now, Bridey . . ." said Michael cautiously.

"Don't Bridey me! You never meant to quit the army at all, did you? What about that paper you showed me—the one that says you're unfit?"

He looked pained. "D'you think I'm unfit?"

"It didn't say anything about that part of you! Did Dr. Brenner really give you that? Or did you just steal it in the hospital an' write in all that stuff?"

"Ah, Bridey, I wouldn't ever do that! I'd get caught. It's real, all right. But, you see, Doc Brenner's naught but a post doctor. Who knows what those big dogs at Division will say about his certificate?"

"It doesn't matter what they'd say!" she shouted. "You never meant to show it to them. You just want that job with the sergeant's stripes that damned general fixed for you. Oh, I know what you're up to . . . god-damn it!" She choked on her fury and burst into sobs.

"Ah, Bridey . . . don't cry!" He came around the table toward her, but she lifted the big iron spoon.

"You touch me, Brennan," she panted, "an' I'll flatten your head like a stepped-on toad! You lied to me! You tricked me, damn you!"

"I did not. I said I was goin' to San Francisco an' I asked you to marry me. You said you would . . . I guess. I'll marry you this mornin' if you'll say the word."

"You know damn good an' well I wouldn't marry you if you mean to wear that blue suit the rest of your life . . . or till somebody kills you! I'll not go to San Francisco with you either!"

He looked astonished. "You'll stay on here?"

"I will not! I've got me a job in San Francisco, an' I'm goin'—but never with you, Michael Brennan!"

"Oh. Well . . ." He shrugged. "We're both goin', an' it's not likely they'll give us a wagon each. I got to keep an eye on you, Bridey. I got to see you don't go an' do anything foolish."

"Keep an eye on me?" she yelled. "I'll see you in hell first!"

"First an' last, love, I'm thinkin'. There's but one end for a pair of rogues like us." He approached her warily, an eye on the threatening spoon.